THE DEVIL'S GAMBIT

THE DEVIL'S GAMBIT

CHRONICLES OF TAROTLAND

KILLIAN WOLF

Grim House
Publishing

ISBN: 978-1-951140-17-5

Copyeditor: Sara Lawson - sarasbooks.com
Cover design: Logan Keys - coverofdarknessdesign.com
Conlanger: Christian Thalmann - twitter.com/thalmach
Map designer: Zentra Brice
Header designer: Etheric Designs - etherictales.com/etheric-designs
Formatter: Michael Davie - grimhousepub.com/plans-pricing

To the reader who wonders if they should just go for it, Tarotland awaits.

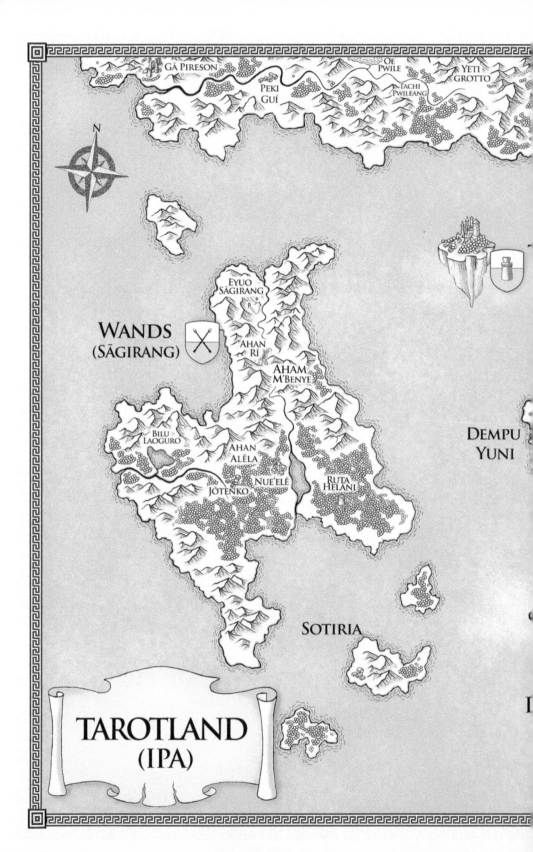

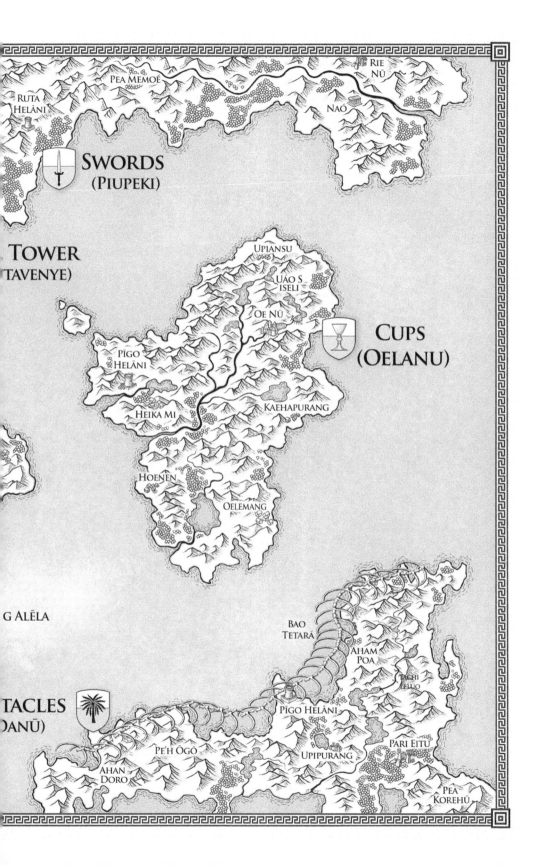

PEA MEMOÉ

RIE
NŪ

RUTA
HELĀNI

NAO

SWORDS
(PIUPEKI)

TOWER
(TAVENYE)

UPIANSU

UÁO S
ISELI

OE NŪ

CUPS
(OELANU)

PĪGO
HELĀNI

KAEHAPURANG

HEIKA MI

HOENEN

OELEMANG

G ALĒLA

BAO
TETARĀ

AHAM
POA

TACHI
LELUO

TACLES
(ANŪ)

PĪGO HELĀNI

PARI EITU

PE'H ŌGŌ

UPIPURANG

AHAN
DORO

PEA
KOREHŪ

1

My thumb traces over the etched symbol of Danū's minted ruby coin: a black palm tree, curved as if it were billowing in the wind. I turn it between my fingers, the afternoon sunlight making it glisten beautifully—a stark contrast to the cringy mauve carpeting with matching mauve curtains in Dr. Peyton's office. My court-appointed counselor. I tap my heel impatiently on the floor, knowing the only place I can get answers is...not here.

This minted ruby coin isn't from the stash Nkella had given me before I came back through the portal. No. It's from my mother's jewelry box, brought to me three months ago by my absent father just after my mother died, and as of late, it's the only thing I can think about.

How did my mother get a Danū coin?

Dr. Peyton stares at me expectantly, waiting for me to say something. I shift positions in my seat, my left butt cheek already tingling from our staring contest.

"Soren, this is your hour."

"Yep, and it's almost up. I have to go to work soon." I don't actually have to work today, but I don't feel like telling her about my relationship with Asteria. This is such a waste of time. I'd rather focus on

1

getting to Asteria's tent before I have my martial arts class, and then I'm meeting up with Talia for a movie tonight. Having to be here and stare at a court-ordered shrink who cannot help me is slowing me down.

I glance at my reflection in the large mirror behind her and move my hair back, letting go of the coin.

"You're still working at the carnival?"

"Mm-hmm."

Dr. Peyton fixes her perfect bangs from her eyes and then folds her hands. "Do you like working there?"

"Honestly?" Not that I'm going to tell her the truth about why I still work there, which is because I'm allowed to make the most money I can without doing something I don't want to, like taking off my clothes. Scamming people with my sleight-of-hand, and giving my former fosters a cut is a win-win for all of us. "I love working there. It's filled with... spirited people." I smile.

She returns a smile, except it's one that says, "I can see right through your hard shell." Well, that's all you're getting out of me, so get used to it.

"Would you like to talk a bit about why you left them for three months without notice?" She flips through her file. "There seemed to have been a mix-up at the county jail..." She hums while she reads something inside the folder on her desk. "A correctional officer lost her job after there were no signs of a breakout, but then you went missing."

I roll my eyes. "Does it say in those papers that I left to work for a different carnival?"

She flicks her eyes from her folder. "And I'm guessing that didn't go over so well?"

I grab my mother's necklace. Flashbacks of Ipa come flooding in, the *Devil's Gambit*, Wands, the crew...Nkella.

Neyuro.

I stifle a gasp. "It went fine," I say a little more abrupt than I'd intended. I can't tell her the truth about where I really was. She'll lock me up in a madhouse for real. "I was hoping to clear my mind a bit after I got arrested is all. But I came back for my sister. She needs me."

Every once in a while, I get a phantom whiff of my captain. Anytime I hear heavy boots on a hardwood floor. Or pass by a bar and pick up the scent of rum. The warm vanilla, mixed with spices and hickory, the leather of his coat. At night, I see him in my dreams. Sometimes it's his dark, menacing stare, the anger flickering behind his eyes, always banked, the devil inside him wanting to escape. Other times, I get his softer side, and I pretend he's holding me while I sleep. But mostly, I try to push him out of my mind. There's no use in ever thinking about someone I'm never going to see again.

I clear my throat. Dr. Peyton crinkles her forehead, her eyes glossing me over, and then writes something down on her notepad. I cringe.

"Talia Landry." She stares back down at her paperwork. "And you met her in the foster system. I think it's really sweet that you look after her. I'm sure it wasn't easy leaving her alone for so long."

I swallow. "No. It wasn't." I twirl the bottom of my hair between my thumb and index finger.

"Would you like to talk about your mom?"

I drop my hair and fold my arms, sitting back on the chair. "What about her?" I shrug a modest shoulder.

"Is there anything you'd like to share?"

I shake my head, and mouth the word nope, no voice coming out.

Dr. Peyton softens her features. "I heard she passed away, and your father was the one who brought you the news." I stay quiet as she goes over the details I don't want repeating in my head, the reality I just want to escape from.

I wish I could go back and visit my mom before she died and tell her I love her even though she wouldn't have known who I was. The corners of my eyes start to itch, and I rub them on my shoulder, not even wanting to move my hands for some reason. Dr. Peyton takes notice of my action. I look away, this time avoiding her fake caring stare.

Something moves in the mirror's reflection behind her.

I glance over my shoulder but see nothing other than Dr. Peyton's framed degrees on the wall. I squint back at the mirror, and my eyes almost bulge as the mirror itself ripples like water struck by a pebble.

My counselor quirks a brow and looks over her shoulder, then back at me. "Soren, are you alright?"

The mirror is now still and solid as a mirror should be.

I blink a few times. Great, I'm finally losing it for real this time.

A concerned expression slips on Dr. Peyton's face as she glances down at her paperwork. "Would you like to tell me about the first time you heard about your mom's diagnosis? Early onset dementia is rare in someone as young as she was."

This snaps my attention to look at her. "What do my mother's medical issues have to do with me being here?" I glance at the digital clock on her desk. Five minutes left.

She presses her lips into a fine line and then jots something down on her notepad. I want to rip it from her hands and shred the pages like shredded cheese.

"It'll help to open up, Soren. Whenever you're ready. You'll see. It will feel good to do so."

My jaw clenches and I stay quiet. There is nothing this woman can help me with. Is she going to help get the harrowing cries from the tortured dead out of my head? Or make me unsee Nkella killing an innocent man after I begged him not to? How about explain to me why an undead crew of pirates felt more like home than any family in the foster system ever did? More than my father ever did? She can't.

Now Asteria on the other hand...she's someone I can talk to, and she can possibly answer the questions burning in my head. Asteria promised me answers, and then she up and left for an impromptu trip back to Greece, making me wait three months for her return. She's now been back one week and interested in my "powers," powers that supposedly mean I'm a "Past Fate descendant" and came out unexpectedly while I was in Ipa—or as I like to call it, Tarotland. Regardless, they don't want to come out now. Meanwhile, all I want are answers.

I just have to appease her by letting her test my powers. "Can I go?"

Dr. Peyton glances at the time. "It's up to you. You have three minutes left. You can leave if you—"

I'm already grabbing my bag and flinging it over my shoulder. "Great. Thanks." Her mouth falls open as I pass her one last look and walk out the door.

The cool November wind brushes my skin as I step out of the beige two-story building. I wrap myself tight with my sweater and stare blissfully into the white winter blanket over the busy street.

Who am I kidding? It's seventy-two degrees right now, and more humid than a UFC fighter's jockstrap, *but* it's winter to us in Louisiana, so I'll pretend however I want and drink all the hot cocoa I can. I beeline to the right and start jogging to catch the bus to Tarotland Circus.

Despite me putting the counselor's office ten feet behind me, I still feel the sting of how she looked at me when she asked me about my mother's early condition. It wasn't easy growing up without her, knowing she had forgotten who I was. It wasn't easy for my dad either.

And it certainly wasn't easy watching her mind go.

It's just...the way Dr. Peyton looked at me...almost as if she was *expecting me* to see something that wasn't there. I swallow, pushing back the ripples from the mirror. I've never hallucinated before, but how can that be happening? It's not like the mirror was a magical Tarot card. I need to get to Asteria.

Anticipation buzzes through my veins as I wait for the bus to arrive and then hop on.

How did my mother have a Danū coin? When did she ever go to Tarotland? Had she lived there? I had wanted to ask Asteria if she knew anything about it, but she had already left for her trip, leaving me only a note. She told me she left to check on her home there, but she's secretive. I still have so many questions for her, but she likes to dodge them; she says she wants me to find things out for myself, and she can't know the past. She means for me to use my magic, which I have no idea how to do. Ever since I came back, my mark disappeared, and I've felt no different than before I left. It's not that I wouldn't want powers, I'm just finding it pointless. And being a "Past Fate descendant"? That sounds like one big ol' responsibility meant for someone else—someone whose life isn't an utter mess, and who can actually, you know, *live in Tarotland*.

All I want is to find out what happened with my mom so that I can put this behind me and move on with my life.

Spots of light glisten in a mosaic pattern on the table in front of me, making me glance in its direction. Philo tilts her head, causing her whole body to tilt upward, her round body having a unique red glass pattern over her black translucent legs. Her large front eyes stare back at me with curiosity. I smile to myself and offer her my palm. She looks at it then back up at my face two times before she jumps on my hand. Philo is a hybrid between a jumping spider and a mirror spider, native only to Tarotland, but they can easily cross dimensions.

"What is it, Philo?" I whisper.

"Oh, she's just craving your attention." Asteria's voice merges with music and laughter as the folds of the tent open. I whip around to her walking into the tent holding two mugs in her hands. The sweet scent of hot cocoa and cinnamon tickles my senses as she sets them down on the table. I graciously take the mug in my hand and smile at the marshmallows. Philo jumps back to the table so that I can use both hands. "Are you ready, dear?"

I sip my cocoa, and nod. Thick chocolate runs down my throat, and I can tell she also added a little nutmeg. I set the mug down and inch to the edge of my seat. Asteria sits on her chair opposite me and uncovers a deck of cards from a red and gold cloth. I watch as she skillfully shuffles the cards in her hands, her eyes closed, deep in meditation.

"Hold the question in your mind, dear."

"Do I close my eyes?"

"It won't matter. Try to open your mind. Your magic is within you, on this land, and in any other."

Taking a deep breath, I close my eyes, holding my question clear in my head. *What did my mother have to do with Tarotland?* When I open my eyes, Asteria has the cards back in a deck. She hands them to me and tells me to cut them in half. I've seen this done at the circus dozens of times, but this time is different. I've seen real magic, and Asteria knows how to use it.

"Choose one card off the deck, and place it on the table."

I pull out the Empress Card. It figures she'd pop up in a reading. I set it down, and the way this goes is the first one stays on the left side of the spread, representing the past, then comes the present, and finally, the future card, which will be to the right.

Asteria has me repeat the process two more times, and the next cards to come out are the Ace of Swords and the Tower. I squint at the last one. What do any of these cards have to do with my mother? I stare at all three cards, getting distracted by the floating colors from the Moroccan lanterns flickering their flames over them. Philo sits next to the third card, looking as confused as I am, or as confused as a spider can appear to look.

"What can you tell me about the spread?" Asteria breaks my already frazzled concentration.

I clear my throat. "Well, I know what each card means... The Empress Card is in "the past" position, so I know she was being a bitch. Wait a minute, how do I know I didn't just pull out a spread for myself?"

"Keep going."

I sigh. "The Ace of Swords means a sacrifice to be made. And the card in the future is the Tower...which means destruction, right?"

"Don't be too consumed by their past, present, and future positions. Your question pertained to your *mother's* past, so this *entire* spread is about the past."

I quirk a brow, and she smiles. I didn't tell her my question was about my mother. I bet she can tell just by reading these cards. "Can't you just tell me what they mean?"

"Certainly."

"Great!"

"But I won't." She smiles. Her large curly hair frames her long face, the light creating bright spots on her round glasses. "Take a moment to pick the card that calls out to you the most in this spread. Concentrate on it for a while. Take your time."

"I can't take too long. The contortionist is expecting me at six p.m."

"Is she still teaching you martial arts?"

"Yep, and she's saving me money, so I don't want to make her wait."

"You have thirty minutes. There's plenty of time. You wanted to know this, didn't you?"

I give her a weak smile and stare back at the spread. I do want to know what my mother was doing in Tarotland. I just wanted her to tell me. I'm never going to get my magic to work here on Earth. I don't know why Asteria wants me to so badly. "Fine, but I don't know what the point will be. It's not like I can change the past and bring her back."

"The power of the Past Fate isn't to change the past, but to learn from it."

I pick up the Tower Card. "That's all I want to do. Learn of my mother's past." The tower on the card differs from the floating island in Tarotland. Asteria doesn't have any more of those special cards with her, and I gave the World Card to Nkella for safekeeping. It's not like I thought I'd ever need it here, and it doesn't belong here, much to Asteria's dismay. But that's another story. Behind the tower of this card is a night sky with hundreds of tiny stars. The tower is split in two, and people are crashing down from the windows. Below it are angry ocean waves in black and white. The entire card appears to be distressing, giving the idea that what was built is going to come undone, or at least, that's what the little booklet that came with the deck says. Not sure if Asteria agrees with it or not, but she doesn't seem concerned with what's written, only with what could spark my power.

My mind drifts back to the Empress's Tower on the floating island of Rutavenye. I try to imagine it burning and tumbling down into the sea. What does the Tower Card have to do with my mother?

Philo jumps on the card, and a tiny gasp escapes my lips.

My vision zeros into the image of the tower in the card, and my peripherals turn black for a few seconds, before they widen to show a full view of Ipa. Suddenly, I'm no longer in Asteria's tent. I mean, my butt is still on the chair, and I still smell the hot cocoa, but my eyes are showing me something else entirely. I'm afraid to move—worried that I might fall as all around me is nothing but sky, and the sight of the floating island far into the distance, but I also don't want to shake the vision. The last time this happened it was my mark working, and I saw Nkella as a young boy with his sister.

A drakon floats next to me. Its hair is a dark smoky gray, with strands of deep red or burgundy. On its back are two people, one Ipani male, and a girl a few years older than me, with red hair and green eyes. I blink a few times as her features strike a stark resemblance to my mother. Hanging by her belt loop is a longsword. Her eyes are fierce—angry— and they're headed to the Tower. The way the Ipani man grips her stomach behind her, pressing his face against her neck as they ride together, makes me think of me and Nkella when we rode on Gari's back to the Karst Temples in Wands. A knot tightens in my stomach, and my vision starts to blur.

My hand holding the card out in front of me comes back into view. Philo has already jumped off and landed back on the table. I blink a few times and set the card down.

"Next time, try it without Philo's help. So, what did you see?"

"I didn't ask for Philo's help, poor spood was probably impatient." Asteria smiles at my use of the word "spood"—something I picked up while researching jumping spiders. I tell Asteria the details of my vision while taking long sips of my cocoa, no longer as hot as it was. "Something I don't understand is, why did my mom have a sword on her?"

"It sounds like they wanted to kill the Empress, but if it wasn't the Ace of Swords, it wouldn't be possible. Or the Death Card."

"My mom? Kill someone? I'm having a hard time imagining her preparing for battle. But then again, I've never seen her without being loopy and silly, talking to spiders and into teacups." I glance at Philo. "Not that I think talking to spiders is silly anymore."

Philo tilts her head and lifts a leg at me.

Asteria sits back in her chair. "To be perfectly honest, Soren, the only thing any of us can do—despite a Fate's powers—is to keep moving forward. You can spend ages looking into the cards and seeing visions, but you might never get the answers you want. The only way might be to ask the people who knew your mother...if they're still alive."

My shoulders slump. Maybe she doesn't know everything. I can't move on, I have too many questions. "So you don't know what my mother was doing in Tarotland?"

"No. I'm sorry, child. But the answers you seek are within you. All you need to do is master your powers. The best way to do that is to go back to the source—where your powers are strongest."

"Go back to Tarotland, you mean. I couldn't, even if we had the World Card."

"No, this is true. Too bad you gave it away."

I sigh. "Sorry. Either way, I couldn't leave Talia behind again. I want to make sure she's safe, and our lives aren't stable enough for me to leave her." Anything can happen to her. She could be fostered by some creeps who are specifically looking for a teenage girl. She could run away and get into trouble. The possibilities are endless. My eyes flick to the time on my phone and I jump. "I'm late! Thanks, Asteria. I'll be back for more practice."

She collects the cards and wraps them up in her cloth. "Take these with you, in case you want to look at them some more tonight."

2

A COOL BREEZE TOUSLES MY HAIR AS I STEP OUT OF
Asteria's fortune teller tent. Bright lights illuminate the pavilions as the
sun sets and the thrumming of a guitar comes from the stage, followed
by a fiddle.

I cross over to the contortionist tent where Sherry is waiting for me.
I quickly take out my phone and slow my step to send Talia a message to
let her know I haven't forgotten about our movie tonight.

My phone buzzes, and I gape at her reply.

> TALIA
>
> Hey Soren, I'm so sorry but I can't make it to
> the movies tonight! I forgot I told a friend of
> mine I was going to hang out…

My stomach sinks. Talia has been dodging my plans for the last two
weeks, and now she's canceling on the night of our plans? Was she even
going to tell me if I hadn't texted her?! I grip my phone tight in my hand
and begin to furiously swipe my fingers across my screen.

> ME
>
> What plans? We've barely hung out at all.

11

"Hi, Soren."

Quirking a brow, I glance up and hit send. Cory, the circus ring-leader, stands in front of me holding a bag of popcorn. He offers me some. "How are ya?"

"Uh, fine," I say. "Kind of in a hurry." I'm now standing in front of the contortionist's tent, staring at the three little dots moving and then pausing, and reappearing. I'm sure Talia is fabricating some sorry excuse to tell me.

He frowns. "Oh. I was hoping..." He stammers. "Well, if you weren't too busy later, maybe you'd like to catch a movie with me?"

I blink up at him. "I'm sorry, I have plans already." I chew my cheek. Was that too harsh?

His face blanks. "Right. Of course. I'm sorry. I'll get out of your hair." He backs away and smiles with a nervous wave. I wave back apologetically. Two of the guys who help with the tent set up stop at the circus tent, looking over with crates in their hands. One of them stares at Cory, and I think I see relief pass over his face as he watches him walk away from me.

Sherry pokes her head out of her tent to see I'm still standing watching him leave.

"One of those guys finally got the nerve to ask you out, huh?" She giggles. She's changed into black sweatpants and a tight white t-shirt, contrary to the usual voodoo skeleton garb she wears for her act.

My cheeks burn. I nod and look back down at my phone.

Her features twist. "Oh, no. Poor guy. Cory's super cute, though, with that swimmer's body. Why don't you ever date?"

"No one ever asks me. Well, until now."

"They're all intimidated. But if you're into girls, let me know, because I'll date you. I'm not intimidated by hot girls."

I stifle a laugh, and glance over my shoulder to hide my burning cheeks. Cory's heading back toward the guys who look like they're about to bust his chops. He is actually really cute. She's right about that. He's also really sweet, and I feel bad for blowing him off like that. It's just...

Gembella.

I shiver. "I have other things on my mind," I tell her. Talia's still typing. You know what? Forget it. I black out my phone and walk inside the tent.

"Feels like the weather is dropping, doesn't it?" Sherry tosses me a pair of boxing gloves, and I catch them, thankful she changed the subject.

I pull them on. "Hopefully." I widen my stance like she showed me and start bouncing on my toes, warming up to get ready. Sherry is not only a talented contortionist, but she's been training in mixed martial arts her whole life and has offered to give me lessons. Well, she stopped me from spending my own money, because I had no idea she knew how to fight. In exchange, I show her how to do my card tricks. If she ever decides to leave this carnival and work for someone else, she'll at least have more skills up her sleeve.

After guiding me through some stretches and warm-ups, Sherry starts off by having me punch the air with three basic combinations: jab, cross, left and right hook. I keep doing this until I work up a sweat, but I barely look at her, as she instructs and fixes my stances. I can't stop my brain from daydreaming. With every punch I throw, my brain jumps from Talia's texts and what plans she could possibly have. I bet she has a boyfriend. That's the only thing that makes sense. Why else would she constantly be ditching me?

For almost four years, we've been more like sisters than best friends. Sure, I do treat her like a sister, and I can be a bit overprotective, but we've been inseparable. If she's been talking to a boy, why wouldn't she tell me?

"Soren, did you hear me?"

"Sorry, what?"

Her forehead crinkles. "You okay, sugar?"

I pause and put my gloved hand over my chest, trying to calm down my heart. "Yeah, sorry. Just distracted today. Talia canceled plans with me, and I'm pissed. I'm back, though. What were you saying?"

"Oh, I'm sorry. Do you wanna call it quits for tonight and talk about it?"

I shake my head. "Nope. I need to let off some steam, I'm good. Let's keep going."

"Well, good, 'cause I was askin' if you were ready to spar yet."

I clap my gloves together and bounce on my toes. "I was born ready."

Sherry chuckles and motions for me to punch her.

I work my way through remembering a few combinations she taught me, but her counterattacks nearly knock me onto my ass. She shoots me a few reprimands and corrections before we pause for a water break.

"Let's go again," I tell her. She gives me a surprised look but doesn't protest.

"Keep your arms up and block your face," she barks, her short black hair bouncing forward as she comes in for an attack. "This time, let's throw in some foot-swiping movements."

I jump back and counter with a set of blocks and punches.

"Good," she says.

I keep my eyes focused on her face, trying to study her movements, any hint of where she might attack me next, but it's hard to keep track of that while remembering the moves.

I keep going, my heart rate picking up speed as I move forward and back. Attack and block. Correct myself. Keep my knees bent.

Gembella

I gasp.

Sherry moves in and swipes my foot forward, catching me off guard and making me fall on my rear.

My heart thuds in my chest as I gape up at her.

She extends a hand out for me, and I grab it. "Are you hurt?"

"Nope." Just distracted by ghosts. I dust myself off and get back into my stance, but Sherry doesn't.

"It's been an hour. Why don't we call it?"

I drop my arms. "That's probably a good idea. I don't want to end up on the floor again."

"No, you were doing great. You're just tired. Keep coming to practice, and you'll get better, I promise."

I give her a sheepish smile while taking off my borrowed gloves, then give them back to her. "Thanks Sher, you're the best." I can't tell her I'm being haunted by the memories of someone I can never see again because he lives in another dimension. And even if I leave that last part out, I just don't want to have that conversation. I'd rather push all those memories out of my mind. Sooner or later, they'll all go away.

"Try talking to Talia about how you feel. She'll eventually learn it's rude to cancel at the last minute."

Right. And that, too, has me distracted. "Maybe. Some people never do."

"I know that's right." She grabs a water bottle from the fridge and tosses it to me. I say my goodbyes and wait until I'm outside of the tent to check my phone.

TALIA

I'm really sorry, Soren. I promise I'll make it up to you. Love you!

Rolling my eyes, I stick my phone into my back pocket and head out for my walk home. She doesn't want to tell me who her friend is. It has to be a boy. I relax my shoulders. I know she's getting older and needs her space, I just wish she'd talk to me. But I guess why would she? I don't think she's fully forgiven me for leaving her in jail, and I don't think she really believed the story I told her about Tarotland. Who would? It sounds crazy.

Sneaking behind the trees, I cross the carnival grounds and walk out the back gate. I don't bother saying anything to the Nelsons, and I don't want to risk them seeing me and making me work. Since I don't live with them anymore, they try to drain me of every ounce of paid labor they can get from me. I was allowed back into the group home after the whole fiasco with me disappearing, and I wanted to be close to Talia. To keep her safe.

The Nelsons let me keep my job so that I can move into my own place when I turn eighteen, in exchange for continuing to help them with their scams. But I made them agree to give me a bigger cut, so I make more here than I would as a cashier in some lame-o job. It's not like there are girls lining up with the same skills I have, no families, and a willingness to cheat people out of their money for them.

I open the front door to the group home and find one of the girls in the living room watching TV. I wave at her and make my way into the kitchen. Almost everyone is either out with friends or at the school library studying for exams. I set a pot of water to boil and open the cabinet to take out a box of macaroni and cheese, then take out hot dogs from the fridge and start cutting them up. A dinner for champions. Not exactly the loaded hot dog with nachos and popcorn I wanted from the movie theater tonight, but after Talia canceled, I don't feel like going alone. I wonder what time she'll be home.

As I let the water boil, I dig out the tightly wrapped Tarot cards from my bag and start flipping through them, inspecting each one. Even though these are store-bought cards, and not portal-opening, life-changing, magical Tarot cards, they're still pretty. And apparently suitable for Asteria.

My mind drifts to the vision I had earlier at the tent. It was the first time I'd experienced a vision like that since I was in Tarotland. Maybe I should feel more excited, but it didn't come from me, it came from Philo. Also, it felt so strange seeing my mom. Instead of feeling the excitement of experiencing magic again, I felt...sad. And now, I was even more perplexed than I had been. She had held the Ace of Swords and was clearly in some sort of relationship with an Ipani. The way he held onto her, how close he sat behind her. I squeeze my eyes shut to keep myself from thinking about...him.

Gembella.

Damnit. And to make matters worse, the word that comes out each time means prisoner. Not neyuro, meaning "brave," which is what he had started to call me toward the end. Nope. Prisoner. And why do I have Nkella whispering prisoner to me throughout the day? I have no idea.

Worst earworm ever.

Maybe it's because I still feel like one.

Once my mac and cheese is cooked, I pour the contents into a bowl along with my cut-up hot dogs and take it up to the room I share with Talia. I switch on Netflix and select a scary movie for some background noise while I gobble up my food. I check the time. Nine p.m. I think about texting Talia, but I don't want to seem overbearing. She'll be back soon.

Setting the bowl aside, I pick the Tarot cards up again, this time shuffling them a few times. My heart starts to race before I can phrase the question in my head. I want to ask about my mom, but mostly, I want to see her again. I know it won't happen without Philo, though. Where is that spider when you need her? I set down three cards on the bed.

This time it's the Ace of Swords, the Fool, and the Lovers. I stare at each card blankly, recalling their meanings and hoping for some wisdom to fall from the sky.

After a few minutes, I give up and put the cards away. Lying down on the bed, I stare at my mother's necklace around my neck, tracing it with my fingertips. I wear it everywhere now; I never take it off. Not only because it makes me feel close to her, but because it speaks of a mysterious life my mother led, a life I had no knowledge of—one we could have shared together. If only I could have seen her, if only I could have talked to her, maybe I could have told her where I had gone. And maybe, just maybe, she would have remembered Tarotland. And remembered me.

But that's just a dream. She wouldn't have remembered me. My chest tightens as I stare at the curved palm tree etched on the ruby. It matched the money—gichang—Nkella had given me before I left Tarotland, so that I could afford a flight to visit my mother in the hospital. We were getting along then; he was being kind, despite his knack for hallucinogenic-type torture. I thought he had betrayed me, but he didn't really. I know that now.

Gembella.

I gasp and let the pendant hit my chest.

Screw this. What I need is a hot shower, to forget about today, and to think about something—anything other than Tarot cards, rubies, and magic. I scoot off the bed and grab my pajamas from my drawer. When I shut the drawer, something moves in the mirror behind me. I quickly spin around but find nothing there. Furrowing my brows, I glance back into the mirror.

A ripple moves down the mirror just like at my counselor's office. I blink a few times, unsure if what I'm seeing is real.

The ripples grow larger, and my eyes widen.

It is real. This is really happening in front of me right now.

The image in the mirror grows hazy and my reflection disappears, to be replaced by white clouds. I take a small step back, a different kind of ripple hitting my nerves. Fear. The white clouds grow sharper until I realize I'm not staring at clouds but snowy mountains. A ship comes into view in the center of the mirror, below the mountains. I can see the waves moving the ship up and down, as white sails billow in the wind. In the top right corner of the mirror is a floating island, Rutavenye. I'm staring at Ipa. But whose ship is that? It's not the all-black wooden boards and horned skull of the *Gambit*.

Three bombs fall from the sky inside the image, one at a time; each hits the ship, one after the other. A yelp leaves my mouth, and I step back. The ship catches fire, and bits fly in different directions. Half the ship starts sinking, as smoke fumes out, covering the mirror in gray darkness. Lightning strikes through the smoke, and now I've backed away so far, I'm touching the bed with the backs of my legs.

The image changes back, reflecting the image of me covering my mouth.

What the hell was that?

I know it has to be of the past—I'm the "Past Fate descendant," and Asteria confirmed all my visions will be of the past.

Panic courses through me. Whose past was I seeing? My mom's?

No... Not unless she wasn't on the ship. No one could have survived that. But then, why was I seeing it?

It takes a moment before my heart drops to my stomach. Wasn't the undead crew going to steal a ship to find the *Gambit* after I left?

"Show me Nkella." I stammer, not knowing if that would work. When the mirror doesn't show me an image, I tap on it. To my surprise, my finger goes through. My eyes widen and I hold my breath as I quickly draw my hand back.

I slowly let it out.

Okay. Get a hold of yourself, Soren. So what if their ship sank? They're undead. And Nkella has ways of disappearing with his wolf. I'm sure they're fine.

But then why was the mirror showing it to me? What if it does have something to do with my mom?

Or what if Iéle was not around and Nkella got killed? Or drowned?

What if he's been captured by the empress and needs my help?

My blood runs cold.

I know I shouldn't care, but I do. Before I can coherently collect my thoughts, a ripple moves across the mirror again, and this time, instead of moving back, I'm moving forward, my curiosity taking me dangerously close.

My hand moves on its own, and I hold my breath as I plan to tap the surface of the mirror. My fingers go through, and I gasp, quickly pulling them out. I swallow the breath I'm holding and stick my fingers in again. It feels like I'm going through water, except it isn't wet.

This time my entire hand goes through, and I ready myself to walk inside the mirror.

3

I PULL MY HAND STRAIGHT OUT. NOPE! NO, NO NO NO. WHAT am I thinking? I don't even know whose ship that is! Or where I'd end up if I go through! *And how is this even possible?*

I don't have the World Card, so how could a portal be opening up in my room?

Not to mention, *I can't go.* I won't go. I'm not about to leave Talia to take off into some other dimension again, clearly straight into danger. She needs me here.

I back away from the mirror, my eyes widening as the ripples stop moving and my reflection comes back. I tap on it a few times and hit solid glass. I'll have to tell Asteria about this tomorrow, because that wasn't normal, and stepping inside a mirror is a little too Alice—even for me.

The bedroom door creaks slowly open, and I blink awake. The light switches on, and I spin around in my bed to see Talia walking in. I sit up.

"Where have you been? It's late."

"One, you're not my mom. And two, it's not late. It's only ten thirty. I just got back from having dinner." She throws her bag next to her bed and grabs her pajamas from under her pillow.

"Where are you going now?" I squint and look around for my phone to see the time; I didn't even plug it into the charger. There's no way it can only be ten thirty. Did I seriously fall asleep binging Netflix on a Friday night?

"To shower," she snaps. "Soren, calm down. I'll talk to you in a minute."

I gape at her as I find my phone between my sheets and tap on the screen. Sure enough, it's 10:35 p.m. I am so lame. I push myself out of bed and follow Talia down the hall. She's in the bathroom with the door slightly open, brushing her teeth. Her curly black hair is tied into a tight bun, away from her brown eyes.

"So did you have fun tonight?" I ask, forcing the door to widen a bit as I lean against the doorframe.

She shoots me a side glare and spits into the sink. "Yeah, it was nice."

"Who did you meet with?"

She scrunches her brows, as if thinking cautiously, considering what she's going to say.

My shoulders drop. "Look, I don't know why you're being so secretive with me all of a sudden, and I get you want your space. I'm just being a concerned sister, okay?"

She rinses her mouth with water and grabs a towel, turning to me. "And we'll always be sisters. But Soren, listen..."

I stare at her, clenching my fists, waiting for her to confirm she needs space from me or wants me to leave her alone. I know I've been overprotective. "Talia—I know I've been overbearing lately, and I'm sorry. I just—"

"Carmen is going to call an afternoon meeting tomorrow." She deadpans.

I blink at her. Carmen is the group home manager, and she usually only calls a meeting to discuss events, activities, house rules...or whenever someone is getting fostered or going home with their real parents. "What does that have to do with anything?"

Her forehead wrinkles. "Nothing, I just thought you should know."

An anvil lands in my stomach. Could her parents be ready for her? Finally, after all this time? She can't be getting fostered. I mean, it's possible, but she and I are too old for anyone sensible anyway...

She must read the assumptions running through my mind because she crosses her arms and gives me an expectant look. "I promise I'll tell you what's going on tomorrow, okay? Just drop it for tonight so that we can both get some sleep. And I promise I'll make it up to you. It's nothing bad, I swear."

"I thought you had a boyfriend or something."

Talia lets out a giggle. "If that were true, I definitely would have told you."

"Sorry...I guess I just felt left out, since you canceled on me at the last minute."

"I know, and I am sorry about that. They contacted me at the last minute, and I couldn't say no. But Soren, I can't always be at your beck and call."

"What's that supposed to mean?"

"I'm just saying, I'm trying to be more independent and have my own life."

"So, you need space from me."

She winces. "It's not like that, but...just a little?" She presses her thumb and index finger close together, showing a little space.

I swallow hard. "Yeah, sure, whatever. Sorry. I'll try to be less up your ass. I just get...worried."

"About what, though? That you're going to end up in some magical land and never see me again? That I'm going to run away and never come back?"

"Or kidnapped, or worse..." I try ignoring the look she's giving me as she says "*magical land,*" but it doesn't go unnoticed. It makes me not want to tell her about the mirror. I can just imagine her standing in front of it, making me try to get it to work again, to prove that I imagined it. She hasn't come out and said she doesn't believe me about Tarotland, but I can read it on her face, and I don't want to go there. Not tonight.

She rolls her eyes. "You worry too much. "

"Maybe. But I have reason to." Getting fostered by sleazeballs time and time again will do that to a person. I don't even want to think about the Ipani trafficking situation in Ipa, not too far off from the child trafficking that goes on here. "We have to look out for each other," I finish.

Sighing, she nods. "Are you still tired, or do you want to watch a movie in the room?"

"Let's watch a movie."

She grins. "Go pick one, whatever you want. I'm gonna finish getting ready for bed."

"Ya'll just gonna stand there and take up space in the bathroom? I gotta pee."

We snap our gazes to our housemate Maxine who's standing there crossing her legs.

"Use the one downstairs," Talia says and slams the door. I give Max an apologetic look and go back to the room. Despite the weight lifting off my shoulders after talking to Talia, I still feel like a pile of bricks has landed in my stomach. She doesn't want to tell me about the meeting tomorrow, and I don't want to press. I'll just have to wait and see what it's about.

The next day, I don't waste any time. I go directly to Asteria's tent and tell her everything from shuffling the cards and trying to do a reading on myself, to sticking my hand through the mirror. I hover over her in front of her desk as she glares back at me with furrowed brows behind her thick-framed glasses, her long curly brown hair over her shoulders.

I think this is the longest she's ever gone without talking.

"Anything?" I finally ask.

She sits back in her chair. "It's certainly different," she says. "It's not something that's ever happened to me. And it happened directly after you pulled cards?"

"Well, not directly after. I was looking down at my pendant, and…it also happened at my counselor's office yesterday before coming here," I say while taking out my mother's ruby coin from inside my shirt.

"What were you thinking about?"

I glance at the coin. "I guess...a few things. About my mom. And about the last time I was there, certain people I met." My cheeks warm.

"So, you were thinking about Ipa." Her eyes look distant as she stares past me. "And you saw mountains, did you say?" I nod. She throws her hands in front of her. "Anything is possible. Somehow a portal opened, and the only explanation is that you opened it."

My face pales. Me? "Are you sure?"

"How else?"

"I don't know. You're the magic expert. You come from there, don't you?"

A surprise look washes over her face. We hadn't actually gotten around to talking about how she came to have the World Card or how she knows of the Empress. She said she would reveal all that to me before she suddenly had to leave, but ever since she's been back, I've felt like she went from wanting to explain it all to evading my questions. I decided not to press it, because...what for? I'm not going back. Although, I have had my suspicions over who or what she is.

Her blue eyes sparkle, and she gives me a toothy grin. "Have a seat, Soren." She points to the chair. "You hovering over me like that is making it seem like you came here for a quick answer. You should know by now that won't be the case with me ever. There are no simple answers."

I deflate and sit down.

"It is not impossible that you opened the portal, but it is surprising."

"Surprising?"

"Long ago, before the modern age, three sisters made the promise to escape this land and start new in a place without war. Their father was mad and hungry for power, but the sisters loved their people and knew that in order to save them, they needed to find a safe haven, somewhere away from this land—somewhere their father could never find them, no matter how many ships and how much magic he had."

I listen intently to her story; I had already heard some of it from Aba in Wands, but I'm curious to hear if Asteria's story is different.

"When the sisters found Ipa, they had intended to create a pocket dimension, with the idea of hiding there until the wars in Greece ended, but they knew that was going to take a long time. When they arrived, they were surprised to find that they opened a portal to a new land, and it was not a pocket dimension at all. Unfortunately, they couldn't turn back."

Okay, that part, I didn't know.

"Their father had forbidden the use of pocket dimensions right before they attempted to create one, and in doing so, they were also trapped."

Philo pops up onto the desk, shares a look with me first, then turns to Asteria. Her big round eyes look cute as she moves her little body back and forth.

My eyes squint down at Philo. "But the Past and Future Fates were able to travel around, bringing stuff back with them."

"So you know the story?"

"Only parts of it."

"Yes, they were able to travel around, but it took years before they could. By then, they were settled, and their people didn't want to leave. Between the cards and the merging of their magic with the Aō, their powers flourished. The three of them no longer needed to be together to open a portal. They had the World Card now, but it wasn't all good. It was savvy magic. And in the wrong hands, it could be destructive and lead the world to burn."

"Didn't the Past Fate descendant of the time betray the Empress or something?"

Asteria's features straighten to look serious. "The youngest sister had just had her baby, before getting killed."

"Because the Empress killed her."

Asteria's brows dip with curiosity as she leans closer to me. "Who told you that?"

"That is the rumor going around Ipa," I say slowly.

"Hmm. The only thing that mattered was the survival of the baby. And I'm not sure the Empress knew if the child still lived after that horrible fire."

"Fire?"

"A fire that broke out in the castle, everyone and everything in it burned. The Empress was blamed for it, but she suffered as well. It's why she wears the mask."

I gasp. She wears a mask because she's been hiding her scars. "How do you know all of this?"

"My child"—her voice quivers—"I was the sister who saved the baby and brought us to this land."

My mouth dries. I guess I had known who she was since I got back. "You're the Future Fate, aren't you? The Past Fate descendant was your sister."

She gives a single nod. "Her name was Adara, and yes, I am. And you are the newest Past Fate. And as it appears you opened a portal last night, you hold greater power than any one of us ever did. You've barely come into your powers, but your magic is dying to come out, isn't it?"

I seriously don't know what to do with this information. "What does that mean about my mom?"

"Your mother never held the World Card like you thought. She must have opened a portal on her own, like you did last night. I've always kept the World Card hidden away, waiting to find the next generation."

"So, you never knew my mother?"

She shakes her head. "No, but I knew when she used magic, which is what led me to you. Unfortunately, when I got here to find your mom, she was already back, and time had passed. Her mind had...well, you know."

My shoulder muscles tense. "Alzheimer's."

"Yes, and at such a young age. I always found it curious."

"Why's that?"

She shakes her head again. "I don't know, dear, but it won't make a difference. The result is the same, isn't it? It's best to let go of the past, no matter how much it goes against your nature." She gives me a sweet half smile.

"I guess."

"So now, tell me, Soren, what will you do with this information, now that you have it?"

I play with the hem of my shirt. I feel like she wants me to say I'm

THE DEVIL'S GAMBIT

going to go practice my powers, I'm going to go back into Ipa, and... do what exactly? "What do you think I should do?"

"Only you can answer that."

"And what about you, then, huh? You're the Future Fate. Why do you stay here? Why don't you go back to take down your sister?"

Asteria's face drops, and her eyes start to swell. "My sister took my leaving her there as an even worse betrayal than that of our little sister. If she were to kill me, I'm afraid it would destroy the future of all who live in Ipa. Aletha may hold the Death Card, but I hold everyone's future in my hands. And the way our magic is merged with the Aō, it might just mean the reversal of everyone's marks. But there's no telling for sure."

"So, you staying here ensures their future? Then why do people die?"

"The Death Card is my nemesis. I can't predict when they'll die. As you see, the balance is broken, which is why I had hoped you would take on the mantle of the Past Fate descendant."

My heart plummets. "But that's not—" My chest pants. "It's just not what I want to do. My life is here—with Talia. I can't live over there forever..."

Asteria raises a hand. "Another generation will come. It doesn't have to be you."

I drop my shoulders and take a deep breath. "So, I'm not...ruining an entire world?"

She tilts her head to the side, raising and dropping her brows. "Hundreds of years have passed. What's another hundred or so?"

My throat dries. This answers a lot of questions. My mother was a Past Fate, which is why she was over there. But it also opens up a lot of questions. How did she end up there? And what was she doing? "Was my mother trying to stop the Empress? Why did she feel it was up to her to do so, if she was?"

Asteria shakes her head. "I wish I knew, but I can't tell you the past." She winks. I refrain from rolling my eyes.

My brows furrow. Nkella and the crew had tried to steal the Death Card but were caught and cursed for it. "Wait. The Death Card is the reason no one can die in Ipa." Philo quirks up at me as Asteria lifts her chin. "But it can also be used to reverse their deaths, can't it?"

27

"That's a dangerous notion, Soren. You can never know how people would come back—depending on how they died."

"But it can bring someone back then? How is that possible if the card means death?"

"The Death Card opens the door for a new life. It holds more power than just an ending—but beginnings."

"What kind of beginnings? Just life after death?"

"And renewal," she adds carefully.

My pulse quickens. "So, would you say, renewal of an illness?"

Asteria taps her fingers on the desk. "A person's mind may not always follow the body once it is gone. The past needs to stay in the past, Soren. Heed my warning."

I nod. "I know, I know. The past needs to stay where it is. Got it."

"Those suffering in eternal torment can only be put to rest, not returned. They want peace, Soren, not to come back."

But my mother died here, not in Ipa, so she isn't in eternal torment. "So, theoretically, could the Death Card—and my Past Fate magic reverse their damages?"

Asteria narrows her eyes. "Theoretically, yes."

I give her a tight smile. Interesting. "Well, this was helpful, but I'd better get going."

Asteria sits up in her chair and starts tidying her desk. "Take care, Soren." I don't miss the look of disappointment in her eyes, like she was hoping I would be moved to go on this extreme adventure.

"Wait," I say. "It just hit me. Does this make you my...great, great, great, like hundreds times great-aunt or something?"

She chuckles. "Yes, we are distantly related."

My eyes round. "So, you're hundreds of years old..."

"I am very old. Indeed."

"And you still look young. Will I live that long too?"

Asteria shakes her head. "Only if you come into your powers. The Ipani live a very long time, hundreds of years even. Did you know?"

My mouth parts. "I didn't know that."

"It's because of the Empress that they've all been stumped."

Just to add more weight on my shoulders. I turn to leave.

"Oh...and Soren?"

"Yeah?"

"If you do decide on going back, look out for that World Card, would you? I don't need my sister crossing over here. She won't be able to find me with my cloaking spell, but she'll be able to make things difficult for the both of us now that she knows about you."

I nod and walk out of her tent.

I spend the rest of the day working at my usual stand at the carnival. It's slow enough for a Saturday, but it's still early. Some people are here with their kids, and none of them are interested in card tricks. A little later is when my particular clientele come. They're either waiting around for a seance or meandering through the creepier nighttime of the carnival. I often wonder if some know they're getting scammed but don't care. Unfortunately, I won't be sticking around for that today. I have to make it back to the group home in time for the dinner meeting.

But in the meantime, my mind returns to my conversation with Asteria.

For some reason, my mother had decided it was up to her to stop the Empress. Did she know she was the Past Fate descendant? If she never picked up the Ace of Wands—which she obviously hadn't because it could only be used once and it had dissipated in my hands—would she have learned who she was? What did she know about the use of her powers? Why was she at war with the Empress? Assuming that's where she was headed with a sword.

After work, I head home, and my stomach slowly ties itself into a knot as the thing I've pushed to the back of my mind all day resurfaces.

Sure enough, what Talia had told me last night was true. This morning, all the girls were told we were going to have a chat before dinner. I wouldn't care if I thought it had to do with some discipline crap, or doing chores, or the variety of mundane things they normally call everyone in for a chat about. I have a bad feeling this time. Talia's face said it all last night, but I didn't want to think about it. I don't want to admit what I fear this might be about.

Let's face it, even if I could steal that Death Card from the Empress, I'd be leaving Talia behind, and I don't want to do that.

I walk inside the two-story group home and shut the door behind me. Talia is sitting on the couch in the living room to the right of the door, next to two other girls. I set my bag down and walk over.

Talia's eyes light up when she sees me, and I smile back. "Hey, Soren!"

"What's up, girls? What's going on?"

Carmen, the group home's manager comes walking down the steps wearing an autumnal red sweater over a pair of blue jeans. Two more girls come through the dining room from the kitchen.

"Good. Everyone's here," Carmen says. "Talia here has some exciting news to tell us." She stares at Talia who is shrinking into her shoulders. I steady my breathing, not wanting to jump to any conclusions, nor make her feel nervous. But my heart is thudding so loud I can feel it in my ears. Talia looks at me and I give her a tight smile, expectantly waiting for her to talk.

"Umm... I'm going to be leaving," she says weakly. My mouth drops.

"What do you mean leaving?" I say. She looks at me apologetically.

"To a lovely home," Carmen answers for her. "I advised Talia to keep it a secret so as to not stir up any emotions...in case it didn't pan out. But Talia agreed to meet with them on multiple outings to make sure it was a good match. She passed all the checks, and they're good to go."

My brain is clogged with this new information, and all I can do is wrap my arms around my stomach. One of the girls sitting next to Talia gives her a hug and gets up to leave the room. I nearly fall to the seat.

"Be happy for Talia, Soren," Carmen says. "This is a good thing."

How is this a good thing?

I smile at Talia. "Congrats," I mutter.

Talia deflates and looks at Carmen. "Can you all give us a minute?"

Carmen nods. "Of course," she motions for all the girls to leave. I stare at Talia.

"I get that Carmen told you to keep it secret in a group home where there's jealousy and sabotaging of shit. I get it. But you could have told me before having me find out this way." Tears brim in my eyes, and I try to hold them back.

"I'm sorry, Soren, but I was afraid you were going to try and make me change my mind."

"Of course, I was," I say, my voice rising. "You don't even know these people. You had a few outings? So what? You think they're good people to bring in a fourteen-year-old girl into their home? How do you know they're actually good? Huh? How?" I'm yelling, my chest rising up and down. She shouldn't have kept this information from me. "I, at least, would have wanted to check them out."

Now Talia's eyes are wet with tears. "You always do this. You always want to control everything. It's my life, Soren."

"Sorry for wanting to be a good sister to you. I promised to always keep you safe, and I was trying to make good on that promise. In fact, I still want to."

"No."

"What do you mean *no*? What kind of an answer is that?"

"You're not going to check them out, because I don't want you to."

I gape at her and stay silent for a moment until I find the right words. I swallow. "We were supposed to stay close together, remember? What happened to me saving up enough money to get us a place together?"

"Soren, I'm doing this for you too."

"How does that even make sense? And don't say for independence. Because I don't need you around me. I'm perfectly fine on my own. I only care about keeping you safe." Hurt crosses her features and I know I sounded mean, but I'm fuming.

"I just want you to trust me," she says, twisting the bottom of her sweater in her fist. "I promise, you'll understand."

"More secrets." I huff.

"Soren, can you just please chill?"

"When do I get to meet this mystery family?"

"I—I don't know. Soon, I promise."

"Fine. Whatever."

"You act like you're never going to see me again, and I swear to you, this is for the best."

I squint at her.

"*Come on!* This place sucks! I'm tired of sharing my stuff and fighting over the bathroom, and things going missing. I'm tired of the constant reminder that everyone's life here sucks and that my parents have practically abandoned me. I just want to be in a nice home, with a full fridge, and be able to see you at my leisure with—no offense—not having to share a room with you. I want my own space." She says it all in one breath. "And these people can offer me more than that. They can offer me literally anything I want."

"That rich, huh?"

"Uh-huh." Her eyes bulge. "Which is part of the reason it's so secretive."

Sighing, I wipe my hand over my eyes. I still don't trust this but now that the foster system is involved, there's not much I can do. Talia has clearly made her mind up, and I don't want to push her away. "Alright," I say, calmer. "You're right. You deserve all that. I'm not going to get in the way of an awesome opportunity for you." After all, she's only fourteen and has four years left until adulthood. Let her at least have a chance to go to a good school and get everything she ever wanted. If this is legit. I try to push out the thought of high-profile abductors fostering children for their own gain. "I love ya, sis. You know you can always count on me if things go sideways."

"Always."

I spend the rest of the night baking a cake for Talia, while I bank away my feelings. Everything I've done for the past few years has been to ensure Talia and I stay together. Not only to keep an eye on her, but so she knows she's not alone. I guess she still knows that, though. And I have to let her go so that she learns to become more independent. I get that. Or at least, I'm trying to.

I don't tell her about the revelations I found out from Asteria, or about me thinking about my mom. I don't want her to worry about me.

I spend the following days working at the carnival and the evenings with Talia until the end of the week. I don't try to spy on her, and I don't try looking up the foster parents. I'm doing my best to respect her wishes.

I did sneak into Carmen's office and pull out her foster parents' file. Hey, I said I wouldn't go looking for them, not that I wouldn't read about them. I trust Talia, I just don't trust anyone else, and I definitely don't trust the foster system.

Pamela and Gregory Sherest. Squeaky clean record, middle-aged, and donate thousands to varying charities each year. Which means nothing. I sigh. All I can do is hope they sincerely want to spend the rest of their lives helping a kid who needs it.

I don't tell Talia I looked into them—I keep that to myself—but since she'll be leaving the group home while I'm there, I wanted to catch a glimpse of what the lady looked like, even if only from a photo. I'm sure I'll see them around. It's not like it's a permanent goodbye.

Talia stares at me from a black Cadillac window and waves goodbye. A tear rolls down my cheek as I press my hand against the glass. Apparently, none of us were allowed near the car and had to stay inside. It doesn't bother me, because I'll catch up to her whether they like it or not. Still, I swallow a sob as the car drives off. The girls watching from downstairs make jokes about how Talia is going to turn into one of those stuck-up, snobby, rich people.

Now it's too quiet in my room. It's even worse knowing Talia won't be coming through the door. I stare at her empty bed, the sheets stripped and everything in her once disaster corner completely empty and clean. Pushing my thoughts about Talia away, my mind drifts back to my mom and Tarotland.

I trace a finger over the place where my mark used to be, trying to imagine the curved spiderweb right above my wrist. My mother must have had the same mark, so she must have known she was different than everyone else there, right? Why weren't there any records of her saying anything. Or maybe there were, and everyone just assumed she was nuts.

And what did Asteria mean by always finding it weird that she had early Alzheimer's and dementia? As I understand it, it's genetic, so I'm probably doomed for the same fate. It's not like being a Fate descendant made us exempt from it. We're still human, and we can still get sick, but Asteria also said that we can live long lives if we come into our powers, so maybe my mother hadn't come into them or, at least, not fully.

I gasp. What if I start losing my mind, and still live as long as Asteria?

I wish I could talk to my mom and ask her all these questions.

I wish I knew what she had been doing in Tarotland. That look in her eyes—she looked so certain of herself. Why did she come back?

The Death Card can bring her back. I know it can. Then, I wouldn't have to worry about ever losing my mind either. I could bring her back and reverse any ill fate for us both.

I sit with my legs close to my chest on the bed. Movement catches my eye, and a buzz of electricity shoots through my veins. I slowly look up at the mirror.

I scurry off the bed and gaze at my reflection between the rippling movements; it's happening again. I watch in awe as my reflection fades away, only to be replaced by the same ship that appeared before. The mountains take up the view in the background, and the waves begin to move. My throat dries, but I stay put.

The Empress has the Death Card. Nkella and the crew were no match for her, but maybe *I* could steal it.

I'd have to work on my powers to be a match for her in case I get caught. Maybe the crew would still be interested in using the card to bring everyone back, and we can help each other. Only this time, I'll be the one stealing it; Nkella just needs to tell me where she has it hidden.

I dip a finger into the mirror, and it causes a ripple. The circles widen as they move away from the ship.

Philo pops onto the edge of the mirror, her puppy-like eyes staring at me. She points a leg to the mirror as if wanting me to go through.

"Were you spying on me?" Of course, she was. "You want me to go back, don't you?"

Philo tilts her head in response.

"Do you think I'll find the answers I need if I go through the mirror?" the spider points her leg harder, and I squeeze my eyes shut. It's not like I have anything holding me back here. Talia doesn't need me. And I have the strongest desire to find out about what my mom was doing in Tarotland. And an even stronger desire to steal the Death Card if it means I have an actual chance to bring my mother back to me—her mind fully intact.

I can't believe I'm saying this but...I have to go back.

Steeling my spine, I pull out a leather box hidden in the back of my closet. Wiping away a thin layer of dust, I slowly open it. The familiar, warm aroma of vanilla and sea salt tugs on my heartstrings as I take out the green tunic Nkella bought me in Wands and caress the soft texture of Ipani woven fabric between my fingers. I turn back to the mirror where Philo is still standing on the edge of the black frame. Okay, if I'm going to do this, I'm going to do it right.

Once I've changed into common Ipani streetwear, I grab the remaining ruby coins I have in a small pouch. This time, I'm going under my own free will, and I'm going to blend in. If that ship that sunk was the crew, I want to make sure they're safe.

Then I'm off to find the Death Card and bring my mother back.

I stare at my undulating reflection in the mirror, and a butterfly lets loose in my stomach. I'm actually doing this. I'm going to see Nkella again. I just hope he's alive.

I move forward, and in a single breath, I crawl into the mirror.

4

Okay, this is not what I expected. The moment I cross the mirror, a cool breeze of humid air touches my skin, but it's not the cold I was expecting from the snowy mountains I saw in the mirror. And for that I am grateful. I wasn't exactly thinking straight. I mean, I would be freezing without a coat right now.

Instead, I'm standing where sand meets dirt at the edge of a dark wooded forest, behind me are the crashing waves of a beach under a full moon, and no mirror is in sight.

My heart lodges in my throat. Okay, no need to panic. If I can't find a mirror, I left the World Card with Nkella. I'll manage to find my way back home.

All I have to do now is find the crew.

Laughter and music come from inside the woods, and I scan the beach. Waves crash methodically, and the aroma of warm sand and spices wafts through the air. It doesn't smell like rotten flesh, so I'm definitely not on Wands. A few boats are parked by the dock, but no one else is around. Deciding to follow the music, I step into the forest.

I don't have to walk far; the music grows louder as I follow the moonlit path up a rocky trail, which leads me to a tavern. I squint my eyes at the Ancient Greek letters decorating the front windows. I know

THE DEVIL'S GAMBIT

this place. To the right is another path that leads down some stone steps. That path leads to a marketplace marina. The tavern is called Cerberus.

I'm back in Dempu Yuni.

I walk up to the tavern and peek through the window. How am I going to be able to ask for directions if no one is able to understand me? Not that I even know where I'm heading from here.

My eyes skim past the bar and the band playing in the corner, away from some broken copper tubing that looks similar to the tubes in the *Gambit* that allowed the flow of potions to make the ship disappear or sail on its own. By the looks of it, it got ripped apart, leaving dangerous sharp points sticking outward, most likely done by the Arcana. I grimace, what a thing to leave sticking out of the wall in a tavern. Real smart.

The stage where Harold and I met is empty. But right there, on the far end of the bar, sitting at a table with three other men, is Nkella.

My breath hitches, and my pulse quickens.

He's comfortably slouched back in his chair, one leg pointed toward the door, while his free hand rests on his thigh. His black hair whisps over his eyes, and his black shirt is open in a V at the collar, the tattoo over the Ipani stripes on his pec showing at the tip. His cheeks look flushed like he's been drinking. In his other hand, he's holding what looks like a couple of glass dice. He tosses a die and so do the rest of the men. They must be playing some kind of game.

I don't recognize the men he's with. I glance around for the rest of the crew but don't see any of them.

One of the men says something to him, and Nkella's gaze intensifies, a red glow briefly emanating from his eyes. He throws down another die.

I almost don't recognize a purple glow coming from behind me until I hear his voice.

"You came back."

I whip around to find Gari's widening grin swirling before me. I can't help but smile in response.

"Gari! How'd you find me?"

A *pop* by my ear makes me jump, and Philo skitters down my shoulder.

"Your shiny little friend was brave enough to tell me." He looks hungrily at Philo. "Good thing I recognized her to be your familiar."

"My familiar?" I don't think I've ever considered Philo as my familiar, but it would make sense for Gari to see her as one. "Hey, how can you understand me?"

"I knew I'd be seeing you, silly, so I drank the translation potion."

"Oh!" Smart drakon. "You wouldn't have happened to bring one of those for me, would you?"

His tail slowly creeps from behind him, clutching a blue glass bottle on the end of his tail like a finger. A label hangs from the top with a word written in another scripture. I recognize it as Ipani because it doesn't look like Ancient Greek. "Whatever do you take me for?" He gurgles. "But you know..." he floats on his back over to my side. "If you're going to stay long, you should really think of a permanent solution."

"Like what?"

"Like learning the languages." He grins.

"Fair enough." I take the bottle from him. "But for now, this'll do." I uncork the top and prepare for the taste of licorice. "Hey, tell me again why this stuff doesn't work on Ipani."

Gari rolls his eyes and bobs his head from side to side. "Because the plant *Indakepoa* that is used to make it and the Ipani are both connected to Aō, while Imboe is only half connected. Lucky for you, most people here are bilingual."

I swallow it all in four gulps. "That was a lot," I gag, wishing I had water to chase it down with.

"That bottle came from a powerful high priestess in Oleanu," he gurgles. "It should stay in your system for a long time. What are you doing back anyway?"

"I saw a vision that the crew was in danger."

Gari squints at me and spins on his head. "Is that all?"

"Yes? Do you know of it?"

"You must really think me omniscient." He turns on his head. "My question to you is if you cared for their safety, why did you leave Ipa?"

I squint at him. "You know why. I needed to get back to my sister."

Gari squints his large eyes back at me and spins on his head. "They're tough pirates, aren't they? They can take care of themselves."

I cross my arms. "That doesn't mean I don't care if they're in danger—"

Something is slammed to the ground inside the tavern, and I spin around to glare through the window.

Nkella stands up, knocking the table to the ground. Some of the people sitting nearby quickly get up and scatter, one man reaching for his drink before scampering off. I see their lips moving, but I can't hear what they're saying through the glass. I open the door to step inside for a closer look.

"Oh, now you've certainly gone mad."

I whip to Gari. "I want to hear what's going on."

"The Devil has gotten stronger since you've been gone, Soren. I'd get away while you still can." He slithers back a little, his hairs flailing in air as he does.

"You go then."

"Don't mind if I do," Gari disappears, leaving the stretch of his smile behind for a split second before the whole of him is gone.

I shake my head and turn back to the tavern. The music has stopped, and people have started pushing each other to get to the exit. I step to the side and let them pass.

"You cheated," Nkella's deep voice sounds deadly. He stares at them, his chin tucked in, and he steps to the side to catch his balance. How much has he had to drink?

"Prove it," says the man with a goatee who was sitting across from him. "I played fair. It's not my fault you suck."

"I rolled a whole shot, and I won. Give me what's mine." Nkella grits his teeth.

Of course, he's playing for something. It isn't like Nkella to lounge around playing games in a tavern. Maybe I can pull him away from there. How will he react when he sees me? Excitement thrums under my skin, as I push my way through the crowd. Some people are frozen in place, staring, probably wondering if there's going to be a fight.

Nkella utters something in Ipani, his stare accusing. The man with the goatee looks behind him and chuckles, then swiftly grabs Nkella's shirt, lifting him off the ground. I gape at him and freeze. Nkella's eyes give off an amber glow as he stares down at the man whose hand is tightening around his neck.

The barkeep backs up and disappears through a pair of double doors behind him.

"Say that to me again. Let's see if you're what everyone says you are," the man says. "I didn't cheat." He shoves Nkella back, and he falls to the ground, collecting himself the moment he lands. He stands, and his legs wobble a little.

Oh man, he's really drunk. I don't think I've ever seen him this tanked before. Everyone in the tavern is standing awestruck, staring at Nkella, while he has his eyes set on the guy.

"Let's go, Guro. He's too drunk," his friend says.

I start walking toward him to help pull him out of here, but Nkella keeps his eyes frozen on Guro, silent as a hawk calculating his next move. His bones crack, and I stare at his tightening fists. A glare on his knuckles makes me do a double-take. At first, I think he has four rings on his fingers, but now I can see they're like metal bumps raised on his skin. Most likely from his curse. That's gonna hurt whoever he punches.

Guro laughs and pulls a vial from his pocket. "You want this that bad? Learn to play better, á?"

Nkella grabs the table and, with a frighteningly powerful lift of one hand, throws it at Guro. The table doesn't just fall; a gust of wind pushes the table, and it crashes against the man's chest, making him land all the way across the tavern, and smashing hard against the instruments now abandoned by the musicians. As he lands, the man's chest is instantly impaled by the sharp piece of copper tubing sticking out from the wall. His mouth hangs open, blood pooling out of it. I gasp and cup my hands over my mouth.

Guro's friends position themselves to attack Nkella. One of them forms what looks like an ice dagger from his bare hand.

I swallow a breath. I did this. I returned ouma to the Ipani.

People are now running out of the building, pushing me against the door, but I fight to stay inside. I have to stop him. Nkella lifts his hand again, and this time, a mini tornado forms in the air.

I stare at Nkella. His eyes are full-blown crimson, and he has a look on him that makes my blood run cold.

"Nkella!" I shout. He's going to kill them all. But he doesn't hear me.

Nkella lifts his other hand, twisting it sharply as a gust of wind makes the ice man's head rise awkwardly. It snaps with a loud crack. My heart is lodged in my throat; my hands start to shake.

The ice dagger shatters to the ground before the man is dropped to the ground.

The barkeep comes running back in with another man, presumably the owner. The owner marches toward Nkella, and I shake my head furiously at him. He points at me and tells me to leave but I stand my ground.

Nkella strides toward the man he impaled.

Someone grabs my arms from behind and starts pulling on me. I glimpse behind me to find a woman with a concerned look on her face. "He will kill you, too, if he thinks you want to stop him."

"I have to try," I sputter.

"He's too far gone. You must save yourself." She steps back toward the door. Two armed men walk past her, pushing me outside without warning. "Hey, let go of me!" I croak, but they're too strong and too fast. I press my face against the window and stare inside. Some people have already left the vicinity, not wanting to be a part of the aftermath.

"I don't know what those guards are going to do. The ouma dampeners haven't reached Wands yet."

I stare at the woman. Ouma dampeners? I don't say it out loud because it's probably something I should know if I lived here. I learned my lesson last time, and I don't want to be questioned about drinking a translation potion right now. I fix my eyes in through the window but have now lost sight of Nkella from behind the guards.

He just killed two people in cold blood.

Over a game.

From the corner of my eye, I see one of Guro's friends pulling his friend's body from the shoulders. Moans emanate from the corpses, and I'm morbidly reminded of what happens when someone dies in this world. I peel my eyes away from the body.

One of the guards makes a fist, and as he does, half his body becomes copper. The second guard grabs Nkella from behind, holding him in place. The owner is still yelling at Nkella about the state of the place and killing his customers.

I can't watch. But I can't look away either.

The guard with the copper ouma reaches far back and delivers a blow to Nkella's face. Once. Twice. Nkella spits out blood. He reaches behind for a third blow, but before he makes contact, a strong and powerful surge of wind lashes out of Nkella, flinging the guards, the barkeep, and the owner back against the bar.

Eyes still burning like fire, Nkella rushes toward the door. The owner stands and yells at him that he's banned.

"He needs to be taken to a dungeon," someone behind me murmurs.

"A dungeon won't hold him. Not with the strength of the Devil. He needs a dampener," another says.

Nkella bursts out the door, and I jump back. The people who were watching through the window with me are now quickly moving away.

He stumbles forward and sweeps the area as everyone scatters. He locks eyes with me, and I gulp. His right eye has red and blue bruises where he got hit. Blood drips under his nose, and his black hair is wet with sweat against his forehead. He narrows his eyes, but before I can say anything, he walks off in the direction of the woods I had come from.

Did he even recognize me? I mean, he is drunk as hell, and I'm sure his vision became blurred after being punched in the face by a metal fist.

I start to follow him through the forest, calling his name. He glances over his shoulder but doesn't stop.

"Nkella? It's me..."

He picks up the pace, almost stumbling into a tree.

"It's Soren," I try again.

He doesn't answer. "What's going on with you?" I ask. "What was all that about?" My hands are still shaking from seeing him kill those two men.

Even though I've seen him kill before and hated it then, at least he could justify it. He honestly thought the goat tender he killed back in

Wands was a danger to us. But what he did in Cerberus just now was a slaughter. He murdered men without a second thought. For what? Embarrassing him? Supposedly cheating in a game? Or because he really wanted that potion, whatever it is?

A slow sinking breath escapes me. Or has he lost himself completely to his curse?

He grunts and continues his walk toward the sound of the thrashing waves on the rocky shore. My senses are swarmed with both the sound and the scent of salt water. He proceeds to walk toward the ocean, and I follow, wondering where he's going. There's not a ship or building in sight, and the woods where he might have a tree house is the opposite direction. Maybe the *Gambit* is cloaked? My heart skips a beat. Maybe we're headed to the *Gambit* where the crew are sleeping safe and sound.

We reach shrubbery where the sand descends to a lower area, the waves are hitting the shore, and the sand is wet. He almost slips on the sand but catches himself. He makes a left turn, and I follow him.

"Nkella?"

This time he slams his hand down next to him. "Go away Iéle. I'm in no mood for your tricks."

My mouth parts. He thinks I'm a hallucination.

Why would Iéle make a hallucination of me?

His breathing becomes heavy.

"Nkella, it's really me. I'm not one of Iéle's projections."

"You are a cruel beast, Iéle."

I roll my eyes. This is useless. He needs to just sleep this off.

"What I would do to see her precious eyes again...to feel her soft skin." He rubs his face.

I feel as though all the oxygen has left my lungs. He's missed me this whole time? My heart thuds loudly in my chest, and I can't help the smile widening in my lips.

"But she left me. Just like everyone else."

I stop in my tracks. He's mad because I left him. Wait. What does he mean by "just like everyone else"? I look around. Where are we going?

Growling comes from my left, and I pause. Iéle is laying on the sand, huddled with three other wolves—the wolves that were loyal to Nkella as their alpha. Iéle slowly gets up, her head prowling low, and her eyes set on me. She starts to growl. She's always been a jealous bitch.

"Hello again, Iéle," I say between gritted teeth. I don't think this wolf will ever like me.

Nkella freezes in place, his eyes glued to his wolf. Then, he slowly moves his body, his eyes moving toward my position until they're staring right at me as if he's seen a ghost.

I raise my hand. "Hi. Told you it was really me."

Nkella parts his lips but then stares back at Iéle. "Enough with your trickery. You cannot convince me. It is impossible."

Is he for real?

Nkella lets himself fall to the ground, his head resting on one of the wolves who starts wagging his tail hard against the sand. Iéle moves closer to him and rests her head on his shoulder, while her eyes are still glued on me. I slap my sides.

Fine. Whatever. I'll be a hallucination. That doesn't mean he won't talk to me.

"Where's the crew?" I ask.

"Kh."

"Amuse me, will you? Where's the crew?"

"Down at the bottom of the sea," he says almost inaudibly.

My eyes widen. "At the bottom of the sea? Why? How?" I gasp, remembering what happens when water touches them. They turn to bones and sink.

"Our borrowed ship was besieged on our way to find the *Gambit*."

That's what I saw in the mirror. It was them.

He reaches into his pocket and takes out the small vial I saw the man holding. The item he was gambling for. He had managed to steal it.

"What's that potion for?"

"Quiet, Iéle. Tomorrow I will drink this and swim underwater."

Nkella covers his hands with his face and turns to his side. He really doesn't believe I'm standing here.

I might as well let him sleep it off; it's late here anyway. It was early when I left, so I can't sleep, not that I want to lie down next to Nkella and his pack of wolves when he just killed two people in cold blood and has blood smeared on his face.

My worst fear is confirmed. The crew did drown when that ship capsized. And Nkella is...a mess. A hot mess. What do I do?

We need to save them.

He said the potion in that vial enables you to swim underwater. Interesting. It makes sense that he was so desperate to have it; he's planning to use it to save his crew.

A *pop* sounds from beside me, and I turn to stare at Gari whose purple and blue glow is casting light over Nkella. I press my finger over my lips and motion for him to follow me out of their vicinity. Iéle growls at me until I'm out of her sight. Empty threats. She knows Nkella will never forgive her if she really hurts me.

"Do you know what happened to the crew?" I ask Gari whose sinuous body radiates a soft blue and silver glow.

Gari shakes his snout from side to side. "That would have required me to be around an exploding devil. No, thank you."

I sigh and look over my shoulder in Nkella's direction. His chest rises up and down as he softly snores.

"What I do know"—Gari turns me back to face him—"is that if the undead crew is at the bottom of the sea, they are both immobile and alive."

I gasp. "Do you think they're conscious down there?"

"It's hard to say, but"—he swoops to his side—"more impossible things have happened."

I turn back to stare at Nkella. He probably hasn't left the ocean's edge since then.

"I have to save them."

"How do you intend on doing that? You'll never find them in the entire ocean."

I squint at him, recalling the time I rode on his back and we swooped into the sea to escape the Empress's Arcana Army.

"The last time we dove, you couldn't hold your breath for long," Gari sings.

"That's a good point."

"And the sea is vast. We don't know where they sunk or how far."

"Also, a good point."

"And don't you forget"—he gurgles as his nose nears mine,

enlarging his yellow eyes in front of me—"the giant sea serpent dying to eat us."

"Right."

"If he hasn't gulped down the crew already."

"Gari!" A sharp gasp leaves my lips. "I still have to try."

"Curious new mark, by the way." Gari winks.

I look down at my wrists. I forgot to look when I first got here, too distracted by where I was. On my right forearm is my curved spiderweb marking, tying me to the Empress. I suppose I should keep it hidden, so as to not draw her attention. I pissed her off pretty bad before I left. A smile curls on my lips. On my left wrist, is a new mark. A simple O, the Fool's mark.

"That's strange," I say. Before I'd left, I had the Six of Swords mark, which meant I had unfinished business with my mom. I guess I failed at that since my mother died while I was here. "I wonder why I was never given the Fool's mark until now."

"You must be coming to terms with what you really need to do.'

I quirk a brow.

"Neyuro..." Nkella's deep voice comes from behind and I spin around. "It's really you..."

"You're awake."

Gari disappears behind me with a loud pop, leaving us in the soft light of the stars and the moon reflecting off the thrashing waves of the sea. I rub my arms together and nod, taking a few steps forward. His eyes flicker amber, and I pause, remembering his sudden violence at the tavern. I miss him. But I still need to be cautious of him; I don't know how far gone he is.

"I-I'm in control. For now," he says, taking notice of my pause.

With a deep breath, I nod and walk over to him. The wind pushes his hair from his face, showcasing the beautiful brutal edges of his sharp cheekbones, his full lips, and his subtly pointed ears. I try to ignore the large bruise on his face. His shirt billows and I can see his Ipani stripes on his neck and chest, hints of his tattoo rising above his collar.

And his dark eyes stare at me, deep and unmoving, shock flickering in them. He takes me in as I walk to him.

"What are you doing here?" he asks.

"I saw a vision that the crew might be in danger. I had to come back."

"And your sister?"

"She's safe."

His throat bobs as he continues to stare at me, and I at him. There's a softness about the way he's looking at me; it's hard to imagine he's the same person who killed those two men tonight. There's so much I've wanted to tell him, but now that he's here in front of me—and not thinking I'm a hallucination—I can't get the words out. Nkella clears his throat and finally looks down at the sand.

"Soren…"

My heart flutters when he says my name.

"I…" He sighs, pressing his eyes shut like he wants to tell me something but can't get the words out. My body tenses.

"What?"

He breathes deeply, and when he opens his eyes, they're heavy. I see something different about them; they're full of remorse. He swallows. "It's my fault," he says, his voice barely a whisper.

"What's your fault?"

"My crew. They're gone because of me." He looks out to the thrashing sea.

"How? What happened?"

He turns to walk back toward the wolves. They start wagging their tails at the sight of him. Iéle curls hers in at the sight of me.

"We capsized before we reached Swords. We never made it to the *Gambit*, and the Empress…she…" He breathes again and looks back at me. "She took the World Card. I thought you were in danger."

My heart drops to the pit of my stomach. "She has the World Card?" Steadying my breathing, I calm my nerves. I don't want to make him feel worse. "I'm okay, Nkella. For whatever reason, she never came after me."

He nods. "I was afraid I had failed you as well."

"Nk-Captain." I correct myself. He raises his eyes at me. "You being the captain means you hold the weight of your entire crew on your shoulders, but it is not your fault the ship you were on went down. If anything, it's my fault. I pissed her off when I left, I gave you the World

Card, and I made all of you a target." My stomach constricts at the real-ization that the words leaving my lips are true. I put them all in danger by leaving the card with them. Would she have gone after them other-wise? She was always after them, but knowing the whereabouts of the card would have made it worse. "How did you escape the Empress?"

"Iéle helped me escape into the Aō, but the Empress had already wounded me and taken the card."

A sob forms at my throat. This entire time I was fooling around back home, I had left them in danger. This is my fault. "I will help you get them back."

"Koj." He shakes his head.

"Yes—Gari will help. He can breathe underwater. We did it before. He can help us search for them."

"I have searched and searched. I cannot hold my breath as long as an oumala merman or a fish." He takes out the vial from his pocket. "But with this I can." He looks at it from the corner of his eyes.

The potion he stole. "What does it do?"

"It will give me the ability to breathe underwater."

"Okay then," I grab his arms, and he pulls the potion away from me. "Let's split it. We can both go on Gari—how else will you be able to carry back everyone's skeletons? We'll need a ship or a boat. We'll have to make several trips, bringing them up to the surface one at a time—"

"Koj."

"Why do you keep saying that? Let me help. This is as much my fault as yours."

"I will not let you drink this, neyuro."

I blink at him. "Why not? What's in it?"

He gives me a long lingering look that sends my heart to my throat. Then, with a voice cold and devoid of emotion, he says, "Because it is rikorō. An Ipani was killed for their ouma to create it."

5

It takes me all of three seconds to process what he just said to me. I stare at his face for any hint of amusement, but there is none. His face is rigid, uncaring, over the word he just muttered.

"Th-the deadly potion the traffickers were stealing Ipani and murdering them for?" My voice comes out quieter than I anticipated. I want to scream at him, but I still don't even believe him. I remember Harold explaining to me that rikorō means "soul-thief" because it absorbs the ouma from living creatures, essentially stealing their life-force. I glance at the black solution in the vial. A solemn expression passes through Nkella's features. "The unstable one?" I deadpan. "The one you hate with every fiber of your being?" My voice raises an octave on the last sentence. There we go.

He sighs but still doesn't say anything.

"And you killed two more people for it?" I hear the disbelief in my voice, and I search for any hint of remorse in his features, but he stares back at me as if he were just doing a job.

I shake my head slowly. "Nkella...this isn't you."

"My crew comes first."

"But not like this. You've said that before. These ends don't justify those means, remember?"

"That was different. I am not killing Ipani to make rikorō to become powerful. I am not a part of their charade. I played for this fairly, and it is only to save my crew."

"Fairly? Two people are dead. And you act like it doesn't even matter. You really don't care, do you?"

"They were not good people, neyuro. They had rikorō to begin with. I did the world a favor, and I will use this potion to save my crew." Silence grows between us, and I just stare at him. He finally speaks. "This is the only way, even if it kills me."

"There has to be another way. There always is."

His eyes dip to the sand. "I have searched for so many ways, neyuro. You don't know what it was like knowing I got them trapped in a fate worse than death, not being able to find them. I've searched everywhere. I almost drowned doing it."

"You've lost yourself, Nkella."

His eyes snap to me. "Not yet."

I shake my head. "The captain I knew would never jeopardize someone else's ouma for his own gain. This goes against everything you believe in, and it's reckless. It'll kill you."

"Kh. I don't have to explain myself to you, daí? Go home, Soren. You are not safe here. You are not safe with me."

My bottom lip trembles. "You always said it's the bancha mistakes that'll get you killed. And there's nothing more stupid than this."

"I don't care if it does. If it brings them back, then let it." The tip of his canines show between his grimacing lips.

"Don't say that." My voice shakes.

He turns the vial around in his hands, inspecting it. "I lost everyone. My parents, my sister, and now my crew. When the Empress took the World Card, I wished there was a way into your world, to make sure I didn't get you killed too."

My heart skips a beat. "You didn't, though. I'm right here. And I'm not going to let you go through this on your own."

"It is my weight to bear."

"Not true. I left the card with you, making you a target for the Empress. It is exactly my weight to bear. Let me help you."

He uncorks the vial. My eyes widen at his action.

"Wait...you're taking it now?"

"I have wasted enough time, and the rikorō might take a while to work."

I reach for his wrist, but he moves it away from my reach. "How can you save your sister if you're dead? You still want to save her, don't you?"

He gapes at me, and when I don't say anything else, he says, "There is talk of a cure. I don't know if it's true or if it will even work, but...if I live long enough to get it, I will drink it."

"Where is the cure?"

"Piupeki." He is holding the uncorked vial in his hands.

Swords. "And that's where the *Gambit* is too?"

"If it is still there."

A memory of the Ace of Swords Card rushes through my mind and then the vision of my mother riding on a red and gray drakon's back follows it. Such fierceness in her eyes. I rub at my temples and force myself back to the present. Nkella squints at me.

Cold water washes over my feet, and wind pushes against my back. Despite Nkella saying he didn't need to explain himself to me, there's something in his expression that tells me he wants me to understand him.

And I do. I would have done anything to save my sister. In fact, I was the one who took poison last time by drinking the potion the Empress told me would transport me home. At least he knows what this is, and he understands the risk.

What wouldn't I do to save the ones I love?

No matter how stupid and reckless.

I approach him closer and can feel his breath brush my skin.

Nkella sucks in a breath at my closing in on him, but he doesn't try to avoid me. "Neyuro? What are you doing?" he whispers.

His eyes dip to my lips, the sharp edges of his features still tense. His head lowers, and I lift my chin, his lips almost brushing against mine.

I place a hand over his, and his lips part. Gently, I put my hand over the vial, not wanting him to think I'm going to take it from him. Electricity sparks under my skin from our touch.

I whisper against his breath, "Do you promise you will find the cure after this is done?"

"Yes," he whispers back.

In one swift move, I slip the vial from his hand and take a long step back. His eyes bulge, and he steps forward, but he's too late. Waves crash against my legs as I raise the vial and take a sip.

"Neyuro," he croaks out, reaching to grab me, but I've already swallowed it. A nasty shot of what tastes like thick nettle molasses mixed with ass burns down my throat. My body involuntarily gags, and he pries the vial out of my hand. There's still some left.

I stumble back onto the beach and collapse on the sand, knees first. Spots and squiggles cloud my vision, contrasting with the dark abyss of the ocean and night sky.

"Why did you do that?" Nkella bellows, but it's hard to hear him with the thunderous migraine blooming in the center of my head. My stomach constricts with a sharp pain, and I'm forced to keel over. Nkella kneels down next to me. "I did not think you would do this, Soren."

"I told you." I cough. "I'm going with you to save them too."

His frown deepens. "You should never have come back here, neyuro." He lifts the vial and drinks the rest.

6

MY EYES FLUTTER OPEN TO THE SOFT GLOW OF SUNRISE breaking the sea. Did I fall asleep?

The last thing I remember was getting a migraine after drinking the rikorō. I only had about half of the small vial, but even that was enough to knock me out cold. I take a deep breath, and something buzzes beneath my skin—something energizing, revitalizing. I breathe again deeply, relishing how the air even *feels* cleaner and letting it fill my lungs with the urge to run, or jump, or...swim. I stare out into the water, and my eyes widen. Tiny specs of gold glisten in the waves as they ebb and flow, backward and forward. The wind carries voices that I can tell are coming from far away.

The wind brushes against my skin as I stand, every minuscule speck of existence around me is known to me, every creature in my vicinity, whether big or microscopic. I can hear hornets buzzing in their nest thirty feet away, I can sense the hard stares coming from the pack of wolves, and I can both hear and sense the multitude of creatures swimming in the sea.

This is incredible.

But there's something else, a soft heartbeat thrumming in my ears, but it's not mine. My heart thrums in my chest, matching the beat of the waves around me in such a rhythm that the only word I can find to describe it is...divine. But no, this is someone else's heartbeat, and despite the many voices and senses I feel and hear, this particular one calls to me specifically. As if it's part of my own...yet it isn't.

Something slams a fin down in the ocean, and I squint at it. Black hair and arms rise above the water and dive in against the next crashing wave, a fin following after. I blink a few times, and my lips part as I recognize Nkella's features. I look down at my arms and legs. I haven't changed.

As Nkella starts to rise over the waves, his fin disappears, becoming legs. The orange and pink hues of the morning sun cast a shimmery rainbow effect on black scales as they quickly disappear to reveal his black baggy pants and shirtless torso.

I walk over to him, my mouth still agape. As I near him, my feet touch the water's edge and my skin tickles. I blink at the shimmery rainbow scales appearing on my feet. I choke on a laugh and glance at Nkella.

Droplets of water glisten over his tattooed pecs and muscular arms. My eyes fall to his cut abs, and I'm caught breathless. I force my eyes up to his face.

"The rikorō was made from the ouma of a merman. That is why I wanted it."

"H-how long will it last?" I ask, moving my hair behind my ears as I collect myself.

"Not long. Rikorō is temporary, and the more you take, the more deadly it is, daí?"

I nod. "I know, it can kill us—even the small amount we took." Hoping it doesn't.

He squeezes his eyes and huffs. "Why would you do this?" he mutters, but I can hear his chest panting hard. I feel it within me.

"Because you're not the only one who's allowed to take risks. And—"

He locks his gaze to mine, a pissed-off expression smeared across his face.

"—the crew isn't the only thing I came back for," I blurt.

"Daí?" His brows furrow.

"I'll tell you later. Let's save the crew first. We don't know how long this rikorō will last." And I don't want to distract him—I'm not sure how he'll react to my new plan of wanting to sneak into the Tower to steal the Death Card. He'll most likely say I'm bancha for even thinking it and scold me over what the Empress did to Ntaoru, turning her into an agentless soldier...besides cursing him with the Devil Card and making the crew suffer under the undead curse. "Just know that I'm trying to train my powers, and I might have a way to save us if the rikorō makes us sick, in case your cure doesn't exist."

"Hn." He quirks a brow, and I stare at him. He has gills close to his pointy ears. I touch my skin underneath mine but don't feel anything.

"I know it's bad for you but...this is beyond words. I can feel everything...I can hear..." My hearing zeros in on a pounding heart. It's coming from Nkella's chest. I place my palm over his heart, and he stares down at it, placing his hand over mine.

"We drank from the same vial. So, for now, we share the spirit essence of the same being it belonged to."

A small gasp leaves my lips. Both regret and gratefulness twist my gut. Regret that someone's life was taken for this experience, but grateful to experience it all the same.

Does that make me a bad person?

Water splashes on my arm and scales appear beneath my skin, almost as if it's erasing my skin. My pulse quickens with the sudden urge to dive into the water and swim. I glance over Nkella's shoulder, but I don't miss the smirk crossing his lips.

"Later, neyuro. First, we need to find a boat."

That snaps me back to the present. "Right. And I'll ask Gari for his help. It'll be wise to cover the most ground we can, and three against a sea serpent is better than two."

We glance at each other in mutual agreement and set off walking back toward Iéle and the other wolves.

Iéle walks over, her eyes only glimpsing me in passing. Nkella bows his head to hers, but she jumps back.

"Calm, Iéle. It is still me."

She whimpers, her head bowing low, not dangerously, though. She seems more suspicious of us than anything else. She sniffs his hand and then sits. She can sense the rikorō in our system; I wonder if she knows we took the same one. She isn't growling at me like she normally does, so maybe she can hear both our heartbeats beating as one.

"You smell different." Gari's gurgling voice whips me around. Nkella stands, breaking his concentration with Iéle, who now turns back to her pack and howls something at them. The four wolves are staring at us all, and with four loud pops, they leave.

"They don't like this," Nkella says. I raise my brows and turn to Gari's attention. I'm not going to worry about the opinions of wolves right now. This is temporary, it'll go away soon, but we need to get going on finding the crew.

"We took rikorō," I tell Gari.

"That explains why you smell like a fish." He sways onto his back. "I thought you might have been swallowed and spit out by the serpent."

"Were you already here?"

"I wasn't, but your little spider friend hasn't left your side. She's hiding in the Aō and told me you needed me."

"Philo's in the Aō? Why didn't she come out?"

"Maybe because you're...different."

My brows furrow. "Can you help us look for the crew?"

"And risk the sea serpent, on purpose?" Gari giggles out loud. "You must think me mad."

"We need to find the crew."

"And why do *I* need to find them?" His sinuous body wiggles back as he purrs out the word I.

"You won't help me? I thought you were my friend." I lean my weight to the side.

Gari swims through the air in a circle around me. "Hmmm. If I do this for you, what's next?"

"What do you mean?"

"Will you go back home to your sister, or will you stay and defeat the Empress?"

My eyes bulge at him. "That's not why I came back here."

"But you're the only one who can do it." He nudges the mark on my arm, and I touch it. "Perhaps, you'll need your crew to help you."

I bite my tongue. He isn't wrong. Not about me needing the crew to help me defeat the Empress, because doing that wasn't on my radar, but I do want their help to steal the Death Card since they have already tried stealing it once. I reach into my shirt and pull out my mother's necklace. I wish I knew what my mother was doing here, but the Empress has the World Card now, and Asteria is no longer safe.

Nkella comes closer and picks up the coin from my chest, peering at it with a smile on his face. "You didn't trade them?"

I swallow at his sudden closeness. "I traded some, but this one belonged to my mother."

He flicks his eyes at me. "Your mother came to Ipa?"

"I just found that out through my power. I-I never got to see her when I went back home." I pause to keep my voice from cracking. "She had died three days before."

His face softens, and he briefly closes his eyes. "My deepest sorrows, Soren. May her soul rest peacefully and not in the eternal torment that curses this land."

I clear my throat as if that would stop my chest from aching. "I just wish I had gone to see her sooner."

"We have a saying here. *E hongu a songu.* It means he who waits, wilts. It's a reminder that we must never hesitate to spend time with those we love."

I stay silent, afraid that if I speak my voice will be weak. Instead, I smile and look back down at my necklace.

He narrows his eyes at the gichang. "But this is not regular Danū gichang. It is royal."

My eyes linger on his finger as he traces the etched palm tree. "What do you mean?"

He reaches over to his belt pouch, which lies on the sand beneath his shirt and coat, and takes out a gichang, then holds it next to the one around my neck. "They don't make royal gichang anymore. The one you have was created before my parents were born. They are only a symbol of status now...or given as gifts." He spins it around to show the scripture on the back. "This says Mikiroro, my family name. Whoever gave your mother this must have been a royal, one of my older relatives who are now dead." I had noticed that the gichang he had given me didn't have a scripture on the back, but I don't know enough about Ipa's currency to wonder about the significance.

"Or they stole it. That is also possible."

Recalling my vision of the man who was with my mom, I doubt it. "While I'm here, I'd like to find out what my mother was doing in Ipa."

Nkella nods.

"It's obvious to me," Gari sings. "Your mother was here to stop the Empress. You both have the same mark, do you not?"

I roll my eyes, peeling them away from Nkella. "But why was it so important to her? And if it was that important, why did she go back home? Why not stay here?" I stare out to the beach, not waiting for an answer. My mom looked so determined in the vision, there had to be more I don't know. I just want her back. I turn to face Gari. "After I get what I came for, I'll stay longer. After that, I'll see where it takes me. Is that enough for you to help us?"

Gari's smile widens. "Deal."

I nod and stare back at Nkella who's staring at me suspiciously, annoyance emanating from his stare. He's waiting for me to tell him what I've come for, but he knows there are more pressing matters. I smile, despite his agitation. "So then, what's the plan, Captain?"

He stares out to sea. Red hues dance over the calm ebbing and flowing of the waves. Seagulls mew as they reach the shore and land on a rock. "We swim."

The softness from the rising sun illuminates his muscles in a perfect way, and I have to stop my eyes from tracing over his body. Too many memories come flooding in at once from the time just before I left Ipa to go back home. The firepit, our first kiss, our almost last one... My eyes stop at the new black ink over his left forearm. It's a skull with horns on its head, the figurehead from his ship. My eyes meet his intense stare, dark and sorrowful, rage hiding just beneath the surface. Usually, when he caught me staring at him, I saw a glimmer of amusement. But not now. I force my gaze away and look at Gari instead.

"Ready, you two? I'll fly us over to where the ship got blown away," he gurgles, "then we'll dive and search."

"So you'll help us?" I ask.

"Who will save you if that poison fails you ten feet under?" He grins.

I swallow and straighten my spine. "Here's to hoping the rikorō lasts longer than that." Nkella leaves his baggy pants on. I, on the other hand, don't want to be wearing soaked clothes when I come back. I pull my shirt over my head, leaving my bra on, then I remove my shoes and pants, until I am standing only in my underwear. They're a matching set, pink with a black lace trim. I may or may not have been paying attention to my undergarments before changing into my Ipani clothes yesterday.

Nkella stops in his tracks and stares back at me. His jaw is partially agape, and his eyes dip to the rest of my body.

My cheeks flush. "I didn't want my only clothes to get wet."

He clears his throat, quickly withdrawing his gaze and looking out to the water.

Just the mention of swimming brings a tingling sensation from my fingertips and toes all the way up to my neck. I have the greatest urge to jump in already. Normally, I would enjoy sitting on the sand and sunbathing, while staring at the ocean from a distance. Not that I don't like swimming, I just prefer to enjoy it from a distance and respect the sea critters while I'm at it.

But right now, all I want to do is swim.

Lengthening his body, Gari floats between us, lowering himself just above the shore, making it easier to climb on. Gripping his hair, I lift one leg over his body, seating myself close to his neck. As I do, waves crash over me, causing yellow and red scales with a rainbow sheen to spread over my knees. Once I'm snug, I grip Gari's back with my thighs as Nkella swings up behind me.

"Hold on tight," Gari sings. He takes off over the water and starts gliding through the air, the end of his tail moving side to side. I lower my head close to his furry neck, holding on as tight as I can, but my gaze is just over the edge of his shoulder. The waves pass close beneath us, and I can taste the saltiness of the air as the wind blows through my hair. The rhythm of Gari's movements serenades me as time passes. Goosebumps appear on my arms and legs as the temperature starts to drop. The caveat of having to take my clothes off. The only thing warm right now is

Nkella's chest radiating heat on my back; I had forgotten how warm his blood runs. His arms are still beside him, grabbing onto Gari's sides.

We travel in silence, as he tries to figure out where the ship capsized.

Finally, Nkella shouts directions from behind me, and Gari glides over to the left, causing me to slide a little lower. Nkella's quickly wraps an arm around my bare stomach, making goosebumps rise from his touch. He grips me tight as I reposition myself, but he doesn't let go. A butterfly releases in my stomach, but I don't flinch. I don't want him to move. Gari swoops down, so close to the water, I could probably touch it with my toes if I wanted to.

I squint my eyes at our surroundings. This is different from my vision. There are no mountains. "I thought you guys were headed to Swords."

"We never made it far enough. The Arcana Army waited until we had our ship. It was a trap."

Interesting. Could my vision have been of a different ship attack?

"Around here, Katergaris," Nkella instructs.

Gari dives headfirst, and from instinct, I brace myself and hold my breath.

Freezing cold water engulfs us, until we're completely submerged. My eyes are squeezed shut; we dove so fast, I don't even remember closing them. A swirl of ice cold water flushes around me, and my eyes open slightly. Something brushes my arm, and this time I open my eyes wide.

Nkella is in front of me, his legs have become a long black fin with beautiful yellow and red trails coming down his sides, a yellow-golden color blending with the red on the top, and then coming out with red on the tips. His Ipani stripes are giving off a subtle glow, emanating a kind of sheen over his skin. Smaller scales spread out over his arms and torso.

I let out a gasp and then another as an open airway reaches my throat from both sides of my neck. I grab onto my neck, feeling tiny fins covering double slits.

Nkella's dark hair sways in the current, sometimes revealing the two semi-grown horns curved back on his head, now a little bigger than the last time I saw him. He can't seem to hide the smile on his face, and I have to admit—this is amazing.

I stare down at myself. Small scales shine down over my chest and stomach in a luminescent sheen, a long black fin grips me at my hips, and the scales go all the way down to split into two gold and red fins, just like Nkella's, since we drank from the same vial of rikorō. The rhythm of his heart still beats in my ears, only now, it's a lot more soothing, like a soft beating drum.

Gari swirls around us, and we both spin around. "Which way, Captain?" Gari's voice comes in a hoarser gurgle.

Nkella opens his mouth, but bubbles come out. He waves his arms at Gari, signaling for him to follow. *"Search the perimeters,"* he says without a sound leaving his lips, and I gape. I can hear him as clearly as if he were speaking to me.

"I can hear you," I think back.

Nkella's eyes widen, and he swims toward me. I reach out for his hand and gently brush between his fingers, a tingling sensation meeting at our touch, almost as if we're feeling each other from the other person. Like we are one. His fingers close between mine, and the look he gives me is filled with the feeling of never wanting this to end. But we both know we have a job to do. Before he moves, I know he's about to turn, and as he does, I follow behind him, letting my new fins do all the work as we cut effortlessly through the dense sea.

I've never felt so free in my life.

With all the excitement of turning into a mermaid, I hadn't noticed how clearly I can see underwater. Back when Gari and I dove into the ocean to escape the Arcana, it was only his illuminating body letting me see what was right in front of me. But with these new eyes, everything under here is brighter.

Colorful and vivid coral reefs line the ocean floor as we swim above them. In the vast distance, rock formations that look like mountain ranges separate parts of the sea. Off to my right, a stone pathway led far ahead with bioluminescent algae between the stones. Carvings are drawn on rocks leading down the path, which is also glowing with algae. There aren't any mer-Ipani around, but in the distance, my mer-vision allows me to see all the way to large castle formations with more of those glowing carvings.

"They are abandoned. We must stay out of sight, daí?"

Nodding, I keep swimming, forcing my vision away from the abandoned castles.

Schools of fish move with the current in the opposite direction. And the farther I swim, the warmer I become, as my body works toward the opposing current.

Despite this potion being created from such a horrible and treacherous act, I can see how it would be addicting. It was giving me new abilities, new powers that enabled me to do things I never dreamed possible.

Gari swims faster than me to reach Nkella. "I'm going to speed toward the right. I'll circle around later," he gurgles.

Nkella gives a single nod. *"Good. He will cover more ground that way."*

I agree and continue to swim behind Nkella, keeping my eyes peeled on our surroundings, hoping to catch a glimpse of wood, a mast, or anything that would lead us to the sunken ship.

It's hard to determine distance. While swimming at a speed faster than walking, we don't want to swim too fast and miss any details that could point to the crew. Nkella's heartbeat thumps harder in my ears, and I know it's not from being out of breath, but from his fear of not being able to find them. All this would be wasted. He would have compromised his beliefs about using rikorō for nothing.

And his crew would be as good as gone.

A wave of emotion emanates from him and swirls in my brain.

A vision of the crew on the *Gambit* in the middle of a storm almost causes me to stop swimming. I can see it as clear as day. They're being shot at, and his worry for Tessa and the others is overwhelming. The ship gets thrown to one side as the serpent lifts them, just as the Arcana Army comes swooping down. A mess of conflicting emotions gets thrown in next, his regret about leaving Danū, his rush to leave Danū, his worry for his crew.

His sister takes charge of the wheel, and Nkella pulls the mast, with Kaehante's help. His mind lingers on his sister for a little while longer as we continue to search. That must have been a memory from when they fled his island. I wonder if mer-Ipani can talk to each other telepathically underwater, or if this is just a result of the rikorō we drank—it having come from the same mer-man or woman.

My mind drifts from his sister to mine. I had left Talia a note saying I was leaving, and that I had left my phone. Let her think I went to find my dad, not that I would. She wanted her space, anyway, and I know she'll be fine in her new home. Hopefully, better than I ever was in any of mine. Guilt surfaces in my throat, and the thought of my mom lying in a hospital bed, alone and dying, forces it's way into my mind. I try to shake it away, but my chest tightens. I refocus on the ocean floor but almost bump into Nkella.

He's staring down at me, his brows furrowed with worry. Sorrow emanates deep within him, and all his emotions flood through me at once. Understanding about me and my past. Guilt over his own family. Understanding over my own guilt.

Fear for his sister, for his crew, and for mine. Fear for my crew. Our fears and worries merging into one as we look into each other's eyes.

This is too weird.

I swim closer, and he opens his arms slightly. He has an urge, a wanting to pull me in, to hold me. But it gets muddled with resistance. I stop swimming in place, and a second later we are moving again, remembering our mission, and knowing that this is only the rikorō merging our emotions and memories together.

As weird as it is, I find it insightful. He hates it.

We keep searching the reef, now passing what looks like deep bottomless caves. Nkella's heart momentarily stops, and I don't need the rikorō to know what he's thinking. A wave of fear and despair crashes into me like icicles piercing my heart. I lock eyes with him and shake my head.

"Don't go there. We'll find them."

He nods once. *"Let's keep going."*

A bright purple and blue light comes toward us, and a flicker of hope sparks in Nkella, knowing it's Gari, wondering if he's spotted the crew.

Gari's crazy eyes zoom toward us, too fast for me to back away. "No luck, but I can tell you the serpent isn't far. We have to hurry."

I glance at Nkella. *"So what do mermaids use to defend themselves against the serpent?"*

"This area is almost directly underneath Rutavenye. Mer-Ipani try to stay clear of it. Use anything you can find."

"Great."

"I thought you knew where the ship sunk?" Gari sings.

Nkella hisses in his mind, agitation emanating from his scales. He spins around in place, his tail swaying effortlessly and pointed down as if he's standing on water. He then looks up toward the surface. The sun shines a blue and yellow light through the waves dancing over our heads in the far distance. He's trying to imagine the location of the ship and how far Iéle took him, but he isn't able to get a clear view. Hopelessness leaves an empty hole in his heart.

I swim toward him, and this time, I grab his hand. I don't care how much he wants to resist me. *"Look at me,"* I tell him.

He flicks his eyes to mine. His lips part slightly, his sharp canines showing.

"We're doing this together," I think at him. *"We'll keep searching until the rikorō runs out, and then Gari can rush us up to shore. We're not leaving yet. Not yet."*

"This is reckless."

"It wouldn't be us if we weren't being reckless."

A small smirk lifts his lips, and he shakes his head. *"Since when did you become the voice of reason, dai?"*

"Since I had a ruthless pirate as my captain who showed me what to prioritize."

"Kh. Let's go."

We head farther into the ridge of the underwater caves, in case anything calls out to us that had either fallen or become lodged in between the rocks. I glare down at the never-ending darkness. If the ship had sunk down into that abyss, there would be pieces of wood scattered around. I don't see anything that resembles the remnants of a ship. Where could they be?

Shock waves blast us so fast that I don't see anything until I land with a hard thud and my eyes are forced open.

But I'm no longer underwater. I'm on a ship in broad daylight. AJ and Kae are readying the sails, while Lāri is on the topmast. Nkella is behind the wheel. I can't see Tessa—she must be below deck. I try to call out to them, but no one notices me. This ship is different as well, it's not the *Gambit*, but it looks just like the ship in my vision.

I gasp. I'm in the vision of a past memory. I glance down at my mark, and sure enough, it's glowing with a white undertone.

A cold breeze passes through my hair, urging me forward. I walk toward the bow of the ship and check on my surroundings. I'm surrounded by ocean. Kaehante shouts something about heading straight north—which I already knew. They were headed to Swords to find the *Gambit*.

Airstrikes whistle down, and the hairs on my arms stand on end. Bombs hit all around us, and the ship lunges sideways, then another hits the other side. Tessa comes out from a room and shoots a potion from her chair cannon to sea. I miss what she was shooting at as another bomb strikes the deck hard, splitting the ship in half. I glance to where the wheel is, but the last thing I see is Nkella turning to reach for Tessa, and Iéle jumping on top of him, then all of them disappearing. In a second, I'm underwater. The weight of the bomb and the blast hits, shielding my sight. But since I'm not really here, I force myself back, and then back up more, until I can get a clear view of the ship and where it landed. The crew instantly become skeletons, lifeless as they fall with the ship.

This ship didn't have an invisibility cloak, and they were attacked too quickly for anyone to do anything.

I watch as the two large halves of the ship sink, and turn so that they're covering anyone who landed underneath. The crew are caught under it, not that they could swim out if given the chance with their undead curse.

What catches my eye is the end of the ridge. Thankfully, the ship hasn't slid down.

"*Neyuro. Neyuro.*"

My eyes flutter open, and Nkella is staring down at me with a worried look on his face.

"Soren," he mouths, but I can hear his terrified voice clearly in my mind. A sigh of relief escapes him as I touch his cheek. Blood circles around us, and my attention is drawn to the slashes on his arms.

I start to get up, but he keeps his arms around me. He must have blocked my fall, and that's why he has coral burns on his skin while I don't. We lock eyes. A fiery glow behind his irises flickers, meaning the devil is agitated, angry, or scared. This time, I know why. He was scared I was dead.

I sit up in a hurry. *"I know where they are."*

7

"Where's Gari?" I shout in my mind. *"Did we really get hit? Or was that all in my mind?"*

"What do you mean you know where they are?" He pulls back, letting me swim out of the coral we were thrown into.

"I had a vision. It's hard to explain."

"You used your mark."

I turn to him. *"Not intentionally, but yes. I saw when the ship was hit, and I saw where they landed. Did you feel or see anything?"*

"I was thrown out of your mind during the explosion." He points up to the surface. *"Something is going on up there. The Arcana Army dropped a bomb. Let us hope there aren't more coming."*

We'll have to worry about that later.

Purple and blue glows behind me, and Gari swims out.

"Gari!" I swim out to him.

"Can't get rid of me that easy." He grins.

"It's okay. I know where they are. Follow me."

A thrum of anticipation comes from Nkella, blending in with my own. He can see the images in my mind now, thanks to the rikorō. I swim fast toward the ridge on the ocean floor. They were headed north toward Swords, so swimming toward the dark and cold and away from where we came is the way to go. Nkella whispers in my mind that he agrees, so we follow the cracked splice, swimming at full speed.

The farther we follow the splice, the farther we are from the Arcana's bombs.

A broken piece of wood sticks out from the sand, and my heart skips a beat. I swim down and grab onto it, pulling it up.

It's shrapnel from the blast. The crew's close.

We swim together, Gari behind us. When larger chunks of the ship come into view, I'm overwhelmed with excitement.

"We found them!" I swim closer to the side of the ship, broken, and cracked on its side. *"They're underneath."*

Gari becomes as small as an eel and zooms past us, fitting through a crack. "Swim back," he gurgles.

Nkella and I give Gari space. As his glow intensifies, he grows longer and wider in size. The side of the ship pushes out as Gari becomes twice the size of the broken walls.

Nkella swims forward and starts grabbing debris and throwing it out of the way. I join him, grabbing anything I can get my hands on. The walls of the ship caved in as well as plant matter and animals bones.

I grab what looks like a red stick and let it go when I realize it's attached to a hand with phalange bones. Nkella stops to look at me, feeling my sudden panic. He comes closer and uncovers a wooden plank hiding the rest of it.

He points to a large black boot. *"It's Kaehante."*

"It seems like someone fell off her chair." Bubbles come from Gari as he sing-songs.

Nkella drops Kaehante's boot and goes to look for Tessa's bones. Catching sight of a shiny object, I lift a string of beads attached to long black hair. My eyes skim the wreck for Lāri, recalling her position high on the cage mast—she could have either fallen farther out or flown away.

"Lāri would have found me if she had flown away. I searched for her everywhere." Nkella says into my mind.

I bite back a smile. I'm still not used to Nkella being able to read my thoughts, and vice versa. *"Fair enough."*

Relief oozes from his energy, but the hesitation is still there. We've found them, but we're not out of the water yet.

"Guys?" Gari swims over to a fallen mast and wraps his tail around it. As soon as I see what he's doing, I gasp. Nkella and I swim over as Gari lifts the beam off the ocean floor, revealing the bones of a large bird. Lāri must have gotten hit in the explosion as soon as she changed form. "That's everyone. Let's grab them and go before the serpent finds us," he gurgles, gripping Tessa's chair.

Nkella lifts Tessa's bones in his arms. I'm already scooping up Lāri because a bundle of bird bones is the easiest to grab.

"We're going to have to make two trips," I think at him. I guess it'll be easier now because we know where everyone is. Nkella lays Tessa across Gari's back.

"Don't drop her, dai?"

"I'll try," Gari gurgles.

Remnants of tendon and sinew hold Kaehante's bones together as Gari lifts him and gently sets him on his back. At least, they don't fall apart. It must be part of the undead curse.

We share a look at AJ and grimace. We both hate leaving him here, but we can't carry everyone and swim at the same time.

Carrying everyone but AJ, we follow the deathly abyss back to where we came, making good time, while staying careful enough not to drop anyone. It was faster getting here, initially, thanks to Gari's help, but it's a little trickier now that we're not on his back.

Nkella's thoughts race with worry. He goes from relief to having found them, to worrying over them being truly dead now, to not knowing how far the undead curse goes, and finally, to worrying about me endangering my life by drinking the rikorō.

"Bancha," he mutters in his head.

I huff but don't say anything back. I'll deal with that later.

We pass the colorful coral reef and start ascending up the surface.

The sun is bright—too bright when I lift my head above water. The air hurts as it passes through the gills of my neck, and I lower myself so that the water covers my chin. The sound of the waves and birds passing by grounds me, as if it almost feels like forever since I thought about life above water. I think I could live undersea forever, as long as the rikorō lasts...

"I'll carry Tessa to the land," Gari says over his shoulder, "and come back for the others."

He's right. He's faster if he flies them over while we stay in the water. As soon as Gari comes back, he takes Lāri's bird bones gently in his mouth. Nkella frowns but he has no choice but to trust Gari. He's been good to us so far, I don't have a reason not to trust him, and Nkella seems content with that. With Kaehante on his back, Gari takes off, leaving us to return to the shipwreck.

Nkella turns to me. "Go with Katergaris. I can go on my own to get AJ. You should keep watch over them." He nods toward the beach. His hair is wet and plastered on his face, his Devil stumps showing more fully than usual. Gold and red shimmer over the light scales on his cheeks and neck.

"Gari and Iéle can keep watch. I don't want to leave you. What if the serpent catches you? I wouldn't know to get help if I'm not there."

He purses his lips but doesn't argue. He knows I'm right.

When we finally reach AJ, I'm urged with a final gust of energy to pick him up and take him back. As much as I have loved swimming, my arms—my whole body is sore. I guess even mer-people get tired of swimming long distances.

Nkella lifts AJ, placing his bones over his shoulder like he did with Kae. As he turns to face me, his eyes go wide, and his face goes rigid.

I gulp, and spin around, coming face-to-teeth with the Empress's pet, the giant serpent, Apeiron.

Nkella shoves into me, and we both move out of the way as the serpent opens its mouth wide, showing three rows of nasty, sharp needle-point teeth. I forgot how large he was.

He could swallow us—and half this wrecked ship—in one gulp. As he opens his mouth, a strong current pulls us toward his throat. A silent, gurgling scream escapes my throat, shattering my ears. I know it shatters Nkella's too. Nkella grabs me with one arm, and swims in full force, until I start swinging my tailfin as hard as I can. As Apeiron closes his mouth, a surge of the current pushes us outward, giving us a lucky boost away from him.

Unfortunately, it's in the wrong direction. But that doesn't matter now. The only thing we can do is swim away. Panic courses through the both of us, the strength of the rikorō blinding my ability to think. Apeiron snaps his mouth shut. I move my fin away just as Nkella grabs my arm and pulls me toward him. We don't look back. We keep swimming, but Apeiron is faster. The serpent whips his tail around, smacking our chests hard and flinging us far.

Nkella cries out in his head as AJ gets flung out of his arm. My heart lunges into my throat as Nkella releases me to swim after AJ.

Apeiron zeros in on Nkella's movement, and I desperately look around for something to grab. I spot a rusty metal anchor on the ocean floor and grab it by the chain. I pull, screaming at Apeiron with all my might—only to send the shattering sound inside Nkella's head instead.

I push and pull furiously at the anchor, loosening it up enough to cause a cloud of sand as I lean my body weight into it. Finally, it lets up. I wrap the chain hard around my arm and start to swim, trying my hardest to gain enough inertia to swing it.

Apeiron snaps his attention to the multitude of bubbles created by my fin moving in his direction, taking his sight off Nkella. I start to swing the anchor around and around, gaining speed. With one forceful swing, I spin the anchor hard enough, hitting Apeiron on the side of his gigantic face. I still have the chain gripped in my hands, and I swing it around again, hitting him square on his nose, as the force of it spins me around too.

Nkella grabs hold of AJ, and swims away from us. I swing the anchor one more time, and Apeiron opens his mouth, closing down on the metal. I let it go and swim back toward Nkella. Yep. He can have that.

"We need to find a way to turn around," I think to him.

"I have to kill the beast first."

"Well, metal anchors are apparently a tasty treat for him, so I'm open to other suggestions."

Nkella speeds ahead of me. AJ's blank skull face gapes at me as it bobs over his shoulder. A tall ocean cliff wall meets us at the other end.

"It's a dead end," he says.

"Keep swimming fast. Full speed."

"Dai?" he quirks a brow at me.

"Just do it. At the last minute, we'll turn around as fast as we can."

Nkella seems to understand what I'm insinuating because he picks up speed, and so do I. We spot a small tunnel off some rocks on the bottom big enough for both of us to swim through, but too small for a giant serpent.

We make a dive for it and swim through successfully. It slows the serpent down, allowing us to make it to the wall. Not a very smart giant snake, is he?

One sharp turn later, we speed in the opposite direction and lead Apeiron right into the wall.

"Bet that hurt." I bite back a chuckle so not to even let that slow me down.

"To the ridge."

We speed to the crack on the ocean floor to follow it back. It only takes about a minute for Apeiron to be back on our tails, only now, there's nowhere to hide and no wall to pull one over him. With no time to think, we swim as fast as we can, AJ's hair flowing over his skull.

Something crashes down on the surface, and I force myself not to pause. Another bomb? No, there's no shockwave. The blue and purple glow grows larger by the second it comes toward us, and my wrists buzz. Gari came back for us! He spots us, and as his sinuous body grows larger, so do his face and teeth. His crazy yellow eyes look past us—and right at the serpent. Nkella pushes me to the left, letting Gari sweep past us and take on Apeiron head-on.

I gasp as Gari clenches his teeth around Apeiron's neck, but then Apeiron wraps around and bites Gari's body. I squeal as blood seeps out of his side.

"We have to go," Nkella says.

"No!"

"There's nothing we can do. We need to save AJ. And ourselves."

I back away, moving over the bottomless rift. Something catches my eye—something white amid the dark—and for a split second, I allow myself a double-take.

The words *North Face* glare back at me.

My eyes bulge. *"What the hell?"*

"Soren, let's go. Now."

Apeiron shakes free, causing a massive wave to push me and Nkella farther out to sea. He grabs hold of AJ's unanimated body and dodges another swing of Apeiron's tail. Gari is wrapped around a pointy rock, blood splotches in the water around him. Apeiron turns over to us, just as Nkella pulls me to leave.

I glance back at Gari. His head has sunk down into his chin, and his eyes are heavy. He looks out of it.

But Nkella's right. An anvil lands in my gut. We have to save ourselves.

We swim just out of Apeiron's reach, and as he opens his mouth wide, Gari swings his tail in one hard motion. White and yellow electricity zaps Apeiron so hard, his body convulses.

Gari strikes him again with the bottom of his tail. Then, he reaches forward, his eyes narrowing into slits, and bites Apeiron on his side. Once, Twice. Then he curls the end of his tail, wraps it around Apeiron's giant head, and pulls him away from us. Blood leaves Gari as he moves back, dragging Apeiron with him.

My heart pants hard in my chest.

"Get out of here," Gari gurgles.

"What about you?"

"Remember, Soren, fate isn't what it seems." Apeiron writhes under Gari's hold, and he sends another shock of electricity into the serpent, causing him to lift his head, then drop it, as he's dragged under the rift.

Nkella pulls my arm. *"Let's get AJ to dry land."*

I nod my head, then pull back.

"Wait."

"What is it?"

"I don't know how, but I think Harold is down there somewhere. That's his jacket." I point to where I spotted it in the dark abyss inside the deep crooked crack in the ocean floor. The last time I saw Harold, the Empress had tried to curse me with the undead curse. But her power ricocheted off me and landed on Harold instead, instantly turning him skeletal and enacting the curse for all to see. Then, she left with him, and we never saw him again.

If he's really down here, it's my fault. It's my fault he was cursed, and it's my fault he's had to endure this pain of being in the bottom of the ocean alone.

I'm already swimming down when Nkella sends a warning emotion. *"The serpent can come back. We don't know if Katergaris killed it."*

"I know but I'm not leaving Harold down here."

Nkella follows me. I grab onto the edge of the rocky floor, and lead myself down, resisting the water flow. Swimming, and letting the wall guide me, I descend deeper into the cave's darkness. Nkella stays close behind, having left AJ on the floor above us, but he's not happy about it. Closer to the rock platform the jacket is on, I can make out the whole thing. I pick it up, just the black jacket with the words North Face over the left chest. My heart plummets. What did she do with him?

Nkella touches my shoulder, and I glance over at him. He points to a hole in the rock formation, like a smallish cave. A blotch of blonde hair moves with the water and my eyes widen. I swim over and reach for the hair, part of me preparing for it to only be plant matter. I push it back, and a skull gets pushed back with it, its large empty eye sockets glaring back at me.

A smile tugs at my lips, and I start pulling at his bones. Nkella lifts him up and positions him over my shoulders. He gives me a questioning glance to make sure I'm okay taking him up, and I nod.

We don't see any sign of Gari as Nkella again collects AJ, but there's also no sign of Apeiron.

We're quiet making our way back to the beach; my heart remains lodged in my throat, and if I didn't have two open slits in my neck from the rikorō, I'd have a hard time breathing from the pain of not having Gari come back with us. And since he isn't here to get us back quicker, it takes us longer to get to shore. Still, we're faster than if we were swimming without tails or unable to breathe underwater.

Harold, being only a pile of bones, feels light on my back. But it's still uncomfortable to carry him since he's just bones. I'm afraid he'll slip out of my hands.

By the time we reach our beach, my arms are shaking, and I'm out of breath. The sunlight hits the surface and I urge myself forward, just a little bit farther. When I finally reach the top, my head pokes out, and the air hurts my throat. The light pains my eyes. I swim out, squinting, until my tailfin reaches the sand. I fall, trying to hold myself over Harold's bones. I lay him down for a second to readjust.

A wave crashes over Harold's skull, and I try to lift him up, while keeping my balance. As I do, something sharp makes contact with my chest. My eyes follow a pointed spear all the way up to the Ipani standing in front of me, a stern look on her face, and purple and blue scales riding up her arms. She nudges the spear to my throat, cutting at my skin.

"Get up, trafficker scum. It ends here for you."

8

I LIFT MY ARMS IN SURRENDER AND GLANCE AT NKELLA who's being held at spearpoint by an Ipani man with pink and yellow shimmery scales on his arms and torso. Even though they're both standing in water, scales shimmer from their legs instead of flukes.

"You don't understand," Nkella tells him. He's now standing, his legs having shifted back. A strange wave of restrained force emanates off him, similar to the waves of emotions that had rolled off each of us other underwater.

"Which one of us did you kill for that rikorō?" The merman shoves the spearpoint close to Nkella's throat, and Nkella inches his face back.

"How do you know we took rikorō?" I squint at them.

"Word gets out from the tavern quick," the merman spits at me. "We had been chasing that vial since Piupeki. Then we were alerted of an Ipani ship escaping from Piupeki and the Arcana bombing them."

"We were checking the waters for survivors but ran into you instead," says the mermaid holding her spear at me.

"This happened today?" They must be talking about the bomb that activated my power when it hit the water.

The mermaid lifts the spear to my throat. "So you know about it, mei?" She smirks. "Don't play games with us. We take rikorō seriously."

76

"So do we," Nkella says, his eyes now giving off a warning glow. "I am Captain Nkella Mikiroro, I'm sure you've heard of me. Put down your weapons." His voice grows hoarse. "I don't want to hurt you."

Both Ipani gape at us and lower their spears. "Prince Nkella," the man says bowing low. "Apologies, but why—"

"It was the only way to save my crew. I would never have taken it otherwise."

The mer-Ipani exchange confused glances, tinged with distaste. Something like a bell rings in my ear, and I quirk a brow.

I feel Nkella's guilt stirring in the forefront of my mind; I know it's killing him to have taken the rikorō. And now that we've surfaced with the crew, we have to worry about how to save ourselves from its poison. I really need that Death Card, not only to bring my mom back from the dead but also to make sure Nkella and I don't die.

Nkella's brows furrow as he glances at me, "What are you not telling me, neyuro?" His frown deepens.

I bite my tongue. I forgot this mer-telepathy works both ways, but it looks like I can only get feelings of emotions and sometimes visions. How much can he read from me?

Grabbing Harold's bony shoulders from the water, I pass him an apologetic look. I'm sitting on my butt not having moved far from the water level. The brightness of the day is starting to normalize, but some things still look saturated, like the sun's reflection on the moving waves, and it's making me dizzy.

The mermaid buckles her spear to her back and reaches for me. "Let me help you."

"We will help carry your men back to shore, and then we will continue the search for any survivors from the refugee ship." The man says to Nkella, helping him with Kae.

Nkella takes a shaky breath, letting the man take Kae's bones off his shoulder. Disorientation is hitting us both, and fear is starting to track up my spine. Once the water is down to my ankles, only the iridescent sheen of yellow and red scales appears on my skin. The bells ring in my ear again and I catch them exchanging a glance.

"What is that ringing?" I ask.

"If you hear the bells, it means we are blocking you from listening in. Only real mer-Ipani can do it," she says.

I swallow a dry lump in my throat. "I think Nkella and I can still hear each other," I say.

Bells ring again, and I can feel Nkella's annoyance. I don't blame him.

"If you drank from the same vial, then I doubt you will be able to block each other's thoughts," she says. The man laughs.

This will be fun. If it doesn't kill us first.

Despite a new sense of nausea surfacing, there is also a fresh feeling of air entering my lungs through my nose, the slits on my neck have now closed. I stare back at the water and wonder if I'll ever experience something like that again. I also wonder how long the rikorō will last. Or how long I have before it kills me.

We step onto the dry sand and watch as the mer-Ipani lay Harold and Kae next to Tessa, who's waking up, bone and skin growing along her arms and neck. AJ is flat on his back a few feet away, hair covering his face, which is now half covered with flesh. I catch a glimpse of feathers above his head; Lāri is still in bird form. A flutter of relief hits me, but before I run to the crew, the mer-Ipani turn back to the ocean.

"Thank you," Nkella says to them. "For...understanding."

That bell rings in my ears as they pause to stare at him. "We still don't condone it, Prince," the merman says. "And I'm not sure you would have understood had it been someone else." The mermaid grabs his arm in warning, pulling him away.

Nkella stands there with a blank look on his face.

"I'm not foolish enough to wage war with the infamous Devil captain, but know that if this were to come out, many wouldn't be so kind toward your hypocrisy. May you both survive the rikorō," he says with a bow, and we watch them go back to sea.

I take a sharp breath and stare at Nkella. His eyes are sorrowful and not angry by what was said to him. A knot ties in my stomach, his guilt twisting it hard.

As badly as I know I'll miss the sea, I want this to pass already.

Nkella fixes his eyes on me, and they're dark and blazing. I can feel his questions burning beneath the surface.

"Can we talk about this later?" I say before he's given the chance to speak. "Let's take care of the crew first and then find food. I'm starving."

His jaw hardens, and I already know he has no intention of letting this go. "If there had not been a refugee boat above us that got bombed," he says slowly, "you would not have had your vision." He pinches the bridge of his nose. "Kh. I could have done this alone."

"Stop saying that. You never would have found them alone. My powers brought us to them."

"It is bancha to rely on luck, daí?"

"Welcome to my life of chance," I say. His intense eyes search mine. His annoyance mixes with anger inside him, and it's pouring into my psyche, the rikorō still going strong. "Why are people escaping from Piupeki anyway?"

He pauses; his features soften. "Piupeki is coming under siege like Danū. Anyone using ouma is put to death. No one is allowed in or out to account for all Ipani the Empress can no longer bind from their ouma."

My breathing slows as his words sink in, and my eyes widen. I used the Ace of Wands Card to prevent the Empress from ever being able to bind an Ipani again, thus returning everyone's ouma, and then this happens. This is all my fault.

First, the crew ends up motionless underwater because I left the World Card with Nkella, making them a target. And now this.

"You did what you thought was right, neyuro." His hand brushes my arm. "You could not have known what the Empress would do."

"How many have died since I left?"

"Neyuro...many would have died anyway."

"That doesn't justify anything."

But I know he feels my guilt, as I feel his. Gari was right—they do need help. A thought makes me perk up. If the Death Card can reverse death, can't I use it to save more than my mom? It can be all of our salvation.

Nkella quirks a brow, letting his arm fall from my arm.

I have to tell him my plan. He isn't going to like it, but I'm going to need his help. "We have to talk."

A moaning-turned-cry leaves AJ's lips, and both Nkella and I turn to him. My heart leaps out of my chest and I run toward AJ as he grabs his head and falls to the sand—both his legs are still all bones. Lāri's feathers flutter as she starts to awaken.

"AJ! Are you alright?" I rasp.

"I'm so hungry," he cries, his long wet black hair showcasing patches of his skull on parts of his head and face.

I pause, and I bite back a laugh. "We'll get you something to eat ASAP."

"It won't matter." His voice cracks. "I'm so sick of this stupid curse." He kicks up, sand flying out in front of him.

"It'll be more bearable, at least, if you eat something," Tessa says. "The curse kept us alive. Although it was torture, it would be worse if we had been taken to the Deep."

I turn to Tessa, who's squeezing her wet hair with skeletal hands. I run to give her a hug, but Nkella calls me back.

He hands me my dry clothes, and I quickly take them, completely forgetting that I had stripped down to my underwear before getting in the water. It takes me two seconds to dress, and then I'm hugging Tessa's neck.

"You call what happened to us not worse than death?" AJ cries out.

"It couldn't have been worse than eternal torture, AJ," Nkella says.

AJ looks up from the sand at Nkella, then at me. His eyes widen as big as saucers, and his lips part. "H-how... What happened?" he finally asks. "Soren, didn't you leave?"

I shrug a modest shoulder and smile. "I heard you guys were in trouble, so I came back."

"We were attacked," Lāri says from behind him. She stands up and holds her head, shaking each talon as they shift to bare feet. "The last thing I remember was a bomb headed straight for us. I turned to leave the crow's nest... But then everything went black."

Nkella sighs deeply. "For three months, I have sought ways to find you in the endless sea to bring you back. We almost didn't find you. It was Soren who did."

AJ's hard stare makes me shiver. He usually isn't this serious, but I know he's been through a lot.

"You...you did something terrible, Captain."

Nkella blinks.

"I can see it all over you."

Red and yellow scales still glisten over Nkella's skin. AJ's eyes move to mine. "And worst, you got Soren to partake in your dirty work and endangered her life."

I can feel the breath leave Nkella's lungs, his guilt intensifying. Amber flashes in his eyes, and I whip my attention to AJ.

"Woah, hey!" I walk over to him and sit down in front of him. Surprise flashes through his features, but he doesn't move. "First of all, Nkella didn't want me to drink the rikorō. I took it myself because I wanted to help you. Secondly, your captain over there? The one standing with unquenchable guilt for taking the one thing he despises the most in this world, apart from the Empress? He thought he would never see *you*—his family—again. Iéle saved him the moment the ship was hit, and he didn't know where any of you had sunk to. He risked his Devil curse taking over and put aside finding his sister—*for you*. Because he loves you, AJ." A surge of guilt and regret emanates from Nkella at the mention of his sister. I look up at the rest of them, glimpsing Kae's bald head as he walks up behind Tessa. His large stature casts a large shadow over her chair.

"He loves all of you," I say. "And he would do anything for you, even if it's compromising his own beliefs. That's the captain you have." AJ's eyes water and he looks away from me. I take his hand, not minding that his pinky is still skeletal, and he squeezes my hand back. Lowering my voice, I tell him, "I'd be thankful that he never gave up searching for you, so that you wouldn't be stuck as a motionless, pile of bones in your own form of eternal torment, above the Serpent's Deep."

My hands are shaking. I never thought I'd speak to AJ like that, and I certainly never thought I'd be defending the captain while doing it. My heart hammers in my chest, and Nkella's heart is beating differently in my ears. A sense of longing is radiating from him, and it makes my cheeks burn.

"I missed you guys," I say, more calmly. AJ gives me a sheepish grin and I pull him into a hug, twining his hair between my fingers. A sob leaves his throat.

"I'm sorry," I tell him. "It must have been hell."

"It was," he whispers into my ear. "But you're right. I'm scared for you now, though, Soren. You and the captain."

I squeeze my eyes shut and nod. "We'll figure it out." I let go of his embrace and walk over to Tessa and Kae, leaving Lāri and AJ to reconnect. Nkella's giving his cousin a hug when I walk over and greet Kae with a hug of my own. He wraps me in a cold and wet embrace, his big, muscular arms eating my torso.

"I always knew there was something special about you," Kae says, his sharp Ipani fangs showing as he grins. "Thank you for helping my cousin."

"Always," I say.

My eyes fall to Harold, who is now sitting on the sand behind Kae, staring at us. My excitement skitters down.

Kae catches my glare and looks over his shoulder. "How did he end up at the bottom of the sea with the rest of us?"

"She must have had her Arcana throw him in after," Nkella says, walking up.

"Him having that curse is my fault," I mutter.

Kae looks back at me and pats me on the shoulder. I cross the sand and walk over to Harold, who looks at me momentarily before he looks past me again. I can tell he's adamantly avoiding looking at the water.

"Mind if I join you?" I ask.

He shrugs. My throat dries up, guilt twisting through my bones as I take a seat next to him.

A few silent beats pass between us as we watch the crew catch up and help each other dry.

"Harold—" I swallow the ball lodged in my throat. "I'm sorry." My voice cracks. He stares at me. "I'm just..." My chest grows heavy. "So sorry."

"Why?"

"That was all my fault."

"What are you talking about? The Empress did this."

I search his blue eyes, confusion sprawled on his face. "What do you remember?"

"Not much." He lays his hands on top of his knees. "I'm trying to remember, but all I can feel is the suffocating weight of the ocean on my chest, even though I was just bones. The never-ending hunger. The fear I'll never see my dad or my aunt again."

I shudder, taking a breath. "Do you remember being at the firepit in Wands after the Empress got there?"

It takes him a moment, but his eyes widen and I continue.

"She meant to curse me." My voice grows heavy, and then it cracks. "But her power ricocheted off me and hit you instead."

He shakes his head.

"Yes. It's my fault you have the undead curse now. It's my fault you still don't have your runes, and you're not back home."

He continues to shake his head. "No—"

"I'm so sorry, Harold."

"Soren, stop."

A sob escapes my throat.

"That isn't your fault."

"What?" I dry my eyes.

"I don't blame you for that. The Empress attacked us. It's not like you aimed her power at me. This is her doing, not yours."

"I still feel guilty about it."

"Well, you shouldn't." He stares out at the crew again. "But I do need to figure out how to end this curse and get to Jötunheim. I still have my family's curse to break."

"Do you feel your ice curse?"

He nods, and ice forms at the tips of his eyes. "Add eternal torment to my frosty curse concoction." He smirks.

"What are you going to do?"

"I don't know yet. I'll figure something out."

A growl comes from Nkella's feet. Harold and I turn to stare at four wolves making themselves comfortable around the crew. Iéle, lowers her head momentarily in my direction, a snarl leaving her teeth.

Harold chuckles. "At this point, I think she's just jealous of you."

Iéle turns toward Nkella, and he absentmindedly scratches her head.

"We should find shelter," Tessa says as Kaehante works to pull two pieces of copper tubing from the back of her chair. Shields of metal form along his hands all the way to his arm as he pries it apart, his power adding to his strength. Water and moss pour out of the tubes, and he shakes them out onto the sand. "Let's go to Cerberus," she says.

"We can't go there," Nkella announces grimly. The crew exchange a glance, and I offer them a thin smile.

"Yeah, that's probably not a good idea," I say. "Is there another inn nearby?"

AJ stands as Lāri finishes tying his damp hair away from his face for him. He's no longer a skeletal figure half-covered with strands of skin. "What happened at Cerberus?"

"I have a place for us to sleep," Nkella says, evading AJ's question. "Understand we cannot eat at any inn, daí? The mer-Ipani said word got out about the vial, so the Columns Inn would be cautious of me as well."

AJ nods and stares at the sand. The crew grows quiet, and I can tell they're piecing the information together. They know he took rikorō, how he managed to acquire it will speak volumes to his control or inability to control his Devil curse. Nkella pushes down a wave of regret, followed by another wave toward the two men he killed. My eyes narrow as the memory of him walking out of the tavern with his face bruised and bloody resurfaces. I squint my eyes at Nkella. With the excitement of everything that's happened, I didn't notice how fast his face completely healed. Maybe it was the rikorō working its magic. Come to think of it, I had completely forgotten how he looked after his fight. I don't think he had any injuries when we got in the water.

He catches me staring at him, and I glance down at the sheen of scales in my hand, now getting lighter by the minute.

We don't leave for what feels like over an hour while AJ, Nkella, and Kae work to get Tessa's chair to hover again. She can roll over solid terrain, although the tires are messed up, but it won't work over sand at all. In the meantime, Nkella sends Iéle and the three other wolves to hunt for food. At least, they're good for something.

Since Nkella and his pack of wolves secured a camping spot before I had gotten here, Lāri, Harold, and I go to check it out, as per Nkella's directions. It isn't where he laid his drunk head last night though—it's a bit more secure and sheltered. As we walk, the telepathic connection between me and Nkella gets lighter, and I feel an enormous weight lift off my shoulders. I feel like me again.

I can think more clearly, and because of that, I feel like I can breathe better.

We find the fallen log Nkella told us to cross. He took a less beaten path to build his camp, which makes sense as he wouldn't want any passerby to scope him out. Lāri walks in front of us, smelling the air with her pointy nose. Having just morphed back from having a tail fin, I can see the advantages of having part-animal abilities. I so envy her. This is going to be gone soon; I can already tell my scales are fading.

"So, what time of year is it back home?" Harold takes me out of my thoughts. "I've lost track of time since I first got here."

"It's November. Almost Thanksgiving."

He lets out a quiet sigh, and I chew my cheek.

"Will your folks be looking for you?"

"No, my aunt knew what I was doing—she made something up for my dad—but it doesn't mean they won't be worried."

We catch up to Lāri who left us behind as she followed her scent, and then pause to see what she's staring at.

"This is it," Lāri says.

Wooden flooring wraps around a thick tree trunk, with a one-story plank for Tessa's chair. He must have been planning for their return. A second floor wraps around the second half of the trunk, with a ladder connecting both stories. I gape at it.

"He built this in three months?" Harold asks.

I shrug. "Guess so."

Lāri morphs into her eagle form and flies to the second floor.

"I'll never get used to that," I say. Although, because she's tall—much taller than AJ—and built, the fact that she can shift to an eagle is no longer any surprise to me. She flies in through one window and comes out another, flying in and out of the hut. When she comes back, she's barely a bird, as part of her has started to shift back into human form as she lands.

Harold stares wide-eyed at the structure. "He cut down trees, carved every wooden plank, and built a two-story treehouse all by himself..."

"Nkella is much stronger, mei?" Lāri says and I bite back a laugh when Harold's eyebrows raise. "He has been living in an empty tree hut," she adds, concern now creeping into her voice.

Harold walks into the hut. I follow, pushing the bamboo straw to the side of the doorframe. Lāri is right. There's a blanket and candle in the corner and a pile of messy clothes to the side. A pile of skinless, licked-clean bones are in another pile—I have the feeling that's where the wolves eat.

Lāri shoves the bones with her foot. "Let's clean this place up."

"Er—I'll go light the firepit outside, so we have somewhere to cook." Harold walks out of the tree hut.

Lāri picks up the bones with her hands and quickly steps out, when she comes back, she has two long palm leaves in her hands. I take one from her and begin to sweep.

"So, what's next for you?" I ask her.

She scratches the back of her pixie-cut hair. "Hnn... First, I need to locate the *Gambit* for my captain. Then, we continue on our mission to stop the Empress. And you?"

I swallow. "I'm on a mission of my own." I pause, wondering if I should tell her now or wait for the others.

Straightening the blanket Nkella used to sleep, I catch a whiff of leather and vanilla rum spices. Two things fall to the floor: one is something metal, and the other sounds like wood bouncing on the wood floor. I bend down to pick up the metal item and then set the empty rum flask on the floor. Stepping back, I scan the floor for the other item.

"Did you lose something?" Lāri asks, poking her nose close to where I'm looking. It really resembles that of a bird.

"Something fell from the blanket when I went to fold it."

She reaches the edge of the wall and picks up something tiny. "Is it this?" She squints one eye. "What is this, mei?"

I gasp and take it from her. A bubble forms in my throat as I hold the tiny item up to my eyes. It's a wooden teacup like the charm I'd lost in the ocean the night I jumped in after Nkella. Goosebumps prickle my arms. He got to hold a teacup when he came for me after I had been poisoned by the itachi vine. He remembered my story and how much this charm meant to me.

And he had carved it out of wood.

"Mei?"

I blink and look up at Lāri. "Oh, umm… It's nothing." I stick it in my pocket, and she goes back to sweeping. Suddenly my mind is feeling too quiet, and I'm missing his brooding and contradicting emotions circulating with my own.

"Well," Tessa's voice comes from the entrance. "My chair is struggling, but it'll do for now."

AJ walks beside her. "We need the *Gambit*. It's where all her tools are. And all the rest of our stuff." Pausing at the tree trunk in the center, he looks around. "This is cozy."

A cool breeze greets me as I step outside. The sun is still out, but it must be late afternoon. The sun was rising when we took off this morning. It almost feels surreal, all that happened on the same day.

It feels surreal to be back.

Harold is hovering over the firepit, furiously rubbing two sticks together. I walk over. "Need any help?"

"No."

I quirk a brow and step over him with my hands on my waist.

"Sorry," he sighs and throws the sticks down. "Making fire was part of my rune magic, but I lost it after enacting my Frost curse."

"Oh… I'm sorry."

He holds his head and shuts his eyes for a second. "And now I'm back to being useless."

"You're not useless, Harold."

His eyes roll in his head and then he continues working. "Just let me have this," he says.

I nod and quietly choose several nearby dry branches, bringing them to him. "I can still help," I say as I take a seat. "It's not like I know how to build a fire."

"I know a girl who's really good at building fires."

"The one in Swords? What was her name?"

"Kenjō."

The vision of my mother riding on the drakon with a sword strapped to her hip pushes itself into my mind. Why do I keep seeing that?

A spark flashes in front of me, and Harold starts to lightly blow at the flame, causing it to grow. I smile.

"See? Told ya you could do it."

"Now I just need to keep it alive," he says.

"Baby steps."

After we eat, we hang out by the fire until sunset. Nkella's emotions start to weigh on me again, and I know mine are pushing their way to him. We've been sitting apart from each other this entire time, hardly looking at one another. And now that the adrenaline from rescuing the crew has died down, it feels weird. We went from thinking we'd never see each other again to sharing thoughts and feelings with one another. We've barely spoken a word since we brought the crew to shore, and after having seen the little teacup he carved, I don't even know what to say. Thanks to the stupid rikorō, he probably already knows I have it.

I excuse myself to walk out to the sand and then take a seat close to the waves hitting the shore so that my feet touch the water. My toes tingle as a bioluminescent light appears from the shimmering scales on my skin. But I resist the urge to jump in. I just want to sit here and stare at the waves. I take the little teacup Nkella carved out of my pocket and twirl it between my fingers. Did my mother ever sit here in Dempu Yuni and stare at the waves? I wonder what her experiences here were like, which islands she visited—besides Swords, of course.

A familiar sense of dark emotions blankets me, and I glance up to see Nkella approaching, his flask in his hand. His hair is mussed over his eyes, but the weight of his gaze has me.

"You found the cup, neyuro."

I swallow.

"I will control my thoughts," he says, staring down at me.

"I don't know how you're doing that. Can you hear mine if I'm just thinking?"

He shakes his head. "Pictures. Feelings. Nothing coherent."

Good.

"Can you hear me, neyuro?"

I gasp and stare at his face. He didn't move his mouth once, I heard him in my head, just like when we were underwater. "So we can talk directly to each other? But otherwise, we just *feel* each other's emotions... I don't know how I feel about you knowing what I'm feeling." I swallow.

He quirks a brow at me and smirks. "This can be advantageous."

I chuckle nervously. "I definitely hate this." I look back out to sea, shoving down the butterflies in my gut as he takes a seat next to me. "I thought you'd want some space from me since we can't seem to control what's going through our minds."

"I don't want you knowing what I have to bear," he admits after a few seconds.

"Those emotions I felt from you before," I whisper, "when the rikorō first started taking effect..."

"I pushed them away as fast as I could. So that you wouldn't feel them."

"No, but...it was from your curse, wasn't it? The curse of the Devil Card." When he doesn't respond, I ask, "How do you live with that every day?"

"Kh. That was only a little. I don't want you near me at my worst."

"How were you able to push it back? I don't think I've been able to hide my emotions from you at all."

"It is what I always do—push them back." He stares out to sea.

"Maybe that isn't a good idea."

He side-eyes me and takes a swig of his rum before offering me some. I shake my head but hold up the teacup charm.

He smiles and swallows a longer gulp of rum.

"So, you missed me?" A smile curls at my lips.

A swirl of emotions surfaces between us, and he pushes them down. And so do I, at least I hope I do.

"I spent many nights all alone out here, worrying I would never see my crew again, that I would not be able to save them. I carve sometimes to take my mind off things."

"Did it help?"

"It reminded me of how you used to anger me, daí?" He glances at me from the corner of his eye and smirks.

"Sure." I give it back to him, but he hands it back to me.

"You keep it, neyuro. You lost the one your mother gave you because of me."

A pain grows in my chest, and I make a fist around the little wooden charm and hold it to my heart. A tear swells in my eyes, but I look away, trying to push them away.

"I never understand why you do some things," he says.

"What do you mean?"

"You say you had to take the rikorō. You do not understand how dangerous it is."

"I do. And because...the crew is like my family too. I don't really have one back home."

His eyes soften. "You have your sister."

"She doesn't need me anymore." This time I take the rum and take a sip. Warm vanilla spices burn down my throat, and I cough.

He chuckles and takes the flask from me, then leans into my ear. "She will always need you."

I nod. "I know, she's young and wants to be her own person. Are you still hoping to save yours?"

"I will never stop." His voice grows hoarse at the last word, and I regret asking him that. Of course, he'll never stop. He's Nkella.

My eyes drift back to sea, and memories from today come in with the waves, but I try hard not to voice it in my head. Something in Nkella stirs.

"I can feel your distress, neyuro. What is it?"

"Gari. I didn't even know he could do that," I whisper.

"Do what?"

"The electricity."

"Drakons are known to use electricity, but it makes them weak. They have to recharge." After a few seconds, he says, "Maybe he survived."

"He was bleeding out."

"Drakons are difficult to kill."

I swallow. I hope so. He saved us.

He slowly and carefully wraps his arm around me, creating electricity with his touch, and my stomach stirs. His breathing grows heavy as he softly pulls me into him. I lean in, resting my head on his chest. He's so warm. His scent overpowers the sea breeze, and I start to get lost in it. I lift my chin. His dark eyes are on mine.

My heart starts to thud loudly, and his thumps in my ears.

I want to kiss him. Badly.

I can feel his uncontrollable desire to kiss me too. An amber flicker ignites behind his irises as he leans down, our lips almost touching.

Hesitation sparks inside him. I can sense his emotions conflicting, dueling with each other.

Maybe we shouldn't... "Nk—"

His eyes widen and he draws back.

"We don't have to—"

"Neyuro, you're bleeding."

I gasp and touch under my nose. Blood smears coat my fingers.

9

NKELLA JUMPS UP AND QUICKLY SLIDES HIS ARMS UNDER MY back and legs, lifting me.

"Nkella, what are you doing?" I wrap my arms around his neck as he stands and carries me back to the tree hut.

"That is from the rikorō, neyuro." He hisses behind his teeth. "That was a bad idea."

"I knew the risks. This was my choice."

Nkella doesn't speak the rest of the way through the dense shrubbery, but I can feel the guilt and regret cocktail he's brewing inside. Blood runs down to my lips, and I let go of one arm to hold my nose. He carries me to where the crew is still sitting by the fire and sets me down.

"What happened?" Tessa's voice is alarmed.

"She is bleeding from the rikorō," Nkella says, his voice heavy with regret.

AJ turns around, sleepily. "Wait, what?"

"I'm fine," I say. "Really, it's just a bit of blood." The flames flicker, smaller now than when we were eating.

"Lāri, take a cloth from inside and wet it," Nkella directs.

Lāri sprints into the hut and comes back a few seconds later with a blue cloth. I honestly don't want to know what it was used for or how clean it is. She sticks it in her mouth then shifts into an eagle and takes off.

Harold sits by me and hands me a dry cloth. "Here. Use this till she comes back."

"Thanks." I take it and hold it to my nose. He turns to grab some more firewood and feeds it to the flames.

"Magician, you know about rikorō, daí?" Nkella asks him.

"I know enough to stay away from it," he says, sticking a long piece of wood into the embers.

Kaehante storms out of the hut, his shoulder nearly taking out the doorframe. He's panting hard, and his arms are in his full armadillo armor mode from his ouma ready for battle. "Captain! We are under attack!"

Nkella gapes at him, "Go back to sleep, Kaehante. No one is attacking us."

Tessa lets out a nervous chuckle.

Kae stares down at me, and I can see concern written across his forehead. He drops his shoulders and sits by the fire next to AJ, rubbing his eyes.

"You big oaf," AJ says. Kae grunts and wipes the sleep from his face.

Nkella flicks his attention back to Harold. "Is there nothing you can make to help her? To prolong the poison until I find the cure?"

"There is no cure," Harold says. The flames burn brightly, causing his face to look orange. "And I would need plants that grow in Piupeki to prolong it, so unless you know someone who sells them on this island, the answer is no. I don't have magic, and even if I had my runes and my abilities, I never connected with the rune that heals." He stares at me dead on. "I do know this, Soren, the more you use power from the rikorō, the faster it'll kill you. So my advice? Don't use it."

I swallow the lump of blood forming in my throat.

Nkella gently lifts my chin a little higher to inspect my face. I squint at him as he searches my eyes. "No more using this ouma, daí?" he whispers, and I give a little nod.

Two large talons land close to my head, and an eagle drops the cloth, Lāri quickly shifts back to her Ipani form and carefully swaps the cloth with the wet one she just brought. Nkella moves over, giving her some space.

"Someone should go collect fresh water, mei?" she says, taking my head to her lap and gently holding the cloth to my nose. I close my eyes as she brushes my hair with her other hand.

"Thank you," I whisper, "I'm okay, though. Really. It's just a little blood."

"For now," Lāri says, "but you don't want to over-exert yourself and have the rikorō work faster."

"Work faster?"

"She's right," Tessa says. "Relax, Soren. There's not much we can do other than keep you comfortable."

My eyes widen at the sound of her words. I think they're all expecting me to die.

"Koj," Nkella says, fear pouring out from him.

Well, everyone except for him.

"There is a cure." Nkella says, bringing his legs up as he stares at me. A subtly pointy ear pokes out from his black mussed hair.

"Since when?" Harold says.

"Word has traveled down from Piupeki that someone has created a cure for the rikorō...stabilizing it."

"And they're sure of this?"

"Koj," Nkella's voice is low. "Words from pirates are never to be trusted." He sighs. "But there is a pirate named Bronte whose word is as serious as the blade. She would not lie."

"You heard this from Bronte herself?" Harold's voice cracks, and he almost leans into the fire as he stares at Nkella. I take the cloth from Lāri and sit up. She tries to lay me back down, but I tap on her hand to let her know it's okay. Wiping my nose, I show her the cloth. No more blood.

"Do you know of her?" Nkella asks Harold.

"She's Kenjō's mother. I was on her ship before you found me at Cerberus."

"Kenjō was the girl Harold was with when he got to Piupeki," I add for context.

"Yes, but she isn't a bad person," he tells Nkella flatly. "She's just in a difficult situation and is being forced to do what her mother asks. She almost lost her life to rikorō because she didn't want anyone else to suffer. If they found a cure in Swords, it was most likely she who made it. That's what she was working on when I met her."

"How can anyone force their daughter to deal with a deadly poison that kills others?" Tessa asks.

Harold shakes his head. "It's complicated, but...she's a little brainwashed."

"If this girl is the one who created the cure"—Nkella stares at Harold, his expression serious—"then you need to get that cure, daí?"

Harold nods and holds his head.

"And you." I turn to Nkella. "How are you feeling?"

"Strong."

The dim, flickering flames dance on his face, showcasing his strong features. He seems completely unaffected by the rikorō.

"For now. You should be taking it easy as well," I say.

He quirks a brow.

"Soren is right," Tessa chimes. "We need our captain. If it is true that there is a cure, both of you need to conserve your energy until we get it."

"It could be taking longer to affect him because he's big," AJ mutters sleepily. Lāri is now resting her head on his lap.

"We also don't know the extent of his Devil curse." Lāri looks over at Nkella. "Doesn't it make you stronger?"

"Kh." He shrugs one shoulder. "But only when it wants me to kill."

I blink at him. "You healed really fast after your fight at the tavern. I thought it was the rikorō, but could it have been your Devil Curse?"

A fury of emotions seeps out of him, and I shift uncomfortably. Nkella buries it. "Stop talking about my curse." His face darkens, and I swallow.

Lāri breaks our awkward silence. "We need the *Gambit*, mei? Is it still in Swords?"

"Right," AJ adds. "We're going there anyway, aren't we?"

"I gave up on keeping track of the *Gambit* when I was focused on saving you. My vessel might be a lost cause. They could have taken it anywhere by now...and sold all of its contents."

"What?" AJ cries out. "We would have to start over. Tessa would have to start over with all her gadgets and potions, Captain! No. We can't give up. Send Iéle to find out!"

"No matter where the *Gambit* is, AJ, we need the cure."

"Well, wait," I say. Nkella flicks his eyes at me. "I still need to tell all of you something." His gaze intensifies as he brings up a memory of us standing in the water, when he asked me what I'm hiding. "I didn't only come back here to help save you. I mean, when I saw that you might be in danger, that urged me to take the leap because I don't want you in harm's way."

"And the other reason?" Nkella asks, his eyes narrowing at me.

A cotton ball forms in my throat, and I swallow it. "When I went back home, I didn't get to see my mother. She had died three days before I got there." I pull out her necklace to show the rest of the crew. "I found out she had been here before, but that's not why I'm back." Eyes widen around me.

"We're so sorry, Soren," AJ says.

I take a deep breath before continuing. "When you guys went...to steal the Death Card..."

"Kh."

I shoot Nkella an angry glare.

"This is what you are after, daí?"

"I can steal it back."

"Oh, Soren..." Tessa warns.

"Do you not see what happened to my crew? To me? This plan is bancha, daí? Kh. Be smarter."

"I am being smart. If you haven't noticed, I have powers that I haven't fully come into. What if I can use them to get past the Empress?"

"And how? Hn? By looking into her past?" He lifts his chin, challenging me.

"Yes, actually. Maybe there is something I can uncover that will help me find the card."

"This is dangerous, Soren," Tessa says from across the fire.

"You had the same plan for different reasons. Why is it dangerous for me to do it, and not you?"

"It was dangerous," Nkella booms. "Look at me!" his eyes twitch with anger, eliciting a spark of crimson. His voice echoes into an animal-istic roar. Anguish radiates from his body, and my bones start to shake. I ball up my fist.

"Captain, let her speak," Lāri says, standing up. Kae is also getting up, ready to hold back his cousin in case he loses control.

"Your voice changed." AJ's eyes are wide as he stares at Nkella.

My chest pounds as I stare at him. "I'm stealing the Death Card to bring back my mother, whether you agree or not. You can help me, or I can leave. Either way, I'll find it. I'll use it to cure both of us, while possibly reversing the undead curse as well. It would be nice if you helped since you know the way around her Tower, but I'm not begging for your help, Nkella. I can go on my own."

Nkella stares at me, his hard breathing making his shoulders rise and fall. Amber flickers behind his dark eyes, but he keeps silent. After a few beats, I hear AJ shift positions.

"Honestly," I dart my eyes at AJ and he rubs the stubble on his chin. "It's not a terrible plan. What's the worst that can happen?"

"True death and eternal torture," Kaehante says.

"Right, but are we just giving up on lifting our curse?" AJ turns to Kae. "The Death Card is the answer to that, isn't it?"

"What got you guys caught to begin with?" Harold asks.

"Kh." Nkella grabs his head and whips around. "You are considering this?"

AJ ignores him. "We snuck in while she was asleep, and she woke up when Nkella was about to kill her with the Death Card. It was all useless. We didn't know non-Fates couldn't use the cards."

"That's still debatable, but it'll be easier for me to get the power to work," I add.

"So this will be different," Harold says. "We're not going there to kill her, and we can sneak in while she's not there."

Kaehante leans in. "Hn. It will be heavily guarded." Tessa nods her agreement from her seat next to him.

"We can dress up as the Arcana Army," Harold suggests.

Nkella guffaws. "Daí? And how will you make your eyes like smoke? We would never pass for them."

Harold's brows raise. "Well, I need this curse taken away and to get out of here. So far, Soren's plan is the only thing that makes sense for all of us. Don't you want to save your sister? Or has that changed?"

Nkella's face goes rigid. "That has not changed."

"So use the Death Card to get her."

Nkella squeezes his eyes shut and then sighs behind his teeth. "How do we get there? We no longer have a drakon who can help."

"How did you get there last time?" I ask.

"We made the *Gambit* fly," Tessa says, "with a floating and invisibility potion."

"I have an idea." AJ sits up. "We can kill two birds with one arrow."

Lāri smacks him on the arm.

"Sorry. What I mean is this. We can still go to Piupeki, get the *Gambit*, and find the cure. That way, if anything happens, we still have the cure. Then we can make the Gambit fly to go to the Tower. Soren steals the Death Card, our curse gets broken, Soren gets her mother back, and you can get your sister back, can't you? The Death Card can bring her soul back from the Deep."

Nkella's face hardens, and I can tell he's contemplating AJ's words.

"Sounds like the Death Card is the answer to all our problems." I cross my arms. "And I'm the one who can use it."

"It will be a long way up without a drakon, or a flying vessel," Lāri says. "I cannot fly that high alone. I should find the *Gambit*, and make sure all our belongings are there."

"No." AJ's voice cracks. "You're not going anywhere alone ever again."

Lāri brings her hand back. "I will go wherever I please. I refuse to live my life in fear because I was once captured."

Oh, I like her.

"Nkella said it's under siege! You'll be killed the moment you're fifty feet from them!" AJ gapes at her, then looks at the rest of us. "We'll all be killed if we don't plan this well. Captain, you barely made it out of Danū alive."

"There are still cargo boats going in. It isn't as bad as Danū yet," Nkella says. "They are securing Ipani and killing at first sight of ouma. If we are going to do this, we cannot use ouma, daí?" He looks at everyone.

Kae nods.

"There's always the Ace of Swords to reverse the curse," Harold says, "and that's in Swords. But someone will need to sacrifice something in exchange for what they want."

I stare at Harold. "Can it bring someone back from the dead?"

He nods. "It's how I saved Kenjō's life, but then, she hadn't been dead for a long time. I don't know if it could work for your mom, but you should know it comes at a hefty price."

"The sacrifice," Nkella says.

Harold nods. "The sword grants one bidding per sacrifice. So make sure you all have something you hold dear to give up."

Lāri gasps, a hint of excitement in her eyes as she cups her mouth and stares at AJ. "So any one of us can use it?"

"Maybe I can give up being a Fate," I mutter.

"Why would you do that, Soren?" Tessa narrows her eyes at me.

"Never mind." I don't want to get into why I'm not interested in killing the Empress and just want to live my life back home with my mom and Talia, without being in constant doom.

Harold turns to me. "Actually, there were written instructions that said only a Fate can carry and use the Ace Card without a sacrifice. Everyone else can do one sacrifice at the temple, and once it's done, the Sword returns to its place on the podium as a card."

Huh. Interesting.

Nkella's gaze falls to the flickering flames of the fire. I swallow. His silence weighs down on my shoulders. When he gets this quiet and distant, I know he's deep in thought about something he's plotting. And he's blocking me from his thoughts. How did he get so good at that already? Or maybe, the rikorō's power is simply wearing off.

"I don't think you understand," Harold says to the crew. "It's a sword. You have to kill whoever you mean to sacrifice."

Lāri screws up her face and returns to look at the fire. I stare at Harold without understanding. Who did he kill?

Nkella scoffs. "The sword is useless to us then, daí?"

"I'm just saying someone can use it if they have someone or something they want to sacrifice, and Soren can remove it from the podium. I hear it's the only thing that can kill the Empress."

"How do you know all this?" I ask.

"Demitri."

I shiver. "Been a while since I heard that name. The image of my mom riding the drakon with her Ipani lover resurfaces in my mind. The sword at her side. Did she kill someone? "Well, I'm not going to kill anyone, so the Death Card is still my choice."

Nkella flicks his gaze to me, disapproval in his eyes.

"I can go on my own."

"Koj," he says. "We will find the cure in Piupeki, then find the *Gambit*. I will help you steal the Death Card. And this time I will not fail. I will bring my sister back to me. And we will lift everyone's curse."

A smile slides across my face.

A magnetic pull from behind Nkella reveals his wolves spread out around him.

"Iéle and the pack will scope out the ship, Lāri—the island is too far. AJ is right, we cannot risk something happening to you when you get there, only for you to send Iéle back with whereabouts of our belongings."

"Thank the Aō," AJ sighs.

"But they cannot check to see if all our belongings are there, mei?" Lāri says. "Or do you trust the wolves to learn what copper tubing is and where to find it in Tessa's lab? I can go, too, and they can protect me."

"I don't like the idea of being separated again," AJ frowns.

"I'll be back. I won't wait for you to come this time."

"It's a long flight."

"I fly fast. I could spot you once you have the ship and are at sea, with Iéle's guidance."

Nkella bows his head, whispering to Iéle. "Iéle will go."

"I can get there faster than the wolves if I fly," Lāri says.

"This is the safest way," AJ says.

"The wolves get distracted and go off to hunt. I'll be faster."

"Enough arguing," Nkella says. "The wolves go without you. Piupeki is under siege, like Danū. It is heavily guarded, and Ipani guards working for the Prefect are hidden inside the Aō. Understood?"

Lāri slumps her shoulders. "Yes, Captain."

"Now with more wolves than just Iéle, we have an advantage. In the meantime, we will find a new ship to get us there."

"Maybe we can find ingredients to keep us hidden—if we can find a ship that takes it." Tessa says.

Nkella lies back. "There is no ship here like the *Gambit*, Tessa. I can promise you that. Tonight, we rest, daî? We have our heading and our plan."

"We have a heading, Captain." Kae jolts forward from dozing off. The rest laugh as he grunts and lies back down.

Iéle growls, and Nkella pats her head. He grabs her from the top of her neck, forcing her to lie down, then rests his head on her like a pillow. Her head faces in my direction, and she fixes her glare on me.

I get up and walk inside the dark tree hut, away from wolves and their jealous glares, and from the prying thoughts of rikorō-induced telepathy.

10

LIGHT TRICKLES INTO THE TREE HUT, STIRRING ME AWAKE. Voices come from the outside and it takes me a few minutes of cold to force myself up. It's been two days since I stepped through the mirror. Two days since I drank the rikorō and swam through the sea as a mermaid.

As I stand, my head spins, and I ease myself back down. The ground moves below me, and a rush of blood reaches the back of my nose. I breathe through my mouth, hoping I don't start gushing out blood right now. My vision blurs at the soft faded sheen of yellow and red scales sparkling over my skin, and I close my eyes, waiting for the nausea to pass. I had expected the scales to be completely gone, but they're still there.

Maybe my genetic disposition for dementia has already taken root. Why else would I have risked my life to drink a deadly potion? I was so sure of myself, so confident in my ability to find the Death Card and reverse the poison.

But I have to.

I have to bring my mom back. I sit back up, but my head weighs me right back down. I stare up at the wooden planks forming a ceiling around the tree.

Kaehante and AJ's laughter booms out from the firepit area outside.

"Nkella's never caught fish so fast in his life," AJ says between laughing breaths.

"He looks good with a tailfin, daí? It matches his eyes," Kae adds.

"Kh." Nkella's voice sends my stomach in a knot. "Maybe none of you are hungry. I can take it back."

So much for not using the rikorō.

"Aw come on, Captain. We're just kidding," AJ says.

"You boys are bancha," Lāri says. "I'm going to check on Soren."

A minute later, Lāri comes in, and I turn my head to stare at her.

"You're awake," she says. "How are you feeling?"

"I'm okay," I respond, propping myself up on my elbow. She hands me a canteen of water, and I graciously take it. Cold water soothes the lining of my throat.

"There is a freshwater stream nearby. Drink it all."

"Thank you."

"How is your head?"

"A little dizzy, but I'm okay. We have to get going."

Lāri nods. "Can you walk?"

I take a deep breath, and clean air fills my lungs. The dizziness passes. The water must have helped. "I think I was just dehydrated," I say, standing up slowly. "I'm fine."

"Are you sure?"

"It's not like I have a choice. I can't stay here."

"This is true." She smiles. "We are getting ready to go to the village for supplies, I will try to find you an anti-nausea poultice."

"You're too kind. I can see why AJ loves you."

Lāri's cheeks turn pink. "You helped my captain save us—twice. It is the least I can do."

I smile back at her. My feet seem steadier on the ground, and my nausea has subsided, at least, for now. I follow Lāri out of the tree hut and meet the morning sun warming my head against random cool winds passing by. It's warm enough to be comfortable, but chilly enough to not want to swim.

"Hello, Soren," Tessa calls from her chair. "How are you feeling?"

AJ glances at me expectantly and waves. "How would you like some fish for breakfast? Or perhaps I can interest you in some more fish, instead? The options here are fish or fish." He grins.

Nkella stands with his back to us as he straps a knife to his belt and reaches for the shirt that's hanging on a tree. The Ipani stripes on his back are soft, in contrast to his dark tribal tattoos of Ipani scriptures. I force my gaze back to AJ.

"I'm fine, guys, really." I stare at AJ. "And fish sounds fine."

"There's also fruit," Harold chips in. He's lying on his back by the fire, eating what looks like an orange.

"That actually sounds even better, thanks." I take a seat next to Harold, and he reaches over and tosses me an orange.

"So much complaining, daî? Wait until we are at sea again and eating stale bread for weeks," Nkella says, as he makes his way into the tree hut, his voice fading.

AJ groans. "Don't remind me."

"Right, we need to see how much gichang we have for the supplies we need," Tessa says. "Here's hoping not everyone's gichang was lost at sea."

AJ pulls out his pockets. "I have nothing."

Lāri shakes her head. "Sorry, Tessa, mine was poured out too."

Kae opens his empty hands and shakes his head.

Tessa reaches into a leather box on the side of her wheelchair and pulls out a leather bag. "Good thing I keep my gichang secured. I have two hundred Oleanu gichang," Tessa says.

I pull the pouch from my pocket, "I have one hundred fifty Danū gichang left from what Nkella gave me," I add.

Nkella walks out wearing his coat with his collar popped up and his captain's hat. "That is not enough," he says. "Gichang rīrō is being used less and less on this island...as well as everywhere else now. Some places are restricting it completely. I was lucky to run into the Hermit since I've been here." He glances at Tessa who gasps. "He still believes Danū will once again rule, and I was able to exchange five hundred, but that is not enough for a ship." He locks eyes with me and walks over.

He inspects me with one of his hard stares, looking me up and down. A fury of emotions seeps out of him, and I'm instantly wrapped in a cocoon of grief.

"If another person asks me how I'm doing, I'm going to scream," I say.

Surprise flashes in his eyes, and he narrows them. "Neyuro..."

"I'm okay." I tap my hand on his chest and quickly bring it down. "How are you doing? Are you feeling the effects yet?"

"Koj. I don't know why."

"Well, you are bigger. It takes you a while to get drunk too. Doesn't mean you should use the rikorō to go fishing though." I pucker my lips at him.

"Hn." He nods, his eyes on the ground. They flick back up at me, and his lips part. I can feel him wanting to say something, but his strong attempts to block his emotions are growing stronger. He said he was controlling them last night on the beach, but I don't know how he's doing it.

"Any chance we can find out of the Hermit is still around and exchange some more gichang?" AJ cuts in.

Nkella licks his lips and peels his gaze from me. "Knowing him, he's gone. But we should go. Maybe we can find him. Otherwise, we'll see what we can do."

"We can steal a ship," AJ says.

Nkella glares at him. "And then what? Slowly sail toward the sun while they bomb us? Kh."

"No stealing a ship," Tessa agrees. "I need to find oil and wood to replace my wheels, especially if we're headed toward Swords. The snow shouldn't be too thick this time of year, but it'll be a challenge with this mess," she points to the wheels on her chair. "Raku explosives and potions will be good things to look for as well."

"And weapons," Kaehante says.

"Should we split up?" Lāri stands, lending AJ a hand.

Harold continues to lie on his back, his hands over his eyes. I squint at him.

He's not doing well with all this.

"Where are the wolves?" I ask Nkella.

"I sent them to search for the *Gambit*."

"Oh. How long will that take?"

"I don't know. It depends on how fast Iéle can trace the vessel. It might take her a day. Maybe two."

A whole day or two without Iéle up my ass? I hide a smirk. "Well"—I clap my hands—"the sooner we get a move on, the sooner we can find the *Gambit* and head to the Tower, right?" I glance at Nkella. "Show us the way."

We follow Nkella through a less-beaten path since Tessa's wheels struggle to move smoothly. Her hovering mechanism worked a little last night and this morning after Kae dumped out the metal tubing, but still it seems to be having some trouble.

We climb the hill toward wooden gates, and a swirl of excitement and nerves buzzes through me. Cerberus is closer to the docks, so I've never been inside the actual village.

Cooked bread and spices engulf my nostrils as the rhythm of steel against steel mixes with the buzz of people talking in Ipani, the clucking of chickens, and the baaing of goats.

The aroma of horse manure wafts through the wind, and I hold my nose and stare at the stables next to the wooden gates.

Nkella makes a right and takes a path back into the woods.

"Where are we going?" AJ asks. "The village is that way."

"To see if the Hermit is still here."

Tessa's wheels crunch over the gravel as we go along a narrower path down the hill. We pass a few tree huts along the way.

"This is too busy for the Hermit's liking," Tessa says, her voice jumping along with her wheels on the rough terrain.

Nkella turns his head. "He was in Piupeki before the siege. He said he was passing through and headed back to an island off Oleanu."

"I hope he's still here," she mutters.

We pass a wooded area with stacks of barrels. A familiar smell of burning hickory assaults my senses. "What's that?" I ask.

"The barrels?" AJ responds. "That's a rum factory. You know the rum Nkella always drinks?"

"This is where they make it?" I stare at the barrels and spot a few shirtless men working around them.

"One of the places." AJ slows and points to a circular wooden structure. "That's where they store it. They burn the rum in hickory barrels, which is what gives it the vanilla and smoky taste."

A smile pulls at my lips as I'm reminded of the many times I got a phantom whiff of that rum while I was back home. I didn't realize how much I'd missed all this. I stare at the back of Nkella's head as we walk. Things have changed between us. We're no longer the captain and his prisoner. Now we're...I don't know what, exactly, but it's a closeness I've never felt with anyone else. I know it's because of the rikorō, but all the memories and feelings we shared will be a part of us forever, even after the rikorō is gone.

AJ is still talking to me about how they make the rum and how long it takes to ferment. Harold has now fallen in step with us and seems more interested in it than I am.

I hear a voice from the side of the trees. "I thought that was you, Tessa."

A tall man wearing a long beige robe with long sleeves and brown pants steps forward holding a wool bag full of what I can assume are fruits or vegetables from foraging. He has a full gray beard and the lines over his lips and eyes tell his age. He wears a warm smile as he approaches us.

"Hermit, it has been a long time," Tessa says. "I was excited when Nkella told me he ran into you and hoping I would see you again."

He glances at Nkella. "I'm happy to see he accomplished his mission. I'm glad he found you all."

"He didn't do it alone, though," she says, glancing at Nkella who stands with a serious look on his face. Guilt surfaces, mixed with impatience.

The Hermit arcs a brow. "Who helped?"

Nkella glances at me, and I wave. "Hi. I'm Soren."

The Hermit's eyes widen and then flick back to Nkella. A smirk tinges his lips. "Is this the girl you told me about? The one from another land?"

My eyes bulge.

Nkella clears his throat. "She drank the rikorō with me to save them."

The Hermit's face pales, and he looks at me.

I give him a modest shrug, and then, with a sheepish smile, I say, "I can't keep myself from drinking potions in this world and making myself sick."

"I might have something for you...if you'll all follow me to my hut." But instead of turning away, he sets his bag down by his feet and walks around Tessa's chair. "The sea was not kind to you."

"No, I need a few items before I can rebuild."

"Let's see how I can help..." He walks around her chair, inspecting it. "So far, it looks like you've kept it intact. I remember when you threw a wrench—it almost hit me on the head."

Tessa chuckles. "I've come a long way, thanks to you."

The Hermit picks up his bag again and motions for us to follow. "I only teach those who are willing to learn, Tessa. And I am certain that, because of you, many more have learned how to survive through innovations. Either from mine that you've passed on or from your own."

Tessa puts her chair into gear, and Nkella lets her go first. We follow the Hermit deeper into the woods, passing what looks like a freshwater stream.

"So," Harold says, picking up the pace behind the Hermit, "is there something else we should call you by, other than the Hermit?"

"I quite like Hermit," he responds. "It tells people I like to be alone."

Harold chuckles.

"And it's a mark I've earned for being who I am, instead of what the world was telling me to become."

I quirk a brow. "What do you mean?"

"Some of you have marks you haven't come into yet. I would have to change who I am fundamentally for my mark to change."

Lāri snorts. "You seem rather friendly for someone who likes to be alone," she says.

He bends down and picks up a stick as we pass the pond to our right. "I'm far more selective than I appear. I already knew Tessa—and Nkella by extension. And when I learned his crew was in trouble, Tessa included, I wanted to help. But don't think for a second I'd stop to help any of you if I hadn't already heard of you." He turns slightly, and I think I see him wink.

Past the pond, a small tree hut with a flower bed on both sides comes into view. This place is a lot more secluded than where we met him. The Hermit leads us inside a warm room with a round table at the center and a large open area kitchen. A counter with two shelfs on the side of the kitchen has a large white shell basin, with a barrel on the top shelf. Tubing feeds through it and up a tree. He goes to it and turns a gear, making the tubes rumble. A few seconds later, water pours out of the tube.

"You built all this?" I ask, staring at the mess of gadgets all around me.

"That's right." He washes his hands and then starts taking jars filled with different plants out of his cupboard, setting them on the center table. "While I do this, why don't some of you help yourself to my garden out back? I can't eat it all myself, and it will go bad if it isn't picked."

AJ and Lāri exchange glances before heading out the back door.

"Are you certain?" Nkella asks. "We have a long journey and would be obliged to you."

"You are always on a long journey. Yes, take as much as you can carry."

"It's nice to see not everyone is so hostile," I say.

The Hermit pulls out a jar with purple seeds and starts mashing them inside a mortar. "It is why I prefer to be on my own." He looks at Tessa. "You know where I keep the oil and wood pilings. There should be extra gears and copper fillings over by that cabinet. Help yourself."

Tessa reverses her chair and gets to work. Kaehante pulls up a chair next to her, and she hands him things to hold.

"How do you travel with all this?" Harold asks. "Or do you have to rebuild each time?"

"This is my home wherever I go," he says.

"I'm not sure I follow." Harold sits back in his chair. Something metal snaps off in Kae's hands, and we all turn to look at him.

Nkella shoots Kaehante a scornful glare as he tries to fix whatever it is he broke.

The Hermit ignores it or, at least, pretends to. "It's why I prefer a hut and not an actual tree home. I can't uproot a tree, however, I can find a nice shaded area beside one. Although that isn't necessary."

My brows furrow, and I stare at Harold. "What?" I mouth.

"I still don't follow."

"And I would rather not give away my secrets. Some favors will cost me my life, so it is something I rarely share."

"Mind your own business, daí?" Nkella says to Harold. "He is helping us."

Harold smirks with a gleam in his eye and leans back on his chair. "That's fair. So what are you making?"

"This here is a potion for Soren and Nkella." The Hermit eyes Nkella. "Although you seem fine."

Nkella gives a small nod. "I do not know why."

"Oh, the Fool and the Devil. Always at war with each other. One wants to journey, while the other feels comfortable in his own chains."

"Daí?" Nkella quirks a brow.

"You each need to take time to explore the gifts the Aō has bestowed on you," he says.

Harold guffaws. "You mean the illegal, magical so-called gifts?"

"Koj. This is a curse," Nkella says, agreeing with Harold.

"No matter what laws come from the Tower, your chains are forged by no one other than yourself." He squints an eye at Nkella as he mashes. "We often give away our power to the thing we most avoid."

Nkella's frown deepens, and he catches me looking at him.

The Hermit glances between us but keeps talking. "Anyhow, this potion will make you sweat, but it should not make you feel sicker. The purpose is to drain you of the toxin before it has reached your soul."

"Will it cure me?" I ask, peeling my gaze away from Nkella.

"It hasn't been tested enough to know for sure. The new cure in Piupeki can cure you, but this will certainly keep death at bay until you get there." He turns to heat up a fire on a burner and pours the contents of his mortar into a metal pot. "Do you like cacao?"

I perk up. "Chocolate? Yes."

"Good, I will mask the taste of the *tetyevisi* with cacao."

"What's the other mark you have?" Harold asks.

The Hermit glances over his shoulder at Harold. "My other mark?"

"We all have two, don't we? Or at least, some of us do. Do you have another mark?"

"You are the inquisitive one, aren't you? I'd tell you, but then I'd have to feed you to the Serpent." He grins.

Harold raises his brows, unimpressed. "I think I know."

"Then keep it to yourself."

The Hermit has secrets? I'm dying to know what they are. "Why are you really helping us? It can't just be because of Tessa."

"Or maybe it is. Maybe I met Tessa a long time ago because I knew she would bring me here, to meet *you*."

I blink. "Me? Why?"

"You are the Past Fate, aren't you?"

I shoot Nkella a stare.

"I did not tell him this, neyuro." His voice sounds calm in my mind, and I relax my shoulders.

The Hermit looks between us, furrowing his brows. "Relax. Your captain didn't reveal much. I'm just far wiser than I look."

"Who are you, then?"

"I am the Hermit and always will be."

Tessa laughs in the background. "I've missed these conversations with you, Hermit."

The Hermit carefully adds the cacao mixture to the potion, mixes it, and then pours it into a wooden tankard. Smiling, he responds to Tessa, "And I, you." He sets the tankard in front of me. "Drink up."

Raising the hot drink to my lips, chocolate and cinnamon swirls under my nose.

"And no more poisonous plants. We need you." He widens his eyes on me, and I take my first gulp.

They need me?

I shake my head, swallowing the sweet hot chocolate mixture. I can't believe he just mashed up some earthy-smelling plants and made it taste delicious. But that's beside the point. "What do you mean you need me? I'm here for—to find something important, but then I'm going back."

The hermit chuckles. "You're just like your captain."

Nkella looks up.

"No point in arguing, though. Some people aren't ready to hear yet what they will eventually come to understand." I squint at him as he regards me. "Figure out who you are, and your mark will change."

A sharp gasp leaves my lips, and I drop my gaze to the Fool's mark on my wrist.

"So cryptic," Tessa chimes in. "I'm almost finished here."

The Hermit scratches at his chin. "I have some wheels upstairs that I was going to use for a wagon. Where are you all off to?"

"Piupeki."

"Then take them. The ones you have there won't last in the snow." He strides across his hut and climbs up a ladder. Over his shoulder, he says, "Kaehante, go grab a jug of oil from the back, will you?"

"You won't need them?" Tessa calls after him as Kaehante heads for the back door.

"Oh, you know I always carry extras, and can always carve more after you leave."

"I forgot it was going to be cold in Piupeki," I say. "I didn't bring a coat."

"We'll find you something to wear in town," Tessa says. Nkella takes out his pouch of gichang and walks over to where the Hermit climbed.

AJ and Lāri walk back inside laughing at something and holding a bag full of produce. The door swings shut behind them and AJ sets the bags down. "This'll last us for more than a week."

"How long will it take us to reach Piupeki?" I ask.

"No ship is going to be as fast as the *Gambit* because no other ship has the infrastructure to take potions," Tessa says.

"Except the ones docked in Danū," AJ adds. "A few weeks."

"We were at sea for like six weeks last time," I say. "It's going to take us longer than six weeks?!"

"Keep in mind we didn't start off with cloaking and speeding potions last time," AJ says.

"And we were held up a few times," Tessa adds. "We spent a lot of time rationing the potion and trying to stay hidden."

"How are we going to stay hidden now?"

"That," AJ says, plopping himself down onto a chair, "is why this plan is so crazy. We won't be hidden, and we're headed straight for the lion's den."

If we didn't need the *Gambit* to fly up to the Tower, I'd suggest not going to Swords at all. "This feels like a bad idea," I say.

"We need the cure," Nkella says, holding his gichang in his hands as the Hermit counts Wands amethysts from his pouch. Tessa's new tires are resting against his leg as they trade currency.

"And the *Gambit*," Lāri says.

The back door slams shut, and Kae walks in, holding the jug of oil. "This is for Tessa, hn?"

"That's right." The Hermit reaches into another drawer beside the ladder and pulls out a different pouch. "How about some Piupeki currency?" They begin to make another exchange. I reach for my pouch and head over. I might as well get in on this, otherwise, what's the point of having any form of Ipani money if I can't use it?

"So the question is, how are you planning to get there safely?" The Hermit fixes his stare at Nkella.

"As soon as Iéle returns with the *Gambit*'s location, she can tell me of any river pathways we can take. Instead of heading true north, we veer to the right and find the open water valleys. Depending on where the *Gambit* is."

"This would be easier if we had a ship with invisibility," AJ groans.

"Even if you did," the Hermit says, "oumala animals are guarding all the routes in and out."

"This is feeling impossible. Is there no way to the Tower without the *Gambit*?" I ask.

The room grows silent.

"Have you heard from Gari?" AJ asks.

An anvil lands in my stomach. I shake my head. "I—"

"Koj," Nkella says. "We do not have the drakon, so the *Gambit* is the only way. And we need to find Harold's friend for your cure."

"Don't you mean our cure? Which, if I can just get to the Death Card, we won't even need. Besides"—I swallow the last of the cocoa—"I feel fine, and now I'm not in a hurry for a cure."

"That's not a cure, Soren," the Hermit says. "You still need one. You just won't be getting dizzy or dealing with nosebleeds so often. Don't let that stop you from finding yourself a cure."

I nod.

"If worse comes to worst," Tessa says, "we jump ship, and you and Soren will have to drag our bones underwater in something."

"No. Hell no." Harold stands, holding up his palms. "Not doing that."

AJ wipes his face. "Must everything be so unpleasant?"

"Let's just hope it doesn't come to that." Tessa reverses her chair. "Are we about ready?"

"Make sure you take anything else you need. You know I'm not easy to find. Ah—" He glides over to a small table beside his kitchenette and opens a drawer. "Take this, Captain." He holds out a scroll, and Nkella takes it. "It's a map of Ipa."

"This is helpful, Hermit. My maps are still in the *Gambit*."

"I hope you all find your way, and—" He stares down at Tessa. "Please know that if I could take you all to where you need to go, I would in a heartbeat. Unfortunately, my fortune runs out if I take more than one."

I squint at him.

"You can't go to the Tower anyway," Tessa says.

"Yes, I stay away from the Arcana, the Empress, and the Tower." He narrows his eyes at me. "But Soren, you shouldn't run from who you are."

"I'm not running. I'm taking care of myself." Like I've done my whole life.

"Ah, well, all in good time. Not to kick you all out, but I have places to go, and you need to leave."

The Hermit and Tessa say their goodbyes, and we thank him and walk out the door.

"Remember to keep your head down in the village. No using ouma, the Arcana has been coming down from the Tower, making their rounds."

I glance at Nkella. "The Empress has taken stricter measures to find the use of ouma," he tells me. "Anyone found will be taken, but I've seen some killed on the spot."

My pulse slows, and I share a look with the others.

"No ouma in front of others," Kae says. "Understood."

Nkella's words brew in my mind as we walk out. After a few paces, I turn back to see his hut and gasp.

It's gone.

"Solerie potion." Tessa laughs. "He always has to leave in style."

11

GUNS, BANDOLEERS, EXPLOSIVES. MY EYES SCAN THE TENTED storefronts inside this cute farm village for items on the supply list Tessa gave us before driving off to the blacksmith. A few people stop and squint at me, but when they catch Nkella's flickering amber eyes staring right back at them, they run off.

The Hermit was right. I've already spotted a few Arcana soldiers floating around the village corners, and I haven't seen anyone use ouma.

Nkella walks quickly before me, leaving a trail of disgruntled thoughts to hit me in the face. Except, I can't understand any of them because they're all in Ipani. But I can feel the angry and frightened emotions all at once. At first, it took me a while to decipher people's looks, until someone literally points at the scales in my arms and calls me a name in Ipani I can't understand.

"Ignore them, Soren," Lāri tells me. "You did what you thought was right—to save us. They don't know that."

"Yeah, it's kind of hard to hide her ears and teeth, plus lack of stripes," AJ says.

My throat dries. Everyone in this village must think I'm a scumbag trafficker or someone who advocates for it. It's obvious I drank rikorō— I still have mer-scales on my skin. I haven't looked at myself in a mirror, but I must have scales on my face and neck as well. And I'm obviously not an oumala Ipani. The mer-people's scales aren't visible on land. I'm evidence of ouma gone wrong.

I swallow and follow Nkella into an armory.

"Choose quickly, daí?" His voice enters my mind as we both walk in. I can tell he wants to get out of here as quickly as I do.

AJ and Lāri try on bandoleers while Nkella picks up a gun. I don't want a gun, but a dagger catches my eye. Ignoring the hard stare of the shop owner, I walk over to it. It has a black hilt covered with red swirls, and the blade is slightly curved at the tip.

"That costs seventy-seven gichang," the shop owner tells me in Imboe with a thick accent, as the translation potion works. He has pointy ears, but his teeth aren't sharp. He must be mixed like Soanalo. Two light stripes wrap over his collar and around his neck.

I take out my coins and count the amount.

He walks over slowly, his pot belly rubbing against the counter. "But I do not sell to *rikukwa*."

I gasp and take my hand back.

AJ comes over with Lāri behind him. Nkella fixes his eyes on him but doesn't say a word.

AJ leans over the counter. "Look, she's not a traitor. She didn't want to drink it—"

"She was poisoned."

I flick my eyes to Nkella. He stares at the man with intensity, one wrong move from the merchant and it's going to be a blood bath. Please dude, just go with it.

"It's okay. I don't need a knife," I tell Nkella.

"Yes," Nkella says between his teeth. "You do."

My heart flutters. Even though things have changed between us, it's the first time he's agreed that I should have a weapon. "No, really. I have you to protect me, right?" I give him a sweet smile. "It isn't worth it. Let's go."

The merchant drops his shoulders. "If it is true that you were poisoned, I will let it slide. There are many traffickers who run through here. I don't want any problems."

I nod and take out my coins, but Nkella beats me to it. I gasp.

"You don't have to," I tell him.

"Save your gichang, you might need it later." He hands me the dagger, and Lāri comes over with a belt and a dark red sash.

"Try this on," she says as she wraps the sash around my waist, then follows it with the belt. "The red matches your hair, mei? I thought it added a nice contrast to your pale skin and brown eyes."

I thank her and slide my new dagger into the small holster that comes with the belt.

Nkella picks out a gun, as do the others, and pays the merchant.

"*Jovoe m'pate.* Peace to you," the merchant says to me. "May your death come without pain."

I pause, then give him a smile, sensing the sincerity in his voice. I'm aware not everyone has heard of the cure in Piupeki, and this is considered polite for the Ipani.

"Do you know where we can find a ship?" Nkella asks before leaving.

The merchant scratches his chin and peers out of the tent. He points to the open ocean and says, "There is a shipping merchant past Cerberus. When you reach the docks, make a right. There might still be some boats for sale, but they are an expensive commodity since Piupeki fell under siege—even more than before."

Nkella frowns but gives him a nod. He reaches into his pouch and hands him another amethyst coin. "We were never here, daí?"

The merchant takes it and silently agrees.

As we turn to leave the tent, two masked soldiers float down the path, looking into each tent. Lāri and AJ stand in front of me, blocking my scales from being seen by them. Some people back away; others stand still and watch as they pass. We wait for them to reach the far end of the market before we head to the marina.

Out on the docks, the ambiance is louder, and the acrid stench of fish permeates the air. Between the hustle and bustle of fish merchants, shoppers, and people climbing up and down ships with boxes of goods, I don't know what to focus on. I keep my eyes down as we pass Cerberus and stay close to Nkella. Harold was distracted and said he'd meet us later. I don't know what that was about.

The last time we were here during the day, I wasn't exactly paying attention to what others were doing—I was a bit preoccupied with going from being a prisoner (thanks to an untrusting Devil captain) to running for our lives with a new prisoner. I hadn't quite pieced together the sort of trading post island Dempu Yuni is.

A lot goes on here, and my mind can't help but skim for the nefarious details that make Tarotland Circus back home go round. Scams, drug deals, you know, unofficial modes of survival.

We don't go unnoticed as some people stop what they're doing to stare at us. My cheeks burn and my eyes bore into the wooden docks as we beeline to the right. The armory merchant said we should go to this area.

"I think it's that." Lāri points to an open-aired hut on the opposite side of the harbor. It has a mast behind it, and I'm guessing that's their marketing tactic. We make our way over, and Nkella stops me.

"Maybe wait outside, daí?"

"That makes sense." I don't want to arouse more suspicion than I already am. "I'll be by the water."

"I will wait with her," Lāri says, offering me a smile.

We take a few steps and then sit, letting our feet hang over the dock. Water claps rhythmically against the wood, and seagulls mew as they land close to the nearby fishermen. We have our backs to Nkella and AJ as they wait to speak with the salesperson.

"At least, no one can see I'm a human with powers that don't belong to me," I tell her.

"Don't worry, we'll figure it out. How are you feeling after drinking the Hermit's potion?"

"Honestly, if I wasn't constantly reminded that I drank the rikorō, I would have forgotten about it. I feel great."

"That is a good sign. Hopefully, it will give us enough time to find the cure."

"Or to steal the Death Card," I whisper. "Why do you think it hasn't affected Nkella yet? Do you think it's because of his curse?"

She shakes her head. "It is strange. And have you noticed the scales are not shining on him anymore?"

I actually hadn't noticed that. Squinting, I glance over my shoulder at him. She's right, they haven't been shimmering on him like they have on me. "Is it just leaving his system?"

"Hnn. Rikorō is unpredictable, but it doesn't go away. Still, I don't know much about it. I don't think anyone truly does, except those who make it."

A slam makes us both jump, and I almost fall in the water. I spin around to Nkella leaning close to the guy, both his knuckles on the table.

Lāri jumps to her feet and dashes over. I should probably stay here, but I don't. I get up and follow Lāri to see what the heck is going on.

The merchant is holding back a man whose fist is positioned to hit Nkella.

Is he nuts?

AJ aims his gun at the guy ready to swing, and Lāri pulls hers on the merchant. A squawk comes from a yellow and green parrot perched on a top shelf to the left.

I...slide my hand over my knife, not that I know what I'd do if guns start firing. Probably run.

"Stand down, Nangraku," the merchant barks at his friend. But then he looks at Nkella and shakes his head. "I cannot sell to you, á? It would send a bad message to our allies."

"Your allies are bad people," Nkella growls.

"Spoken by someone who wanted what was in the vial." Nangraku has his eyes trained on Nkella; his voice is deadly as he speaks. "You will pay for killing who you did." He has a tattoo of a snake in strike position on his right cheek, its fangs painted just over his cheekbone, and a scar that goes straight down his left eye.

AJ leans close to me and whispers into my ear. "His name means snakebite."

I scoff. "Suits him."

Something about Nangraku makes my insides curl, like he doesn't care who he murders as long as he gets what he's after. And based on what he just told Nkella, he must have known one of the traffickers Nkella murdered at the tavern the other day. My eyes land on a black whip tied to his belt. His gaze finds mine, and he smirks at me. My stomach churns.

"We should call the Arcana on you," the merchant says. "You are lucky we are letting you go."

"Call them, daí?" Nkella tilts his head. "And I will tell the Empress who you both are and your involvement with trafficking ouma."

"I am not involved," the merchant says, "and aren't you wanted by her? Why would she listen to you?" He furrows his brows, releasing his hold on Nangraku who's stretching his neck. "What would someone like you want with rikorō anyway?"

"That is not your business. And if you are protecting them, you *are* involved."

"So are you, then." The merchant crosses his arms. "Either way, I am not selling you a ship. I need you all to leave now."

Nangraku grimaces, and they both stare at us.

"Wait," I say.

Nkella's eyes widen as he flicks his gaze to me.

I lift up my sleeve. "You wanna know why you should sell us a boat?"

The merchant looks at my arm. "Enlighten me."

"Because I'm related to the Empress." AJ smacks his face, and Lāri sighs, but I ignore them and continue. "She might not listen to him about you. But she'll listen to *me*."

The merchant and his friend lift their eyebrows and stare at the curved spiderweb of my mark.

"I can tell her whatever I want about you, and she'll listen," I lie. "Why do you think she let him go?" I tilt my head to Nkella. "They're all with me now."

A tiny smirk appears on Nkella's face. I keep my eyes glued to the ship merchant.

The merchant rubs his chin and glances at his buddy, then back at me. "You are the reason why Piupeki is under siege, á?"

A flare of agitation emanates from Nkella, but he banks it. I keep my poker face.

"Hey, I'm on your side. I returned ouma to the Ipani, and my aunt got mad. Family doesn't always agree, am I right?" I switch between the merchant, AJ, and Lāri. They nod in agreement. "So why don't you just take this captain's gichang and let bygones be bygones, and I won't tell my auntie what you and your friends have been up to. Deal?" The merchant squints at me when I say the word auntie, and I realize that may not have translated well, but he gets my drift all the same.

Nkella stares at the salesman.

The merchant squints his eyes at us. "Hnnn." He glances at his friend. "I think I have one ship left I can sell you."

I widen my award-winning smile at him, showing my teeth. "See?" I glance at Nkella, then at the other guy. "I knew we could be friends." Nangraku scowls, and walks away, shouldering AJ hard as he does. "Or not. But that's okay, we can't all get along. Business is business though, right?"

"Yes," the merchant grins at me. "Business—business." Turning to Nkella, he says, "Your new ship costs 700 gichang."

"Kh." He reaches into his pouch and pulls out the money, emptying out more than half its contents to show he has it. Ouch. If he hadn't traded with the Hermit, we'd be out of luck. Then he pours it back into his pouch. "Ship first."

The merchant scowls but turns to grab a metal key from inside a set of drawers behind him. "Follow me."

The Arcana floats along the boardwalk where the ships are docked. We follow the merchant until we reach a medium-sized two-story boat. The *Ugly Kraken* is faintly showing in dark paint on the boat's side. Its rickety sails waver in the wind, and holes decorate the sides of its walls. I'm waiting for him to keep walking when he points to it and says, "Your new ship."

AJ smacks his face and stomps his foot, looking behind him as if waiting for someone to come out and call the joke.

"Is this a joke?" Nkella's voice darkens.

"There is no joke. What is wrong with it, á? This boat is strong and has traveled around Ipa twice in one journey."

Lāri steps up from behind me. "There are seven of us, and one person is in a wheelchair."

The merchant raises his palms. "If you don't want it, do not take it. It is all I have available now. Times are rough, á?"

"I am not paying 700 for this."

"As I said, take it or leave it." The merchant starts to walk away.

A seagull mews over our heads as we stare at the rickety boat.

"Captain," AJ steps toward him and lowers his voice. "We'd never make it to Piupeki in that."

"We could fix the sails," Lāri suggests, "and add planks over the stairs for Tessa. It's smaller than what we're used to, but I have seen smaller boats make it from one island to the other."

Nkella shuts his eyes. "Wait," he growls.

The merchant pauses and looks over his shoulder.

Nkella takes out his gichang. "We'll take it."

The merchant takes out his large metal key and unlocks the padlock attached to a chain, leaving the ropes to keep it in place.

AJ climbs over the rope and jumps in. He stomps his foot on the flooring a few times. "Feels safe enough," he shouts. "Actually, it doesn't seem as small from in here."

Nkella scoffs.

"No really," he shouts. "It isn't as big as what we're used to, but it's big enough—ow." He steps through a floorboard. "It'll need some maintenance, though."

The merchant turns to leave. "Yes, very safe." He glances at me. "We are good, yes?"

I give him a salute, not that he knows what it means, but I nod for emphasis. "All good."

Lāri raises her arms and waves someone over. I glance behind me and spot Kae and Tessa making their way onto the docks. They spot us and come over. Kae has a confused expression on his face as they approach, and I bite back a laugh.

"Like our new ship?" I ask.

"Koj. Captain, this is madness."

"It was the only vessel available. Go back and get some wood planks for Tessa, daî?"

Kae stares at the ship a bit longer and then turns to do as asked.

"We will make it work," Tessa says. "It's only temporary until we find the *Gambit*. At least it has two floors." She arches her neck. "Where's Harold?"

I shrug. "He said he'd find us."

The clucking of a chicken makes me spin around, and my eyes

bulge. Harold comes carrying a bag over his shoulder, and a cage with a chicken in the other. My brows furrow.

"Harold?" I shout. He spots us and quickens his step, a smile on his lips as he raises the chicken cage.

"What are you going to do with that?"

His features twist, as if it's obvious what he's going to do with it.

He gets closer, and Nkella shouts. "Good thinking. Now we'll have more than fruit and stale bread for supper."

"See?" Harold says as he climbs onto the dock. "I'm useful. And what'd you think a chicken is for, Soren?"

"I just didn't know you knew what to do with one. Aren't you from Boston?"

"Hey, I can figure it out, and if not, one of them can. But don't you want eggs for breakfast?"

"Okay, okay. Sorry."

AJ lowers the gangplank, and Nkella steadies it, planting a firm boot on the wood to make sure it can hold the weight. Tessa moves her wheelchair into gear and boards the ship, followed by Harold carrying a bag of produce and his chicken. Lāri and I follow suit.

Tessa parks herself by the bow and stares over the rail, muttering something under her breath.

The floorboards creak as I step to the center of the main deck, not unlike the *Gambit*, except for the visibly large holes in sporadic places on the hardwood floor. A large dent decorates the side panel, and there are *no cannons*. Not that I'm expecting to get into a ship fight, but I wasn't expecting it last time I was here either, and it happened. Crossing my fingers that Nkella's plan to get a better route from Iéle works.

The main deck isn't large, and there are only stairs to the quarterdeck on one side, with the captain's quarters directly behind it. I walk over to a large wheel at the center and push at one of the poles sticking out of it—it barely budges as I lean into it.

"Careful, Soren." AJ steps next to me. "We need to untie the ropes before we can hoist the sails. Then, we'll raise the anchor with the capstan. The *Gambit* didn't operate this way, and Kae did most of the heavy lifting."

As Nkella climbs up on the quarterdeck to check the steering, Lāri heads to the topmast and unties a rope, letting it drop down with a thud. AJ grabs it and starts untying a knot. Lāri drops another rope down, causing the chicken to startle. I walk over to the rope and start tugging at a knot to loosen it, copying what AJ does. When we're done, we walk back, pulling the sails open. Kaehante boards the ship, holding several long planks over his shoulders. He walks to the first set of stairs and sets down a plank to make it easy for Tessa to drive up and down. The chicken clucks, and he stares at it.

"Is that what we are having for supper?"

I snort.

"Watch it," Lāri calls down from above. "No one is eating any birds, mei?"

"It's for eggs, you big oaf." AJ chuckles.

I gasp. "Is it an oumala chicken?"

Harold walks up the plank. "Don't be looking at my chicken like that. That's so all of us can have eggs."

"If it's oumala, it'll disappear," I warn.

"It isn't. I asked before I bought her." Harold picks up the cage and brings her down. "And I found the kitchen, so I'll take this." Turning, he makes his way back down.

"Are you this ship's chef then, Harold?" AJ asks. "You should have grabbed more than one if you wanted eggs."

"I could only afford one. And I'll do whatever is needed of me," Harold replies dryly. "Not like I'll be able to enjoy my food anyway, since I can't taste anything."

AJ passes me a look, and I shrug.

"He's not doing very well with the curse. Remember, he already had one when we met him, and he was supposed to go on this journey to beat *his* family's curse."

"Right. What's he going to do?" AJ fidgets with loosening another knot.

I shake my head.

After we're all settled in and the ropes and sails are hoisted, we raise the anchor. Lāri, AJ, Kae, and I push with the poles, but no matter how hard I push, I know it's Kae doing most of the work.

A wave of strong emotions comes from behind me. Determination.

Ambition. A longing to finally be done with all this. I shift my gaze toward the quarterdeck.

Nkella stands over the wheel, his collar popped and his captain's hat on his head. He's turned to face the open sea as he backs up the ship. I stare at his back as his coat billows in the wind. It feels strange being on board a ship with him again and not being his prisoner this time.

The warm sun contrasts the cool breeze hitting the back of my neck as we sail away from the Dempu Yuni harbor.

"This ship needs re-bedding," Kae mutters.

"I wouldn't bother," Tessa cuts in. "It's not like we're going to keep it."

AJ grabs the two bags of produce and swings them over his shoulder. "You never know when you'll need a backup boat. I think I can get used to this little ship."

I follow him down the ramp, curious what the sleeping situation will be like. When I first got back home from Tarotland, I would wake in the middle of the night, thinking a cannon had gone off and wondering if we'd gotten hit—only it was just Talia snoring in the other bed. Even though I was happy to be home, I missed my personal room in the *Gambit*, the room I was given after being allowed out of the brig.

At the bottom of the ramp, AJ sets down the produce and lights a lantern hanging from the low ceiling. Something scuttles by my feet, and I jump.

"It's a rat." Harold steps into the light. "There's rats on this ship."

"Great," I choke.

The bottom floor has an open floor layout, with sandbags stacked along both sides and two barrels behind the board we just walked down. Two rows of hammocks are on either side of the floor, with three hammocks on each row. Small circular windows let in light from the outside. Chests for—I assume—storing clothes are next to each hammock. At the far end of the room, toward the stern, a set of stairs leads to a door.

"What's through there?" I ask, walking over.

"The kitchen," Harold says, plopping himself next to the hammock closest to the door. Clucking sounds come from behind the door, and I already know this is going to be one noisy, uncomfortable experience.

"Cozy," I say, opening the door to a small kitchenette. It had a sink, a burner, one round table, and a chair. AJ walks in right behind me and sets down the two bags of produce. He scans the kitchen, then walks to the back and opens a pantry next to where the chicken is. A rat runs out of it, and he lifts his leg to let it run. I yelp.

"We're going to be eating and sleeping with rats," I groan.

"I'll get rid of the rats," AJ says.

I nod and let out a sigh. "It's okay. I've been through worse." I remind myself this is a means to an end. Get the *Gambit*. Get the Death Card. Bring back my mom. I can do this. "What's on the bottom floor?"

"More rats," Harold mutters under his hands. Gross. "But there's also a lot of sandbags, and from what I could tell, possibly a leak that they're keeping sealed."

My eyes bulge. "Is this ship going to make it the whole way there?"

"It'll make it," Tessa responds. "A ship like this was used to carry oils and spices. Downstairs is more storage area for amphorae. Big clay carriers."

"No brig?" I ask.

She laughs. "Not on this ship. We should go up to meet the captain. He'll want to plan the route with us."

Kaehante lets out a big yawn before swinging his feet off a hammock he chose close to the exit. Makes sense that he'd choose that one since he's always battle ready. That way, he'd be the first to protect us.

If I thought we were cozy in our thin-walled rooms on the *Gambit*, this family is about to get a whole lot cozier.

We make our way up through the quarterdeck, and into the captain's quarters. I don't know what I was expecting, but this was not it. The captain's quarters in the *Gambit* was a large room with window panes all the way around, giving Nkella full view of our surroundings. This room is small with a cot against the back wall and a table in front of the door. Nkella lays out his map, putting his gun on one edge and a dagger on the other to keep the corners from rolling up.

Tessa leads the crew inside the tiny room, and Kaehante's broad shoulders struggle to fit through the doorframes—and he looks uncomfortable as he does. I'm the last to enter. The room is warm from everyone's body heat, and I look for a spot near the door, leaving it propped open. A familiar magnetism comforts me, but it's not the one I felt after spending time with Nkella underwater or by his tree hut. It's a specific type of magnetism—it smells like him. Feels like him. It's like having his warm voice inside of my head, his vanilla and hickory leather scent, his battle between rage and control. Right now, I sense a peace in him as he concentrates. Being out at sea and staring at a map is his comfort zone.

Being away from him when I was downstairs made me forget about our connection. The farther away we are from each other, the less connection we have. But when we're close together, it's like the consciousness of the mer-Ipani this ouma came from wants us together—like the *Aō wants us together.*

He flicks his eyes at me and pauses. A flash of what I think is the same recognition crosses his features, and a small smile tugs at his lips but then he returns to staring at the map.

A butterfly has gotten loose in my stomach, but I beat it down. Especially now, since I don't know if this is because of us or because of the rikorō. We almost kissed the other night before my nose started bleeding, and I haven't allowed myself to give it much thought since then. Because well, what's the point? I have my mission, and he has his. Then I'm going home, once again.

Nkella points at a small peninsula on the northern land mass on the map. "This is where the Prefect's Tower is. I suspect the ship will be somewhere here," he points to the far right.

"Close to the Ace of Swords," Harold says.

"Daí. If it was Demitri's crew who stole our ship, then that is what he was after." Nkella grunts and points back to the map. "This map does not show the river entryways. But I know there is a pathway big enough to allow a ship through."

"Won't it be secured also, Captain?" Kae asks.

Nkella goes on to mention Iéle and what he's expecting. I squint at the map and notice the land mass in the southern region. "Is that Danū?"

Nkella stops and stares at me. "Yes."

"Wands is much bigger," Harold says now hovering over the map of Ipa. "It's interesting that Danū used to be the superpower."

Irritation simmers under Nkella's skin, and Kaehante laughs.

"The caverns in Danū run deep. It's much larger than it appears on the map," Nkella says.

A vision of a beautiful underground cave-scape emerges in my mind, different from the first time I saw a vision of Danū. Waterfalls with red steam crash next to tall, curved staircases leading to different alcoves, and lights shine through with cascading rainbow effects to glisten on underground ponds in a cavern. There's more to that island than meets the eye, and from what I can see...it's breathtaking.

Nkella's eyes cut to me, and I smile at him.

"What is the plan if Iéle does not find the entry route?" Kaehante interrupts. Nkella peels his eyes away from me and looks back at the map, continuing to talk about the plan.

My eyes skim over the room past Tessa and Lāri, and land on a small broken piece of green glass on the floor, an oxidized hatchet next to it. The spiderweb mark on my arm buzzes and a magnetic pull urges me over. Nkella's voice fades into the background as I zone in on the items.

I bend to pick it up, my fingers touching the dirty wooden hilt.

My vision zooms into the blade, and my surroundings blur around me. In an instant, I'm still standing in this room, but the crew isn't with me. Instead, two Ipani men are arguing outside the captain's quarters over the pattering of rain.

A thunderclap shakes the wooden walls.

The hairs on my legs and arms stand on end. What the hell just happened? Where's the crew?

"Help me get him over the rail. The serpent will eat him."

"Too risky." One of the Ipani takes out a hatchet—the same hatchet that was just here on the floor is now in his hand. "We have to chop him up first. Then he'll never be washed up, and no evidence will lead to us."

My eyes drop to the man in question, and I almost pee myself. A tan-skinned man, his eyes bloodshot and open, lies unmoving on the floorboards. The haunting moans of a dead person's soul being torn apart in the Deep emanate from his throat. The moans vibrate through my bones as if I could sense where they come from, even all those leagues under the sea, and I shiver. The Ipani swings the hatchet high over his head and plunges it down on the man's skull. Brain matter spurts, and I scream.

I jump back and cover my mouth, but they don't hear me. I had a feeling, but this confirms it; I'm witnessing the past. They can neither see nor hear me. The man hacks and hacks, cutting the dead man into pieces, while the other takes the pieces and throws them overboard. Bile rises up my throat, and I hold my mouth tight.

"This wasn't worth the gichang," the Ipani says.

"It's worth it for the resistance, for the cause. Now if the Tower's Arcana come sniffing, their psychic abilities won't catch on to what happened."

"It's the Danū Prefect," the other man says. "The Empress will only reign with a heavier hand. This was foolish."

"It was necessary. He needed to die," he shouts over the pelting rain.

"They've already put in a new Prefect. You heard them this morning. It'll be days before they find us."

"Relax. I have a buddy who will help us get rid of this ship. They'll never catch up to us. We have enough gichang to live off the coast of Oleanu if we want to."

I gasp. This ship was meant to be scrapped?

"Better get rid of the whole ship fast..." He stumbles back, knocking over the lantern by his foot. It shatters, and he kicks it to the side. Thunder roars above our heads, and it starts raining harder, washing away some of the blood. My vision blurs and a magnetic tug urges me back.

"Neyuro!" Nkella's voice shakes me, and I blink. His dark eyes stare back at me, worry lines creasing his forehead. Tessa is next to me, holding my hand. "Neyuro?"

"I'm fine," I sit up.

"What happened?" Tessa asks. Nkella moves back, giving me some space, and I see the whole crew staring at me.

"I had a vision." I swing my legs over the cot, and a wave of dizziness threatens to drag me back down, but I force myself up anyway. "We bought a bad ship."

"What do you mean?" Nkella demands.

Lāri barges into the room. "Captain! I've sighted a ship. And they have their war flags hoisted on us!"

12

Nkella looks over his shoulder, his body still positioned toward me. "How far away are they?"

The hairs on the back of my neck stand on end. The last time we were attacked, Arcana soldiers were all over the *Gambit*.

"*Who* are they?" Tessa reverses her chair. "What could they want with us?"

Hanging onto the door with one arm, Lāri peers at the ship. "I can't tell who they are, but they are still too far away to hit us with a cannon."

AJ leans into the doorframe. "They have their war flag hoisted alright."

"Can they catch up to us?" Kae asks.

I start to walk toward the door but Nkella turns back to me. "Stay there, neyuro. We aren't finished."

"I'm fine. It was just a vision."

Tessa reaches for my arm and gives me a gentle push. "Yes, but perhaps you hit your head?" I gape at her, but she turns to face Lāri who is securing her bandoleer.

Harold shifts his gaze from Nkella and squints at me. "You're getting visions now?" he whispers to me.

"Yes," I shoot Tessa a stare, and she quirks her brow. "None of you were around when my mark started working last time I was here. I can see the past."

"It's true," Nkella states, bringing his bow and arrows over his back. "It's how she got the Ace of Wands to work and how she helped me find your bones." He stares at Tessa.

Tessa's eyes widen, but then she looks at the others. "We don't have a way to make this ship go faster. What are our options?"

Lāri shakes her head, her features twisting into visible worry. "I will watch their moves from the crow's nest." She shifts to an eagle and flies up to the topsail.

"It's fight or go down with the ship," Kae says, walking out the door.

AJ smacks his forehead and wipes his face. He pulls his gun out of the holster. "We don't even know who they are."

The rest of us follow Nkella out to the stern to take a look at the ship. Tall beige sails—one bearing the image of a skull—face us.

"Yeah, they're not friendly," Harold says.

"I knew this little ship was a stupid idea," AJ stammers.

"We'd still be stuck on Dempu for an unforeseen amount of time if we hadn't taken it," Tessa says. "What do we do, Captain?"

Nkella is staring through a spyglass. I absent mindlessly run my fingers over the dagger he bought me at Dempu.

"We have ingredients to make raku bombs. From the Hermit's house," Harold suggests.

"Make as many as you can, quickly." Nkella lowers his spyglass. "I cannot tell who's captain, but I see their crew. And their cannons."

Harold bolts through the door with Tessa behind him, heading for the supplies to start making bombs. Nkella turns to AJ and Kae, "Hoist the topsails to pick up speed. We are going to try and stay ahead of them."

AJ starts walking but twists his features. "Their ship is faster, though—"

"Not much faster. It is not like the *Gambit*. This will give us time to prepare for a fight. Then, we will lose speed on purpose."

"Captain?" Kae's eyes bulge.

"And we will prepare to board."

I do a double-take. Did I hear him correctly?

"From what I can see, he has a crew of ten." He holds his spyglass up. "We will be outnumbered, and there are most likely more crew on the bottom floors."

"How the hell do you expect our small lot of a crew to take on even ten of them?" AJ says, waving his hands in the air.

"I do not expect any of you to." His eyes give off a sharp glow, and they back up.

AJ and Kae both widen their eyes in understanding. "Yes, Captain."

An image of him killing the two men with his powers resurfaces in my mind. "Nkella..."

He turns to face me. "You will not get in my way."

My eyes narrow. "What does that mean?"

He takes a step closer to me, and I fight the magnetic pull that makes me want to like it. His dark eyes linger over mine, and he parts his lips, showing the tips of his canines. "Do not try to convince me not to kill them." His voice darkens. "They are coming to kill us, daí? Let me do what I need to do in order to protect my crew."

I swallow. "You have the power to restrain them all. You don't have to stoop to their level and kill them."

"Kh." He shoves past me. "Do as I say, Soren."

I ball my fist and my eyes bore into his back as he walks toward the wheel. "Don't forget, the more you give in to your anger, the more you give yourself away to the Devil Card."

He pauses for a second and glances down at his shoulder. "If that is what I must become to protect you...then so be it."

I reach him and pull at his arm. "Try to restrain them."

He quirks a brow.

"Your crew needs you," I say. "You can't be there for them or your sister if you're lost to the Devil inside." I shudder a breath. I know I can't stop him from killing these men, but I can at least try.

His eyes soften, and his lips part. A warm magnetism grows from the rikorō's psychic connection between us, and I hope that's him understanding me. He gives me a slight nod, then keeps walking. Here's to trying. I make my way down to help Tessa and Harold create the explosives while Lāri keeps an eye on the enemy ship, completely armed and ready.

It's a mess of a setup. Without a lab like Tessa in her quarters of the *Gambit*, we're sitting on the kitchen floor, mashing up plants and doing the best with what we've got. Between the clucking chicken and the fear of leaving anything deadly on the table where we also plan to prepare our food, my nerves are on end. But we work fast. The enemy ship is on our tail.

My mind is fixed on my vision as I work. Despite the impending doom that's upon us, I don't forget the strange vision I had and the warnings it might bring. Twenty minutes pass before Nkella joins us, followed by Kae and AJ.

Nkella stares at our work in progress, and Kae starts picking up the already-made raku bombs, attaching some to his belt, while looking for something to carry the rest in. I push a few I've made in his and AJ's direction when I feel Nkella's intense stare hanging over me. I can tell he's feeling my thoughts. When I glance up at him, he's staring at me.

"What did you mean when you said, 'This is a bad ship'?" he asks. The others stare at him.

"This is about Soren's vision?" Tessa asks.

I glance at her. "Yes. Were you aware that the Danū Prefect is dead?"

Nkella's face blanks, and he stares down at the floor, his brows furrowing. "I... heard the Empress had added extra Arcana to Danū. They stopped the cargo ships from entering."

Kaehante lifts his head as he fills a bag with the explosives. "Daí? No cargo ships?"

"Koj." Nkella shakes his head sadly.

Kae balls his fist. "How will they eat?"

They stare at each other, a pregnant pause in the air, and I can feel Nkella's guilt stirring inside him. "I was unable to investigate...and was trying to save you first."

"W-was the Prefect a friend of yours?" I ask, wincing as the vision of the hatchet in his skull re-emerges in my memory.

"Koj. He kept my people hungry." He growls, readying himself to leave the kitchen.

"Seems like they'll be hungrier now," Tessa mutters as she puts her chair into drive.

"It was a resistance attack," I say, now standing. The floorboards creak underfoot as I step toward Nkella. "Two Ipani men in my vision were disposing of the body to throw off the Psychic Arcana from the Tower. Not sure if they were the ones who killed him, but they were definitely involved, and their next plan was to get rid of this ship... One of them mentioned having a friend who could do it."

AJ glances up from his hand, his eyes wide. "That bastard who sold us the boat. He set us up."

I squint at him. "But why would the resistance kill the Prefect? It seems like it would be pointless without an army. That was a rash decision if you ask me."

"Hn," Nkella squints. "Reckless. But not pointless."

"What do you mean?"

"It was done to make the people angry. So they will take action and join the fight against the Empress. It is what Soanalo would have done."

"Are you sure?" AJ asks.

Nkella shakes his head. "Koj. Maybe they were desperate. But in either case, it was bancha, and it can be seconds before the Arcana find us. But that enemy ship is not Arcana. This we can be certain of."

"Yet," AJ says, "we'll have the Arcana to worry about later."

Back on the main deck, we're all armed and ready, our bandoleers are full of raku bombs, and I'm feeling better now that I have more than just a dagger.

AJ rubs his chin. "What are they doing?"

They've been slowly following us, knowing they have a faster ship.

"They're trying to intimidate us," Kae says.

"Or they're feeling us out," AJ suggests.

"Be ready to cover me," Nkella says as he walks past us with nothing but his pants on. My heart skips a beat.

"Wait. You're boarding them now?" I whisper.

"I'm jumping in away from their line of sight. They won't see me coming."

"Are we forgetting what I said about how often you use the rikorō?" Harold asks. "This still applies to you, too, you know—not just Soren."

Nkella quirks a brow at him. "We do not know that, daí?"

I squint at him, then look at Harold.

Harold shrugs. "It's your funeral."

My stomach ties itself into a knot as I watch Nkella dive into the sea from the window in the back of his room. His legs shift into the black fin, with red and yellow shimmering on his scales, and gills form at his neck as he disappears below the surface and swims out toward the enemy ship.

"They're picking up speed," Lāri calls as I walk back down to meet them on the main deck.

"That was almost on cue," Harold says. "Did they see him jump in?"

Tessa cranes her neck to where Nkella jumped from. "How? He left from the back so they wouldn't."

My throat dries. I clutch an explosive bottle and join the crew, readying for an attack. I study the waves, looking for any sign of Nkella swimming underwater, but I know he plans to surprise them and infiltrate. He's going to swim deep enough not to be spotted. My heart hammers in my chest as the anticipation builds. The ship is getting closer, and now we're meant to stay put to attack anyone about to attack us or Nkella if they spot him raising his head.

AJ nearly jumps down from the rail, and I startle. I clutch my knife on my belt. "What's the matter?"

"Something just jumped from their ship. No, make that two somethings."

"What?" I lean in. Sure enough, two lines are zipping through the waves so fast I can hardly keep sight of them. "What is that? They're too fast to be mer-Ipani, right?"

Tessa backs up her chair. "This is bad."

Kaehante cocks his gun and points to the water; he shoots once and misses. AJ takes a shot, but they're too fast. They're coming in hot. I grab an explosive from my bandoleer and tug it off. Within seconds, they're reaching our ship. I stare into the distance, trying to find where Nkella might be.

A *pop* comes from behind me and I jump, spinning around to face a green and yellow parrot perched on the rail. My mouth gapes, and AJ curses.

"*Utwa*," Kae gasps. Spy, he means. "They knew our Captain would jump ship and leave us alone."

AJ's eyes widen, and he points his gun in my direction. I gasp when hands grab my face and jerk my neck backward. "Shoot and she dies."

The parrot disappears with another *pop* in front of me. My heart is beating so loud I can hardly make out his next words.

"You won't be needing this." The man unlatches my bandoleer with his other hand and another man comes from the side to help lift it over my head.

He lifts my sleeve and checks my mark. "Red hair and the Empress's mark. It's her." He has unnaturally green eyes, tinged with a bit of yellow. They almost look as if they're glowing. His fingers brush over my stomach as he taps my sides and hits the hilt of the dagger on my belt. A zap makes me jump at his touch. He stares at me, and his smile widens, showing sharp canines as he removes my dagger. The two of them laugh, and I arch my neck to get a good glimpse at the one holding my mouth tight. He has the same eyes, the same hair, the same cheeks, except the one grabbing me has a mole above his lip. They're twins.

Lāri lands on the floorboards with her talons and quickly shifts to her Ipani form. "Let her go," she says.

"One meaningful zap from me and she'll be dead in an electrifying instant, mei?"

"Electric eel twins?" Lāri asks. "What do you want?" The crew circles behind her, their guns pointed at both twins, but I can tell they're unsure about what to do. If they shoot one of the twins, the other will kill me. Or miss and hit me instead.

"Who are you people?" Tessa asks.

"I'm just here for the girl. Right now, your captain is being captured and will soon be tortured. As for the rest of you"—he tilts his head at his twin—"your fate rests in his hands."

I squirm in his grip, and squeeze my fingers through his hands, gripping his pinky. I yank down hard, but right as I do, his hand morphs into a slimy serpent-like tail. My hand slides off, and he grips my mouth harder and laughs. With his other hand, he pokes the side of my stomach. I start to violently shake as an electric current jolts through my bones. I hear the crew shouting my name, but the ringing in my ears is overpowering. He backs up, pulling me with him, squeezing his arm over my torso. Lāri advances toward me, and the second twin pulls her back, my dagger now in his hand. My eyes bulge as he brings the point of my dagger to her throat, drawing blood. AJ screams, moving his gun to point at the twin. I squirm harder, but the man brings me down to the sea; we fall with a loud crash. The sound of a gun firing up above rings in my ear as terror shoots through my bones.

My legs instantly shift to the fin, and I feel re-energized and ready to swim. This sensation is killed instantly by the giant net closing in around me. The electric eel swings his tail at my arm, sending a shock of electricity coursing through me. It's enough to disorient me, but not enough to kill me. Arms grow out of his body, and he grabs the netting and starts to swim fast. My body hits the back of the hard rope, and I can't see around me as we zip through the ocean currents.

I'm blinded by the brightness of the day as soon as I'm pulled from the water. Air passes through my nose and the gills on the side of my neck. Gripping the rope net, I try to spin myself around to get my bearings.

"Looky here, a damsel in distress." A bearded man says between laughs. He wears a heavy brown belt over a blue sash under his sagging belly. Beads decorate his beard.

"Is their captain here yet?" the eel twin asks as he jumps into the ship and pulls at the netting. The bearded man hangs the top of the netting on a hook.

"We've lost sight of him, but we have members of our crew under water and in flight."

Three birds fly in a circle above the water. My pulse quickens. He hasn't made it here yet. I gape at the ocean below me, looking for any way of escape.

The netting drops and swings with my weight as the hook is pulled over the ship and lowers me onto the deck. The rope drapes over my head, and my fin shifts back into legs.

The electric eel Ipani and the man who hooked the netting stand above me, with hungry crazed looks in their eye. "She has a taste for rikorō, it seems."

"By the looks of it, so does the Devil captain. So much for what they said about him, á?"

I ball my fist. I'm not about to explain shit to them.

Heavy boots on the floor make my head turn. The man from the store with the snake tattoo on his face casually walks in front of them, his eyes serious and glued on me, his whip held tightly in his hand.

I gasp. *"You?"*

"Here she is, Captain. Just as you asked," the eel says.

My eyes drop to the whip he's holding. What is he planning to do with that?

He drapes the heavy whip around his neck, grabbing onto it with both hands. "That crew dead yet?" he asks them, his eyes still glued to me.

"My brother cut one of their throats before I jumped ship with her. The rest should have followed shortly. My brother's electricity has a long range." His grin widens at the last word. My gut sinks, hoping what he's saying isn't true.

"Good. Take her to the cages."

"And her captain?"

"He may have gone back for his crew. He won't know we have her yet."

"What makes you think he'll come back for me?" I spit.

Nangraku leans in, "Don't act ignorant. I knew taking you from him was the way to hit him where it hurts the moment I saw how he looked at you."

I blink at him.

"Taking you will hurt him, and I'll make him watch as we torture you first."

My heart hammers in my throat as he straightens his back to walk away. "Who were they to you?" I ask.

He stares at me.

"The people he killed. You must have really loved them."

He spits at me, and I grimace. "He killed the love of my life."

My eyes widen. "One of those men was your boyfriend?"

"My *aovate*. And your captain killed him for a vial of rikorō he could have bought."

"That's not how it happened," I say.

"I don't care how it happened. The result is the same. Now you and everyone he cares about will suffer the same fate."

I stare at the back of his head as he walks away.

"So we're just leaving her in the cage until he shows up?" the bearded man who called me a damsel asks after him.

Their captain responds over his shoulder. "Do with her what you want. The result will be the same when he gets here, but I'd prefer it if she were kept alive for him to hear her screams." A worrying ache pulses behind my eyes.

The men come over and untie the knot. As the bigger one grabs my wrist, I immediately twist it down, letting me loose and bringing him close to my face as I punch him hard in the nose. The Eel guy grabs me from behind, and I kick back hard, missing him. I try kicking again, but he comes around and clocks me in the eye. He clocks me hard too. The bastard. I grab at my face.

I do the only thing that's left to do, so that someone—anyone who could possibly hear me and want to help—might respond. I start screaming. I'm unsure if the crew is still alive and can hear me or if Nkella is out there somewhere. Hopefully, he's still alive too. I'm in the company of very bad men with powers.

"Tie her feet. She's a feisty one."

A hot searing pain strikes my legs, and I scream. My stomach hits the hardwood floor, and the air is stolen from my lungs. I gape at the snake face tattoo standing over me with his whip hanging over his left shoulder. The tip of the whip has morphed into a cobra head with fangs, and it hisses at me.

"Get out of line again, and I'll show you what real pain is. Understood?"

I'm shaking. Blood oozes from my leg, which is now swelling where the snake bit me. I stare at him and nod.

"Good." He nods at them and then walks away again.

They take me down kicking and screaming. Though, my leg feels numb and I can hardly kick. I hope to God this isn't going to kill me quicker. But I'm not relenting. So as soon as I'm dropped into a dark, damp room, one of them gags me with cloth and ties it tightly behind my head. A wretched stench of piss and vomit makes me want to puke. I have to hold my breath, letting it out slowly. Tears sting at the corners of my eyes.

"Aw, don't worry, princess," the Eel says. "This isn't venomous enough to kill you. You just won't be able to walk for a bit. Perfect for us." He winks and looks back at his friend who laughs.

"Now, sit there quietly while to torture your captain." The bearded man blows me a kiss and slaps my cheek twice. I wince. As they shut the door, little light illuminates my surroundings. People shift places in what appear to be cages stacked upon cages. Trafficked Ipani.

13

ROWS OF UNBOUND IPANI PRISONERS STARE AT ME FROM inside cages. Some of them mutter words that I can't understand, while others groan and appear to be drugged. My jaw hurts from my mouth being tied open. Despite my legs coming back, the soft sheen of yellow and red scales glows, remnants of the rikorō. Since I used the power again, who knows how much time I have left. I stare at the ground, water dripping from my wet clothes and hair, and try to avoid the judgmental eyes of the trafficked Ipani.

They probably think I'm a traitor. And they're probably confused over me being captured.

It's been hours, and I can't hear anything happening outside. Nkella would have been here already unless he went back for the crew the moment he saw the eels pass him by. Or the rikorō could have caught him the moment he used its power as Harold warned. I haven't felt the magnetism from the rikorō between us, and I can't hear him.

Something's happened, I can feel it.

I raise one knee up to my chest, almost forgetting I can't wrap them because my arms are tied up and my other leg is temporarily paralyzed. I try moving it, and it tingles, meaning the effects are probably wearing off. Goosebumps form on my skin from the cold temperature.

THE DEVIL'S GAMBIT

Being captured and kidnapped makes me realize how defenseless I truly am. How am I supposed to steal the Death Card from the all-powerful Empress if I can't even defend myself against some pirates? They might be a crew of powerful pirates, and we were outnumbered and outsmarted, but the Empress has an entire army at her command.

I'm such an idiot. Tears sting the corners of my eyes. I just want to bring my mom back.

The door creaks open, and the bearded man walks in. The caged Ipani start moving back in their cages, and a few of them let out scared whimpering noises. By their reactions, I can tell that this man has been abusing them. He walks closer and towers over me. I arch my neck to see a sick look in his eye. He glares down at me. His upper lips form a smirk as he reaches down and grabs my arm, pulling me up to my feet. It's hard to stand since my ankles are tied, and one leg is still out of commission. A moan escapes the back of my throat, even though I know I can't speak through the cloth covering my mouth. He pushes me against the wall, and I lose my balance and hit the ground. The cages bang around me. I squint past the man, some of the Ipani are saying something to me but I have no idea what. I climb to my knees, and the man picks me up by my shirt. He pushes me back so that my back is flat against the wall, and I'm balancing with my feet tied close together. I'm breathing hard, with my eyes looking at him and my chin up.

"My captain gave me orders to hurt your captain when he comes around." He grins.

I narrow my eyes at him.

"You know what would hurt him more than my knife?" He spins it in his hand. "Finding out his aovate was defiled by me."

My breathing slows to a complete stop.

He moves his hand up to my chin with his knife, lightly touching my skin. I move my face to the side, my eyes still trained on him. If my ankles weren't tied up, I'd kick him in the balls. He moves the knife slowly down my throat, stopping at my collar. Then, in one savage motion, he rips the front of my wet shirt all the way down, exposing my bra.

My heart pants in my chest. The man licks his lips as he stares at my breasts. And I turn away from him, but when I do, I fall onto my side. A

143

few Ipani make whimpering sounds. I had almost forgotten all their eyes are on me. He's going to abuse me here in front of all these prisoners, with everyone looking.

He unbuckles his belt and begins unbuttoning his pants. I start to crawl away on my elbows, my face touching the floor. I kick furiously, trying to loosen the rope even though I've tried so many times, only for it to become tighter and tighter. I scream through the cloth, my throat becoming hoarse. He leans down with his knife and cuts the cloth. I scream loud, but he yanks my hair back and presses his hot breath to my ear.

"Scream. No one here will care. And if your captain hears you, good. That is what we want. There are thirty men aboard this ship and only one of him. He will hear your screams while we torture him, and then once we have him tied up, we will make him watch as we all have a turn with you."

My scream turns into a sob as he drops his pants.

I clamp my eyes shut and turn my face to the floorboards. He tries to lift me up by my jaw and crushes my cheeks, his other hand finding and squeezing my ass. I try lifting my knee to push him away from me, but he pushes himself between my legs. As he lowers himself, he lets go of my face just a little, letting his fingers slide over my mouth. I bite down hard.

He lets out an angry yell, lifts me up, and throws me against one of the cages. A scream shatters my eardrums as I hit the floor. He reaches me and picks me up again, this time backhanding my face. I let out a grunt, and then he shoves me back against the wall. Tears are streaming down my cheeks, but I'm not going to let him do what he wants without a fight. I don't care how hard he hits me.

Banging comes from somewhere above the room, and my muscles tense. I'm expecting more of these assholes to come down here.

He presses his face to my ear. "Do that again, and I'll take pleasure in your corpse."

I open my mouth to scream but then I shut it. Something in the air shifts. A dark magnetism—Nkella.

Loud banging comes from above the ceiling, followed by a terror-izing scream.

He's here.

The rikorō stirs inside me; it's fueled with rage. My eyes widen as I stare up at the man, my lips forming into a wicked grin. I can't help an estranged giggle that escapes my throat.

He stares at me, awestruck. I don't care how crazy I look right now. Maniacal laughter leaves my mouth, and I can't stop it. "He's going to kill you," I choke.

The man gives me an evil grin. "Not if they kill him first." He wraps his hand tightly around my throat, making me face the ceiling. He moves his hands over my waist, and I start screaming Nkella's name in my head.

The metal door breaks open and flies against one of the cages, causing the Ipani inside to scream. I'm instantly dropped to the ground, and I grab at my throat. Turning my head, I see him standing there, shirtless, with blood pooling down his chest. But he looks unhurt. His eyes are glowing something furious, and he moves his hand up. A strong gust of wind forms around him. The bearded man is lifted from the ground, his face staring at the ceiling. He can't even get a word out as he starts to choke.

I stare at him as his face goes from tan to blue in seconds. His eyes bulge, and his feet kick in the air. Normally, I would plead with Nkella to stop—not to kill him. But this time, I don't. Not for all these Ipani prisoners he's abused, and not for me.

The man's skin starts to swell, and his veins start to bulge. His eyes look like they're about to pop out of his skull, and his tongue sticks out. I back away, making my way to Nkella. I glance up at him from the floor, and it looks like a dark shadow has eclipsed his features. His eyes are crimson, and the horns on his head are bigger than I've ever seen them.

I gape at the man, who starts to blow up like a balloon as Nkella fills him with hot air. I fall back on my arms, staring as he grows wider and wider.

Blood and brain matter shoots out in every direction. I shut my eyes and scream into my arm. My heart pants furiously in my chest.

Metal cages start to rattle, and the surrounding screams grow louder. I lift my head from my arm, afraid to see why they're still scream-ing. Nkella has his arms raised again, his eyes still a fiery red.

"Nkella?" I croak. He doesn't hear me. One of the cages flies off a shelf and bursts open. The Ipani inside doesn't come out. He raises his arm to another cage, and it starts to shake. Fury and rage ooze out from him. He doesn't mean to free them. He's not in control. He's going to kill them all.

"Nkella!" I reach for him and grab onto his leg. "Stop. You can stop now!"

The cage door rips open, and with one gust of wind, he forces the Ipani out. The girl screams as she's thrust into the air.

"Nkella, listen to me. You're about to kill an Ipani prisoner." He still doesn't hear me. I force myself up, gripping his arm as I shift my weight to my one working leg. I hold onto his arm and call out to him. "Listen to my voice. It's me, Soren."

The cages rattle harder, and the poor girl has stopped screaming. I gape at her as she starts to turn purple. No...

Quickly, I reach for his shoulder. "It's me. It's Soren."

He stares at me hard, his face blank and unreadable. A tear rolls down my face. "Remember? Neyuro..."

His eyes twitch with anger, and a gasp sticks in my throat. But then a small gasp escapes him as well, and his eyes widen. He looks down at me...and slowly sets the Ipani girl on the floor. She takes a huge gasp of air. My shoulders drop.

"Soren..."

"Nkella." A nervous chuckle escapes the back of my throat. Blood is smeared all over his face, chest, and hair. My hands are shaking as I glance around the room. Blood is splattered everywhere, and Ipani pris-oners are still screaming.

"Are you okay?" he whispers, his eyes returning to their normal dark shade, but a glimmer of amber flickers beneath them. A sob is stuck in my throat, so I only nod. He reaches down and cuts the rope from my feet and arms. Then he helps me up.

I'm still shaking as we lock eyes.

"I-I could feel you from the rikorō," he croaks, "but I couldn't reach you."

Some of the Ipani have stopped screaming. I think they are beginning to realize he isn't going to kill them.

My heart is still pounding hard. "I thought—I thought I had lost you. You—"

"I know," is all he says. "I'm here now. Because of you."

My breath hitches as I stare into his eyes. "The crew?" I ask.

"They're safe."

"And Lāri? I saw—"

"She will recover."

"I thought you were captured."

"I was."

I gasp. "How—"

"They caught me underwater. When I realized my mistake, I fought them to get back to the ship and found you were gone. I came as soon as I could."

I shudder. Then, he pulls me in unexpectantly and presses me against his chest. He grabs my hair, and I close my eyes into him, not caring about the blood. He holds me tight—and that's all I need right now. My arms close in around his waist, and I pull him in tighter, not letting go. A sob escapes me, and my eyes tear up. "Maybe some men do deserve to die," I say weakly.

He squeezes the back of my hair. "From now on, neyuro, I will always keep you safe. Even if it kills me."

I lift my chin to stare into his eyes. "You won't die," I say. "You're too strong."

He smirks, and then we pull away to look at the Ipani still trapped in cages.

"Can you walk, neyuro? Are you hurt?"

I shake my head. "I'm fine. I want to free them." I glance at the girl who had been suspended in air. She gets to her feet and runs to help the Ipani who's still stuck under the cage. Nkella reaches the cage, and she flinches away, but he lifts the heavy metal cage, freeing he young boy who's shaking beneath it. He tells them something in Ipani, and by the look on their faces, they seem to relax a little.

"Captain!" A voice rings out from above, and I jump.

Nkella runs to the now-open entrance and calls out to Kaehante. I relax my shoulders realizing the crew has boarded the ship.

"What about the rest of this ship's crew?" I ask carefully.

He shoots me a stare, and I know they're all dead.

"Did the crew come with you?"

"Koj. I jumped while Kae sailed."

"So how did you kill the entire crew by yourself? I thought there were thirty of them."

Nkella doesn't respond, but something stirs between us. Something dark. Unnatural. It wants to rise to the surface, but Nkella banks it down. It sends a shiver down my spine.

"I told you once, neyuro. If protecting you means I must lose myself, then so be it."

My breathing shallows.

Kae barges through the opening and pauses. His eyes widen at the scene. AJ follows him and his eyes also bulge.

"I'm not even going to ask," AJ says, eyeing the blood and guts drenching the room.

"Then don't. Hurry up and help us release these prisoners."

"On the double, Captain!" AJ stretches a leg in, wary of stepping on the wet blood, and starts opening the cages. Kaehante doesn't seem too bothered by the mess as he also gets to work releasing the prisoners.

"I'm guessing Tessa and Harold stayed to help Lāri?" I ask. I mostly just want to know where everyone is because I'm afraid something terrible happened. Although, AJ wouldn't be so chirpy if something bad happened to the crew. And he doesn't ever need to know what almost happened to me. In fact, none of them do.

AJ laughs. "Lāri is fine, Soren. She has the undead curse, remember?"

I gasp. I had forgotten about that. I had seen Kae get stabbed before and then reach down to pull the sword out.

"Tessa and Harold are protecting the ship and watching our backs, while Lāri checks out the rest of this ship.

Releasing a sigh of relief, I open the cage holding the Ipani girl who had been calling out to me before. I hold my hand out to her, and she takes it, letting me help her out. Once she's on her feet, she gives me a big hug. My eyes widen, but I don't hug her back at first. I'm covered in blood, and I thought they hated me seeing how I obviously drank rikorō.

"Engi."

I don't need to speak Ipani to understand she's thanking me. I look from her to Nkella. His eyes are filled with sadness as he stops to glance at her. We work fast, and as more Ipani are released, they release the others.

Kaehante and AJ lead them all outside. I count thirteen of them. Despite the multiple scares I just had, I feel as though a weight has been lifted from my shoulders. I glance behind me and realize Nkella is actually the one feeling that weight being lifted. He stares past me, his eyes softened, before he quickly glances at me. I smile back at him. He didn't just save me; he saved thirteen trafficked Ipani from a horrible fate.

"Now what?" I ask him. "Are we taking them somewhere?"

He wipes his neck. "There are too many of them to look after. I hope they have somewhere to go."

I nod.

He grabs my wrist, and we stop on the stairs, letting the rest of them climb onto the main deck. "Neyuro..."

"Yes?" I hold my torn shirt together, suddenly remembering that creep had destroyed it. We won't find another shop until we reach Swords, and Tessa and Lāri have also lost all their stuff.

Blood stains hide the creases of his concerned face as he looks at me with his worried, dark eyes.

"What's wrong?"

There's a pregnant pause, and the magnetism we share from the rikorō shifts; he wants to tell me something, but he's pulling back. I furrow my brow. He clears his throat and lets out a sharp sigh. "Walk straight to the ladder to board our ship. Do not look out over the deck."

"What? Why?"

"Just do as I say."

"Okay..." He lets go of my wrist, and I continue up the steps. AJ's voice projects across the deck, and I hear Lāri speak after him, but it's muffled by loads of people yelling and some crying.

149

"Lordy!" AJ croaks. "Alright, step away from the bodies, everyone. Follow me."

Nkella places his hand on my left shoulder and urges me to the right, but it's too late. I make it to the top and gape at the scene. It's a bloodbath. There are pieces of people everywhere, and no one knows where to step.

"Didn't you see it when you boarded?" Lāri asks.

"I had my head down. I was on a mission to find Nkella and Soren," AJ says.

"I saw the whole thing. He was...unstoppable."

My eyes skim the crowd; people are huddled together, some have their heads down, afraid to look up. My heart breaks for them. Each of them was abused, drugged, raped, and sentenced to death for their ouma. I can see the hope lost in so many of their eyes, and now they have to witness evidence of a bloodbath. My eyes stop at a familiar face behind AJ. The snake face tattoo is covered in blood, his scarred eye staring up at the sky, and his head is on a pike. The blood drains from my face, and my eyes slowly meet Nkella.

He's staring straight ahead. He pushes past me, his heavy boots silencing everyone as he makes his way toward AJ. Everyone moves back, giving him space, watching him in awe. Some are visibly scared of him and recoil when he passes by.

"Those of you who have the ouma of flight, fly. Of the sea, swim. If your ouma is of fire or land, then find a way back home. You cannot come with us. We have a small ship and are wanted. You will not be safe with me."

"So much for taking this ship," AJ mutters under his breath. "You couldn't have made less of a mess?"

Nkella shoots him a hard stare. "Kh."

My eyes wander over my surroundings. He didn't just fill them all with air and blow them up. Pieces of the deck are blown out, the captain's quarters are—well, the bed is overthrown on the wheel, and the captain's quarters are no more. Planks are missing, and there's a gaping hole in one of the walls. The ship is utterly destroyed.

"We need to sink it." Kaehante breaks the silence. "We cannot leave it behind for the Arcana to find, daí?"

"He's right," Nkella states. "The Empress is after anyone using ouma. And this ship is full of it, even without the traffickers to blame. If you are found, you are all in peril."

"Not to mention, we can't feed you," AJ mutters.

"And we're headed to Swords, which is the last place any of you will want to be," Lāri adds.

That last statement makes me realize this ship was on its way to Swords, despite the siege. How were they planning to get in?

An Ipani man speaks up. "Some of us are still drugged and cannot move far."

"Yes, but if I stay on this ship any longer, I will most likely die from the stench," a woman says.

"How are all of us going to leave? There are so many of us, and many are too weak to use our ouma."

Lāri raises her hand, and they turn to look at her. "How many of you can fly and feel strong enough to carry one person?"

Four raise their hands.

"And swim?" Nkella asks.

Another five raise their hands.

"Dempu Yuni isn't far south. The seas are dangerous. Move quickly and be careful."

"And look out for one another," Lāri says. "May the Aō guide you."

Chatter disperses among the rescued prisoners as they help each other and decide who is taking who.

After we're finished, Kaehante is the last one to leave. He lights a match and catches the enemy ship in flames.

I know it's not the *Gambit*, but after spending the day below that horrible ship, I'm happy to be back on our rickety *Ugly Kraken*. Away from traffickers and bad men. Tessa gapes at me as she drives up to us. Nkella and I are drenched in blood, and I really want a shower.

Kaehante and AJ handle the sails, but before I go down to get cleaned up, I take one last look at the ship bursting into flames as the sea eats the sun behind it. Nkella stands at the edge of the deck, the light from the orange flames dancing on his skin. Our magnetism grows, and something tells me we're both reveling in the destruction of the vessel of blood.

14

THE SHOWER ROOM IS SMALL, JUST LIKE EVERYTHING ELSE on this ship. I had forgotten about the charcoal mixture they use to clean themselves, but with a hard sponge, it does the job of removing all the blood. I sit on the bathroom floor for longer than I should, thinking about the events of the day, and how close I was to not getting out of there alive, or...

I guess the good thing is the number of people we managed to save. Or that Nkella saved. I was completely useless.

Sighing deeply, I pick myself up and grab my towel. A wave of dizziness rushes through my head, and I lean against the wall, closing my eyes until it passes. Being taken into the sea activated by the rikorō, which was probably the worst thing that could happen. I don't know how long I have left. I need to move forward with getting the Death Card. Once I have that in my hands, I can save myself and bring back my mom. And heal Nkella...although he still doesn't seem affected.

The dizziness passes, and I open the door to see Lāri hunched over one of the chests on the guys' side of the room. The flickering light of the hanging lanterns casts shadows on the floor as I step out. "This might be too big," she says, "but it should work until Tessa finishes sewing up your shirt."

"Oh, I didn't know she was doing that."

"Of course." Lāri hands me a pair of pants and a tan shirt. I take them and get dressed.

"The night is quiet," she says.

"For now."

"The fire is almost out, and the ship is nearly gone."

"Until something else comes."

She takes a seat on her hammock, and I lie down on mine, moving my wet hair to hang over it.

"Do you want to talk about what happened?" she asks quietly.

There's a loaded pause, and I swallow. "I would rather just forget it happened. Not that anything did happen, but...if Nkella had gotten there a second later..."

"Good thing he came when he did."

"They removed my weapons. I had nothing. I wasn't strong enough. I even took fighting lessons back home because I never again wanted to be at the mercy of anyone, and I still wasn't strong enough. How am I going to be able to steal the Death Card? Or protect my sister? Or myself?"

Lāri sits up on her hammock, the flickering lights hitting the top of her short pixie-cut hair. "Sometimes, we are overpowered. There will always be someone stronger, no matter how strong and powerful we are."

I glance at her. She, too, had been kidnapped for her rikorō and kept in one of those cages. AJ was a wreck until he found her. He even risked his own life and was caught by the Arcana trying to go where she was being kept. I don't want to imagine the awful things that they must have done to her during that time. Those bad men were after more than making rikorō with ouma.

"But we must endure," she says. "We must always hold on to who we are—no matter what they do to us—or we let them win."

I nod.

"We must stick together, we are stronger in numbers, mei? And we must never give up."

"Stick together. Got it."

"None of them out there are stronger than the undead crew."

"I'm not undead."

"No, but you're still part of the baddest crew around. We don't pillage or abuse, we have our mission, and therein lies the love we have for each other and for Ipa. We never give up on going against the Tower because our hearts will always be true, be it for the love of our brothers and sisters or for the life we dream of having. We may steal, we may even kill, but it is never without regret or for the game of it. We are pirates, but we are different from the rest. Pirates against the Tower." She smiles.

"Pirates against the Tower." I agree.

"Promise me, you won't lose your shine, Soren. You might not realize this, but you have brought hope to this crew. Even to our Devil captain himself." She offers me another sweet smile.

"Thank you."

AJ knocks on the kitchen door and pokes his head into the room. "Is everyone decent?"

"As we can be," Lāri says.

"Who's ready for a feast? Before these veggies go out of date."

Lāri gets up from her hammock and extends her hand out to me. "Ready?"

"One more thing," I say, taking her hand. "How do we know we're safe now?"

"We never know if we're safe. We cherish every moment and choose to make light of things when they're grim. But keep your weapons on you at all times, mei? Always be ready. Let's eat."

After dinner, the crew scatters to their corners. I think we all need some quiet after today. My brain won't let me sleep, so I make my way up to the main deck and find Nkella at the wheel. He's clean and fully clothed; the popped collar of his coat edges his stiff jawline, his hat on his head. I wrap my arms around myself, thankful that the shirt Lāri found is made out of wool, as the temperature is dropping.

He focuses straight at the sea, a serious expression on his face.

Strong winds whip my hair around my face as I start to make my way up the wooden steps. The ship hits a few hard waves, so I grip the wood tight on my way up. The strange magnetism from the rikorō starts to grow. He flicks his gaze in my direction.

His lips part when he sees me, and he swallows, looking back to sea. "You should sleep."

"I should do a lot of things, but I don't."

He keeps his vision focused in front of him with his hands gripping the wheel tightly. I stand next to him, staring out at the dark sea, it's hard to see the parting of sky and sea when looking straight ahead. If not for the purple swirls moving in a nautilus dance straight above our heads, I'd find myself immensely disoriented.

He reaches into his coat and pulls out his flask, taking a swig. He offers it to me, "Maybe this will help you sleep."

I take it and have a drink. "Thanks." Silence passes between us, and I narrow my eyes. "Is the rikorō wearing out?"

He glances at me. "I expected it to be gone already. It is supposed to be temporary."

"This must have been a stronger dose than what you're used to seeing."

"They have been working on making it better," he grimaces. "I wish I hadn't drunk it. I wish you hadn't either."

"I know, but we saved the crew, and that's what counts, right?"

He scoffs. "Your life is in danger, neyuro. Why do you take this lightly, daî?" He cocks his head, eyeing me from the corner of his eye.

"I'm not taking it lightly. I'm just not talking about it."

A pregnant pause passes between us. "I know. I can feel your worry. And your pain."

"I can feel yours too..."

"Kh. I've been trying to block that."

"You've done an okay job at it so far."

"Hn. I think it is my curse that tries to keep my thoughts private. It does not like others knowing my secrets."

I blink. That's the first time he's spoken of his curse as if it's a separate being or entity inside of him. "It doesn't like it? Not...you?"

"I don't," he corrects, "but the Aō also manifests itself through our marks. Understand?"

"I'm trying to. So you haven't been blocking me on purpose?"

"Koj. I cannot control my power. I try hard. But when the time

155

comes for it to take over..." He looks away from the wheel...and from me. "It does."

I nod.

He quirks a brow and reaches into his coat, taking out my dagger. The red swirls in the black wood shine from the lights in the sky. "Keep this on you, daí?"

I take it and put it back on my belt loop.

"Thank you...for...saving me back there."

He flicks his eyes at me and blinks.

My cheeks redden, and I stare hard at the wheel.

"Are you still sure your mission is worth the cost of being here?" His tone is serious, dark. I glance at him.

"Bringing my mom back to life is what I want most in this world, and I'll risk anything to do it. Don't you feel the same about your sister?"

A sigh escapes his lips, and he rests his arm against the wheel. The ship jumps on some thrashing waves, and I fall against him as I catch my balance but then rectify myself.

"I always put my family first. So, yes, it is worth it for me. I don't require thanks for saving you, Soren. I could not have lived with myself had I been too late."

The magnetism shifts to something darker and more intense, and I suddenly want to change the subject, but I don't know how. I don't want to talk about what happened. I want to chalk it up as something that didn't happen and keep moving forward. He must interpret my emotions because he stays quiet, although the silence is heavy. Still, I appreciate him not pressing.

I stare out to sea, and I'm not sure if I should excuse myself and try to go to sleep or stay. Despite the shift in energy, I want to stay.

"Do you want to steer the ship?" he asks suddenly.

I do a double-take, not sure I heard him right. "What? Me?"

He moves back to let me in front of him. "It would be good for you to know how. In case I need you to someday."

"But Kae and AJ can steer it..."

"In the middle of a battle, anyone who can take the wheel should." He moves his hand for me to step in front of the wheel but continues steering with the other. Nerves tighten in my stomach. I don't even drive a car. I mean, I have my license, but since I can't afford one, I take the bus everywhere. I don't have much practice driving. "What if I crash the boat?"

He chuckles. "That is hard to do on open sea, daí? And I won't let us drown."

Steeling my spine, I take the wheel and step in front of him. "Don't let go, though!"

He laughs again. "I will not." His breath fans against my neck, causing goosebumps to form over my skin. "Keep it steady, like this." He moves his right hand over mine, making me gasp for breath at his touch. He gently tightens his grip so that we're both keeping the wheel steady, but it's hard to focus on how the wheel is tough and fighting against the current when my mind is going back to our last kiss. My throat dries, and my breathing grows shallow.

I lick my lips.

"In the *Gambit*, a lot of this is automatic with the right potions," he says over the wind. "But it is important to know how to steer a manual ship. The potions do not last forever."

I nod, gripping the wheel tight in both hands and trying to keep the boat from moving to the side. Wind pushes my hair in front of my face, but I'm afraid to let go, even though Nkella is doing most of the work. I feel the boat leaning too far to the right, so I try moving the wheel over to my left to keep us from tipping over.

Nkella's fingers whisper over my neck, moving my hair back. My breath hitches. He lets go of the wheel to move his hands over my arms. He pushes them down gently. "Relax your arms. You are too tense."

A butterfly lets loose in my stomach, and I back it away, keeping my focus on the dark ocean. He leans in, the warmth of his body warming me through the cold winds, and he points up. "Do you see the direction the *bayoa* is moving?"

My brow puckers as I stare at the sky. "The purple lights? I thought they were just moving around in a swirl."

"They are moving in a shape. Watch."

The lights move in a pattern, forming a nautilus shell. It takes me a few seconds to notice they repeat the pattern. It isn't random. His fingers move my hair behind my ear, pushing it away from my face. I can feel the trail of his touch on my back as he strokes my hair, eliciting a wave of electricity down my spine. "They're beautiful," I say breathlessly.

"Yes," he whispers into my back. My stomach twists. "When the lights move wide apart, you know you are headed true north."

My eyes widen. "Oh. That's good to know." I loosen my grip on the wheel, and the ship jerks to my left, catching a large wave and bouncing Nkella into me. His arms grasp my stomach, and he quickly takes the wheel with his right hand, steadying the ship. But he doesn't remove his left hand.

"I said, don't let go of the wheel," I tell him. "I don't know what I'm doing."

He laughs. "We are safe for now, neyuro." He loosens his grip on my stomach but doesn't move his hand away.

And I don't move it away either. Instead, I let go of the wheel and let my fingers explore the skin on his hand. His breath hitches behind me as I thrum my fingers over his knuckles and twine my fingers between his. He curls his hand, enclosing mine in his, and for a moment, we still, caught in each other's presence, allowing the rhythmic movement of the ship moving up and down with the waves to cocoon us in a moment I don't want to end.

He tugs at my hand, and I let him spin me around with one arm, his other hand still on the wheel. Not that I'm concerned about the ship capsizing. I know he knows what he's doing. And I feel safe. I'm just acutely aware of what he's doing with his hands.

"Earlier..." He clears his throat. "When I...almost lost control." He speaks just above a whisper. "You were my bayoa. My own guiding light. Chaotic like those purple lights in the sky, but purposeful. Brave." The corner of his lip tugs into a smirk.

I lick my lips and stare into his dark, soulful eyes, as he stares back into mine. The wind is blowing my hair back now, and he has me clasped at the waist, his breathing deep and steady, his full lips so close to mine. I want to taste them.

His eyes dip to my lips, and he kisses me softly. I close my eyes as we both revel in the moment, the magnetism pushing us even closer together. He lays another gentle kiss on my lips, his tongue kisses me at the seam, and I part my lips, granting him access.

My hands reach for his back, sliding inside his coat, which warms me as I find the seam of his shirt and feel the touch of his skin. He explores my mouth with his tongue, and I arch into him. His legs widen, allowing me to move closer to him, his body molding into mine.

Wind circles around us, and it feels like we're being cocooned inside a magnetic force with the wind surrounding us. I'm not sure if it's the natural wind from the sea or from his ouma, but the thought of the latter makes me crave him more because it means he wants me with every part of himself that he's been holding back. I bring my hand around to the front of his stomach and start exploring his chest. I tug on his pants, but only hook my fingers to the top of them. He lets out a primal growl and kisses me deeper. My heart pants uncontrollably in my chest.

The ship moves to the right, but I don't care. He struggles to keep it straight, but he doesn't stop kissing me. He refuses to let me go.

The ship jumps on a wave, and we both hit the wheel. His arm protects my back from getting hurt, and he laughs into my mouth. A breathless giggle escapes me, and with one motion, he lifts me up. My legs wrap around his waist, pushing him back in his chair.

"Kaehante will take the wheel soon." His tone is breathless, and he kisses my neck. I run my fingers down his chest, inside his shirt, and close my eyes, relishing in his touch.

Heat surfaces between my legs, and I press myself against him. His eyes meet mine, and his irises dilate, a flash of amber flickering beneath them. His pulse quickens beneath me, and he stands, keeping his arms tightly around me, my legs still wrapped around his waist. The ship moves as he lets go of the wheel, and we are pushed against the rail, my back pressed against it. My neck arches slightly over the rail, my hair billowing in the wind. A mixture of arousal and the thrill of hanging slightly off the ship and at the mercy of Nkella's strength sends a buzz of excitement swarming through my belly. He moves his head down to my neck, his lips planting soft kisses on my skin. His sharp incisors trail over my flesh, brushing against it, teasing to nibble on me.

I can feel his arousal rising like the waves crashing against this boat.

My knees tremble, and my legs nearly give out. If his arms weren't firmly wrapped around me, I'd be swimming with the kelp at the bottom of the sea.

His lips whisper against the flash of my stomach, sending shivers down my spine, and my eyes roll back as I stare at the nautilus swirls in the sky. I grab a fist of his hair, and a moan escapes my lips.

"Capt—" Kaehante's voice carries in the wind, but Nkella doesn't respond. Instead, he pulls back, taking me with him. I can barely see Kaehante's features as he runs to grab the wheel. I kiss Nkella's neck as he carries me to his room, kicking the door open and laying me down on his bed. He only turns long enough to shut the door and light a match, quickly lighting the lantern by his bed. I remove my shirt, leaving my bra. I'm not ready to remove that yet.

His eyes zero in on the action, and they linger over my body. He lets out an appreciative growl, and takes off his coat and his shirt. My eyes stare at his cut muscles, studying every marking, every Ipani stripe, and every tattoo on his skin. He's so beautifully adorned. His eyes move down my body, drinking me in. I start to unhook the button on my pants, but he reaches down and stops my fingers from doing so. His eyes meet mine, and he pauses.

"Neyuro...we don't have to..."

Lifting his chin, I kiss his soft lips. "Let's just see where it goes."

"Are you sure?"

"Yes."

He smiles into my lips, and draws his tongue over them, tasting me. I part my lips, and he enters my mouth, licking the top of my teeth. I kiss him back furiously, my body moving to wrap around his. The entirety of his body now molds perfectly into mine, and his hand caresses my back, lifting me against him. The girth inside his pants hardens, and my pulse quickens. The magnetic force from the rikorō is trying to merge us together as one, and it's the strangest feeling but the best feeling I've ever had in my life. Bonding us like we were always meant to be together and never apart.

Our breathing intensifies as our bodies move, twining into each other with the rocking of the ship. It's as if our spirits want to join with each other just as the waves crashing against this ship want to merge. I get lost in the taste of him, the feel of his lips against mine.

I start to tug at my pants, sliding them down my legs as I reach for his hips. He removes his pants, and only our undergarments are between us. The candlelight flickers over our bodies, casting both a warm red light and shadows that dance to our rhythm.

His mouth chases mine and his breathing intensifies as our bodies press closer together and I'm submerged in his warmth, his girth pressing hard against me. My pulse quickens, but his pulse beats even faster. I can feel it in my fingertips as I touch him. He pauses.

"Nkella?"

His breathing is hard as he stops to look at me. A dark red glow flickers in his eyes, and his lips are parted but he doesn't speak. He stares at me so intensely it sends a dark shiver down my spine.

"Are you okay?" I ask.

The red glow darkens, and he comes up to my lips. I take that as a yes, and I kiss him back. His kiss is sensual but quickly becomes a fury neither of us can stop. Every touch is magnetic like magic sparking electricity after every kiss, every stare. And I'm now addicted.

He kisses me so deeply, my eyes close and my breathing stops. He does it again. Until warm air fills me with a rising tide of his arousal.

I take in his ouma, and a wave of red overwhelms me. My lungs fill with air, and I become lightheaded. My eyes flutter open. Something is wrong.

He moves in to kiss me again, but I pull away.

He blinks. "Soren?"

I part my lips, but no words come out. No breath comes out. I can't breathe.

His eyes furiously search mine, and I shake my head and hit my chest. I don't know why I do it, but I also don't know what else to do. "I can't breathe," I mouth, a hoarse whisper coming out of me. His eyes bulge, and he shakes his head.

"No! No no no." He props me up. "I don't know how to stop this."

I can feel my cheeks burning as my body temperature rises.

He stands up and runs to the door, yelling something in Ipani. Then he says the word, "Help," and whips back around to me. I've fallen on the floor, and the room is darkening around me. My chest grows so tight, it burns. My vision starts to narrow, and all I can see is the candlelight flickering behind Nkella. Dizziness makes the walls cave in around me, and I fall to the floorboards as my oxygen is cut off. Nkella screams somewhere in the distance.

The next thing I see is Lāri's face. She's yelling something at Nkella. He yells something back as she tries to prop me up, but my head bobs down.

The light flickers in and out.

15

NKELLA GRABS MY CHIN AND PULLS ME CLOSE TO HIM. I think he's going to kiss me again, but then he says, "Open your mouth, Soren."

I part my lips slightly, finding it hard to move at all. He leans in, his lips close to mine, and begins to suck in air.

Suddenly, I feel a weight being lifted from my chest. The oxygen comes crashing back in, sending a wave of nausea and pain down my temples. Sweat trickles down my forehead, and queasiness overtakes me.

Lāri is standing over us, holding her neck, her eyes wide with shock. Relief falls over her face as I blink up at her.

"Soren?" Nkella is out of breath. I try standing but collapse. He catches me by my arms, lifts me up, and carries me to his bed. My eyes grow heavy and I let them close, biting back the nausea coursing through my head. I hear Lāri ask him what happened, and Nkella grows silent, then the door shuts. Even with him outside the room, a lingering unease swirls between us from the rikorō.

My chest still aches from the air that was trapped in my lungs; it's hot, painful, and still growing. An image of the man Nkella blew up from the inside out forces its way into my thoughts and now a different ache hits my chest. One that I don't feel like confronting right now so I let my mind drift off to sleep.

When I wake, Nkella isn't in his room, but there's a pillow and a blanket on the floor in the corner. Not that he and I would fit comfortably in this small bed, but he shouldn't have had to sleep on the hard floor.

The covers are pulled up to my chin. I'm not sure if I did that in my sleep or if he covered me, but there's a cool draft coming through the window. I'm thankful for it. The way I burned up with hot air last night terrifies me. Images of me and Nkella at the wheel last night flashes through my mind and I lay my head back down, trying to ignore my body's aches for it to happen again.

AJ's voice fights against strong wings and the thrashing of waves. Tessa's voice comes next. I'd better head down before someone comes to get me, thinking I'm dying. Not that anyone other than the captain will walk inside the captain's quarters—I swing my legs over the bed—especially since I'm still in my underwear. I reach over for the wool shirt and black pants on the floor and slip them on. I close the door behind me, hoping to see Nkella at the wheel but find Harold instead.

"Hey," I say to him.

He arches his head and widens his eyes at me. "Back atcha," he says with a smirk on his lips.

I roll my eyes. "What?"

"Nothing." His smirk stays pasted on his face. "Was wondering where you went." He chuckles. "I fell asleep early last night, and when I woke up, you weren't in your hammock."

"You know? I thought maybe sharing a room with you all would be fun, but it turns out, it's a lot like the group home."

"What do you mean?"

"Everyone's so nosy."

"Oh, come on. It's not like we didn't know you two were..."

My brows rise to the top of my head.

"I mean, I didn't know. Last time I saw you two, you were his prisoner. Then, you save me from an eternal life underwater, and now you guys are all cute together." He shrugs.

My lips pucker, and I glance to the side, trying hard to hide the stupid smile that wants to creep on my lips. Harold laughs.

"Adorable. So did you two..." He clears his throat.

"No!"

"Uh-huh."

"Lāri didn't tell you?"

"Tell me what?" He notes the seriousness in my eyes. "Did something happen? I did see her run out, but after waiting a few seconds and not hearing news of being under attack, I went back to sleep."

Well, it's good to know she isn't a blabbermouth. "We, uh...didn't get past kissing last night. He...kind of...lost control of his power, I think."

Harold's jaw drops. "Are you okay?"

"I am now." My eyes squint as I recollect how he managed to keep me from dying. "He ended up sucking in the air he filled my lungs with. I don't understand how."

"It makes sense. He controls air. He's just having a hard time controlling it."

I nod, glancing at the floor.

"He'll be able to. He just has to practice. When Kenjō was coming into her power, she needed to practice turning in order to remember she was a person and not just a jaguar."

My eyes widen. "A jaguar?"

His lips thin to a smile. "Imagine my surprise when I woke up to find bloody rabbit bones beside me in the middle of the night. I had no idea what was going on. But I helped her figure it out...well, before we realized the more she used the ouma from the rikorō, the quicker she'd die."

"That's interesting. The rikorō we drank granted us the power, but we didn't have to try hard to learn it."

"It might be different for full-on shifters. But even when I was learning my rune magic, I still had to practice in order to control it. He'll get better, Soren."

"Yeah."

"I'm glad you're not dead, though."

I snort. AJ's voice comes from the hall of the quarterdeck. "Harold, the sea is calm enough to let it sail. Come and eat."

My stomach roars at the sound of food, and we both make our way down to the kitchenette area. A butterfly gets trapped in my gut when I hear Nkella's voice coming from the hall.

The aroma of fried eggs and fresh bread fills my nostrils as we walk through the door. Tessa and Lāri are sitting next to Nkella who's hovering over a map while taking a bite of his bread. AJ and Kae are both standing by the stove with plates of food in their hands.

"It's a small ship, but at least the food tastes better," Harold says.

"Hi, Soren." Lāri perks up when she sees me. "How are you feeling?"

"A little dizzy, but I'm better," I say, staring at Nkella whose eyes are still glued to the map. He glances up at me, and I see relief wash over him, but then he's back to studying the map.

Harold fixes himself a plate, and I do the same. It feels good to get some sustenance in my stomach. Lāri pushes a chair over to me, and I take it. Nkella clears his throat and points to an opening with his pinky.

"Iéle returned this morning with bad news."

"It's such a shame," Tessa says. My eyes widen at her.

"Why? What happened?" I ask.

"She was unable to find the *Gambit*," he continues, "and they came back because they were being hunted by oumala animal traffickers."

"Poor girl," AJ says. "Do you think she's traumatized?"

I raise my brows. "Traumatized?"

Nkella nods, and stares down at the map.

AJ takes a sip from his canteen. "Back when we all met, Nkella saved Iéle from an oumala trafficking ring."

Oh. That's why she's so bonded with him.

"But at least she came back," Tessa says, "instead of trying to carry on with the mission and getting herself and the pack caught."

"So, now what?" Harold asks, dipping a slice of bread into his fried egg, and taking a bite.

"We're going to veer to the right, away from the Prefect's Tower. She did find some openings around here that are not on the map," he points, "as I suspected. And she will try again to find the *Gambit*, only with us in close range."

"How long will it take us to get to Swords?" Harold asks.

AJ cups his hands over his mouth and sneezes loudly. "Piupeki!"

"Sorry," Harold corrects. I snort. "Piupeki. Swords is easier to say."

"If we had the *Gambit* and were heading straight to the Prefect's Tower, then two weeks. Especially hidden and going along their coast. But in this ship, with no speed, probably four weeks."

"A month at sea?" I gape.

"I can make it in three."

"Nkella would live at sea if it were up to him." AJ leans over his chair, placing his hand on Nkella's shoulder. Nkella stares at it and AJ removes it, rolling his eyes. "You're in a good mood," he says sarcastically.

"Nkella would rather live on a farm," Kae says with straw in his mouth. "Away from people...out in the middle of the volcanic dunes of Danū."

I flick my eyes to Kae. "There are farms in volcanic dunes?"

He nods, the light shining over his big shiny head. "Special farms that have a fruit called *saechi*." He closes his eyes. "Sour and sweet at the same time."

"Like Nkella," AJ snorts. Tessa laughs.

"Kh." Nkella straightens the map and tilts it a bit at the corner, studying something in particular. "AJ is right. I belong at sea."

"Harold," Tessa backs up. "Shall we start making some more raku bombs?"

"Who's taking over the wheel?"

"I can," AJ says, putting his plate in the sink barrel. "And you can do the dishes and clean the deck," he says to Kae, who grunts.

"I'll help you, Kae." I get up and start collecting dishes when a wave of nausea forces me back down.

"You look kind of pale, Soren. Paler than usual," AJ says. "Maybe you should rest up and conserve your energy until we find you the cure."

"Oh, that's right," Tessa says. "You were forced to use ouma when that eel grabbed you." She turns to Harold. "Do we have any more of the Hermit's potion?"

Harold nods with a grin. "Of course. I grabbed some."

The floor starts to move beneath me. "Sorry, Kae..." I croak. "I'll make it up to you." I sniffles and wipe my nose to see blood coating my fingers. AJ jumps up and hands me a cloth.

Nkella's eyes bore into me, and I can sense the worry flooding into him. Ignoring that, I say, "So the wolves are back, huh?"

"Yes. They will not bother you."

"Great." I stand and make my way into the next room, dropping into my hammock. I don't realize I knocked out until Harold nudges my shoulder.

"How long was I asleep?" I ask, sitting up. My hand touches something soft, and I pick up my green tunic. I trace the threading where it was ripped the night before.

"Not long. Maybe twenty minutes. Here. Drink this."

I take the potion, and hot cacao warms my tongue. I drink it all, hoping it will buy me enough time to find the Death Card. "Thanks."

"No problem." He takes the cup from me. "Looks like Tessa fixed your shirt."

"Yeah, it looks almost new. So have you decided what you're going to do about getting out of here?"

He stares at the empty cup. "The only thing I can do is help take down the Empress."

"Why? This isn't your fight. It's neither of our fight."

"The way I see it, she's blocking any portal out of here, including into Jötunheim. Unless you can open a portal to somewhere other than your home?"

I shake my head. "Sorry. I found out through Madame Asteria—who's the Empress's sister by the way, and my great, great, great....aunt—that the only reason I was able to walk through the mirror was because I have a connection to this land."

"Figures. So, the Empress's sister? Which Fate does that make her?"

"Future."

Surprise washes over his features. "Why doesn't she come back here to stop her sister? Isn't she powerful?"

"When I asked her that, she said if she comes back, her sister will kill her. And because she protects everyone's future, her death would destroy everyone here."

"Bummer."

I snort.

"I'd better get to making bombs with Tessa so I can start cleaning. This place is disgusting, and if I have to sleep another night in this fifth, I'm going to be sick before we get to Swords." I nod at him. "Coming with?"

"In a bit." I watch him leave, then I change into the shirt Nkella had bought me in Wands. The awkward silence between us is maddening. I have to focus on finding the Death Card, getting stronger, and coming up with a plan to steal the Card once we get the *Gambit* and fly to the Tower. But I can't focus with dread twisting the air around us or—worse—with the rikorō still in our systems letting me know his feelings. And I'm sure he feels the same way, which is probably why he's avoiding me.

Not that I think he's focused on avoiding me. I know he's steering the ship, and busy being a captain.

But he's too quiet, and I don't like it.

After freshening up, I make my way to the quarterdeck. My eyes search the ship. He's not at the wheel; AJ is steering. I know he's not in the kitchen—I would have felt his presence. Lāri is sitting in her usual spot high up in the nest, scribbling away on her drawing pad. I walk up the steps and wave to AJ as I make my way to the captain's quarters and knock on the door.

Nkella's voice is deep. "Enter."

I creak the door open, and a growl greets me inside. Iéle's red eyes stare at me as she moves her head up.

"Calm down, Iéle. You know Soren."

Ignoring her, I step inside and shut the door behind me. Nkella is lying on his bed, with one hand over his forehead. I swallow. Maybe I shouldn't have come to find him; he obviously didn't get much sleep last night. He glances at me, but doesn't say anything, expecting me to speak first. I take a seat on the corner of the bed. His hair is mussed, and he wears his black tunic, its collar open in a V.

Iéle slowly lowers her head, but her gaze remains on me.

"Where are the other wolves?"

"They do not always stay. They roam as far as they like, only to come when she calls them."

"Oh." We fall into silence.

"Why have you come, Soren?"

My stomach turns. The way my name just left his tongue makes my stomach sink. What happened to neyuro?

"I wanted to make sure you weren't beating yourself up about what happened."

He sighs sharply. "I almost killed you."

I knew he was feeling guilty about last night. "But you didn't. You saved me in the end, which means you're learning to control your ouma."

"Kh. As long as I'm the Devil, I will never be able to control my ouma."

"But what about what the Hermit said? You did manage to control it, Nkella. You will again."

"Wise tales from a wise man." After a few beats, he shuts his eyes and says, "Next time, there might not be any coming back for me. I felt it taking over."

I swallow and reach for his hand. He retracts from me, and my breath hitches. "Nkella..."

"Go, Soren. It's better if we're apart, daí? No ouma meddling between us. No outside forces."

"I kind of liked it."

"How do we even know what we were feeling was real? With all that rikorō around us?"

My eyes sting at the words. I swallow a dry lump in my throat. "You don't think it was real?"

He stays quiet but avoids my gaze.

I grab his hand. "Look at me, and tell me it wasn't real."

"Stop, neyuro. Daí?" He looks at me. "Ko quela mu. What difference will it make? You will go home, and I will stay here. What is it you want?"

My lips part. Anger fuels the magnetism between us. Angst. Raw emotion. He brings his legs in to sit up on the bed, planting his feet on the floor. He stares down for a beat, then speaks. "They thought you were mine."

The traffickers. *He will come for his aovate.*

"That's why they took you. He thought we were together." He glances at me. "Even if I had no ouma, as long as you are with me, you are in danger. I cannot let that happen. I let this go too far."

"I can take care of myself, just like I always have. Even if you hadn't gotten there in time, I would have found a way out—I always do. It wouldn't have been the first time something like that happened to me. I grew up without parents, remember?"

He stares at me, shock in his eyes.

"But you saved me. You were there, and that's what counts. We're a crew, and we're here for each other," I say, repeating Lāri's words to him.

He shakes his head. "Still. I cannot control my powers. I almost killed you," he growls. "And you are unwell because of the rikorō. My word is final, neyuro. We cannot be together." His voice is cold and devoid of emotion, and it sends an icicle through my heart.

I hold my breath, trying to keep my bottom lip from shaking as I stare at him. I wish back the memories of last night, and how I so want them to mean something. Forget it. "You're right." I stand. "It meant nothing. You mean nothing to me." He blinks at me as I turn and start walking out. Sadness and conflicting emotions brew from the rikorō, and now I just really want to push it back and get away—far away from him.

"Soren..."

"It's fine. We'll just be friends," I say to him, changing my tone to more neutral and trying to hide my anger, although I know he can feel it.

I let the door slam behind me, but he doesn't come after me. AJ calls out for me, but I run down the steps too fast to stop. I don't want to talk to anyone right now.

16

Filled with rage, I go through a closet in the room below the hammock room, trying to find something to do. I grab a broom and start furiously sweeping the floors.

I honestly don't understand what I'm so upset about. He's right, I am planning to leave again after I steal the Death Card and bring back my mom. I'll help them first by bringing back their loved ones, but it's not like I'm bringing my mother back to Ipa to live here with me.

So what was I expecting from this, really?

A relationship? With a pirate captain, an estranged prince, in a foreign dimension? It doesn't make any sense.

Him recoiling from me makes my cheeks burn. I sweep the floor harder, my fingers in pain from gripping the handle so hard.

Someone clears his throat at the entrance, and I glance up to find Kaehante standing there holding a sword. "Do you have any knives that need sharpening?"

I reach for my knife and take it out, handing him the hilt.

He takes it, but then stops and says, "Have you ever sharpened knives before?"

"No."

"Come on. Put the broom down."

I'm about to protest because I just want to be alone but finally drop the broom with a wooden thump on the floor. It might help to sharpen some knives. Why not? I follow Kae up the steps to where the crew is hanging out in the sun. Tessa is cleaning out her chair cannon, and Lāri is still in the crow's nest. Checking my peripherals, I take a look at who's sitting at the wheel up in the quarterdeck. A sigh of relief escapes me when I see it's Harold. Nkella is nowhere in sight, and that's fine by me. I take a seat next to Kaehante, and he hands me a whetstone.

"Hold the knife like this." He grabs my dagger from the hilt, and positions it at a slight angle, so the blade touches the stone. "Move it from the front of the stone to the back, daí?" He starts to slide the knife over the stone, making a steel sound. I take it from him and give it a try. "Try more slanted," he positions my hand a little, and I try again.

When he's satisfied with how I'm doing it, he nods and proceeds to sharpen a sword over his larger stone. AJ comes by with his pack of knives and drops them down beside us.

"Lunch will be ready soon, kay?" He glances at me, concerned wrinkles on his forehead. I smile at him and keep sharpening, slowly, one swipe at a time. This isn't as cool as it sounded like it would be. It's kind of boring, actually; at least, sweeping was more physical. I let out a sigh, and Kaehante glances at me.

"We will find the *Gambit*. In due time," he says.

I bite back a chuckle. He thinks I'm sighing out of impatience. Well, he's not wrong. "Three weeks at sea," I mutter under my breath.

"We will make the time go quick. We can practice fighting."

I glance at him. "Here?"

"Yes. There is space. We will take turns sparring."

I perk up. Learning to fight from Kaehante and AJ would be great. I've seen them both fight, and Kae has the same fighting style as Nkella since they learned together as kids. "I was learning back home before I got back."

"Daí?" He quirks a brow. "And have you learned to fight?"

"I think so. Or, at least, I thought so but I was useless the other day."

"There is no use in thinking that way. You do not have enough experience fighting yet. But more importantly, there were guns and ouma involved. There is only so much I can do, and I am big and have experience, daí? The important thing is knowing when to use what during a battle."

I slow my sharpening as I take in what he said. I guess none of us had a choice that day; we were caught by surprise and given a terrible ultimatum. I don't know what I would have done if Talia had been taken.

The sound of boots comes down the steps, and a butterfly lets loose in my stomach. I plant my gaze down at the stone and continue to sharpen, unsure of when to actually stop sharpening. Nkella approaches and sets down two knives and a sword next to Kaehante. My stomach ties itself into a knot as I get a side view of his face in my peripherals. I hate how he can do that to me.

"Is that all you have, Captain?" Kae asks.

I steal a quick glance up at him, but he's also avoiding my gaze as he nods once to Kae and walks away. I return my gaze back to the whetstone, but I don't miss Kaehante's stare that flickers between Nkella and me. My cheeks redden, and I continue sharpening.

"That one is sharpened now, Soren. Start another." He passes me the knife Nkella dropped off.

"Oh." I stick my dagger back in its sheath on my belt, and pick up one of AJ's, ignoring the one Kae was handing me. Kaehante zeros in on my choice of knife. What? Am I being petty?

Maybe just a little.

After a few moments of silence apart from the sound of knives sliding against stone, Kaehante lets out a sharp sigh. "Whatever is going on between you two, he is still your captain." He glances up at me.

My throat clogs. He had walked in on us at the wheel last night and didn't miss the awkward way we just were.

"Do not let your emotions get in the way of your mission. Whatever happens, he will have your back. And you need to have his, daí?"

My breathing shallows and I try to push back a tear. I clear my throat. "I know. I will. It's just all too fresh right now. I'll be better when the time comes."

"I want to make sure you have the crew's backs, too, and your mind is not elsewhere, daí?"

"Yes. Understood, Kae."

"This is what he is doing. Understand."

I put AJ's finished knife down, and pick up another. Kaehante takes it from me, and hands me one of Nkella's.

"Never forget. While on this ship, he is your captain first." I stare at him. "He is my cousin, daí? But you hear me call him captain in front of others."

I let out a shuddering breath and take Nkella's knife in my hand. I study the sparkly dark blue swirls inside the dark hilt and then start sharpening it.

Kaehante sighs. "My cousin has lost everyone he has ever loved and loved him in return. Except for me. Yet."

"We're not losing you, Kae." I've grown to care and love this crew as a family. I don't like hearing them talk like today is their last, even though we're constantly in danger.

"My point is, he does not know how to be with someone as...aovate, daí? He has never had a chance for one. There have been girls, yes, but never anyone he cares about. If my cousin pushes you away, it is because he cares."

"Or because he thinks it's just the rikorō making him think he cares."

Kaehante guffaws.

"What's so funny?"

"I do not know about rikorō, except what it does to Ipani. But Nkella is a fool if he thinks the rikorō is making him have feelings." He laughs.

"I don't want to talk about this anymore."

"Hn." His shoulders shake with his chuckles. "That one is done. Sharpen another."

In the two following days, we work hard at making the ship squeaky clean. Kaehante even managed to take part of the wooden planks he'd collected for Tessa and cover the biggest gaping hole with it. Nkella and I have yet to speak a word to each other, and my chest is tight from it.

Outside, the night is calm. The crew chats on the main deck, while Kaehante steers. I don't know if Nkella is out there with him—I haven't heard his voice. But I've done a good job at making myself scarce and almost invisible except when there's a task to do. I avoid looking in his direction, although, sometimes, I feel as though he's staring at me. Especially because whenever I think he is, the magnetism between us gets stronger. I know it's just the rikorō causing that effect, though. It's just half of the mer-Ipani's spirit trying to reconnect. It has nothing to do with us.

I lie on my hammock, twirling the wooden teacup between my fingers and trying to pick out a memory of me and my mom, but all I see is him. It's been hard getting anything done without Nkella popping into my head, and now this stupid teacup reminds me of him because he carved it. Because he listened to my story and knew it meant something to me. He carved it to remember me by.

Kaehante has been good about keeping things quiet. And Lāri and AJ don't ask me any questions, but I have been trying to avoid them as much as possible. Whenever there's nothing else to do, they cuddle up next to each other, kissing.

Not that I don't want to see them happy. I'm just not in the mood to be around that right now.

Earlier today, we sparred. I took turns with everyone except Lāri. I'm not used to sparring with guys, as my instructor is a very flexible contortionist. She's limber, and fast, but petite. Lāri is taller and stronger.

I did hit Harold pretty hard on his face, and he has more fighting experience than I do.

He blamed it on being tired, but I think I'm getting faster.

Kaehante says it's good for me to fight men, because that's who I'm predominantly going to be up against, and he's right. And I'm glad for the sparring experience, especially going up against him. He lets me use him as a punching bag to work on my throws and then blocks me to make me quicker. Then we switch so that he's throwing punches and I'm blocking them, all while keeping a low stance.

And the entire time, Nkella is staring hard at me, and I'm not sure what to make of it. Is he judging my stance? Is he remembering when he started teaching me how to "walk quietly" and fight while in Wands? Does he think I'm doing it wrong and Kae is just humoring me? Does he think I'm improving? Or is his mind wandering to the other night?

Then it's our turn to spar with each other, and I don't miss the reluctant pull in his energy and in his eyes.

He's your captain first.

I lower my stance and get in position. His dark eyes stare back at me with intensity, but he doesn't move first. We're at a standstill, and I know he's trying to intimidate me, to make me nervous so I lose my footing.

Or he's afraid to hurt me.

I move swiftly forward, as I'd practiced many times with Sherry, and send a punch to his face, which he casually sidesteps to avoid. I move away in a circular motion, like he had taught me before, and throw another punch. He quickly avoids my throw and swipes at my feet, causing me to land on my rear on the hardwood floor.

My cheeks burn. He extends a hand to help me up, but I don't take it.

"Captain—" AJ starts but Kaehante shushes him. I hear AJ sighing behind his teeth.

I get back in position, burying my embarrassment...and annoyance. I should have expected that, he's done it to me before. He's testing me. Trying to see if I learned what he taught me back in Wands. This time, I act like I'm going to punch his face. He moves away, and I punch at his chest. He swiftly blocks my punch and hooks his leg under my knee trying to bring me down. I twist my wrist, breaking loose from his grasp, and jump back, catching my footing. I'm not letting him trip me up again.

He keeps a straight face, his eyes staring into mine. Why won't he attack first?

I throw another punch, this time, at his face. He blocks me with one arm, which sends me spinning around, and I come out on the other side. I kick toward his chest, and he blocks my leg, throwing off my balance. Once again, I land on my ass.

"Time." Kaehante calls.

I avoid Nkella's hand again—funny he's still trying—and get myself off the floor.

I ignore Kaehante's call for time. This time, I throw four consecutive punches, two toward his face, and two at his chest. He works to block me, but I push him back, and give him another punch in his chest.

"Time!" Kaehante repeats.

He grabs my fist tight and pushes me down. A smirk befalls his face. "Do you feel better now? Kh."

"Good job. You win," I tell him.

"It is not about winning, daí? It is about experience and learning control."

"What do you know about control?" I hold my breath as the last word rolls off my tongue.

Something that looks like hurt flashes across his features, and he straightens his face. "We are done here."

"Great. I'm tired anyway."

I leave the deck, and the crew stares down at the floor as I pass them.

"Why do you have to be such an ass?" I hear AJ saying.

"Kh."

Back to the present, I stick the teacup in my pocket and roll over in the hammock.

Lāri taps at the wooden frame, and I glance up at her. "We are going to drink a little and let loose. Are you coming?"

I quirk a brow. "Oh? What club you guys going to?"

She screws up her face. "A club? Like for fighting? What do you—"

"Never mind. Stupid joke."

"Come on, it will be good for you to get some fresh air. Better than sitting here alone in the dark."

And looking pathetic. Fine. I get up from the hammock and follow her outside. The stars are shining brightly, but the air is cooler. It's becoming more evident that we're headed north toward some snowy mountains.

Tessa is laughing so hard her cheeks are turning pink, and AJ is cracking up into his hand.

"What?" Harold has an amused look on his face and both shoulders shrug.

"You've changed her name like twelve times now," AJ says.

"I'm particular about names. And I needed something to call her by. You guys don't even know what you're laughing about. You're laughing because I keep changing her name, but if you knew where the name came from, you'd be laughing harder. Just ask Soren.

I take a seat between AJ and Harold, "Who are we talking about?"

"The chicken."

I gape at him. "You named the chicken?"

AJ bursts out laughing. "See? We don't name our food."

"Hey, she's providing us breakfast—she's family now."

"And no one is eating her," Lāri agrees.

Kaehante huffs. "If we get hungry, she will be the first one eaten." Lāri smacks his shoulder and he scoffs.

"So, what's her name?" I ask.

"Harley Quinn." He smiles at me.

I snort, and then burst into laughter. "Harold, no. You can't name her Harley Quinn."

"Why not? I named my yeti friend, Alfred."

"You must really like Batman, huh? What about Robin?"

He gapes at me. "How is calling a bird the name of another bird any better?" He stares into space, and I think he's about to have an aneurism.

AJ and Tessa start cracking up again, even though they have no idea what we're really talking about. Lāri shakes her head. It's nice to be in the crew's company when we're all having a laugh and not in imminent danger. At least, not for now.

Kae pours something into a cup and hands it to me.

The aroma of sweet citrus wafts under my nose, and I lift it to my tongue to taste. "What is this?"

"I made it," AJ says, leaning into me. "I fermented some oranges with sugar and left them in a cabinet when we first set sail."

"Alcohol ferments faster here," Harold adds. "Still doubt it's strong though."

"Tastes sweet. Thank you."

I take another sip of the orange concoction when the magnetism of the rikorō comes near. Nkella takes a seat next to Tessa with his back against the wall. Even with a few people between us, I can feel the magnetism, but it's not as strong. Maybe it's finally losing its effects.

The ship hits the waves a little hard but goes back to being calm. " Are the seas this far north always so calm?" I ask.

"Only after a storm," AJ responds. "If they start getting choppy again, then we have to worry."

"It is getting colder, though," Tessa says. Kaehante reaches for AJ's bottle and offers it to Nkella, but he shakes his head and averts his eyes.

A swirl of emotions festers from his direction, but I can't look. This is becoming no different that the intense silence he used to bring into a room anyway. So I take a longer chug from my drink.

AJ and Lāri whisper something to each other, and Tessa stares at me. I avert my gaze back to my cup, my cheeks heating. Apparently, everyone is talking about us.

"We need to discuss what we do with the *Gambit* once we arrive," Nkella says. "We cannot go there without a plan to get to Tower, daí? Do we have any solerig? We need to have potions for invisibility and floatation and be ready to leave as soon as we find my *Gambit*."

"Our *Gambit*, right Captain?" AJ asks.

Nkella flicks his eyes to him and takes a swig of his drink. "Keep messing around. That is how we were attacked last time."

AJ gapes at him, and Lāri buries her head in her face, peeking one eye at me and shaking her head. I lend her a half smile.

"Tell me you're joking," AJ lowers his cup, nearly spilling its contents. "We were sitting ducks. We weren't messing around."

"Be ready. That's all I am saying."

"We're always ready, Captain," Lāri says, patting AJ on the shoulder.

AJ grits his teeth and sighs. "We need ingredients to make what the *Gambit* needs. It won't hurt to stop by a village, blend in a little, and get those supplies." I flick my eyes between the two of them.

"Kh. How? Those supplies are even more illegal in Piupeki than before."

"I'm sure we can forage for some ingredients," Harold says. "A lot of what we need grows in those mountains."

"That will take ages," AJ whines.

Nkella flicks his eyes at him and scoffs. "We will be discreet and quick. We will need to make camp—"

"Must we talk about this now?" Tessa interrupts, staring at her drink.

"Yeah, we were having a good time," AJ says. "We can have this meeting tomorrow."

"I kind of agree with Nkella," I say above a whisper. AJ darts a look in my direction, and I shrug. I can feel Nkella's hard stare from my left. "We need to know what we're doing and what we're up against as much as where we're headed." Kaehante nods in agreement, and I keep going. "If we don't do it now, what happens if the sea serpent comes up and causes trouble?"

AJ sighs and nods.

"Or if we're attacked out of nowhere, or the mer-Ipani decide to strike because they know Nkella and I drank rikorō from one of their family members. I'm just saying, anything can happen, and I don't want to lose track of the mission. I want to steal that Death Card to bring my mom back, but also to help all of you. Bring back Kae's wife and Nkella's sister. If something happens where we get separated, it'll be easier if we have a clear idea of what the plan is."

"Fine. You're right. Let's talk it through now." AJ lowers his legs in defeat and shoots back his drink.

Harold leans his head back against the ship's wall, giving Nkella a clear view of my profile. I glance at him to see that his face has softened and his lips are parted. He closes his mouth and gives me a nod. My lips curl into a half smile, and I drop my eyes back to my cup, glimpsing at the tip of my new mark. The Fool's O. I trace it with my finger.

"Right then," Tessa says, perking up. "I'll start the list. Magic ingredients for the ship. We are going to need to go to the village for coats, because none of us are prepared."

"How cold is it there now?" Harold asks.

AJ lets out a high-pitched laugh. "Freezing. Piupeki is always covered with snow ouma."

Harold's eyes shoot up. "Snow *ouma*? That's why trees and plants grow as well?"

Everyone grows silent. He looks at me, "I mean if it were just snowing year-round, wouldn't it be a wasteland? But since it's ouma, I'm guessing the plants thrive in that environment... It probably fuels the ouma they grow with!"

I can't help but chuckle at Harold's enthusiasm about nerdy information.

"Why is Swords so special?" I ask. "I mean, besides the Ace of Swords, why are the traffickers focused on it?"

"It's where the rikorō plant grows," Harold says. My eyes widen. Oh.

"No ouma, daí?" Nkella looks to all of us. "They will kill you on sight if they see it used. There are no more binding Ipani, so do not give them a reason to send you to the Deep. In any case, they should be busy searching for traffickers."

"And we're not traffickers," AJ says, "so what are we telling them?"

"Let them search you. Let them search the ship. We have nothing to hide. No one gets out, and so far they say, no one gets in. Like on Danū. But maybe I can persuade them, daí?"

"How do you plan on doing that?" I ask him.

He grins, showing me his pointy canine. "I can be persuasive."

My cheeks heat.

"I will tell them we are there to join their cause. We go undercover."

"And if they don't believe us?" AJ asks.

"We fight," Kae says.

"Koj. We cannot take them. Let me do the talking, daí?"

"Er," Harold perks up. "Are they going to search our marks? I don't have a great track record with the Swords Prefect."

Nkella's eyes widen, and I realize none of us thought about the illegal Magician mark. "Let us hope they don't. If they do, we still carry on with the mission."

AJ winces. "Sorry, Harold."

He raises a hand. "Nope, that's fine. Keep going. I'll deal with Alec."

"That's the Prefect's name?" I ask. He nods.

They discuss how they'd break Harold out of the Prefect's Tower if he gets taken in, or if we should until I steal the Death Card when Nkella stands from his spot. He walks toward the quarterdeck momentarily stopping in front of me. AJ glances up at him, but he stares at me.

"Can you come with me?"

I blink. Okay... I stand and follow him up the steps, holding my breath when he reaches the door of his room and opens it.

He shuts the door behind us and turns to look at me. "Soren," his voice is deep, full of regret. I swallow against the thickness of my throat, and stare at him, twisting the corner of my shirt in my fingers. "I—" He sighs.

I bite my bottom lip.

"You don't have to say anything," I start. "I was being a jerk earlier. You were right, we're better off as friends."

Shock creases his features.

"I am going back after this. I can't stay in Ipa—there's nothing for me here." I chuckle nervously. "I mean, I need to get my life together back home and find what I want to do in life, without worrying about foster parents. My sister is being adopted, and I need to make sure she's okay in her situation, and have a solid situation myself in case she needs a place to crash—which is very likely to happen."

He quirks a brow but keeps silent as I wrap my arms around myself and flick my eyes to the floor.

"You were probably right about the effects of the rikorō, and they seem to be wearing off so..." I glance up to see something like disappointment wash over his face, but then it's gone.

He parts his lips to say something, but then closes them, giving a nod in agreement.

Iéle's tail wags from the corner of the bed, and I swear that wolf can understand more than she lets on.

Good. Now we can go back to being captain and crewmate, and I can move on with my life. Just thinking it tastes like a lie, but it's what has to be. Silence descends on the room. The way he's looking at me conjures up images of the other night, and I eye the door, preparing to leave.

The high-pitched whistle of the Arcana spins me around. Worry pulses behind my eyes.

He shifts his gaze toward the door, opening it just as AJ runs up the steps.

"What's happening?" Nkella demands.

"The Arcana are here." AJ's voice is out of breath as he leans over the railing. Pivoting back around, he grabs the gun from his holster.

17

THE BLOOD DRAINS FROM MY FACE. "MY VISION."

Nkella cuts his gaze to me. "They are after this ship." He pulls his gun from behind his coat and flicks his eyes to Iéle who is already charging out the door.

"That means they aren't after us," I say. He stares at me. "They're looking for whoever killed the Danū Prefect. Is the Empress still after you?"

"Always. If they find us here, they will take us to her." He opens the door and calls out for AJ. "Do not shoot. Tell the others not to shoot. Hide below deck."

They will take us. The last time the Arcana grabbed me, they delivered me to the Empress herself. Even if she were to put me in her Tower dungeons, I'd be closer to the Death Card. I'd be in.

I'd have to escape her prison to find it, but it wouldn't be the first time I've escaped from behind bars. An Arcana soldier lands on the quarterdeck, the soulless dark eyes of his mask moving slowly across the floor. The clasp of his robe is of a shield, wrapped over his left shoulder, the emblem is of the Tower. Perfect.

I reach for the door, but Nkella shuts it.

I stare at him. "What are you doing?"

"Neyuro. You are thinking about getting captured."

I gasp. "You can still hear my thoughts?"

His mouth parts. "I do not have to hear your thoughts to anticipate your actions."

"Well, I'm not thinking about getting captured."

He grimaces and his voice darkens. "You are lying to me."

I drop my shoulders. "We need to go out there. The crew needs us." He won't be able to stop them from taking me the moment they grab me.

His eyes flare. "Soren."

I gape at him. "I thought the rikorō was wearing off."

"It is. But right now, I can feel your thoughts like the beating of my own heart."

I grimace and reach for the door, but he blocks me.

I grit my teeth. "I'm doing this." I step to the side and grab for the handle, but he spins me around and picks me up. A yell escapes my throat. "What are you doing?"

"Keeping you safe."

"No! I can do this."

"You're going to get yourself killed." He drops me on his bed, and I sit up straight away.

"You can't keep me locked up. There's no brig here."

He yanks rope from beneath his bed, and my eyes widen. I push myself off the bed, eliciting an angry flicker in his eyes. He pushes me back down hard. In one fluid motion, he drags my arms to the bedpost and starts tying a knot.

"Ow. You're hurting me," I tug my wrist but he finishes too quick. I kick at him, but he moves back as he growls. "Be still."

"I'll scream," I say.

"Please don't make me do this."

My eyes widen. "Make you do what?"

He sighs behind gritted teeth and tears off a piece of the black shirt on his table. Following his actions, I move my face away.

"No...Nk—"

He fastens it around my mouth, gagging me to keep me from screaming. Tears sting the corners of my eyes, and I stare at him with disdain and kick at him.

"This is for your own good."

I stare at him wide-eyed as he walks away. He gives me one last glance before leaving the room and locking it. Stars of fury blast behind my eyes as what he did hits me like a pile of bricks. I tug at my wrist, but his knot is too tight. From the window, I can see the Arcana moving slowly around the ship. The candlelight flickers.

Whispering from the crew comes from outside.

I slow my breathing to try to hear what they're saying. It's eerily quiet. What is the crew doing? What's their plan?

I turn to face the window and pull back. A white mask presses against the glass, its pearly white glare a contrast to the endless darkness coming from where his eyes should be. I suck in a breath and hold it.

It stands there, staring in then fixes its gaze on me. Shadows writhe to life as smoke-like tendrils ooze up against the window-frame.

I may want to be taken, but not like this. Not tied up and gagged.

I duck low, managing to wiggle off the bed except for my arms still held by the rope. My breath is hot and wet against the fabric. Good job, Nkella. Yeah, this is working to keep me perfectly safe. I let out my breath slowly, so not to make a sound. My eyes land on my dagger inside its sheath. If I can only reach it and cut the rope off...

The masked soldier floats away from the mirror. I can't believe Nkella left me here to go hide below deck with the crew.

The door flings open. I yelp.

Nkella barges in with AJ and Lāri, and they shut the door quietly.

"Quiet, neyuro," he whispers. AJ's eyes bulge when he sees me.

"What the hell, Nkella?"

Nkella bends down and unties me with one pull of his hand. I rotate my wrists and scowl at him. "I could not risk you doing something bancha," he says, taking off my gag.

"You're an asshole," I push him away from me and stand up. "It was a good plan."

"What was a good plan?" Lāri asks.

"She was going to let herself get captured to reach the Empress."

"That was a terrible plan, Soren," AJ says.

"It would have gotten me into the Tower."

Nkella whips around to face me. "Alone. And how would we have saved you, daí? With less time to find the *Gambit*."

I narrow my eyes at him. "Why do you care?"

His face goes rigid as he stares at me, but he stays quiet.

"Soren," Lāri breaks the awkward silence. "We can't be sure we'll find the *Gambit*. Losing you would have put everything at risk."

My heart thunders in my chest. "Fine. It would have been impulsive."

"Bancha," Nkella says.

I shoot him an angry stare.

"Alright." AJ whispers loudly. "We're wasting time. The Arcana are still out there. What now?"

"We can't fight them—there are too many of them," Lāri says.

"We wait for them to collect the information they want." Nkella lowers his head to gaze out the window. "They are not after us."

I rub my wrists from the rope burn. "The men I saw in my vision said they needed to get rid of the ship. Maybe they'll be able to read the information from the ship with their psychic powers?"

"But what if they take the ship?" AJ asks.

Nkella shakes his head. "And what good would it be to provoke them, daí?"

"They must know we're here, though," I say. "They're psychic."

"They know the ship isn't empty, that's why they're roaming around," Lāri adds. "But they won't know who is here... I don't think."

"They would have found me or Soren by now if they did," Nkella says.

"They don't seem to have a big range," AJ adds, "unless they're directly in front of you or given information for what to look for."

A shadow falls through the billowing curtain as a masked soldier slowly floats before the window. Lāri holds a finger to her lips and looks at us. I swallow. AJ points at the flickering candle, and I quickly blow it out, snuffing out the only light.

Darkness looms over us as silence thickens. We stand there, afraid to move. The soldier doesn't move from his spot for what seems like an eternity.

Then it creeps toward the door, and this time, both AJ and Nkella move their hands to hover over their guns.

A minute passes, and the soldier moves away.

We let out our breaths, and AJ wipes his face.

"Do you think they've already been below deck?"

AJ shrugs in the dark, the moonlight hitting his back from the windowsill. "They were hiding in the kitchen last."

A few beats pass and Nkella checks the window. "I think they've gone."

"How can we be sure?" I whisper.

He nudges the door open, and AJ, Lāri, and I follow close behind. Cold sea breeze smacks my face as we step onto the quarterdeck, looking all around us. We quietly descend the steps, and Nkella walks through the main deck, and onto the bow, while the rest of us walk down the hall toward the kitchen.

"They are gone," Nkella says from behind me. AJ opens the kitchen door and lets the others know.

AJ rubs his chest as he flops down on his hammock.

"Don't get too comfortable," Nkella says to him. "They may come back."

"They must have gotten what they came for," Tessa says.

Stepping out onto the plank, I stare out at the calm sea. There's a stillness in the air that wasn't there before. What happened to the wind? It's too quiet. Like the quiet before the storm. "Something still doesn't feel right."

Harold walks past me and stops at the top, staring out.

"What makes you say that, Soren?" Tessa drives her chair over to the side by her hammock and starts searching for something in her chest drawer.

"I don't know. I'm just getting a strange feeling." I glance at my mark. A soft sheen has covered it. That's weird.

Kaehante flips his gun to point past me, and Nkella quickly puts his hand over Kae's arm. My eyes widen, and I spin around. A masked soldier is looming behind Harold who's now walking back down the board.

I hold my breath and point behind him. Harold's eyes widen as he slowly turns. Just run over here, you idiot.

The masked soldier grabs him, and Kaehante shoots. AJ spins off his hammock and lands with a thump as he scurries for his gun. I run to Harold and grab his hand pulling him away.

"Soren, move!" Nkella's voice booms as I yank Harold's hand. The soldier lets go as AJ shoots the mask. The soldier disappears.

Tessa drives past us, now holding her handgun, and yells for us to run.

"She's right." Kae runs after her. "If they blow up the ship, we don't want to be on the bottom."

Out on the deck, hordes of Arcana soldiers are shooting down from the sky and landing all over. We move to the center of the main deck, our backs against each other as we stare at the dozens of soldiers floating over the sea.

Everyone with a gun points it at them.

But we're trapped like rats in a sinking ship.

One of the soldiers glides forward, and a blast of power shoots at us, sending a tidal wave over the boat. Shots are fired, but I lose sight of what's happening as the ship is blasted from all sides. Large waves crash over us. I hit the wood hard and slide against the side panel. A strangled scream sticks in my throat, and I gasp for air as another wave submerges me fully.

My fin reappears, and with the water coming in and out, I can't walk or swim.

"Jump ship!" I hear Nkella shout between crashing waves.

Another blast hits us, and the entire side of the ship rises at an alarming height. My nails scratch at the wood as I slide down hard to one side. My scream is muffled by water.

My heart pounds. I know we must have lost the crew again to sea and bones.

The ship lands with a deafening thud, and the air gets crushed out of me. A hand reaches for me, and I grab it. I feel the Devil's bumps on his knuckles, and I hold on tight as he pulls me close to him.

Another blast hits us; he wraps his arms around me, and I close my eyes, burying my head into his chest as shrapnel flies over us.

Nkella lifts his head. Wind picks up around us, and we move back with a push of his power. Then another blast hits us, and we're plummeting with a deafening—no time to catch our bearings—crash as we get separated and land with our backs somewhere on the ship.

The pole of the top sail comes crashing down, and I scream. Something that looks like a giant arm—or no, sand?—grabs it and tosses it aside. My heart pulses in my chest as I try to make sense of what I just saw. Wet, wooden splinters are driven into my arms and legs as I struggle to get up, my eyes frantically searching for Nkella or the crew.

It quiets, and the ship sways from left to right, but the temperature drops. An Arcana soldier emerges in front of me, and I back up. It wraps an icy arm around me, and my surroundings spin around fast as it carries me away.

18

I'm dropped on a black wooden floor, and I gasp as I'm released by the Arcana soldier who took me. Springing to my feet, I look around me. The crew is on the floor, getting their bearings. I let out a breath of relief.

"What happened?" I ask, my gaze stopping at Harold huddled on the floor beside me with his chicken cage between his legs.

Kae points a finger to the *Ugly Kraken*, our ship, now sliced into two large pieces from being slammed so many times. The Arcana are still surrounding it, looking for us.

"Welcome aboard the *Ghost of the Sea*." A woman's voice comes from behind me, and I turn around. She's wearing a black and red embroidered long-sleeve coat, wrapped in a corset at her chest that flows down over dark brown pants. She's standing in front of the wheel as she steers. Beside her, a slim man with his hair in a long braid, and two sand-whips coming from both his arms smile at us.

Sandwhips? A memory I witnessed of Nkella's childhood comes to mind. Was he the same little boy who used to bully Nkella as a child?

To the woman's other side, a man with a clipper cut hairstyle walks out from behind her, and I gasp. Demitri.

"My, how far you've fallen. That your ship?"

Nkella springs forward. "You."

Demitri skims the waters around us. "Yes, me. That's quite the mess you've made. Good thing I've come. Don't worry about them," he says, motioning toward the psychic Arcana. "This ship is invisible."

Lāri's face goes rigid, and AJ places a hand over her shoulder.

Tessa points her chair canon at Demitri who twists toward her.

"Is that a way to treat the person who just saved you?"

"Why did you save us, daî?" Nkella demands.

"Would you rather us put you back?" There's a tinge of amusement in his tone as he stares at Nkella.

"State your purpose."

"Relax. We've come to make a truce and offer you safe haven."

My crew scowls.

"Kh. Why?" The way he has one hand on his gun but is keeping an eye on the crew standing behind Demitri, tells me he's measuring the ship. Can we take them all? Probably not.

Harold inches toward me. "That's Bronte," he whispers.

"Who?"

"Kenjō's mother. The one who held me in her ship before I was taken to Dempu."

Lāri laughs. "We would never go with you."

"You must be Lāri," Demitri says. "My men picked you up, and I didn't know you were part of the Devil's undead crew. You have my sincerest apologies, and if you come with us, you will never be subject to kidnapping again. This I promise you."

"It never would've happened in the first place if you weren't a scumbag," AJ yells, with his hand on Lāri's shoulder. "We're getting off this ship, my love. Don't worry."

"Not to mention your ex is here." She grimaces. My eyes widen.

Demitri holds up a hand. "Please, I have many apologies I am ready to make, but I believe we have a common enemy. We all want the same thing, which is to take the Empress down," his eyes find me, and he smiles. "I heard you were back. Couldn't stay away?"

"What can I say? Home is where my crew is." I can see AJ smiling in my peripherals. Nkella scoffs. They know I'm joking.

"I feel we got off on the wrong foot," Demitri continues. "I hope you'll consider my terms."

"Terms?"

Nkella glances at me, my brows furrow, and I shake my head. He stares at Demitri and Sandwhip. "Where is my *Gambit*, daí? We know it was you who stole it."

"Your *Gambit* is docked near the Ace of Swords Temple in Naó. I have it well hidden and guarded."

"Why is it there?"

"It's waiting until I need it. But if we help each other, you can have it back."

"Why do you need our help?" I ask. "You seem to be accumulating an army on your own." I glance at the chrome-faced soldier who brought us aboard his ship. His hollow eyes stare aimlessly, waiting for instruction.

"And yet, you are the key, my dear."

I blink at him.

"I will be transparent with all of you. As soon as I heard from two mer-Ipani searching the waters that the Prince of Danū and the red-headed girl were roaming around, I knew we could help each other."

"I don't see how I can help you," I cross my arms.

"Leave that to me. You want the *Gambit*. I want use of the Sword."

"I want the Death Card," I correct.

His brows raise. Nkella shoots me a scowl, but my gaze doesn't leave Demitri.

"I was her advisor." Demitri walks casually toward me. I steel my spine and lift my chin. "I know where she keeps every card, and I know the extent of her power. I can help you get stronger. I can *train* you. You won't get stronger with *them*," he says, eyeing the crew. "Let me train you, Soren. I was there when the Empress lost control of her magic years and years ago. It's how I became the Hierophant."

I stay quiet, considering his words. I don't like him, and I don't trust him. But if what he's saying is true... The Death Card is what I'm here for. If he can help me get it quicker, then that's all I need.

"Besides," he says, looking back at the *Ugly Kraken*. "You're stranded at sea if you leave our ship. Still, the choice is yours."

The crew quiets. Our temporary ship is now sinking, not that it was salvageable after being split in two.

"He's right," Tessa says. "We're stranded."

"Are you kidding me?" Lāri says. "Do you think I am going to sleep in the same quarters as AJ's ex-boyfriend?" She waves her hand at Sandwhip.

"Sandwhip guy is your ex?" I ask AJ.

"His name is Mūhī, and regrettably, yes. Even so"—he grabs Lāri's hand—"you have nothing to worry about. No one hates him more than I do."

I glance at Mūhī as he turns and leaves with a grimace.

"I have plenty of room for all of you, so I'll even sweeten the deal," Demitri says. "Your crew gets their own wing. It'll be easy sailing into Swords, as the Prefect is with us and is a friend."

"Hn? The Prefect is on board with your methods?" Nkella asks.

"I always thought the Swords Prefect was entirely with the Empress," Tessa says. Harold mutters a yep under his breath.

Demitri shakes his head. "Not entirely, but he's coming around. Unfortunately, he cannot hold down the Empress's commands in Swords, and we can't afford for the entire island to act with treason, like Danū. It's bad enough with the Arcana killing any Ipani who use ouma, but he is working to keep the peace. He doesn't want to see his friends get killed any more than any of us."

The crew and I exchange stares.

"So, what do you say? Climb aboard the *Ghost of the Sea*. We can let bygones be bygones, and after we both have what we want, we can go back to hating each other."

Nkella looks over his shoulders at each of us.

"Should we vote on it?" Tessa asks.

"You are really considering joining forces with him?" Nkella asks.

Lāri shrugs. "I probably hate it more than you do, mei? But he is right about one thing. Our little boat is done for. We will be stranded after he leaves. Trust me, I do not want to be anywhere near the head of my captor or AJ's ex-boyfriend. If this is the only way, then I will do my best to make myself scarce while on the ship."

Nkella sighs. "All in favor of joining Demitri?"

Each of us slowly raises a hand, except for Nkella and Harold.

He looks around at us and stops at me with my hand halfway up. I give him an apologetic look. What choice do we have right now? And I want to know how he can help me get the Death Card.

Nkella shakes his head. "Kh. We will join you as far as Swords. Then we part ways."

"Excellent." He turns to a crewmate standing nearby and tells them to get our rooms ready.

Bronte's boots thud on the wooden floorboards as she makes her way down from the quarterdeck. "Take off your weapons."

Nkella steps before her. "I give orders to my crew, and they will not take off anything."

"I am the only captain of this ship, and you will follow my command."

Demitri holds his palm toward her. "Easy now." He looks at Nkella. "Let's get along. Nkella, Captain Bronte here just doesn't want any fights among crew members of her ship. You understand, don't you?" He turns to Bronte. "He's not going to stop being their captain, and we need them, remember?"

Bronte narrows her eyes at Nkella and then looks at each of us. I steel my spine as she passes a glance over me and then pauses when she lands on Harold. She raises her chin and gives him a toothy grin. Harold keeps a straight face.

"Despite Demitri needing you on board, I have no use for disobedience on my ship, especially from boys with unstable curses." Bronte stands a foot away from Nkella. "Any trouble and I'll cut my losses one at a time, è?" Nkella stares at her head on but doesn't say anything. I swallow.

Finally, he cracks a smile. "There will be no trouble. But my crew sticks with me."

"Just make sure you all abide by my rules," she says. They stare at each other for another moment until a girl's voice comes from the wheel.

"Harold?" A gorgeous girl with long black wavy hair, light Ipani stripes, and round brown eyes stares at Harold.

Harold nearly drops the chicken. "Kenjō." He walks toward her, and Kenjō jumps down, practically flying into his arms. This time he sets Quinn on the floor and holds her tight.

After a few moments of all of us watching them embrace, Bronte clears her throat and they let go. "Why don't you show your new crewmates to their sleeping quarters in the west wing?"

"Yes, *Ama*." Her cheeks turn a deep red.

The pathway she leads us to doesn't go straight down like the other ships I've been on. It leads toward the stern, with several areas to take a board path down to lower levels.

Copper furnishings decorate the inside of the ship, from copper lanterns to matching copper tubing reaching from one end to the other. We pass a communal area with black couches and a black table with a black-framed mirror.

"This will be your area," she says then points to a door behind her. "Through there are your beds. But the kitchen is upstairs, è?" She smiles at Harold and reaches to take his chicken. He moves the cage back, causing Quinn to cluck.

"Where are you taking her?" he asks.

Kenjō furrows her brows. "To the kitchen. Where else?"

"I don't trust others with Quinn. They might eat her."

She rolls her eyes. "You and your strange names."

"*Strange?* What was wrong with Alfred?"

Kenjō shakes her head, and her eyes display a yellow sheen, almost cat-like. Harold's jaw drops.

"Kenjō..."

Her face straightens. "È? What is it?"

"Your eyes. The last time I saw you, I-I sacrificed my power to bring you back, after I..."

"My ouma came back," she says weakly.

Disbelief washes over Harold's face. "Oh. I'm happy for you," he says without smiling.

"And you? What about your ouma?"

I smile to myself as she referenced Harold's magic as ouma.

Harold shakes his head. Realization dawns on Kenjō's features.

"Oh, Harold. I am so sorry. That was my fault..." Her breath hitches, but Harold just brings her into his chest and wraps his arms around her again. I know what they're going to be doing tonight.

"This is all very touching," AJ interrupts, "but we're on an enemy ship now. To stay." He clears his throat awkwardly. His eyes are wide open but pointed to the floor, his hand scratching the back of his head. "And can somebody explain to me how this ship is invisible? I thought the *Gambit* was the only one with those alterations."

Tessa drives up, her eyes glued to the copper tubings lining the walls. "Looks to me like they've made some alterations of their own."

"Yes," Kenjō says. "Demitri took the plans from the *Gambit* and had these created."

"Can it fly?" I ask.

Nkella, who's been quietly observing Kenjō and his surroundings, flicks his gaze to me.

"Sadly, no." Her eyes skim my shirt. "They managed to only make the ship do one thing at a time. With a ship this size, it would require too much of one *taevenye*, and it would run out quickly. Invisibility is slow acting, so we are safe with that for now." She stares at AJ. "We are not your enemy."

"For now," he coughs out.

She frowns. "I'll leave you to get ready for dinner, è? Demitri wants everyone at the mess hall in one hour." She turns to me. "I have a coat you can wear. It will be cold where we are going."

"Oh, you don't have to do that—"

"You are friends with Harold, è? I have plenty of clothes." She turns to face Lāri. "I can lend you one of my mother's, since you are taller."

"That won't be necessary," Lāri says as she bumps her shoulder, making her way to the room with the beds in it.

Our new quarters are larger and by far more comfortable than in the *Ugly Kraken*. We don't have private rooms like on the *Gambit*, but at least, we have beds instead of hammocks. Nkella picks a bed in the far corner, next to Kae, and far away from me.

I glance over my shoulder at him, but he's looking down, cleaning his gun. The last thing I said to him before we were attacked was that he was right about us being better off as friends and that we were just feeling the effects of the rikorō the night we kissed.

It's not like he tried to argue it.

The rikorō's magnetism should finally be wearing off. I can't say I don't feel relieved, but... I don't know. I guess I'll miss feeling as if we have some sort of connection.

"Big ship, huh?" Harold's voice breaks my concentration.

"Where have you been?"

"Talking with Kenjō."

I raise my brows, and he rolls his eyes, hiding a smirk.

"At least you found her, right? And she's safe."

"As safe as she can be, I guess." He lowers his tone. "I don't like her mom or the fact she trusts Demitri so much."

"Yeah, what's up with that?"

He shakes his head. "Anything to take down the Empress, I guess."

Lāri lies on the bed next to mine with her arms wrapped over her face. We kept the same layout as on the *Ugly Kraken*. I arch my head to look at her, but she refuses to move. I can tell she's pissed off. I would be, too, if I had to be here with my boyfriend's ex and the people responsible for kidnapping me. She raises her arm when she sees us staring at her.

"Mei?"

"You okay?" Harold asks.

"Hn." She shuts her eyes again. "Wake me up when we're in Piupeki."

AJ walks into the room and pauses at the end of Lāri's bed, concern on his face. He glances at us, and I give him a tight smile and a shrug.

"There are chrome masks standing at the ends of the ship," he mutters, distaste in his voice.

"The Arcana?"

"Mm-hmm." He nods. "Part of Demitri's guards."

"Any idea how he was able to infiltrate them?" I ask.

"I think it has to do with being a Hierophant," Harold answers.

"Even after he betrayed the Empress?"

He gives a modest shrug. "That doesn't mean the Aō will give him a new mark."

"Oh, that's true." She doesn't control the marks. The Aō does.

Harold takes a seat on the corner of my bed. "Kenjō told me she has a new Hierophant already, and they've been keeping her busy."

"Wow, the Aō doesn't waste time," I say.

"Weird." Harold furrows his brows. "Wonder how that happened."

"What do you mean?"

"Well, the Hierophant gets their mark by being able to hold great influence over people, even if they don't believe what they're preaching. Who else besides Demitri would be that gross and nefarious?"

"Maybe this one's different?" AJ suggests. "Maybe they'll use their mark for good."

Harold chuckles. "Right. Either way, I wonder how she found them. Did they just walk up to her and be like, 'Hey, Empress, guess what mark I have.'"

I laugh.

"Maybe she appointed one." AJ raises his brows. "Can she train someone to act a certain way so the Aō gives them the mark?"

Harold rubs his chin. "They'd have to truly believe it."

"Kh." Nkella puts his gun down on his bedside table and walks out the door. He doesn't even look my way as he leaves. My stomach ties itself into a knot, but I push it down.

AJ, Harold, and I exchange glances.

"Where's he going with that attitude?" AJ asks.

I shrug one shoulder and look to the side. "Where's the rest of the crew?" I ask.

"Kae and Tessa are in the 'community room,'" AJ says with air quotes. "This place is too fancy—makes me sick."

I chuckle.

Kenjō's voice comes from the other room telling Kae and Tessa that dinner is going to be served. She walks in, and Harold stands. I stifle a snort. She eyes him and then smirks. "Did you hear what I told them?"

"To go up for dinner?" Harold asks.

"Yes, come. I'll show you the way."

AJ does a fake, sloppy salute in her general direction. "Wouldn't want to get lost."

The mess hall is large and full of pirates. Lanterns flicker on either side of the long room, between arched windows facing the sea. Three-piece candles are lit along the long table in the center, creating elongated dancing shadows along the walls.

Nkella leads us in, followed by Tessa, then the rest of us. We spot an empty space at a circular table by the entrance, away from the main table, and go to it, when Demitri's voice booms through the room.

"Devil's crew, that won't do. I've saved all of you seats up here with us."

Nkella grimaces and looks at us. AJ shrugs and grabs Lāri's hands.

"Better do what he says or jump ship, Captain," AJ says.

Nkella faces him and growls. "You are the one who voted to be here, daí?"

"Not like we had a choice." AJ and Lāri let the rest of us walk ahead of them.

A flicker of agitation comes at me with rikorō magnetism, and I perk up. It's not wearing out? Or he's been doing a good job keeping it from me.

Harold takes a seat next to Kenjō, whose mom is scowling on her other side. Demitri sits at the far end table next to Bronte, holding a seat for Nkella. The rest of us scatter around them. I take my seat next to Kae and Tessa. Lāri and AJ try to be the farthest away from Demitri.

Mūhī sits down in front of Nkella, between Demitri and Bronte, causing Bronte and the rest to scoot over. He grins at Nkella.

"Long time, old friend."

"We are not friends, daí?"

"Come on, you still hate me? We were children."

Nkella guffaws. "You think I care about when we were young? You traffic Ipani." Nkella is leaning into the table, hissing with each word. "You are the worst kind of Ipani."

Mūhī straightens his features. "What I do is for our kind."

"Weak words from a weak man."

Mūhī bangs his fist on the table, and I jump. The chatter throughout the room stops and people look our way. "You think you are better? You deserted our island. Your people are starving."

"I had to leave to save my sister." Nkella growls as he leans in.

"And she is worth more than our entire island? They looked to you. You gave them hope."

"Saving Ntaoru is for Danū. She is to be queen. Going to Piupeki to find the *Gambit*—my *Gambit* that you stole will help us get the Death Card. And the rikorō cure."

Mūhī grips his nails on the wooden table. "You keep chasing cards and dreams, daí? The only way to conquer Ipa and Danū is with power. At least, I understand that the road to power has casualties."

"At what cost? The cost of your people," Nkella hisses.

"They look up to you." He bangs another fist. "Not me. If I were the prince, I never would have left them to starve." Mūhī is shaking, and Nkella's eyes give off a glow, but he stays silent. I don't need the rikorō to tell me he's struggling to keep the Devil inside him banked, but there's a conflict and anger simmering beneath the surface I had never recognized in him. His breathing turns heavy as they stare at each other.

Demitri starts to laugh. "Alright, everyone, settle down. The food is coming. While we're on this ship, let's all work to get along. There is strong ouma within these walls, if anything gets too out of hand, we'll all be serpent fodder." He looks to the room and waves. "As you were."

Chatter starts up again until everyone is laughing and talking. I glance at Nkella—he's looking down at the table, silent and deep in thought. Mūhī is muttering something to Bronte.

The aroma of seafood invades my senses, and my stomach is immediately reminded I haven't eaten anything in hours. Platters of shellfish on top of orange egg roe are placed at the center tables, along with bowls of what they tell me is some kind of pea porridge.

Plates get passed down the table, enough that everyone can grab food for themselves. AJ digs in first, then I copy the rest. "So Soren," Demitri starts, sticking food in his mouth. "That's a pretty royal necklace. Did a certain prince give it to you?"

Nkella stills, and my cheeks heat as I grab my mother's necklace. "Oh, um... No."

"No? One of those is hard to come by these days, with Danū being under siege and all. That's not a regular Danū gichang."

"It was my mother's."

His brows reach the top of his head. "Your mother's? Well, that is interesting. She was in Ipa?" He looks down at his food, an inquisitive look on his face. "So your family travels here?"

"That's what I've been trying to figure out. She—" My throat clogs, and I stare at my plate. Demitri takes notice.

"Oh. My condolences." I can feel his stare as I turn my food over with my fork. "But I do see you two have gotten along better since our little...trade last time, eh?"

A sigh sounding like a hiss escapes Nkella, and Demitri chuckles.

"Let me guess, it was all a ploy to get inside my operation. Well done, you two."

I look away, a swarm of memories flooding back. Demitri's gaze flicks between me and Nkella, and then he chuckles. What the heck is he laughing at now?

"I see." he rubs his chin with a gleeful smirk. And, pray tell, has the Lovers mark been planted on either of your wrists yet?"

Now my cheeks are flushing hard. I twist my wrists over to check, but then let out a sigh of relief. Nope. Just my Spiderweb mark, and the Fool's mark. I hadn't even thought about the Lover's mark. My gaze flicks to AJ and Lāri, who are smiling over their marks. I recall seeing AJ's Lover's mark while we sat around the barrel in the *Gambit*.

"Kh. Why would we, daí? Mind your own business."

Now Tessa snorts, but she quickly straightens her face and goes back to eating her food. Demitri chuckles and sticks a mussel in his mouth.

"Why are you looking for a rikorō cure?" Kenjō asks, dismissing the awkwardness of the conversation. I like her already.

I'm about to respond when Harold cuts me off. "Well, you see, the Empress cursed me."

Kenjō's eyes widen, and she gapes at him. "Another curse?"

He nods. "To be like them—undead. And then she sent me to the bottom of the sea, where my bones weighed me down. I was still alive, feeling the time pass."

She gasps. "Harold! I didn't know."

"But then, I was brought to the surface. These two brave pirates drank rikorō so they could find us. They risked their lives and their morals to save us all." He smiles at her, and she blushes. "But now, Soren is very sick."

Kenjō turns her gaze to me. "I can help you. I developed the cure. But I do not have enough of the ingredients here to make it. When we get to Piupeki, I will save you, Soren."

I smile weakly at her. "Thank you. And for Nkella?"

"Yes, of course."

Mūhī darts a look at Nkella. "The ends do not justify the means, daí?" He laughs as he stands. "I am going to bed." He leaves, scoffing to himself. Nkella shuts his eyes and grimaces.

"If he even needs it," Tessa tells Kenjō, ignoring what's going on in the table. "He doesn't appear to be sick."

Kenjō stares at the captain who looks down at his plate, ignoring everyone. "You have the curse of the Devil Card, è?"

Nkella nods once but doesn't look up.

"Hnn."

"Do you know anything about that?" Harold asks her.

"Koj. But we can figure it out. I will need a blood sample."

Nkella laughs and shakes his head. "Worry about yourselves, daí?"

"How often are you having nosebleeds?" Demitri asks.

"Not too often," I say. "I've drunk some chocolate drink potion to ease the effects and prolong my life."

Demitri nods, sucking on a bone. "I'd like to get started on your training bright and early. Maybe your power can cure the rikorō entirely, you never know. You're different than anyone here. Remember that."

I blink at him.

"And what makes you think you know how to train her? Hn?" Nkella pushes his plate away from him and crosses his arms. He stares at Demitri.

"I know a lot more about training power and the Fates than you know, Captain Devil."

Nkella scowls. "She will not meet with you alone," he says. "I will be there. Or one of my crew."

I swallow my mouthful of pea porridge and stare at him.

"Actually, I'd prefer if she and I worked alone, without the judgment and stares of anyone else."

"Judgment or stares?" AJ asks. "There is no judgment between us. Soren trusts us just fine."

"Yeah, I'm not worried about that, Demitri. Thanks," I say.

"I insist," Demitri combats. "We work alone."

Nkella laughs. "I do not trust you, daí? She will not be alone with you."

Bronte leans in and speaks low. "This is the last time I will say this." I take a deep breath. This woman intimidates me, and she's been silent the whole time. "This is my ship. I am captain. Whatever Demitri says goes. And Soren"—she looks at me—"you do not need men to speak for you, è?"

My cheeks warm, and I feel Nkella's hard stare. But she's right, I don't need anyone speaking up for me. And I want to find the Death Card. If that means coming into my powers, then I'll do it. "It's okay, guys. I can meet with him alone. I can take care of myself."

A flash of concern mixed with surprise washes over Nkella's face.

AJ shrugs. "I'm sure Nkella will have Iéle watching over you. And if anything feels wrong, any one of us will be with you in a heartbeat," he mutters. I nod and smile.

Demitri claps. "Excellent. Bright and early then. There's much to do."

19

Someone taps on my foot, and I startle awake.

A shadow looms at the end of my bed. I bring my feet in, almost jolting out of my sheets. The shadow brings a finger up to his mouth, and now I can see the long braid in his silhouette.

"It's time for your lesson. Demitri is waiting upstairs."

"Oh...okay." I blink and yawn into my hand. Moonlight spills through the round windows, and I know it's god awful early.

"Hurry up." Mūhī backs up and leaves the room.

I squint at Lāri beside me; she's sound asleep. I debate on whether I should ditch this plan and go back to sleep, gravity calling me back down to my pillow, but I think the better of it. The last thing I need is for Demitri to come hunt me down himself, he was adamant about starting early. And I do want that Death Card.

Tiptoeing my way outside, I'm careful not to wake a soul. Quinn ruffles her feathers next to Harold's bed, and I almost jump out of my skin. Out of the room, the lights are dim in the communal area.

"I was beginning to think you went back to sleep," Mūhī muses.

"I thought about it."

He gives me a disapproving stare and starts walking. "Let's go."

A pair of red eyes glow from the corner of the room, and I gasp.

"Iéle?"

She growls, and that's when I see Nkella's shadowy silhouette on an armchair in the far corner of the room.

"Have you been there this whole time?" Mūhī says to him. "A bit creepy, daí?"

Nkella stands. His hair is mussed like he either slept in that chair or got up earlier than I did just to be here waiting. "Soren. Why are you doing this?"

I open my mouth to speak but Mūhī interrupts me. "The captain said to follow Demitri's orders. That is why."

Nkella keeps his gaze on me, ignoring Mūhī.

"I want to know what he knows," I tell him. "If he knows a better way I can get the Death Card."

"He is likely lying."

"Possibly, but if he's not, then I want to know."

"She wants power too," Mūhī purrs. Nkella's face is emotionless and hard to read, but his eyes bore into mine as though he's trying to read my mind. I'm sure he can still feel the tug of my emotions, which at the moment, are tired and just wanting to get on with this.

"Don't go," he tells me.

My brows furrow at him. "Why not?"

"I don't trust him." He takes a step toward me. "If he doesn't want me there, he has something else planned."

"So send Iéle."

"Not going to happen," Mūhī says with a bored expression. "Sending your wolf is as good as you going. He won't allow it. And you're making us late."

Nkella takes another step toward me, but this time I back away and walk toward Mūhī.

"Why the hell do you care about what I do or who I go with? I told Demitri I'd go, and that's what I'm doing."

Nkella looks away from me, but I don't miss the look of disappointment on his face.

Turning to face Mūhī, I tell him, "Lead the way."

We walk quietly to Demitri's quarters. I want to ask him about his and Nkella's past. I only witnessed his memory that one time, and it wasn't great. At the same time, I have to remind myself this guy is gross. For whatever reason, AJ broke up with him, and he makes Lāri feel uncomfortable. Not only that, he's involved in the ouma trafficking circle that stole Lāri and was the cause of so many others' suffering. I know why Nkella despises him, and that's probably why he's so pissed at me for walking with the creep right now.

Shit. I wasn't thinking.

Maybe I shouldn't have come.

"We're here." He stops in front of a dark wooden door and knocks.

"Enter," Demitri's voice sounds muffled through the door. Mūhī opens it wide.

"Ah." He stands by a window to the right of his office. All the wood is a deep red, with upholstered chairs of leather cushions. "You made it. Come in." He looks at Mūhī. "That'll be all. Go to your post."

Mūhī gives him a nod and closes the door behind me. I stand at the entrance of his office, and suddenly every hair follicle on my body stands on end. I am wholeheartedly regretting this stupid decision. This is the man who wanted to buy me from the tavern. The man Nkella was adamant about me staying away from. The man who wanted to use me to become Emperor. The man in charge of the Ipani trafficking. And here I am, like a fool, letting him train me.

"Don't be afraid." Demitri walks around his desk, and I take a step back. "Sometimes, Soren, we all do things in desperation, things we regret."

"Like trafficking people?"

He stands with his back against a chair in front of his desk, his hands folded in front of him. "I don't mean you any harm, and I hope that our lessons will help you see I only intend the best for Ipa. When you met me, I was running out of time, and making rash decisions. I have no problems admitting that is my fault, and not my proudest moment."

"No offense, but you come across as a creep."

He laughs. "I wear my ambitions on my sleeve."

"Whatever." I sink my weight into my hip. "So are we doing this or what?"

His brows rise, and he smiles, letting out a soft chuckle. "Marvelous. Let's get started." He points to the chair he's leaning on as he steps to the side. "Have a seat."

I do as he says, keeping my eye on him.

Returning to his desk, he takes a seat in his own chair. "As you know, until recently, I was the Empress's advisor, a position I held for many, many years."

"How many years exactly?"

He puckers his lips and looks to the corner of his eyes. "Oof. Let's say, more than a century."

My eyes widen. "You're that old?"

He chuckles.

"No, sorry. I don't mean to say you look old. You don't. I just didn't know people here lived that long." I recall Asteria telling me that Ipani lived for a long time, if not for the Empress's eternal torment. "At least, not the humans anyway."

"This is true. The Ipani live for as long as it takes for them to feel their task in their life is complete. Until the Fates came and reworked the Aō's influence. You see, people—Ipani or human—do not age the way my ancestors did in Greece long ago."

"I'm listening."

"They could live forever if they wanted to."

"Are you part-Ipani?"

"Oh, no." He chuckles. "The Fates like to mess with people's lives. My family lived on the island she calls the Tower. They were close to her family back in Greece, and we were nobility. So"—he sits back in his chair—"they kept us alive for longer than we should have lived as humans."

"And now you're dying, aren't you?"

He raises his chin. "You catch on. You're quicker than I thought you were."

I stay quiet, considering his words. When I don't say anything, he continues.

"Because of the Death Card—because of the Fates and the mess of all those powerful Tarot cards—Ipani life expectancy is shortened."

"Everything here seems shortened because of her."

"Well, not only because of her."

My brow puckers.

"There were others involved."

"The Past and Future Fates."

He nods.

"And what do you want with me?"

"I want you on my side, Soren. The Empress knows you can help her restore balance to this world. But you can also be a threat to her. You used up the Ace of Wands, and took a piece of her power away. No one could have done that."

"Some good that did."

"Well, but it was a start. Now for the Ace of Swords. It is the only sword that can kill her."

"I don't want to do that."

He plants both arms on the desk, and his face goes blank. "I understand you don't want to get your hands dirty. But with your power, you could revert the sword's direction so that I could use it."

"I can?"

"You're a Fate." He points to my mark. "You can do anything with those cards. But most of all, you can change fate with your power."

"How do I do that?"

"Why do you want the Death Card?" he asks.

"I want to bring my mother back from the dead."

He smiles. "That's my girl. In order to do that, you'll need to wield power over it. How easy was it for you to use the World Card?"

"It wasn't easy. I needed to use my mark, and I didn't understand what that meant at the time. I still don't."

"So, say you acquire the Death Card. You won't know how to use it either, and then you'll have a brutal chase with the Empress on your hands. She's protective over her deck, but especially with that particular card."

"Makes sense as that's how she controls people's deaths."

He nods. "Precisely. By the way, where is the World Card?"

"Oh, um. The Empress has it now."

He raises his chin and looks over his shoulder. "No one is safe now. Do you understand?"

"I mean, no one has ever been safe."

"Yes, but now she can see directly where people are."

I blink at him.

"I'll explain. From what the Empress confided in me, each of the Fates have had different powers. They don't all carry on the same way, so I don't know what your powers are or what you should be expecting. What I do know is the way for you to attain her cards, which are yours by birthright, is to come into your power and learn how to use it. Only then will you be her match."

"I don't want to be her match. I just want to bring my mom back."

"And you can do that"—he leans in—"by knowing how to use those cards, and you get there by..."

"Learning my power."

He smiles. "What have you done with your power so far?"

"I've only been able to see into people's pasts. Their memories."

He squints, looking past me. "It's a start... The Empress, being the Present Fate, can detect everyone's current ability, or turmoil, but she can't see where people physically are because time is ever passing—none of her Fate powers can affect you, of course. None of the Fates can affect each other." He pauses to think. "You should be able to either travel to or affect the past somehow."

My eyes widen.

"I'm not saying that is what you can do, remember. I'm only saying what is possible."

"Right."

"How does it happen? When does your power start to work?"

I shake my head. "It's random."

"How has it happened before?"

"At first, it would take something extreme. But recently, I had a memory of the past owners of the *Ugly Kraken* disposing of the body of the Danū's Prefect. All I had done was touch a piece of a glass lantern that was there. And that's how I knew it was a wanted ship."

"So by touch, so probably also smell, taste, etcetera." He waves his hand. "You need to learn to do it at will. The Empress can suspend people's lives, so I'm willing to bet there is more you can do as well."

I gulp.

"Let's do this. "Close your eyes."

I stare at him.

"You're going to have to trust me, Soren. It's the only way you'll learn."

My stomach tightens. The only person I've come to trust recently is Nk—I ball my fists. "Okay," I take a deep breath and close my eyes.

"Take a few deep breaths and quiet your mind." I do as he says, and then he asks, "What were you feeling the last time you had a memory?"

My mind swarms with emotions, trying to draw out exactly what I was feeling. Nkella was there, and I was feeling conflicted about him, but I don't tell him that. "We had just gotten on the ship, and I remember feeling...a sense of déjà vu, but with a warning...like we didn't belong there. It wasn't our ship."

"Anything else?"

"I remember being mad at you for taking the *Gambit*."

"Would you say you were feeling cautious?"

I hesitate. "Yes."

"Bask in that feeling for a minute. Describe it to me."

I twist my features. How do I describe feeling cautious? "Um. Worry. Conflict. The odd feeling of being watched."

"Keep feeling that, like you're swimming in all that worry and conflict."

This is stupid. I take another deep breath and I envision myself touching the green glass. What I felt before was...a magnetic pull. And it was filled with a strange sense of emotions. Strange, because in all honesty, it's hard to put a limit to them. Like there're multiple pathways for every path ever taken. Like a web moving backward.

A tug of magnetism pulls me into that web, and I let it, riding the wave.

I open my eyes, and I'm in the Empress's Tower, except this is far in the past. Demitri is young, and his father is standing beside him. The Empress is shouting something and pointing at his dad. Suddenly, spiders fall from the ceiling and wrap his father in their web. Demitri starts crying and pulling at his dad, tears rolling down his face, as the spiders sink their long fangs into him.

His father is wrapped in a cocoon and carried up to the ceiling, his horrible screams becoming muffed and suffocating as the web thickens.

Now the Empress climbs off her chair and walks to young Demitri. She presses her face close to his and says, "Worry not, my child. You did not betray me—your father did. You won't have to suffer for his misdoings, but you will have to prove yourself worthy. Serve me as my advisor, and you will maintain your eternal youth and never want for naught." She holds out a gloved hand.

Young Demitri stares at it, tears in his eyes.

"Take my hand, boy. You must learn to seize the opportunity when your Fate gifts it to you."

Young Demitri slowly takes her hand, considering it cautiously. He stares up at the high ceiling where there is no longer any trace of his father.

The vision blurs, and I gasp, Demitri's present vulpine face coming into view.

"You had a memory. Showing improvement already." He claps. "Tell me, what did you see?"

"I—"

"Yes?"

My bottom lip trembles. "I'm so sorry."

He features twist. "Sorry?"

"About your father..."

Demitri's face goes rigid. He's silent for a bit, and then says. "I see."

"What did he—why did she?"

A calm and collected voice. "My father slaved over her for very long. Too long. Ever wanting our status back—what was promised before coming to this new land—both of them were too impatient for their own good, and my father suffered for it."

I wipe the sweat from the back of my neck.

"I think that's good for now. Come back tonight." He turns in his seat and looks tato the window.

After a beat, I stand. "Thanks?"

He lifts two fingers in acknowledgment without responding.

"I wish I could know more about the Empress's younger sister," I say. "The Past Fate descendant, Adara."

To this, he glances at me. "It would be helpful to know what her power was. Let's try to dig into her past after dinner, shall we?"

213

I nod and leave the room.

The air grows more crisp, and the winds are picking up. I wrap my arms around myself as I step out to the main deck to look for the crew. It's taken me almost an hour to find my way around this ship. I get lost, finding myself in the right wing where Bronte's crew hangs out. I bump into a burly man with a towel wrapped around his waist and a tattoo of an Ipani woman on his chest. I had walked in looking for my crew just as he walked out of the shower room. He grins down at me. I pivot and walk straight out.

Gross.

I manage to find my way to the mess hall and snag a piece of bread and an apple while I continue searching.

Lāri's voice carries on the wind, and I squint up at the topsails. Sure enough, she's in one of the crow's nests with AJ. I decide to abandon my attempts to find the others and walk out to the rail to stare out at sea. Cold wind whips my hair around my face, and I start braiding it.

If I'm being honest, I don't mind having some time to myself. I'm sure everyone is going to be asking me how my first session with Demitri went, and I know they're going to be judging me, despite what AJ said about no one judging anyone. Nkella is angry I went, and they all hate Demitri. They have every right to.

And I'm not saying I don't hate him. But after seeing his past, I can understand him a little better. One thing I've learned from being in the foster system is that whenever I have a great opportunity to elevate my life, I should take it. No matter if it's from shady people. That's what the Nelsons were to me, and now it's Demitri. No one in the crew is above that, and I'll remind them if I have to.

"Aren't you cold?"

I turn to face Kenjō whose hair is in a tight ponytail. She wears a dark tanned coat with fur on her neckline.

"Yes, but this is all I have."

She smiles. "Come."

I follow her back inside, but this time she takes me up to the same floor as Demitri's office.

I'm not surprised to find she has her own room. Her mother is the captain, and they're somehow in deep with Demitri. Her bedroom is small, about the size of Nkella's bedroom on the *Ugly Kraken*, which makes sense for a ship. This ship having enough rooms for more than one person is extreme in itself.

"So, you and Harold, huh?" I ask, throwing myself on her bed and making myself at home.

Her eyes widen, and she looks away.

"Oh, come on. He and I are friends. You can tell me."

"I didn't think I would see him again," she says. "My mother... She promised me to someone else."

My eyes bulge. I was not expecting that. "Does Harold know?"

She grows quiet as she reaches a chest on the floor and opens it.

I sit up. "Wait. You haven't told him?"

"What is there to tell, è? He is going to leave Ipa anyways."

I shut my mouth. She has a point. My mind drifts to Nkella. Not that either of us want to pursue anything, but even if we did, what was the point? I can't stay here. This isn't my home.

"I'm sorry," I tell her. "I know he really likes you, so that's got to be tough. I'm guessing the other guy doesn't know?"

She stands holding two coats in her hands. "Alec is a good man. I do not want to hurt him. You will get to meet him today."

"Why does that name sound familiar?"

"He is the Swords Prefect."

I gape at her. "You're with the Swords Prefect?" Damn. Girl's got friends in high places.

"After Harold left—"

"You mean, after Demitri kidnapped him, and your mom kept him in a cage until he was traded—and then, he was finally rescued by Nkella." I give her a wide, sarcastic smile. She frowns, and her eyes are puffy. "Sorry, that was rude of me."

She takes a seat next to me. "I don't always agree with their methods, è? But there is nothing I can do to stop them. I did not know my mother had him on her ship. I couldn't have known—I wasn't there. They don't tell me everything. I never would have wanted that to happen to Harold. You must believe me."

I offer her a half smile. I want to believe her, I'm just not sure I can yet. But I'm also not trying to make enemies with the girl dating the

Swords Prefect, not to mention she's lending me a coat. "Harold wouldn't care so much about a person if she had bad intentions."

Kenjō nods. "Yes. That is true." She stands and holds up two coats. One is dark blue with fur trim on the neckline—this girl really likes fur! —and the other is black leather with onyx buttons and no fur. That's more my style. "Which one do you like?"

I point at the leather one, and she hands it to me.

"Thanks," I say, slipping it on. "How do you say 'thank you' in Ipani?"

"*Engi.*"

"Engi," I repeat.

I stretch my arms out. It's snug, but I think it curves around me in all the right places. The bottom is long enough to cover my butt, which is good for the cold, but it's also tight enough to accentuate my shape. She smiles at me and leads us out of her room.

"Do you know where my crew is?" I ask.

"I know Harold and the one on wheels are making explosives in my lab. That is where I am going. The big one is with the cannons. He said he wanted to be there. But I don't know where your captain is."

"Oh, that's okay. I wasn't looking for him. So, does your mom have tasks for everybody, or..."

"I think your task is only with Demitri. Her crew is big, so everyone already has a task. But if you see something that needs to be done, no one is going to stop you, è?"

"Makes sense. I guess I can go with you to make explosives."

She grins. "You know how to make hū raku?"

"Oh, yeah. Tessa and Harold taught me all kinds of stuff. I heard you taught Harold."

She blushes.

We walk down a corridor with a red carpet running over black wooden panels to a room at the far end. Round windows facing the sea illuminate the path, but as we get closer, a small bit of magnetism tugs at me.

The door opens, and Nkella steps out, pausing when he sees me.

I frown as a butterfly gets trapped in my tightening stomach. Maybe it'll finally suffocate and die in there.

216

"So how was your lesson with Demitri?" Kenjō brings me back to look at her. Her forehead wrinkles.

"It was"—I lower my voice to keep him from hearing—"interesting."

"How?" Nkella asks as we approach. So much for him not hearing. His dark eyes seer into me, a flicker of amber igniting inside them as I walk closer. His collar is popped at his neckline, revealing him in all his badass glory. His expression is unmoving and intense but also magnetic. I can't tell if that flicker is from anger that I went to see Demitri or because I'm near him. And the butterfly starts to fight for freedom. Die, insect!

"I learned a lot," I say to him. "Found out some stuff out about myself. And him."

He quirks a brow and the magnetism from the rikorō surfaces between us. He's fighting back the concern he has for me. He doesn't want me to know.

I hate what that does to me.

"What did you find out?" His frown seems permanently plastered on his face.

"About me or him?"

He blinks a few times, then his eyes dip.

"I will leave you two to talk," Kenjō says as she walks into the lab before I can protest her leaving me out here with him. Harold and Tessa's voices ring out as the door shuts.

"Soren..." He steps toward me, and I hold my breath. What is he doing? He pauses and lets out a sigh. "What did you find out about yourself?"

Now I quirk a brow. "Is that really what you're interested in knowing?"

"Can't a captain be concerned for his crew?"

Crossing my arms, I let myself fall against the wall. "Apparently all the Fates have more to their power. The Empress knows everyone's present state, but she can also stop people from living—suspended in time. Demitri thinks I can learn to do more than look into people's pasts."

"Like what?"

"I don't know. It could be going back in time for all I know. It would help to know what the previous Past Fate could do. But that's something we'll try to work on later."

"Later?" his expression darkens.

"Yeah, after dinner." I scoff. "Did you think I would just have one lesson?"

He nods once. "Understood. But I do not trust him."

"Neither do I. Look..."

He stares at me.

"I understand why you're upset. Demitri is a grade-A asshat..."

Nkella's features twist. "Ass on hat? What does that mean?"

I suppress a laugh. "What I mean is, I know he's responsible for so much bad shit that's happened. But I thought about it, and if there's one thing I learned growing up without parents, is to take every opportunity that comes my way. Can't you relate to that?"

He stares at me without speaking so I keep going.

"Nkella," I take a step closer, and his breath hitches. I bite my cheek. "If I could become as powerful as the Empress—not saying I could or even that I want to be, but... I could bring my mother back to life. Could you imagine having that kind of power? I really want this." I stop when we're an inch apart from each other.

His chin raises slightly, and his eyes lower. "Be careful, Soren, daí? The chase for power is a dangerous one. You heard Mūhī last night. It brings casualties. He was right about that." He looks down at how close I am to him. I can feel his body heat radiating against me. He licks his lips and swallows.

"I'll be careful," I say.

"Don't be bancha, daí? I am still your captain. Come to me for help if you need it."

For a moment neither of us move from where we are. His eyes drift to my arms and chest, and I can feel his desire to touch me. Is it the rikorō? What if it isn't? We kissed before going into the Temple at Wands, and we almost kissed a second time before I went back home. And then, when he saw me again at the beach...

Are we being stupid?

"Nk—"

"Soren, I can't." He backs away, and the butterfly in my belly plummets as he turns to walk down the corridor.

"Yeah…" I step back and walk into the lab.

Tessa, Harold, and Kenjō stop talking when I walk through the door. They avoid my gaze, going back to their work, and I get the feeling they heard our entire conversation. Wrapping my arms tightly around me, I lean my back against the wall and squeeze my eyes shut.

"I hate rikorō. I want it gone and out of my system."

"What happened?" Harold asks. Kenjō snorts.

I quirk a brow at them. "Okay, don't pretend like you couldn't hear outside the door if you did."

Tessa starts to giggle, and my cheeks burn.

"What does the rikorō have to do with you two?" Tessa asks me, a serious expression now on her face. "I have my suspicions, but I want to hear from you what exactly is going on."

I drop down on a seat and cover my head with my hands. "The rikorō we drank from seems to have given us a telepathic connection because it belonged to the same Ipani. Like, there's this magnetism every time we're close to each other." I grit my teeth. "I hate it. I just want this to wear off already."

"Hnn." Kenjō squints like she's trying to piece something together.

"I can't imagine being able to share thoughts with Nkella." Harold wipes his face. "I feel so sorry for you."

I sigh. "At first, it was useful. We could hear each other underwater."

"If it is still in your system, you probably still can underwater," Kenjō says.

"Maybe, but now we just feel each other's crazy emotions, except he can control his better than I can for some reason. Like, he can block his feelings from me, but I can't from him."

"I don't think it works that way," Kenjō says. "And an Ipani would not feel a romantic connection with themselves, è?" She smirks. "Knowing the way each of you feels could have made that stronger, but if you had drunk it with..." She looks at Harold and Tessa. "With Tessa," she says carefully, "you two would not fall in love."

Tessa laughs, and now so do I.

"You would only feel a close bond. Maybe like siblings."

I pause.

"That makes sense," Harold says as he mixes two solutions together over a burning flame.

My head is starting to hurt from all this. "Well, it doesn't matter. We can't be together, regardless. I'm leaving, remember?"

Kenjō's cheeks redden, and I bite my tongue.

Tessa breaks the silence. "Kenjō, do you have any idea why my captain can control the rikorō? I keep thinking about why it is not affecting him like it is Soren."

I reach over for one of the ceramic burners, and Harold passes me two of the solutions.

"Hnn. I think it has to be related to his curse. It can't be because of anything else, è? He is Ipani like me, and I got very sick."

Harold mutters a "Yep" under his breath but doesn't look up. I wonder how he's doing—being so close to Kenjō—and if he's trying to deny his feelings for her too.

"Why would a curse be saving his life?" I ask suddenly.

"Self-preservation?" Harold speculates. "If he dies, the Devil dies, too, right?"

My brows rise. I hadn't thought of it like that.

We spend the rest of the day making loads of raku bombs for not only our crew but Bronte's crew. We take breaks and walk around the main deck for fresh air from time to time to avoid being stuck indoors and getting seasick.

Part of me wants to join Kae in cleaning the cannons. I think it's because it was the first task I was ever given on the *Gambit*. And I like hanging out with Kae. He's quiet, but he feels like an older brother or cousin.

20

Before dinner, I catch up with AJ and Lāri in our quarters. The ship is sailing smoothly with occasional large waves causing us to drift from side to side, in slow rocking motions.

Lāri throws herself on her bed. "Do we have to eat at the mess hall?"

My brows perk up. "Oh. Is it optional?"

AJ stands at the end of her bed and grabs her feet. "And miss all the fun between our captain and the rest of them?"

She snorts. "I can do without that entertainment for the rest of the trip, mei?"

AJ's shoulders lift and drop as he lets out a long sigh. "I'll see if I can bring us both a plate and eat here." He glances at me. "Hey, Soren, you eating there or here?"

"Here." I chuckle. "If that's an option. I'd rather be away from hard stares and awkward conversations. Why don't we all eat here?" I ask. "The whole crew."

"Because Demitri has ordered everyone to the mess hall." Tessa drives in from the communal area.

Lāri lifts her head. "But for what purpose? We are not part of their crew. They don't want us here any more than we want to be here."

"He says the Prefect is arriving and he'll want to scope us out. We don't want to cause problems. Come on."

Kenjō did say the Prefect was coming tonight.

Lāri and I exchange a glance, and we climb out of bed. It takes me a few minutes to straighten my hair and put on Kenjō's coat, then we're headed to the mess hall.

In the long hallway, my chest tightens as a coughing fit befalls me. I clench my coat in my hands and lean against the wall. AJ grabs my arm to help me balance as I struggle to breathe.

"Take it easy, Soren. Long breaths."

My chest constricts, and my throat lets out several long wheezing coughs. After about a minute, it's stopped. I rub my face to see a spot of blood smeared on my fingers. "Great."

Lāri shares a concerned look with AJ as she pulls out a handkerchief and hands it to me.

"I'll go tell Harold and Kenjō to make you more tetyevisi," Tessa says as she drives off in a hurry.

I nod to her even though she's already taken off. Another wave of nausea overtakes me, and the motion of the ship makes me feel like puking. "I don't think I can eat dinner."

"Try eating some bread. It'll be worse if you starve yourself." AJ crouches down and places his hand on my head. "You don't feel so hot."

"I'll be fine. Just need more of that cocoa drink."

After a few minutes, the nausea subsides. I stand and the three of us walk to the mess hall.

Once there, we spot Tessa at one of the corner tables. I glance over at Demitri with his usual posse of regulars, but he doesn't make any attempts at calling us over today. I guess he wanted to speak with us last night when we had first gotten here. Lāri and AJ sit down with their backs facing Demitri, and I take a seat next to Tessa. I'm about to ask her where everyone else is, just as Nkella and Kaehante walk through the open doors.

Nkella stands at the entrance. He nods toward Demitri, but then his gaze falls on our table, stopping on me. He narrows his eyes and walks over.

"Soren." He glances at Tessa. "Did you make her more tetyevisi?"

"Harold is bringing it now," she says. He nods once then pulls up a seat across from me.

"I'm fine," I tell him. "I won't die yet." I smirk, but he frowns.

AJ tilts his cup to me. "Not funny, Soren," he says.

I roll my eyes.

A tall and lean man wearing a yellow wool coat buckled at the corner, similar to how the Arcana wear their robes, stops at the entrance. He has a square jaw and muscular features. His straight brown hair is neat, and he skims the mess hall, raising a hand to Demitri who stands up and welcomes him.

"I'm guessing that's the Swords Prefect?" I whisper to the crew.

"Yep," Tessa says.

Nkella squints in his direction, his eyes following the newcomer as he walks and talks with Demitri's group. Kenjō gets up from her seat next to her mom. I hadn't even seen her there, she's so petite. They are lost in conversation, disguised by the loud chattering of the mess hall. Alec takes Kenjō into his arms and smiles. Then he leans down and plants a kiss on her lips.

Lāri gasps and I turn my head to see what she's looking at. There, at the entrance of the room, is Harold, a hot drink in his hand. His face is blank, emotionless, as he stares at Alec and Kenjō. He quickly shifts his gaze to us and walks over. He places the hot drink in front of me, pauses, and backs away from the table.

I stand. "Harold? Are you okay?"

He's turning to leave when Kenjō calls his name, but he speeds out of the mess hall.

The Prefect steps forward, his brows pinched together. "Harodscot?"

Kenjō whips around, placing her hands on Alec's chest. "Let me talk to him alone."

Alec rights himself but then agrees.

Tessa reaches for my arm. "Leave them be, Soren. Drink your tetyevisi."

I take my seat, picking up the cup. My eyes scan the room and land on Bronte. She has a malicious smirk on her face that makes my skin crawl. She whispers something to Demitri who had been watching the whole thing. He leans in and laughs at whatever she just said to him.

"I'm taking it Harold had no idea about the Swords Prefect and Kenjō?" AJ asks.

I shake my head. "Nope."

"Kh." Nkella shakes his head once. "It is for the best if he stays away."

I don't know why that makes my stomach tighten but it does. Harold can do better.

They bring out the food, and I guzzle down my drink and eat supper in silence while the rest of them talk.

When we finish, Demitri approaches our table and places a hand on my shoulder.

"Meet me in twenty minutes?" he asks, and I reply with a nod.

Nkella's eyes flare as he stares at us. Demitri passes Nkella a long look before he leaves, but he's too busy staring at the shoulder Demitri just touched. I shrug it off and turn to Tessa and Kae instead.

It's colder than a polar bear's ice hole in Demitri's office. He ignites a flame inside a burner-type thing, which I assume is this ship's version of a chimney. As long as it warms the place up, I don't care what it is.

"That should do it," he says. "We're getting closer to Swords, so the temperature will be dropping more every day."

"Fun," I say dryly. "I'm not used to the cold where I'm from."

"Well, let me know if you need anything else to keep you warm, and I'll have it brought to you. Whatever you want."

I quirk a brow and smile sweetly.

"In fact, I would like you to know, that with me, you'll never want for anything ever again."

A chill crawls up my spine. From my experience with foster parents, whenever they say that, it's because they want something in exchange. It's no different with him. Only thing here is I already know what he's after—my help to become emperor. Not that I'm planning on keeping that promise because I don't trust him. Despite seeing his past and what's brought him here, I don't believe he has the right motives to save Ipa. His methods of getting himself to his current position is evidence of that. But he doesn't have to know what I think. I keep a poker face and let him go on.

"How are you feeling?"

"Fine. That drink really helps."

"I'll have Kenjō keep some at the ready. Should you start to get a nosebleed again, it's good to keep that handy. And when we get to Swords, she'll get busy making you the cure."

"And that entails killing Ipani?"

"No," he says. I raise my brows. "That was before. Kenjō has found another way—by use of a rare type of ouma—which is why it is unnecessary to kill so many."

"So, instead, you're only killing one? What type of ouma is so rare?"

"The healing kind. And don't worry, they weren't Ipani."

I stare at him. Not Ipani? "So oumala animals then?"

"While we're off-topic"—he folds his hands on top of his desk—"what is your relationship with the undead crew?"

"What do you mean?" I deadpan.

"Well, with each of them. How fond are you of them, for starters? Last I saw you, your captain had you in binds. Weren't you a prisoner on his ship? He planned to trade you for his sister, so forgive me if seeing you friendly with them came as a shock."

"Oh." Okay, I guess that checks out. "The rest of the crew treated me like family. I don't know why, but one of them believed I was telling the truth, and the rest eventually followed."

"And now?"

"Now they're the family I always wished I had."

He sits back in his chair. "Right. Home is where your crew is. Isn't that what you said to me yesterday? But after this, you're planning on going back home? Once you take the Death Card, that is."

"I can't stay." I sit back and fold my arms. "Why do you ask?"

"No reason. Just putting the pieces together. If you say they're your family, why would you want to go back?"

I blink. "For starters, we don't have Arcana shooting down from the sky."

"So for safety."

"I mean, not entirely. There's also my sister."

"Ah, right, your infamous sister you fought hard to get back to. She must have been ecstatic to see your return." His face is straight as he stares at me, and I'm suddenly feeling like I'm back at my therapist's office. What's his endgame here?

"To be frank, I guess what I'm hoping for is"—he clears his throat—"that you would stay here and see this through. Say, after you get the Death Card, you lead me to the Ace of Swords, give me hold over it, and the Empress has something else up her sleeve—"

"So what you want from me is security. I'm not even sure I'm capable of that."

"I'm confident you will be."

"Yeah. I want to go home to bring my mom back, and I'm not bringing her back to Ipa. She, Talia, and I are going to be a family."

His face slackens. "Understood. I can manage. So what of your captain?"

"What about him?"

"You two seem...close all of a sudden."

My cheeks heat to an unnatural level, and I avert my eyes. "Can we get to the lesson now?"

"Of course," he says, sporting a smile on his face.

I shift uncomfortably in my seat. I'm not unaccustomed to people trying to get information out of me, but he's starting to get on my nerves.

"So, this morning you said something before you left, that you wish you knew more about the Empress's sister, the Past Fate descendant. And I got to thinking." He stands at his desk and walks to the window. "The Fates can't affect each other, but what if it's possible, if the one you wanted to look into the memory of was dead?"

I scrunch my features.

"What I mean is," he touches his chin. "I wonder if you could somehow reach her memory."

"How would I do that? The only times I've had these visions, I've either touched something belonging to the person or actually touched that person."

"What if I have something that belonged to her?"

My brow perks up. "Oh?" Of course, he could have stolen something from the Tower. I sit at the edge of my seat as he bends down to unlock a cabinet. Inside is a chest. He picks it up and sets it on his desk.

It's black, with brass bindings that wrap all the way around. He pulls a key out of his inner coat pocket and unlocks the chest. As he opens it, he tells me, "I would appreciate it if you don't mention this to anyone. If you do, the Empress will be down here in seconds. Do you understand?"

I nod.

He opens the chest, and a single black Tarot card with a gold trim stares back at me. A purple sheen glosses over the face of what appears to be the Hierophant, who looks—identical to Demitri.

I inch closer. The cards belong to the Empress, but at one point they belonged to the Past Fate, as she's the one who brought them here. "How...?"

I claimed my card so that she would never take it away from me. Even though the Aō determines our marks, my own card can be used to keep myself hidden from her. I can sway the masses, and I can seize one Arcana soldier at a time."

I gasp. "That's how you have all those Swords Arcana. But why don't you take them all?"

"They're too many, and they're engrossed with her Ancient Greek magic. One at a time, I have the Aō to aid me, but all at once, I'm overpowered by her magic."

"So you think I can see into her sister's past—see what powers she had because she brought the cards from my world. What if it shows me the Empress's past, or her other sister, Asteria?"

"Then we can still use that information to our advantage."

"That's fair. Okay, so what do I need to do?"

He hands me the card. "Take it."

"Wait, I heard the Empress has a new Hierophant. Wouldn't you having this card make that impossible or difficult?"

"No. Again, the Aō gives them the mark. She doesn't even know I have it. The new Hierophant—whoever it is—won't have their full potential, but they'll still do her bidding. My image on the card hasn't changed yet."

Yet.

"So with this card, the image changes to whoever holds the card's full power."

"I have no doubt in my mind that the Empress is training her new advisor to reach the full potential of the card. And once they've attained it, the card might possibly disappear and go to them. Which may be why she hasn't bothered to take the card out and see it's missing."

"That's possible?"

"The way I attained this card, is...well, I heard it calling my name. It was hidden in the Empress's chest. It might work differently than other cards."

I stare at the card and take it into my hands.

"I'm trusting you with this, Soren. Try to get a memory out of it. I know the Fates are different than anyone else."

"Would I be able to harness its power?" Demitri doesn't respond. "Never mind. Stupid question." I was able to with the World Card and the Ace of Wands, and I'm expected to do the same with the Ace of Swords. I'm probably able to harness any of the card's powers. I stare at the figure on the face of the card.

The Hierophant wears a conical black hat and a loose black robe with the emblem of the Tower embroidered on it, symbolizing who he serves. I turn the card over in my hand and face the back, so that I'm not looking at the magical glare the card brings or the creepy eyes in Demitri's image staring back at me. So weird.

"Let yourself relax. Close your eyes."

I do as he says, letting my shoulders rise and fall with my exhale.

"Good. Now try to recall that feeling you get when you're about to have a vision."

"The magnetism."

"Yes, good. See if you can get there quicker. Feel the magnetism."

I don't know if I can just feel the magnetism. Is that how he helped the Empress? I can't imagine her going along with that. I purse my lips, gripping the card in my hands.

"Try to imagine the Empress's sister, holding that card in her hands. Try to evoke her presence."

"I don't even know what she looked like."

"Maybe you can get a sense of the way she felt."

I open my eyes. "What?"

"I'm only trying to give you an idea. Please proceed."

Letting out a sigh, I close my eyes again. This time, I work to block him out. What happened last time? Oh, right. I saw into Demitri's past, but then he was right here. This feels impossible.

"Ouma is directed with intent. So how you choose to go into your vision, make sure you are intentional." His words spark a memory of me and Gari, when he first gave me the ouma ipononchi, the cookie which turned me into a specter. The more I learned to be intentional, the better I became at climbing the rope to fix the sail, and the next time I chose the invisibility, I even remembered to keep my clothes on.

He's right. "Intent is what I need here. But I can't have intent if I don't know what I'm looking for."

"Why don't you start with, who was the Past Fate descendant?"

Who was the Past Fate descendant? Adara...

That's a good place to start. I repeat the question a few times in my mind.

My mark is starting to pulse on my wrist. My eyes blink open, and I drop the card on the desk. I don't bother taking off my coat, I just focus on that area and keep repeating the question. The pulsing grows slower but somehow deeper, like I can feel it touching my bones. The air grows crisp, and fog escapes my lips.

My eyesight narrows, and it gets darker.

"Demitri?" I call out to the dark, I can no longer see him or any of the furnishings of his office. I'm still seated on the chair, though, unsure if I should stand or stay where I am.

"I'm still here. You haven't gone anywhere."

"I-I think I'm having a vision, but..."

"What do you see?"

"Just darkness."

Footsteps splash on the water as a girl runs past me, gripping a journal close to her chest. She has long, luscious, curly red hair billowing behind her, and I instantly know I'm in Adara's memory. The scene spreads out beneath my feet, and suddenly I'm sitting on cobblestone—around me is a garden. The entrance to what looks like a labyrinth is to my right. The girl stops running, looks both ways, and walks inside.

"Soren?" Demitri's voice echoes through the vision.

"Wait."

I stand to follow her through the labyrinth, but my vision transports me to her location.

The girl runs and sits under a tree inside the labyrinth. A tall Ipani man walks out from one of the corners. His large muscular torso is defined by a sleek black tunic, with a long sword hanging from his hip. He has dark eyes that remind me of Nkella, an intense stare, and high cheekbones. Adara quickly stands, leaving her journal open, and they embrace. He kisses her deeply, his hands gripping the sleeve of her dress, and she wraps one leg around his.

Feeling like I shouldn't be watching this, I turn but then sit down when something inaudible makes them both cut their gaze to one direction. The scene disappears into tiny fragments of color, leaving behind the darkness I first started in.

The next scene wraps around me in stone from floor to ceiling. It takes me a moment to realize I'm in the Tower. Next to a window is a table where the Past Fate descendant sits, scribbling furiously in her journal. Banging from the door causes the girl to nearly jump from her seat, but she still doesn't look up. She keeps scribbling. When she stops, she picks up the book and holds it to her chest. She turns to take out a small box from under her bed. A tear rolls down her cheek, and she sticks the journal inside and locks it. A purple film of magic sweeps over the box.

More banging comes from the other side, but she continues to ignore it. I watch silently as she takes the chest and walks over to the open window, placing it on the windowsill. She tosses it out in one throw, then climbs out herself. Getting up from my chair, the scene rushes me forward to where she now stands at the edge of the sea. The cold wind blows my hair as I witness her walking into the water until the waves are over her waist; then she tosses the chest out to sea.

The scene dissipates, and I'm back in Demitri's office.

My eyes adjust to the light. Were they closed this whole time?

Demitri opens his mouth to speak but I cut him off. "I saw her."

His eyes widen. "The Past Fate descendant?"

"Yes." I stand and walk to the window and explain the details of everything I saw, from the Ipani man she was with to the banging on the door and her throwing the journal out to sea.

"This must have been before the Empress suspended Rutavenye in the sky."

I stare up into the cloudless night sky, too dark to see a floating island, but I can imagine it being there. I try to imagine who the person banging on the door was that could drive her to climb out the window. And what was she writing in her journal?

"Legends say the man she was seeing was Tetalla, the Danū warrior sent to fight the newcomers who meant them—us all harm."

The story Aba told me around the fire back in Wands resurfaces in my memory.

"But," he says from behind me, "love conquered and then caused a war."

"I wonder what she was writing in her journal." The mirror shows him getting up from his desk and approaching me.

"Yes, that would be beneficial to know." He glances out the window next to me, then hums, looking around his office. Walking back to his desk, he pulls out a tan leather map. "Since we're headed to Swords, do you know where we are right now?" I stare blankly at him, waiting for him to tell me. "We are sailing right under the Tower." He taps his chin with his index finger. "But we'll have passed it by morning."

"What are you talking about?"

"The chest the Past Fate threw into sea, of course. It would be right below Tower Island."

My eyes widen as it dawns on me. We're sailing over the chest. "How would we find it?"

"It would be difficult. We would need something with a lot of light, and it would be quite a long shot. Far too impossible."

An image of Gari crosses my mind, and my stomach twists.

"Too bad. But it's probably useless."

"What do you mean?"

"Well, she could have been scribbling anything. Love notes, for all we know."

Silence falls over the room, and my breathing grows loud in my ear.

"Although, I'm sure there would have been some secrets about her magic casually passed. Ah, well, no use thinking about it. We don't have a way to get to it."

I swallow. "Are there any mer-Ipani around under these waters?"

"Not this far out, I'm afraid."

My shoulders deflate.

"You know what I find curious?" Before I can answer he says, "That she put it inside a chest and threw it in the ocean. That could only mean she was hoping to find it again someday."

"She must have written something important in there."

His brows rise as he nods, his hands crossed in front of him. "Good job today. You managed to see into the past quickly, and without the person being here. That's an improvement."

I give him a half smile. "Thanks, but how do I find out what other powers I have?"

"You'll just have to keep searching. It will take time. I have all the time in the world—we'll get you there."

All the time in the world. But I don't.

"Bright and early?"

"Absolutely."

Outside Demitri's office, shouting comes from inside Kenjō's room. Harold's voice projects from the bedroom followed by Kenjō's.

They're still arguing? I tiptoe over for a closer listen.

"I was not dishonest, Harold. I hugged you because I missed you. We did not kiss."

"But you didn't tell me you and Alec were a thing."

"A thing?"

"Together!"

After a moment of silence, her voice sounds shaky. "I thought I would never see you again. I have always been promised to Alec."

A shadow eclipses the wall in front of me, and I spin around.

"It is rude to eavesdrop." Alec stands there with his hands behind him. Concerned lines decorate his forehead, and I can tell he's uncomfortable.

"Sorry," I say. "I was just leaving Demitri's office."

"It's okay. I'm curious about them too. Is Harodscot your friend?"

I chuckle. "Harold?" I emphasize the ending of his name, and Alec smirks maliciously. Oh, I see how it is. "Yeah, we're friends."

Alec nods. "I don't know what to do about them," he says, taking a seat in a communal lounge chair. "On one hand, I want to give her space and allow her to have this conversation. On the other, he is an outlaw Magician, and I don't trust them to be alone together."

I take a seat next to him. "Do you trust Kenjō?"

He glances at me from the corner of his eye and gives me a strange smile. "I want to, but I know they spent time together. If you know what I mean."

I give him an apologetic smile, and his face pales as if the expression I gave him confirms his suspicions. "When you say 'outlaw,' you mean because of the Empress's laws? But you're here on Demitri's ship..." I let that linger to see if he catches on.

"I have come to realize the Empress does not have the best intention for my people. I will not give Harold up to the Empress, if that is what you're wondering."

"I wasn't." I mean, until now that he'd said it. "What I mean is, you do know what Demitri has been doing, right? To the Ipani for their ouma? What Kenjō has been making?" I hold my breath, realizing I might be telling him some sort of secret.

Alec takes a deep breath and stares down at the floor. "I am not okay with Demitri's methods. And I was not okay with finding out what Kenjō had been doing and hiding from me all that time. But I understand she has helped others and is helping you?"

I tilt my head.

"She told me about you. How you took rikorō to save your friends."

I give a modest shrug. "That's me. Helping my friends."

"Well, I don't think we were properly introduced. I'm Alec."

"Soren."

He smiles tightly and then stares back at the door.

"Listen," I say, resting my elbow on a cushion. "You don't have anything to worry about. I'm sure they'll be friends—or not—but nothing more. He's planning on leaving this world anyway, you know? Just like me. We're not from here."

Alec stares at me. "I appreciate you saying that, Soren. But I fear I still would not be content if her heart lives somewhere else."

My eyelids flutter. "I...understand that."

The door opens, and Harold walks out. He stops when he sees me and Alec sitting next to each other, his brows quirking.

Alec sighs and gets up. "It was a pleasure to meet you, Soren." He stops at Harold. "Harodscot."

"Hi," Harold says flatly.

Harold doesn't talk the whole way to our wing...which is completely understandable and fine by me. Too many things are buzzing through my mind. Adara, the journal, being right under the Tower where the journal could possibly be. with no way to get to it. And one more thing...

"I fear I still would not be content if her heart lives somewhere else."

Out of all the things swarming through my mind, why is that the thing that stuck out to me the most, causing my stomach to twist?

We're get into our beds quietly, careful to not wake anyone up. I glimpse Nkella, turned over and lying flat on his stomach. A memory of his body close to mine follows me into my covers. I smile as I wrap the covers over my head despite the sinking feeling living in the pit of my stomach. I just need the Death Card, so I can go home, and get on with my life. Keep my eye on the prize. Bringing my mom back. These sessions with Demitri are good, they're getting me there. Before, it felt like a hope or a dream. But now, it feels like a reality. I am going to get my wish.

I lie awake, not able to think about anything else other than the journal and what secrets it could hold. Secrets about her powers, about the Empress, about how to control the cards. About my own possible powers.

Demitri said it was too bad we don't have anything with a light and that we'd be searching without finding anything. But I can't help wondering if I could get it myself, if I could use the rikorō I have left in my system and swim, using the glimmering light I emanated when I first shifted to a mermaid.

Would it kill me?

I feel fine. And if anything, Harold or Kenjō would make me more of that chocolate drink.

Sitting up, I glance around the room. If I don't do this now, it'll be too late; we would have sailed past it by morning. What other chance will I have to read the Past Fate's journal and learn whatever I can about my power?

Climbing out of bed in a pair of leggings and a long-sleeved shirt Kenjō brought me, I sneak out into the communal area. Glancing behind me, I make sure no one is waking up. No signs of Iéle either. I half tiptoe, half run down the hall, and make it outside to the main deck. Freezing cold winds send goosebumps bursting through my arms and legs. That water is going to be freezing. But I know, once I'm in and my legs shift to a fin, my body temperature will acclimate.

Pressing my body against the wall of the ship, I slide against it until my hands land on the cold metal of a ladder. My eyes follow it all the way down to the dark blue void of splashing water, and I gulp. Gripping the cold metal tightly, I swing my legs over and start to slowly climb down, the deafening winds pushing my hair over my face. Shaking, but carefully slow, I climb all the way down to the last step, still a few feet above the water.

I arch my neck back to make sure no one is watching.

And then with one giant breath, I jump into the frigid, cold ocean waves.

21

I'm immediately blinded by pain. It feels like I hit a block of cement. I swallow ice-cold water, worsening the shock in my system, but the moment my skin touches the water, a soft orange glow emanates from me. My legs morph into a long mermaid tail, and the slits on either side of my neck open up. I tread water until I'm re-energized to dive in, and my body temperature warms enough for me to move, just as I had hoped. My mark pulls me forward, but I resist, trying to catch my bearings.

My body sets off a glow that illuminates the dark ocean depth perfectly. I'm immediately filled with vigor and the urge to swim fast. My tail automatically glides from left to right, and my body zooms forward; I almost lose sight of where I'm headed. I can't stop the smile spreading over my face.

I feel free! My mark pulses, and magnetism pulls at my wrist instead of in my head. What is this?

Should I follow it? I'll have to hurry. I don't know how long this'll last, or if I'll even make it. To be honest, this was crazy. I should have told someone I was doing this. But no one in my crew would have let me go.

A school of fish passes me as I search the ocean depths around me.

The ocean floor looks pretty deep. I don't even know which direction to look toward.

Yeah, this was definitely ambitious.

I guess I could have told Demitri. He could have at least had one of his Arcana guards keeping watch.

But it's not like they could have come down here with me.

Focus, it's too late now. No one else could have come to help me, and anyone I could have told would have just used it against me in some way. I'm on my own.

And I have my power.

My wrist pulls me down again. I'm starting to realize it isn't because of the rikorō, it's because of me—my Fate magic.

I glide to a halt, with my tail facing down as if I'm standing, and stare at my mark. A yellow and red glow shimmers over my faint scales. *Come on.* Where did the chest fall?

Could I even see the past of something non-sentient?

My vision zooms into focus, and I see the chest, fallen on top of dead coral. The magnetism pulls me down, and I decide to follow it. I don't know why, but I feel like it's the same pull I get whenever a vision comes to me, as if it belongs to a Past Fate or something.

The water gets colder as I descend deeper, and my ears pop. A big ugly fish with a pointy hook at the end of his face scurries away when it sees me. I almost swallow my tongue but relax when it leaves.

The water is definitely colder in these parts of the ocean. Even with the rikorō allowing me to be comfortable fully submerged, there is a difference. It's unsurprising since we've been sailing north toward a freeze-zone. The space around me starts to darken, and I can only see the light coming from my glowing sheen. I shiver, too afraid to question if it's the rikorō finally wearing off and taking away my ability to see underwater, or if it's just darker so far down below.

It must be the latter, because I can still breathe underwater. My pulse quickens, as I know that at any second, I can run out of this magic and be too far down to come up for air. Probably get the bends.

Focus, Soren. I keep swimming toward the pull of my mark, letting it guide me, weary of any apex predators that may be lurking and watching me. Keeping the vision of the chest in my mind, I search as far as I can see on the dark rocky floor. My wrist urges me to head straight down, so I steel my spine and go for it. At this point, turning back would mean having gone through all this for nothing. I hope for the best and dive straight down.

At first, there's nothing but rocks and dark trenches. But then I see, wedged in the crevice of a trench, a piece of metal sticking out. Anticipation buzzes through me as I head straight for it. My mark is pounding now, becoming almost painful. My tail flows behind me as I try to climb down against the rock, the ocean current pushing against me. Stopping right at the crevice, the metal comes into view—it's the latch of a chest. I found it. I start to tug on the metal, but it's stuck in there pretty tight. Gripping with both hands, I give it a strong pull. It sends me backward but with the chest in my hands. I got it. The shiny silver metal reflects off my soft shimmering glow as I turn the dark wooden chest over in my arms. My mark pulses for a few long beats and then stops.

This is it. I can't believe how easy it was.

Time to swim back to the surface.

I hope that by just swimming upward, I'll see the ship and get back. While following my mark to the chest, I didn't keep track of how many turns I made or the direction I went.

I keep swimming up.

Pressure weighs down on me, and I fight against the current. I pass the chest from one arm to the other, but my muscles are growing tired, and I'm getting tired of swimming. My vision starts to blur, and with the pressure coming down on me, I'm not sure if I'm even facing the right direction anymore. The more I move my arms up, the farther I feel I am from the surface.

And no one even knows I left.

I let my eyes close. I'm so tired, but I keep swimming with my one arm, and my tail—God, I'm so glad the rikorō hasn't run out yet. Still, I'm slowing down, my breath is catching up to me, and I really want to give up.

My eyes squint open. It's a little brighter, at least, and I can see better than before, but my vision is still blurry. I'm not sure if the rikorō finally in running out, or the water is just hazy.

Finally, I think I see ripples on the surface, and I force myself to gain speed, swinging my tail back and forth as hard as I can. I reach out to the surface, and the cold frigid wind strikes my fingers. My pulse quickens. I'm here. I made it. My head rises above water and my lungs burst into a fit of coughs. Rainwater drips over my head, making it difficult to see. I spin, searching for the ship.

Something grabs me.

"Soren!" Nkella's voice shouts over the rain, he holds me up under his arms. My head arches back.

"The chest." My voice is barely audible.

"Do you have a death wish?" he growls. I can hardly see his face—those dark eyes of his—through my blurry vision and the rain. I move the chest toward him. He must have grabbed it from me because the next thing I know, I'm leaning over his shoulder; a second later, I'm unconscious.

I wake up soaking wet and trembling. Nkella is leaning over me, his face close to mine, and his hand is gripping the back of my hair. Worry lines crease his forehead, and he's calling my name. Rain patters around us, muffling the sound of his voice.

Someone approaches from behind and throws a warm wool blanket over my shoulders. Nkella grabs the edges and tightens it in front of me before helping me up. My legs are wobbly as I climb to my feet, but I'm glad they're back, instead of the tail fin. Demitri walks onto the deck.

"What is the meaning of this?" His eyes fall to me, and they widen. "What happened?"

My jaw is still trembling from the cold, I can't speak. The chest! I step back, but Nkella blocks me. "No," I mutter. "Where is it?"

"Kh. Go inside." His face is rigid as he stares at Demitri.

I resist, but he lifts me with one impossibly strong move and drapes me over his shoulder. I'm too beat to resist.

When we're inside, he sets me down on the couch, making sure the wool blanket is still covering me. His hands warm my sides as he looks deeply into my eyes. Then he narrows them. He's about to say something when Demitri comes back inside with Kenjō.

Nkella darts a look in his direction, and with a fast swift move, he has his elbow lodged under Demitri's neck as he holds him up against the wall. Demitri's chin is pointed up as he struggles to speak.

I stand, and Kenjō runs at Nkella.

"Nkella," My teeth are chattering. "Let him go. He had n-nothing to do with this."

Kenjō pulls at Nkella's arm, but I grab her and shake my head. She doesn't know what monster he's battling inside.

"You did this," Nkella hisses to Demitri.

Demitri chokes on a word, and Nkella loosens his grip to let him speak.

"I'll have you know I've no idea what you're accusing me of, but if you don't unhand me, I will have you sleep in the brig and leave you there to die."

"Nkella," I say. "He did not make me jump." I start walking back outside, but now Kenjō is stopping me.

"Soren, what are you doing, è? Are you trying to freeze to death?"

"The chest," I tell her. "Where is it?" I glance at Nkella who still has Demitri pinned to the wall.

"Outside," he says.

"I will get it," Kenjō pivots and braves the rain.

I turn back to Nkella. "Let him go. My mark was showing me where to find the Past Fate's journal. I took a leap of faith and went and got it."

Demitri brings Nkella's arm down from his throat, and Nkella lets him, his face awe-struck at my words.

"Brilliant girl," Demitri says. "You took a risk and executed it perfectly. I'm proud of you."

Nkella whips back to him. "Bancha. She could have been killed, daí? You put things in her head."

"I haven't put anything in her head that wasn't already there. She is mastering her abilities."

Kenjō walks through the door holding the chest and sets it down by our feet. I drop to my knees to take a closer look. It has a lock with the spiderweb symbol on it, but no hole to fit a key. I trace my thumb over it. "How do we open it?"

"The rikorō is killing her," Nkella's voice is hoarse and serious as he stares at Demitri. She should not have jumped."

"Stop," I say. "I'm the one who had the vision, and I was following my mark. This was worth it," I tell him. "Believe me."

Nkella breathes heavily, without speaking. Kenjō hands me a hand-kerchief.

"You are bleeding."

I take it from her and hold it under my nose.

"You need rest," she says. "I will make more tetyevisi and bring it to you."

"Thank you, Kenjō."

"We'll get it open tomorrow, Soren," Demitri says. "For now, Kenjō is right—you need to rest. We all do." He glances at Nkella who steps back, giving him space to walk away. He's still not talking.

Demitri nods at the chest. "Your captain isn't wrong though. As much as I applaud your risk, you should have told someone what you were doing."

I sigh, still holding the cloth to my nose. "I didn't want anyone to try to stop me," I say with difficulty, trying to breathe from my mouth.

"Kh." Nkella pinches his eyes with his fingers and looks away.

"At least, you're alright," Demitri says. "Good thing your gallant prince cared enough to jump in after you."

Nkella's face pales. "I would do it for any of my crew."

My eyes narrow. "How did you find me?"

"I saw you leave the room. When you did not return after an hour, I went looking for you. The one steering the ship saw you jump."

Oh.

"Well, I'm off to bed. Shall I take the chest?" Demitri asks. I place my hand on it, and he narrows his eyes. "Or you can take it and bring it tomorrow if you please, just don't leave it here in the open where any pirate can take it for loot."

He turns to leave but then pauses, glancing over his shoulder. "Of course, you probably shouldn't walk into my office carrying it yourself. I suppose I can send someone to collect you."

"I will walk her," Nkella says.

I sigh behind my teeth. It's not like he can open it without me. "Just take it. I'll see you tomorrow."

He nods and picks it up. "Very well. Let's make our meeting for the afternoon. You'll be needing your sleep."

I rub my nose with the handkerchief and check for blood. When

I'm convinced it's dried up, I roll it up and stick it in my pocket. Nkella is staring at me, but I walk past him.

"Where are you going?"

"To bed," I say. "Where else?"

"Kh. You tell me. Maybe to the Tower by yourself. Or to fight the serpent. Daí?" He grabs my arm and spins me around. I face him and cross my arms. "Answer me."

"I get it. It was bancha. And no, I don't have a death wish," I say. "I want the Death Card. And what's in that chest is my shortcut to getting it, understand?"

"Koj. You have expedited your death sentence, Soren. For power? It is the bancha mistakes—"

"That gets us killed. Why do you care so much whether I live or die, huh? Why would you risk your life for me just now?"

Surprise flashes across his face. "I do not want you to die, Soren." He huffs. The magnetism from the rikorō swirls between us with unspoken words. His heart feels heavy, but he's holding back.

"Whatever." I turn to leave, but he stops me again. His hand touches my arm, this time eliciting electricity to run down my spine. I turn and lock eyes with him. He parts his lips, wanting to say something but doesn't.

"Why didn't you turn?" I ask.

"Daí?"

"Into a merman. When you found me, you didn't have gills on your neck...or fins."

"I don't know."

"It isn't in you anymore, is it? Your curse took care of the rikorō for you," I say recalling Kenjō's theory. "Can you even feel me anymore? Hear my thoughts?"

He shakes his head once. "Koj." His eyes are soft when he looks at me, even though I know he's furious.

"I can still feel yours," I whisper. "Not always, but...sometimes. It's fainter than before."

His breath hitches, realization probably crossing his mind. His eyes dip to my mouth, and he licks his lips.

"Let's go to bed," I say. "I'm getting dizzy."

He carries me the whole way to our quarters and leads me to the tub room where I can properly wash myself and get dry.

The next morning, I sleep in.

I vaguely remember Kenjō coming in and giving me the healing chocolate drink. I can never pronounce the name right—*tetyevisi*. I remember chugging it down and then falling straight to sleep. My muscles ache from having swum; every stretch of my neck or arms feels like my body is going to rip apart.

Dizziness clogs my mind whenever I do try to get up, so I lie back down and drift off to sleep. The crew takes turns checking on me. First, Lāri comes to check my temperature and to bring me breakfast. Then AJ comes to bring me lunch. Sometime during the day, Tessa and Kae poke their heads in to ask me how I'm feeling and see if I feel up to some exercise. When I try to stand, my nose starts bleeding again, so I stay.

Harold comes in to give me more of the chocolate drink, in hopes that more will make me feel better. The dizziness comes and goes, but otherwise, I feel fine; I'm just exhausted. At one point, I wake to see a silhouette of a man standing at the door, watching me. A tiny magnetic pull comes from him, and it makes me feel safe. I smile and turn over, drifting back to sleep.

It isn't until the light outside starts to dim through the windows, that I begin to toss and turn in my bed, tired of being on my back. Images from the night before come in waves, my mark urging me. Why did it do that? Was it because it wanted me to find the journal? Did it sense the journal because I'm a Past Fate, and I was meant to find it? Or was it because I wanted to find it? I need to get that chest open. Stepping onto the floor, I slowly stretch my arms and legs, waiting for the nausea to hit. When it doesn't, I decide it's time to talk to Demitri. Maybe that extra drink did help.

I knock on his door, and he tells me to come in. "Sorry I slept so long," I tell him.

He's sitting in his usual spot at his desk, and he starts to fold a map he has in front of him.

"No apologies necessary. Your body needed time to recover. Have a seat. I was just about to take a look at this chest." He motions to the chair opposite his desk with his hand. The chest I retrieved is sitting right on top of his desk, now dry, and the wood looking brittle.

"It appears there is no keyhole." He scratches his head. "I suppose the fact that she used magic to guard something is more good news, a testament to what else you might be able to do. Silver linings."

I pick the lock up, and as he described, the chest is securely fastened with the lock; my spiderweb mark has the same emblem on it with no hole for a key to fit inside. My mark pulses, and my brow perks up.

Without prompting, I tug on the lock, and it snaps off. A small gasp leaves my lips. I reach into the chest and pull the journal out. My mark gives another quick pulse, and I know I used my magic—it just didn't actually feel like I was doing anything, like I wasn't really trying.

Demitri covers his mouth with his hand. "Astonishing. She must have used blood magic."

I turn the journal in my hand. It's a plain leather journal, dyed in red, and wrapped with a piece of leather cord. As I unravel it, the smell of old leather and handmade pages tickles my nostrils. I take a seat, and Demitri leans in. I open it to the first page, anticipation bubbling in my chest.

The first page is in Ancient Greek, I can tell by the scripture, but I can't read them. The translation potion is blurring the lines between English and Greek for me, unlike when I first saw Cerberus change before my eyes. I glance at Demitri.

"Well?"

"I can't read it. Do you read Ancient Greek?"

His forehead crinkles. "Ah, I always forget, you speak a different language." He opens a drawer in his desk and takes out a small vial. "I never learned Ancient Greek, so I keep this handy for those ancient special scrolls the Empress has." He hands me the vial, and I cautiously take it.

"That should give you a boost on top of the one you took when you got here."

Right, I forgot about that. I uncork the vial and the smell of licorice assaults my nostrils. Yep. It's legit. I take a deep breath and shoot it back. Yuck. I gag and lick my lips. I hate licorice.

Looking back down at the journal, it takes a few seconds for the words to become clear. The letters dance as they shift from Ancient Greek to English and then move around to make sense.

> *Dearest diary,*
>
> *Today I started writing to you because I fear that if I keep these feelings trapped inside, I will fall ill, for it will madden me to the point of no return. When I first laid eyes on him, I knew of Aletha's plan. I cannot deny I knew it. She wanted him for the benefit of a union between his people and ours. To end war. They sent him to kill us. But once I gazed upon the cruel face of that warrior, something inside him called to me. Something deep and surreal. The way he looks at me, as if I've changed something inside him, too, makes me believe we were fated to be together. And I believe it is true for he no longer wants to kill us. I have begged and begged Asteria to look into our future, but she denies my request—as always, the wise one.*
>
> *Love,*
> *Adara*

I feel my cheeks redden and set the journal down.

"What does it say?" Demitri takes the journal and opens it to the first entry. "I see." He flips through more pages and takes a seat. "Well, Soren. You might have to read through all this. Hopefully, it isn't all useless, but this seems to be a declaration of her love for Tetalla."

My shoulders slump. "There has to be something in there."

"Oh. Oh wait—there is." He stops on a page and reads on before turning it back over to me.

> *Dearest diary,*
> *Yesterday Asteria and I needed to get away. I told her I had something dangerous to tell her and I couldn't risk*

whispering while the spirits of the Aō are still a mystery. She took me to the future of Rome, where we found this beautiful deck of cards. I couldn't believe I had left you behind and dipped into the past to retrieve you, just so I could write you this letter. That way, Aletha couldn't have found you. Even now, I'm afraid to write what I told Asteria for fear of Aletha spying on me. Perhaps I'll have the courage later, but for now, Asteria thinks, somehow, giving her something else to focus on would take away her sorrow at Tetalla's and my betrayal. But really, he was never hers.

Love,

Adara

I read it over twice, stopping where she wrote "dipped into the past to retrieve you, just so I could write you this letter." I read it out loud. "What do you think she meant by that?"

Demitri places a finger on his bottom lip and says, "You know what you need to do." He smiles.

I place the journal on the desk and sit back, getting comfortable.

"Practice makes perfect," he presses. "Deep breath, now you have something of hers for certain so this should be easier for you."

Leaving one hand on top of the leather journal, I shut my eyes and take a deep breath, this time feeling straight for the pull of my mark until it starts to pulse.

It works quicker this time. But it's different. I'm standing on a large spiderweb, it's bouncing beneath me and I'm rigid, hovering like I'm about to fall with my hands spread out for balance. In front of me, I see Adara sitting on the silk web, alone. She's looking inside one of the open spaces within the web, her feet dangling off it. Colors—or an image—come into view inside that open space as I take a careful step toward her. Then, she leans her body to the edge, and I gasp as she jumps down into the image.

Reminding myself this is just a memory, I do the same, following her down through the web.

I recognize her bedroom from my vision of her before she jumped out the window. She picks up the journal from her desk and says, "No one has to know I'm here, so this can't change the past." With that, she glances up at the ceiling, and to my disbelief a web flies from her fingertips. She latches on and is whisked away.

The scene changes, and I'm back.

Demitri's face comes into focus, and I stare down at the diary. I'm not sure I understand what I just saw. Or maybe, I do but it's just too...unbelievable.

"What did you see?"

"I—I think she was able to take objects from the past without altering them."

Confusion spreads on his face. "Something like a lost object?"

"Or an object no one knows about," I explain to him the details of the vision.

"Fascinating," he looks down to the side. "Give it a try," he urges.

"I wouldn't even know how to start, visions for me have always just been....visions."

"Have you ever felt anything in these visions? Wind? Heat?"

"Yeah, I guess, but..."

"If you can feel, then maybe you can pick up tangible items."

I rub at my eyelid. "Doubtful. My visions always feel almost dreamlike. But I'll give it a try." I close my eyes and take a deep breath. "I wonder if I'd be able to pick anything up from any memory, or only from my own."

"Why don't you just start with your own for now and work your way up."

My mom comes into view, and I get whisked away into a memory. I'm sitting at the breakfast table and she's smiling at me. I'm five years old, and making a mess of my cornflakes. I reach over and touch the fork. It feels...solid. That's good. My mom whispers something in front of me and I focus on what she's saying, but I can't hear her. She has her mug up to her face, and she's talking into it as if there's something inside. I reach for her, but when my fingers brush her hair, she startles.

I gasp.

Then, she giggles at me and grabs my hand. My throat dries, and I get the urge to pull her. Can I bring her with me? I tug at her hand, but it becomes like whisps of air, a phantom disappearing in front of me. The kitchen changes the same way, then the table.

I'm back with my heart lodged in my throat.

I shudder and shake my head.

Demitri sits back in his seat. "I think that's enough for now. Are you alright?"

I nod, but don't say anything for fear my voice will be shaky.

"Do you want to talk about it?"

"No," I mouth.

"We can try again tomorrow." He starts to pick up the journal.

I clear my throat. "I'd like to read that before bed if you don't mind." I speak more formally than I intended.

"Oh." He squints at it and closes his hand. "Go on then, but Soren... I would keep it away from your captain."

"Why?"

"It seems to me he doesn't want you to develop your power. What if he takes the journal from you?"

"He wouldn't do that."

"Can you be sure? I overheard your argument, and I can't help remembering his entire motivation for being here lies in bringing his sister back, and nothing else. He's with you because of your promise to find the Death Card. I'm only laying it out flatly. Don't forget he betrayed you last time."

"It wasn't a real betrayal," I counter, balling my fist.

"Even so, he kept it from you. That's his strategy, keeping things hidden. What else would he keep from you? He isn't infallible, quite the opposite, in fact, with that hideous curse of his. He makes mistakes. He can put you in danger. And he has. "

"He saved me last night."

"He saw his one chance at getting his sister back in peril."

My chest tightens. "You're wrong. I've felt his feelings from the rikorō we drank. I've been able to hear his mind."

"Well, admittedly, that's a first. If he feels so much for you, why aren't you two together?"

I swallow. "I'm not staying here after this. I'm going back home. Why start anything new?"

"That makes sense. But a man like Nkella would stop at nothing to get what he wants, and he wouldn't let you go. I noticed he hadn't shifted last night when he came back. No trace of any rikorō in his body. Can you still hear his thoughts?"

"No... But I can still feel some things."

"Well, as long as you're not mistaking feelings for what they aren't. You're a brilliant girl, Soren. I don't want to see you getting hurt."

He does try to hide his feelings from me. He somehow managed to block all that out shortly after finding the crew. I thought it was because he didn't want to admit his feelings to me, but maybe it's something else.

"Come to my table for dinner tonight," he says. "Take a break from your crew for a night. Come on. It'll be fun."

"Umm..."

"Think on it." He pushes the journal forward, and I bring it up to my chest.

22

I CLOSE DEMITRI'S OFFICE DOOR BEHIND ME AND HOLD THE journal up to my chest as I walk back to my wing. Voices come from down the hall where Kenjō's lab is, and I pause. Part of me wants to join them, but the other part of me wants to be alone. I need some time to reflect on my visions and what I just learned about my power. If I walk inside the lab, I'm going to be put to work making bombs. And as much as I'd like to chat, I need to focus on getting stronger so I can take power over the Death Card when I get it.

When I get it.

This is definitely feeling like more of a reality.

I start to walk out of the hall when the door shuts, and Nkella catches sight of me. I bite my cheek, pushing back what Demitri suggested about him. I don't want to believe he only saved me for his gain. Not again.

But maybe I should.

He approaches me, and I hold the journal tighter against my chest.

"How are you feeling?" he says, his voice low.

"Fine. The second drink worked."

His eyes fix on what I'm holding, and he nods to it.

I shrug.

He lets out a chuckle. "What is it, daí?"

"Oh, it's what was in the chest."

His brows rise. "You opened it?"

"Yep."

"Was it worth it?"

"Definitely."

"Hn." He looks at it, and I keep it covered. "What does it say?"

"I'd rather not talk about it. I'm going to go."

He blinks at me, and I think I see hurt washing over his features, but he erases it not a second later. He nods and pivots back to the lab. A set of red eyes emerge through the doorway, and I know it was Iéle who told him I had come out of the office.

Before dinner, I head back to my wing, but no one is there. Grateful, I stick the journal under my pillow and straighten myself up.

At the mess hall, AJ calls me over to the table. I glance in their direction and wave but keep walking to Demitri's side. AJ's face slackens, and he gapes at the others. Before I see Nkella's reaction, I take a seat next to Demitri, facing Alec and Kenjō.

Demitri gives me an approving grin, and he quickly glances at the table where my crew is. I avoid looking at them.

Alec greets me with a nod and a smile; he has his arm wrapped around Kenjō's shoulder.

"How are you feeling?" Kenjō asks me.

"Better, I think." I bring my arms in as someone sets down a large tray of what looks like a giant serpent. The aroma something citrus blended with meat swarms my nostrils, making my stomach growl. People start cutting off pieces of meat, and I wait until I get a chance.

I gape at it. "That's not the serpent, is it?" I ask no one in particular.

Alec chuckles, and Demitri smiles. "Not that one, no. But we do have very big eels in this part of the sea. Demitri takes a butcher knife and chops a piece of eel, then puts it on my plate. It catches me off guard, and I stare at it. I know I've been spending time in his office, but I still don't trust him. Knowing his intentions and what he wants me for...these little acts of kindness are only to win me over. And I'm not falling for it.

"Before it's all gone," he says to me with a wink.

"Thanks."

"Are you leaving tonight?" Bronte asks Alec.

"I'll leave early in the morning and be back tomorrow evening." He rubs Kenjō's shoulder. "I need to make sure Swords stays in line. I have soldiers letting me know if there are any problems, but I'm confident my men can handle it."

"Your men know not to mess with our ship?" Demitri asks.

"Absolutely," Alec says as he takes a bite of the eel.

I stick a piece of meat in my mouth as I repeat his words in my mind. He has a soldier bring him to and from the ship. I lean into Demitri and whisper, "Is it possible for you and my crew to go straight to the *Gambit*?" Why are we stuck on this ship if he has soldiers by his side that can do what he asks?

"Clever," he says. "Unfortunately, the Swords Arcana still reports to the Empress. We can get away with our large cargo ship as Alec is giving us free passage to bring in supplies. If we sneak in via my Arcana, there is no doubt that we will be caught, as her Arcana are guarding the Aō in Swords now as well—especially near the Ace of Swords, which is where the *Gambit* is."

"Can't you use your Hierophant magic and turn them all to your side?"

Demitri chuckles as he takes a sip of his drink. "I admire your ambition, but that is a war we are not ready for. I need the Sword first."

"Right." I take another bite of my food.

"That is a nice necklace," Mūhī says a few seats down. "I still wonder how your mother acquired it."

"È?" a man in front of him says. The man is now gaping at me with a full mouth. "How many of you muse people are there?" His sleeves are cut off, broadcasting a pair of muscular arms. His right arm has a tattoo with some Ipani lettering over his stripes.

"Muse?"

"Spider," Demitri says. "That's enough. Leave the girl alone."

"I'm only wondering," Mūhī says.

"She must have been fucking an Ipani from Danū." The guy with the scripture tattoo remarks. "Only way to get gichang like that."

I ball my fist, and my tongue absorbs all the saliva in my mouth.

"A royal," Mūhī says. "It's a royal gichang."

"Like mother like daughter then, è?" Laughter bellows out of him as food spews out of his mouth. I grimace. He leans over and turns to me as he cuts a slice of his meat. "What happened to your mom? She left?"

My heart starts pounding loudly in my chest.

Before I can answer him, he says "I bet the Empress got jealous."

Another man from the other side joins the conversation and leans in. "A! Didn't the Empress get jealous of her sister too? Looks like she's always jealous about bitches taking her men." They join in laughter.

I feel my body temperature rise. "My mother was not a bitch."

"I said, that's enough." Demitri's voice booms.

"What is it with Danū men wanting *guyuti* anyway, è? What is so special between their legs?"

"Oy!" Bronte warns. "Do you want to go overboard?"

The man laughs louder, clearly not hearing his captain, and smacks his friend on his shoulder. "The Empress must have golden web between her legs by now." He perks up. "Maybe all muse women have golden web, è?" He looks at me, and smirks.

More laughter erupts from the table, but I ignore whatever insult he threw at me. Alec and Kenjō are frowning, and Demitri motions for them to shut up or he says he'll have their throats, but it all becomes background noise as my vision darkens, and I'm no longer in the crowded room.

I'm standing in front of my mom. Her hair is loose, and she wears a loose tan shirt over dark tan leggings. She looks so beautiful. A shadow eclipses her and I turn to see the Empress standing in front of her, holding a pretty purple vial in her hand.

"Drink this," she tells my mom, "and you will be able to attain all your gifts. You can stay here forever with your love and raise your child without harm."

"So we have a truce? And you'll leave me and my family alone?"

"It is my gift and my oath to you, Diana. I only ever wanted for us to weave together as Fates, to make this world stronger."

"And it won't hurt the baby?" She touches her stomach, and confusion clouds my brain.

My mother takes the vial and lifts it to her lips. My heart starts to hammer in my throat. I recognize that vial. *"No!"* I shout. *"Don't trust her. It's itachi."* Tears well in my eyes as my mother drinks the whole thing. The vial drops to the floor, and a few seconds later, my mom's eyes grow wide and glossy, and she, too, falls to the floor. I reach for her, but everything turns to smoke as the scene changes.

The Empress is standing in front of the Ipani man I had seen flying on the drakon with my mother. She has him suspended as an Arcana soldier slices his throat, and blood seeps out. My lips tremble. Where's my mom? How did she end up back home?

The scene changes. My mother is crying over a hand mirror. I don't know what kind of itachi the Empress gave her, but she seems to be back. Maybe she was strong enough to come back alone.

"Go now," an Ipani woman in a red tunic tells her. "Do not die here in eternal torment from the Itachi."

I gasp and let out a huge breath as my surroundings all come back to me at once. People have jumped out of their seats, and Demitri and Nkella are both shouting my name.

My hands are shaking, and I see red.

My mother didn't develop early-onset Alzheimer's. The dementia she had was somehow induced by the itachi she drank.

The man that was talking shit to my right says something along the lines of calling me dumb, and Nkella reaches over and slams his head down against the table. A fight almost breaks out, but Demitri waves his hand, and an Arcana soldier comes and takes the man away. A few of the pirates in his crew gape, but Demitri says he deserved it, then returns his attention to me.

"Soren? Can you hear me?"

Nkella is now sitting next to me. He takes my chin and turns my face to him. His dark eyes search mine.

"Neyuro. Say something."

"I—"

"Where did you go?" he whispers.

I gasp as webbing covers his shoulders. I gape at the table. A few others are also drenched in silk spiderwebs. Kenjō is peeling it off Alec's back, and it's covering Kenjō's hair. Bronte has a displeased look on her face. Where did all this webbing come from? I stare down at my hands, and the silky web is draped over my legs. "Was that me?" I whisper mostly to myself.

"It was fascinating," Demitri says. "You had a vision. What did you see?"

"She killed her." I curl my fist to abate the shaking.

"Who killed who?" Demitri says.

My throat dries. Nkella touches my hand, but I pull away. I jump back off the seat. "No."

Confusion sprawls on his face as I back away. Demitri stands, but Nkella holds him back. Nkella glances at me, his face serious. I give him one last look before I dash out of the mess hall. Eyes stare at me as I leave. I hear AJ calling my name, but I ignore him and start running.

I run down the hall and up to the freezing cold main deck. I don't know where I'm going or even where I want to be, so I lean against the rail and stare out to the dark waters of the sea. I don't even care how cold it is. Tears well up in my eyes, and I drop to the floor as they fall down my cheeks. I grab onto my legs. My shoulders shake as I cry into my knees.

Everything I thought I knew about my mom—my life—was wrong.

It was all a lie.

"Soren..." Nkella's voice cuts through the wind. I lift my head to see his boots in front of me. He takes a seat next to me. "Neyuro..." A wave of worry and conflicted emotion emanates from him, and I know he's actually concerned. Despite the rikorō being gone from his system, I can still feel him because it isn't out of mine yet. I glance at him, tears blurring my vision. He wraps his arm around me, and I let myself fall to his lap. I squeeze my eyes shut as the tears start flowing out of me again.

He places a gentle hand on my hair and starts to stroke it. He doesn't press me for my vision; he just lets me cry.

I cry until my back starts to hurt from being in this position, so I prop myself back up. I find his gaze on me as I do, but he doesn't say anything, so I decide to tell him.

"My life would have been so different. I would have had a mother. A loving family. I never would have been a foster child. The Empress killed her. She did this to me."

"What did you see?" he whispers.

I tell him my vision. How my mother died, what we thought she died from. I tell him everything from how I was raised to my father giving me away to the foster system. "I thought he never cared," I say. "Now, I know he didn't. He wasn't even my real father."

"Daí? How can you be sure?"

"My mother was pregnant before she left."

"To a Danū royal?" Nkella asks.

I nod, wiping my cheeks. "I never got his name."

"My family used to be large, but not too many have come from your land. I will find out for you."

I gasp. "Would this make us related?"

He shakes his head and smiles. "Koj. It would not have been anyone directly related to me. I would have heard about it."

"I hate her so much," my voice shakes. "She k-killed my mom."

Nkella wraps his arms around me once more, and I sob into his coat.

"Let's get you inside where it's warm, daí? We are going to freeze out here."

I let him help me up and take me back to our wing. The crew is already inside and sprawled on the beds. They stop talking when we enter the room, and I walk straight past everyone and go to clean my face up. I can hear Nkella tell them something through the door, but I don't mind. I don't have any secrets from the crew, and it's good for them to know. I splash water on my face and walk back out.

AJ is standing outside the door. He gives me a hug. I almost start crying again but hold back my tears.

"We'll get her for you, Soren," he whispers into my hair. "The Empress is going down."

"Thanks, AJ."

I make it to my bed and get in. The others glance at me but no one presses me for any information, even though I know they're curious.

"Sorry, guys. Do you mind if we talk about this tomorrow?" I ask. "I kind of just want to be alone with my thoughts." And by alone, I mean not talking, because there's nowhere else I can sleep.

"Get some rest, Soren," Tessa says. "You don't have to share anything you don't want to. We're just glad you're okay."

"Well, I *would* like to know about the web that came out of you like Spider-Man," Harold says from his side of the room. "But it can wait."

Ignoring him, I pull the covers over my head, dimming the light of the room. I have no idea how the web came out of me, but I'm guessing it came out of my fingertips. But why did it? When I saw Adara do it, she was going through some interdimensional area. What would prompt it to happen to me?

"What is a Spider-Man?" Lāri whispers loudly.

I smile to myself as Harold tries to explain it to the crew. Hearing him describe the adventures of Spider-Man as if it's some epic tale since he doesn't know how to describe movies or comic books makes me want to crack up and join them, but I don't move.

They chat for another thirty minutes while I try to force myself to sleep. After they snuff out their candles, I become restless. Taking a peek over my covers, I notice no one snuffed mine out. I feel for the journal under my pillow, reach over and grab one of Lāri's pencils, and scoot close to the light. If I can't sleep, I might as well try to distract myself from my thoughts.

I open to the second journal entry.

> *Dearest Diary,*
> *Aletha hasn't left me alone. I never wanted to come here, I wanted to stay in Athens. Asteria is trying to keep the peace, as always. But I need to be alone. I miss him dearly, I can't think. I can't sleep. It isn't fair Aletha banished him from seeing me. He does not wish to have her as his suitor.*
> *Forever trapped in perpetual madness,*
> *Adara*

I get it great, great, however-many great grandmother.

My whole life, I'd thought my mother had a genetic disease. I thought what was happening to us also happened to others—it sucked, but it's life. I didn't know she was murdered, and my whole life was stolen because of your sister. My dad isn't even my real dad.

What am I supposed to do now? I want the Death Card to bring my mom back, but...

All I can think about is wishing I had the power to crack open the Empress's skull.

> *It was all a lie.*
> *Lies*
> *Lies lies*
> *She killed her*
> *The empress killed my mom.*
> *I hate her. I hate her so much.*
> *I hate her I hate her I hate her I hate her I hate her I hate her I hate her I hate her*
> *I hate her I hate her I hate her I hate her I hate her I hate her I hate her I hate her*
> *I hate her I hate her I hate her I hate her I hate her I hate her I hate her I hate her*
> *I hate her I hate her I hate her I hate her I hate her I hate her I hate her I hate her*
> *I hate her I hate her I hate her I hate her I hate her I hate her I hate her I hate her*
> *I hate her I hate her I hate her I hate her*
> *And I want her dead.*
> *I'm going to kill her and no one is going to stop me.*
> *—Soren*

23

I WAKE TO THE CREAKING HINGES OF THE DOOR SLOWLY opening. I narrow my eyes in the direction of the sound. A figure casts a shadow over the dark wooden floor. Before the man steps through, I get a glimpse of his collar popped at the neck. Nkella nears my bed, and I stare at him. What's he doing up? I fell asleep on the diary's open pages. I quickly shut it and stick it under my pillow. He stands over me, wearing his black pants and black tunic under his coat.

"Get ready."

"For what?"

A small smirk tugs at his lips, "For your training, neyuro, daí? You and me." I blink at him, and he raises his chin. "You have five minutes. Hurry up." He softens his features and I swear I just saw him wink, then he turns and leaves me to get ready.

That was...uncharacteristic of him. What the hell is going on?

I sniffle and wipe my eyes. A few minutes later, I'm dressed in the green tunic Tessa had sewn up. I meet Nkella in the communal area where he's sitting with Iéle by his feet. He glances up at me and stands.

"What are we doing up this early?" I ask him. "And why are we doing it?"

"I told you already. Let's go."

259

"Training for what?" I follow him down the hall and to a different hall to the right I haven't been to yet.

"You have not trained in days, neyuro. You are too weak to fight. Sweat more in training. Bleed less in battle, daí?"

"Nk—" I take a deep breath and pinch the bridge of my nose. "I don't exactly feel like training right now, okay?"

"I am not giving you a choice."

I gape at the back of his head. He's serious right now. He opens a door and leads me to an open room, with swords and daggers on the walls. Sunlight comes in through the circular window on the left.

"Are we even supposed to be in here?"

He scoffs. "Since when do you care about places you are not supposed to be?" He quirks a brow, and my cheeks heat.

He takes a fighting stance and instructs me to do the same. Then he motions for me to come at him. I take a step and throw a punch. He grabs it with one fist instead of moving away like he normally does.

"Kh. Harder, neyuro."

I throw another punch, harder this time. He takes my fist and shoves me back. I catch my balance and grimace at him. I throw a harder punch, and he lightly blocks it.

"Again."

I throw another.

"Again. Harder."

I punch him again. And again. And again. My fists start to hurt, but this time I don't care. I keep punching him, and soon I'm hitting him hard against his chest. Tears are streaming down my face. He doesn't budge. He doesn't even act like he feels it. He just lets me hit him. And now I understand why he wanted me to do this. It wasn't because he wanted me to train. He just wanted me to let it out.

I glance at him, and he's smiling at me. "Does this feel good, neyuro?"

"Yes."

He opens his arms and wraps them around me. I stop punching him and let him hold me. I dry my tears. "Last night... I wrote in the journal."

"Daí? What did you write?"

"I'm just so mad." I pull away from him and stare into his eyes. "I wrote that I want to kill her." My breath hitches. I can't believe I just admitted that out loud.

"You are allowed to feel that way." He wipes a tear from under my eyes. "But, neyuro, you are no killer, hn? Keep focused on bringing your mother back. That will be your revenge. Life. Not death."

"You kill."

"I am already gone. You are the light in the sky from the Aō that guides me in the darkest storm, daí? Do not change."

My chest grows heavy, and I swallow.

"But this does not mean you cannot learn to defend yourself. Choose a sword." He lets me go, and I stare at the wall.

"How do I choose?"

He takes the swords down, one by one, and lets me hold them, measuring them against me until he decides which one I should try.

"Now," he says, moving back to the center of the room. "Let us blow off some steam."

He teaches me a set of movements. They feel almost like a dance as he swings his sword along with each step. Then he teaches me each move slowly, having me hit his sword with mine. It's hard to focus as his moves are so swift and masterful. He's brutally handsome and elegant as he goes through each motion. I get lost in the sight of him.

The room grows hot from our practice, and he pulls off his tunic, showcasing his lean muscles and the tattoos over his Ipani stripes, glistening with sweat.

A few times he catches me staring at him, and he scolds me for not paying attention, but I don't miss the gleam in his eye, and the smirk he tries to hide. Every once in a while, I feel the wave of rikorō carrying his emotions, but I ignore it.

I know we're just friends now, and that's what I need to concentrate on.

And I appreciate his methods of trying to distract me; I think it's exactly what I needed.

After two hours, we hang the swords back on the wall. Sweat sticks to the back of my hair against my neck, and I wipe my brow.

"I better go to Demitri's office for my session."

He frowns but nods. "Be careful."

"I know."

When I reach Demitri's office door, I hear voices arguing inside, so I wait before walking in.

"I cannot do it, Demitri. It would attract attention from the Tower if I make you second-in-command."

"No one in the Tower needs to know. Not yet. It is in your best interest we do it this way."

A pause. And then, *"It wouldn't be fair. I cannot allow it."*

"You will not allow it, you mean."

"I'm sorry, Demitri. You are a friend, and I do not wish to upset you. I just can't do it."

"Let's discuss this later, Soren should be here soon."

I step away from the door and act like I'm getting here late. The door opens, and Alec walks out, looking flustered. He glances at me, and I wave as I walk in, but he doesn't say anything coherent as he walks past.

Worry lines cross Demitri's forehead as I take a seat in front of his desk. "I didn't think you would make it this morning."

"Sorry, I'm late. I was training with Nkella." I don't tell him I heard part of his argument with Alec.

He frowns. "Oh?"

"Yeah, it helped to get my mind off things."

Demitri raises a brow. "I bet it did." He folds his hands and sits back in his chair. "I want to apologize to you on behalf of this ship's crew. They can be most unruly and difficult to control."

"You don't need to apologize for them," I tell him. "They were just being themselves."

"Even so, them being themselves shows the worst this world can bring, and it shouldn't go unpunished." He glances at his hands and then back at me. "Would you like to discuss the vision you had at dinner? I know whatever you saw made you feel severely uncomfortable, but, Soren, you showed another great power."

I stare at my fingertips. "The web."

"The web," he repeats. "And I have a feeling it is only the tip of the iceberg of what you can do."

"I don't know how I did it."

"It seems it was prompted by your emotions. What were you feeling during your vision?"

I inhale deeply and look away as my eye starts to itch with the threat of tears. I swallow, and it feels like acid going down my throat.

"Sadness?" His voice is soft. "You don't have to tell me what you saw. I just want to figure out what is prompting your powers."

I clear my throat and look down at my hands. "Mostly anger," I say. "Oh."

Before he can say anything else, I say, "The Empress killed my mother."

Confusion and then something else flashes in his eyes. Recognition? Remembrance? It was like he just realized something.

"Did you know my mom?" I ask more directly. "You were around back when she came."

He purses his lips. "I do remember now. I wasn't certain she was your mother because others have come, and well, the Empress has a problem with every newcomer who has ever found their way to Ipa. Or Fateland as she prefers to call it."

"Tarotland," I say with a smirk.

"Tarotland?" he chuckles softly. "Is that what you call it? It's fitting." I smile back at him.

"But yes, your mother and the Empress had a feud." My stomach clenches. "It seems your mother reminded Empress Aletha of who she used to be. Back then, I advised her to make your mother her friend and become her family as she and your mother—and well, you—are very distant relatives. With your powers, you both could keep the balance of this world from falling apart."

"Falling apart?"

His gaze becomes distant as he visibly tries to remember. "The balance is off, you see. The Aō should never have adopted new magic, and the more one magic tries to overcome the other, the more likely it is that this world might collapse one day. The problem is the Empress fears anyone who holds power."

"Because all she cares about is ruling."

"I would assume it's because out of the three Fates, she feels she is the weakest. The present is ever-passing. It goes from being out of reach to somewhere behind her in a matter of seconds. Pausing the present is useless if nothing comes from it."

"Sounds lonely. She should probably give up and just die already." I force a fake smile.

"Severely lonely. But she has lost anyone she's ever loved due to power in one way or another, so this is how she copes. She'll only ever let one person into her life at a time, and I was that person. Now, I assume her sense of trust is even more tarnished."

"I don't blame you for turning on her though," I say, recalling the vision I had of his childhood.

"I appreciate you saying that, but I never turned on her because I was never her friend. She merely trusted the wrong person. That's always been her failure. Her power is greater than she knows, but she will never become good at it, because she refuses to become one with it."

"What's her greatest power? Just a second ago, it sounded pretty useless."

"Keeping the peace of one's nature."

My brows furrow.

"No matter. I pity the poor soul she has encased into her clutches. Whoever her new Hierophant trainee is will suffer a great deal of pain."

"Sucks for them."

He laughs. "Yes, well, that will only matter to us when they come into their power and act as her advisor and spy. For now"—he taps on his desk—"we want to get ahead of that. What would you like to work on today? Your newfound web powers? Or perhaps what we were doing yesterday, picking something physical out of a past memory?"

"Did you know she was going to kill my mother?" I ask, ignoring his question.

"Or we could talk about that." His frown deepens as he stares at me.

"I did know of her plan. I can't say I did anything to stop it—I would be lying to you if I said that. What I will say is I would have wanted to befriend her, to get her on my side once she saw the real Aletha."

"And do with her what you're doing to me?"

"Precisely, yes. I know it's my ambition. I know I sound opportunistic, but I'm honest."

I relax my shoulders. That's probably the truest thing he's ever said to me. "Wait—what do you mean the world might collapse? Won't getting rid of the Empress make it worse?"

"You're smart, Soren. Yes, but it has survived for hundreds of years with just her. There can be one Fate, two, or none at all. But if there's to be only one, wouldn't it be wiser to have the less evil one?"

I swallow, carefully considering what he's telling me. My mother could have been Empress. The only Fate. And it would have been better because she wouldn't have had people in eternal torture after death, or be against ouma, or have agentless soldiers. "Wait."

His brows rise.

"That's why you want me to stay—but I can't be Empress. And don't you want to be Emperor? How would that work?"

He smiles. "There can be an Emperor and an Empress. We could rule together, you and me. Or you don't need to at all."

Ah. There it is. "Us rule together?"

"But just because you're a Fate, that doesn't mean you need to lead. You can live happily in the forest, or at sea, if that's what you like. Don't meddle in people's lives, especially their past. Leave things how they are, but stay here to restore the balance while I do all the heavy lifting."

"So if I stay, I don't have to rule?"

"Of course not. Empress Aletha is controlling and power-hungry."

"But what about the Tarot merged with the Aō?"

"What about it? It will continue to do what it does. If I need you to control it, I'll come to you. That can be your only job if you like. Or take up the throne. The choice is yours. The Aō won't give you the Empress mark unless you are ready for it."

The ship rocks back and forth, and I sit back in my chair.

"We'll be reaching the peak of Swords soon, and then we'll make a right and sail toward the Temple where the *Gambit* is."

I nod. "I was thinking...maybe I don't need the *Gambit*."

"Why is that?"

"If I can pick something out of the past, can't I pick out the Death Card?"

He blinks at me. "Clever girl."

"Then I can even use it to bring back Nkella's sister. I'd bring the *Gambit* back, but that's a little heavy."

"Yes, you'll have to be meticulous with how you use that power, though. And you'll have to be careful not to change anything—no taking the card before Nkella is cursed."

I part my lips. "Why not? What would that change except saving everyone from being cursed?"

"Who saved you when you first came to Tarotland?"

"The crew."

"And what were they doing?"

"Seeking refuge before curse day."

"And what do you think would happen, if they were never cursed? If Ntaoru was never taken as an Arcana soldier?"

My eyes widen. "I never would have met the crew."

"And possibly, you would have drowned."

"Understood. I'll be careful." I recall how Adara reclaimed her diary only because she knew her sister hadn't known about it.

"Good girl. Now, if it's okay with you, we should begin. Once we dock, we won't have time for so many lessons."

"I don't want to go into a memory right now."

Demitri's shoulders drop.

"But..." I squint. "When I saw Adara's memory, I noticed she didn't zone out. I don't think she had to see a memory to activate her power. Webbing just came out of her at will. I'd like to be able to do that without suffering through a traumatic revelation."

A smile slides across his face. "I'd like to try something if you're be okay with it."

"What?"

"Since you don't even remember your web coming out of your fingertips, and it happened because you were angry, why don't we try to focus on that anger alone?"

My throat dries up and I glance down at my feet. "I wanted to kill her," I mutter.

"Many of us do."

"I still do," I say a little more hoarsely. "My entire life was stolen from me because she took my mother away."

He leans over his desk. "Then kill her, Soren."

I blink up at him. "What?"

"Take the Ace of Swords—it's the only thing that can kill her—and do it. Master your power. Take back what's yours. You can have it all. The Death Card, the Sword. Revenge."

"I've never killed anyone before. I don't think I can do it." Sweat starts to form along the back of my neck.

"There's always a first time for everything. Why give me the sword, while you can do it yourself?"

"Don't you want to be the one to kill her? After what she did to your father?"

"It would please me just as much if you did it or if we did it together. Don't you want your mom back, without having to worry about the Empress finding her again and taking her away? I would be worried if it were me." After a beat, he starts talking about the new exercise he wants me to do, but I tune out.

The air escapes my lungs. I hadn't thought of that. What's to stop her from taking my mom from me again after I bring her back? She has the World Card now. She can still find us. My heart starts beating as realization consumes my thoughts. I have to kill her. He's right. The Empress must be stopped, and the only way is by getting the Sword. "I'll do it," I finally say.

"The exercise? Marv—"

"No. I mean, I'll kill her. I'll do it." My hand starts to shake, and adrenaline surges through me. "I just—I don't know how."

His face darkens. "Leave that to me. I'll show you how. But first, your power."

I nod, my chest slightly out of breath despite my not having moved. "Right. The exercise."

"Think about your vision last night. Without going into it. Feel the anger, Soren. Feel the rage." His voice gets louder at the last word. "When you learned the Empress poisoned your mother."

My cheeks heat, and I ball my fist.

"Your life was stolen from you," he preaches.

My blood curdles.

"An orphan in a strange world. When you should have been *here*."

My throat clogs. I should have been here. I gasp. My father wouldn't have been my dad. "Did you know my real father?" I ask.

Demitri blinks, and his eyes move from side to side, trying to picture who I'm talking about. "Sehu."

"My father's name was Sehu?"

"He was adopted by the royal family. He was from Oleanu originally. But the Empress killed his family, and he was taken in by Nkella's grandparents."

My chest tightens, and my eyes fill with tears again. I smile. "He was adopted like me. We already share something in common."

Demitri quirks a brow but stays silent for a moment. Then he says, "You might have even more in common. There was a secret about him, about his family but..."

"But?"

He purses his lips. "We're getting ahead of ourselves. Focus, Soren. Focus on your anger. You never met your real father. The Empress killed him. Killed your mother. Left you as an orphan, to be raised by—"

"Someone who gave me away to be taken by bad people. Because he couldn't accept the responsibility of having me." My blood starts to boil again, and I start to see red.

"Yes," Demitri says. "Good, feel that hatred and let it manifest into something greater. Powerful. Don't let it stew. Release it."

"She ruined my life." My mark starts to pulse.

"Yes."

"She took my family away from me." My wrist grows unbearably heavy as I'm blinded by rage.

"Yes."

"And she almost killed me. She thinks she can stop me. Well, she can't!" I shout. Silky webbing releases from the fingertips of my right hand, I gasp as the sensation is tingling, yet releasing. "But if none of that ever happened, I wouldn't have met Talia." I pull my hand back, and gape at Demitri as he spits webbing out of his mouth. Gasping, I stare at the web covering him and his desk. "I'm sorry!"

"Perhaps we should continue your lessons outside my office from now on." He pulls the web from his face but then smiles. "You did very well. Take a break, and meet me after dinner?"

Picking up the silky thread from his desk and examining it in my hands, a wide smile covers my face. "Absolutely."

24

A SMIRK SMEARS MY LIPS AS I WALK TOWARD THE MAIN DECK —not because I feel lighter, and not because I feel better. But because now I have a plan I feel strongly about. All this time I've hated Demitri, thinking he was sneaky and a creep, however, he's only been that way because of the Empress. She made him the way he is, he just got carried away when he was close to failure. I get it; she killed his father, probably both his parents. And he lost everything his family ever had.

If I were in his shoes, I'd probably want to take everything she has away from her too.

But me? I'm only interested in the Death Card to bring my mom back. Only now I understand that in order to be successful, I have to kill the Empress—or she'll stop at nothing to take her away from me again. I can't let that happen.

Plus, she'll try to kill me again too.

She can try. Now that I've been training my power—and I know she's afraid of it—I'm going to survive this. I'm going to kill her.

"Soren?" Kenjō's voice comes from the open doorway. Harold is standing in front of her, with his back to me as he leans against the wall. I guess they're friends again. He looks over his shoulder at me and smiles.

"Hey, guys." I walk over to them. "What are you two up to?"

"Just talking," Harold says.

"No making bombs today?"

"We're out of supplies now," Kenjō says. "We have made a lot."

A chill breeze makes me wrap my arms around myself. "Demitri says we should be docking soon."

"Yes, we are getting close. Like another day or two." She smiles. "We were about to go watch the games. Want to come?"

"What games?"

"The crews are playing *mō nalo* at the mess hall."

"Oh, sure. Lead the way."

I fall back into step with Harold and nudge his elbow. "So, you two are friends again?"

A gives me a modest shrug. "Sure, why not?" He grins sheepishly.

Cheering comes from inside the mess hall as we step inside. I avoid looking over to the left where I sat last night. Even though Bronte and Demitri aren't there, I don't want to relive what happened. I follow Kenjō and Harold to where our crew is sitting at the far right of the room. AJ is playing a game that looks like the one I saw Nkella playing in the tavern against one of Bronte's crew members. Kae is playing on his team, and Nkella has a hand on his shoulder. I spot Tessa and Lāri and smile at them as they wave us over.

AJ jumps up and claps Kaehante on the shoulder, making Nkella step back. A wide grin is plastered on Nkella's face.

"Good work, daí? Maybe bet on this ship next round," he tells AJ.

The two men they were playing against fist the table and shake their heads. They get up and swap places with two others to play against the winners. My eyes widen when Mūhī takes one of the empty seats and stares at AJ. AJ glances at Lāri who's frowning.

"Kick his ass, love," she tells him.

This should be interesting. I lean in against Kenjō. "So how do you play?"

She starts to explain the rules, but I get distracted. Watching Nkella let loose, not fighting, not brooding, somehow briefly forgetting that the weight of the world rests on his shoulders, brings a smile to my face.

He shifts his gaze to me and narrows his eyes. He starts to make his way over to me...

"You look different, neyuro."

Kenjō stops talking and steps over to the side.

"What do you mean?"

"You seem happier."

"Maybe this morning really helped."

His face darkens. "What happened during your lesson?"

I resist a sigh. "I found out who my real father was."

His face slackens, he takes my hand and leads me out of the mess hall. Aww. I wanted to watch AJ kick Mūhī's ass.

"Who was he?" he asks as we reach the brightly lit hall.

"His name was Sehu, and he was from Oleanu. Your grandparents adopted him when the Empress killed his parents."

Realization flashes in his eyes when he hears the name. "I have heard of him. He was a good man. Kaehante's parents told me he was on a rescue mission to save me from the Empress."

My eyes widen as I stare at him. "When she kidnapped you?"

"Yes."

"My father helped rescue you...which means my mom did too." My voice vibrates with excitement, and I grab his hand. Shock spreads over his features. "They were both riding the drakon in my vision...heading to the Tower..." I let go of him and turn as my mind races with new information. I glance back at Nkella, his face is hardened as he stares at the floor, I can see the gears turning in his head, and he's probably asking the same questions I am.

"Don't you know what this means?" I ask him. He stares at me. "My parents helped rescue you—they knew Kae's parents!"

He nods. "What else did you learn? Just this? Or did you work on your power?"

My gaze falls down to the floor, and I pivot a little. "I realized that if I take the Death Card without taking care of the Empress, it would all be for nothing."

"What do you mean *taking care of?*"

"I think you know what I mean."

Nkella guffaws. "Why don't you enlighten me."

I frown at his laughter. "I've changed my mind. I want to get the Ace of Swords first."

He lifts his chin; his features darken. "Hn. You mean to kill her. Did you already forget what I told you this morning?"

The corner of my lip curls. "It was cute, Nkella. But the reality is, the vision I had last night changed me." Surprise flashes across his features. "I thought you, out of everyone, would understand why I need to do this. If I don't, she will only go after me and my mom again. And don't forget. She has the World Card now, too, so she can come to my world. We'll never be safe with her still alive, and I'm the only one who can carry the Ace of Swords out of there, I'm the only one with power matching hers who can get close enough to kill her."

Nkella's face pales as he stares at me. He knows I'm right.

"Neyuro—"

"Don't you want your sister back? I can get her back for you. I'm not afraid of her anymore."

"I will get my sister back. I don't need you to compromise yourself for me."

I step closer to him. "I want to do this," I say darkly. His gaze intensifies on me as he zeros in on my movement. "I can't even explain the feeling I had when I was in my vision." Every fiber of my being starts buzzing with revenge, and the rikorō still running between us stirs. "I'm not above murdering anymore. I have changed. I *want* to kill her. I *want* to see her suffer in front of me for all she's done—"

A flicker of crimson flashes behind his irises, and his expression darkens. His gaze dips to my lips, and he looks up and down my body, hunger reaching his eyes. Something inside me stirs until all I want to do is rip that tunic off him and crash into his lips.

He walks forward quickly, crashing into me as he pushes me back against the wall. I gasp as his forehead rests against me, and his lips are above mine. He holds my arm against the wall, and I have my other hand involuntarily placed on his chest. My breathing increases, but before I can reach his lips, he whispers against my ear.

"Be careful speaking dangerous things, neyuro. It makes me want to do dangerous things to you."

My heart is at my throat. I grip a handful of his shirt, and he inches his lips closer to mine, ever so lightly brushing against me. I chase his lips but he's pulling away before I can properly taste him.

He violently turns away, wiping his face.

An exasperated sigh leaves me.

"You won't hurt me," I say out of breath.

"I will." His voice is husky, dark.

"No. You can control it."

"I can't." He faces away from me.

"Captain Nkella Mikiroro. I want you to kiss me."

He turns back to face me. "Neyuro..."

"Nkella. Kiss me."

He rushes back to me, lifts my face, and kisses me deeply. Electricity runs up my spine as I take in the taste of him and kiss him back furiously.

Air fills my lungs, and I gasp. For a moment, I'm paralyzed with fear. He pulls away, shock on his face, then he comes back and slowly sucks the air out of my lungs just like he did that night on the *Ugly Kraken*. My knees weaken, and he holds me up. I smile up at him. "I know we said we'd just be friends but..."

"I can't, Soren," he says hoarsely. He lets go of me, and I have to grab onto the wall to hold myself up. "Just don't do anything you'll regret, daí?"

I stay quiet, my throat full of too much hate to even speak.

He heads toward the mess hall without looking back; I turn and rush out of there as fast as I can. Back at our wing, I'm glad to once again find myself alone. Instead of burying my face in my pillow like I would have ordinarily done, I take out the journal and get to reading.

Dearest diary,

Today I saw him. I snuck out and met him in the gardens. Aletha doesn't suspect a thing. We made love under the olive tree as the bright swirling lights of this magnificent world danced among the stars. I know not when I can see him again, but at least I have this night to accompany me forever.

Love always,
Adara

I slam the diary shut and shove it back under my pillow. I squeeze my eyes shut. And all I can see is him. On top of all my rage, he has to torture me too? Sticking my hand in my pocket, I find the little wooden teacup. I trace my fingers around the intricate carvings. Such a fierce fighter, and yet, he can also be so gentle.

Despite the rikorō that coursed through our system, giving me insight into his thoughts, he remains a mystery to me.

I have to focus on my power. That's all I can do. Forget about him. Forget about this wooden teacup. I want revenge, and I won't get anywhere with him distracting me.

I sit up. What I want most is to bring my mom back from the dead, and to do that, I have to kill the Empress. Revenge will feel good while I do it.

I don't need this stupid teacup. It's an anchor to him, not to my mom. I raise my hand to throw it when—wait.

I can use this. I lean against my pillow with my back to the window. Twirling the teacup between my fingers, I focus on the day I lost the one my mom gave to me.

My mark pulses, and I'm there. I'm getting faster. Better.

Good. Keep it up. I stand by the railing of the *Devil's Gambit* as I watch myself jump after Nkella. Demitri's voice rings in my mind.

Be careful. Don't change the past.

Knowing I can't get hurt inside a memory, I jump over the rail and float close to the surface of the water. From the moment I find Nkella, I wait for the exact second he accidentally snaps my bracelet off. Ignoring what happens next, I watch the silver teacup sink beneath the surface. I quickly cup it in my hands and pull it up. A smile spreads over my face as my surroundings change. I'm back on my bed, as dry as can be, with my mother's teacup safely in my hand.

A maniacal laugh erupts from the back of my throat. I cup my hand over my mouth as I laugh even harder. I laugh so hard, tears well up in my eyes.

"Hey, Soren! We won—uh, Soren?"

I glance up from my hand. I can only imagine how red my face is from laughing. AJ and Lāri walk in, hand in hand. Lāri twists her features as she lets go of him and walks over to me.

"Are you alright? Have you been crying?"

A burst of laughter escapes me. She deadpans and looks at AJ.

AJ giggles. "Lordy, you haven't cracked, have you? What's so funny?"

I hold up the teacup for them to see, but I don't think either of them knows I ever lost it.

They exchange a glance. "Someone is making her crazy," Lāri says.

"Mhmm. I wouldn't be surprised if it were a certain Devil."

I breathe deeply, hooking the chain back around my wrist. Drying my eyes, I let out another giggle, but then shake it off. "Gotta go, guys. See ya later."

AJ and Lāri frown as I hop off the bed and briskly walk out of the room.

I spend the rest of the day going over knots with Kaehante. It's not exactly what I had run off to do, but I couldn't find Demitri to tell him about my accomplishment, so it'll have to wait until after dinner as planned.

I figured spending time with Kae would be good for me anyway. AJ and Harold soon joined us while Lāri was up on the sails, and it was almost like my first trip on the *Gambit*.

During dinner, the crew decides it's best to bring the food out to the communal area of our wing and eat here. This time, I agree and stay with them. Demitri didn't try to stop us when he watched us grab plates and leave the mess hall. He did call me over to ask if I was still going to our meeting, to which I responded that I couldn't wait. He gave me an inquisitive look, but all I did was smile.

AJ takes a large gulp of his drink. "So did anyone else know Lāri and I found Soren sitting alone in the wing, laughing like a crazy person by herself?"

I gape at him. Tessa squints at me, and I shrug. "I won't deny it."

"Daí?" Nkella says. "When was this?"

Oh great.

"Much earlier today," AJ sticks a forkful in his mouth. "Sometime after breakfast."

Nkella quirks a brow at me and narrows his eyes. Steeling my spine, I get up and dare to move closer. I show him my wrist where my little silver teacup hangs from its chain.

"Remember this?"

His eyes widen, and he grabs my wrist. "How?"

I pull my wrist back and smile. "I developed a power."

He stares at me expectantly.

"Wait—" AJ leans closer, and now, so does Harold. "A new power?"

"Is that the teacup you lost?" Harold asks.

I point to him. "Bingo."

Harold's jaw drops. "And you didn't—?"

"Didn't what?"

"You didn't, like, go diving in to find it, did you?"

A high-pitched giggle leaves my lips, and Nkella gapes at me.

"No. That would have been nuts. We lost it too far from here. No, no, with my new power, I—" Should I be telling them this? Demitri warned me what would happen if I took the Death Card before they were all cursed, but what if they asked me to do that? I mean, that's something *I* would ask...

"Yes?" Tessa urges. "Before I fall out of my wheelchair in anticipation."

I chuckle. "Sorry, it's just a hard one to explain. Let's just say I'm able to retrieve certain objects that mean something to me."

Tessa's eyes widen. "That is a peculiar power indeed. Congratulations, Soren."

"Man, what I would do if I were able to grab my runes from my past," Harold says. My gut twists in guilt. Now that's something I'm not sure I can even grab for him, can I? I don't even know what they look like. And how might it change the past and affect the present?

"That's amazing, Soren," Lāri says, glancing at AJ. Her boyfriend has a confused look on his face, but he smiles and agrees anyway. Kae nods in approval. My eyes fall to Nkella, but he stares at me with that permanent frown on his face. Something that feels like suspicion mixed with worry brews through the rikorō. I reach into my pocket and pull out his little wooden teacup.

"I guess you can have this back," I hand it to him, and he takes it. Sadness hits his features, but it's quickly erased as he stuffs it in his pocket.

I'm a little surprised he took it back, but I don't say anything.

A popping sound makes me jump.

"Iéle!" AJ calls, pointing a bone at her. She ignores him and turns to Nkella. I give them some space as they communicate in silence. It's been a while since I've seen them do that. Once they pull away, Iéle backs up, fixes her eyes on me, and growls. I narrow my eyes at her, and she looks away. Then she walks up to AJ and grabs the bone off his plate.

"Rude," he mutters. Tessa laughs.

"Why does she still growl at Soren?" Lāri asks, half laughing.

"Cause she's a jealous bitch, that one," AJ responds.

"What did she say, Captain?" Kaehante asks.

"We will be docking in a day. When we do, we part ways with their crew, daí? Iéle found the *Gambit*." His eyes fall on mine, but I keep a straight face. I hadn't even realized he'd sent her back to search for the *Gambit*.

I'm not entirely sure I want to part ways with Demitri so soon. Not when I'm making so much progress, and he's helping me achieve what I never thought I could. He wants the Empress dead as much as I do—not that Nkella doesn't, but he doesn't have the ability to do it. With Demitri's help, I do.

25

DEMITRI INSPECTS MY LITTLE TEACUP BRACELET UNDER HIS light, and then taps it gently on his desk. "And you didn't have to use a portal or anything like you witnessed the Past Fate do?"

"Nope."

He hands me my bracelet back. "Most impressive. You're advancing at a remarkable pace. What were you feeling when you retrieved this item?"

I twist my shirt with my fist. "I was...frustrated. And upset."

Demitri nods. "Anger again. Good. I believe that is the key to raising your power the quickest."

He isn't wrong.

He stands from behind his desk and motions for me to follow him. "So today, I would like you to relive the vision you had the other day— the one where you found out the truth about your mother."

My face blanks.

"Getting the Ace of Swords and the Death Card are only the first steps. If you want to kill someone as powerful as the Empress, you'll need to match your power to hers. Don't you agree?" He has his hand on the door as he waits for my reply.

I take a deep breath and nod. "Yes."

"Excellent, I thought we'd go to a training room instead of decorating my office with spiderwebs."

I wince and follow him out to where Nkella and I trained yesterday morning. An image of us sparring together with swords, Nkella glistening with sweat, flashes in my mind, and then I quickly push it back. I need to focus.

Can you revisit that vision on your own, or do you need me to guide you?"

"I think I'd like to try going there on my own. I've been able to do it lately, so I don't want to rely on anyone."

"Very well." He leads me to a corner of the back wall where a target is placed at eye level. "I'd like you to explore the extent of your power, which could be more than shooting webs. But for now, let's start with what you know."

I position myself about two feet in front of the target.

"When you're ready, go to your vision. And aim there." He points at the target.

Standing with my feet shoulder width apart, I concentrate on my mark and search for the anger that brought me to my mother's memory.

She comes into my vision. I smile at how strong and healthy she looks as she walks on the beach, shouldering a thin rope. I don't think I've ever seen her that way in my life. Wind breezes through my hair, and the saltiness of the sea tickles my senses. I take a moment to lean into them, feeling the sand beneath my feet and the warmth of the sun on my head. I wiggle my toes. The sand is pink, with occasional iridescent granules. This feels even more real than last time. I know it isn't the right vision, but I want to stay and explore.

The scene expands, and my mother walks up to a man who stands in front of a waist-high flat boulder, his back to her. As she steps closer, he glances over his shoulder and gives her a smile. He has brown eyes, tanned skin, and dark hair. The man who was with her on the drakon. I'm struck by grief. This is my biological father.

I walk up to him, even though I know this is a vision and he can't see me. I startle when his eyes meet mine for a split second, but I know it's because he's looking at my mother standing directly behind me. I touch the corner of my eye as I stare into his. We have the same eyes. I had always thought my eyes were the same shape eyes as my mom's and got my dad's brown color, but now seeing Sehu up close, I can tell he's definitely my biological father. I swallow the lump in my throat.

An agonizing cry breaks my concentration. The body of a human boy around my age is lying flat on his back on the smooth surface of the boulder. His face is twisted in pain, and his hands grab at his leg. A sharp stick impales his right calf. I grimace as I make my way around the boulder so that I can get a clear view of both my parents. My mother takes the rope and ties it around the boy's thigh.

I hold my hand over my mouth as my mother takes the boy's hand and lets him squeeze tight as Sehu works to remove the stick. Blood pools on the boulder, and I scrutinize the boy's garments. He has a gold sash that's bundled over his neck from his fidgeting. An emblem of the Tower catches my attention. But then, a shirtless Ipani holding a bow marches up to the flat rock. He has a disgusted frown plastered on his face.

"This is what is taking so long, á?" He stares at the wounded boy. "You are lucky. I would have left you for dead." He glances at my biological father. "Why help him? He's part of her living army."

Living army?

Sehu frowns. "It is not their fault they protect the Empress. They were raised to believe ouma is dangerous. They think we are the enemy."

My mother hands the newcomer a torn rag. "If you are going to be here, help. We will not kill, and we will not leave them to die." Sehu and my mother share a loving look, and they keep working to remove the stick.

My heart sinks to the pit of my stomach.

There's so much love between them. I wonder if they ever wanted to kill the Empress. In these memories, she didn't look like she'd ever tried. What was she doing? What were they doing? Were they trying to make a truce? In the last vision, my mother sounded like she had hoped to make a deal but was tricked. Maybe murder never even crossed her mind. I can't imagine my mother wanting to commit murder, and it's not something my "dad" ever taught me. He may have taught me how to scam people for money, but he always told me to know the difference.

Between petty crimes and the real bad stuff, I never realized he was setting me up to give me away. I guess he felt if he could teach me to be resourceful, he wouldn't have to worry about me.

The vision grows more distant as my thoughts stray. How would my life have been if the Empress hadn't been a threat? I would have been raised here, in Ipa. Would I still have met Nkella?

Of course, I would have. We probably would have played together as kids.

I gasp, and my surroundings change back to the training room. Demitri has a bored look on his face. Then his eyes widen when he sees mine are open.

"What happened?"

I look down at my hands. No web. "I—" I glance at him. "Do you think I have ouma? Like my father would have?"

An annoyed expression crosses his face. "Where did you go?" He avoids my question.

"I tried to go back to the vision with the Empress, but I went to a time when my parents were helping someone. I think it's because I've had my biological father on my mind."

He rubs his chin. "You lost focus."

"Sorry."

"No, it's alright." He raises his hand. "You have questions that need answering; in order to focus, perhaps, you do need to look for some of those answers. I get it—I do. But we're running low on time. We'll be docking soon, and then we're heading to the Temple for the Ace of Swords."

"I understand. I just...couldn't help but realize if Sehu was my father, then..."

"There's no saying whether or not it could have been passed down to you. Some who are born half-Ipani and half-human never develop ouma, and stay more human, despite any Ipani characteristics they may have. You may never get ouma on your own without rikorō of course, or it might be taking a while to develop because you weren't born here—with the Aō."

I twist my lips. I wonder what type of ouma I would have.

"There's no use in thinking about it, though, Soren," he says as if reading my thoughts. "It may only lead to disappointment. Nine times out of ten, a halfling won't develop any ouma. I'm sorry. But you do have your Fate powers—and that's certainly powerful enough. Focus on strengthening those abilities."

I nod.

"Now focus."

"Wait."

His brows furrow. "Was there something more?"

Twining my fingers together, I stare at him. "I was thinking, maybe I shouldn't do this."

"Do you need a break?"

"No, I mean, maybe I shouldn't"—I lower my voice—"kill the Empress."

He lowers his chin. "What changed?"

"The vision I just saw..." I part my lips, trying to think of the right words. "My mother would have never wanted me to resort to murder. My dad didn't raise me that way, and—"

"Your mother is dead, Soren—"

A knife cuts through my stomach.

"—because the Empress poisoned her."

Tears sting the corners of my eyes, and I mouth, "I know." I swallow. "But when it comes time to kill her, I don't think I'll be able to move. I can't imagine taking someone's life like that. Even someone like the Empress."

"I understand."

"You do?"

"Sadness makes you weak."

"What?"

"In your vision, you say your mother was helping someone?"

I nod. "They were both helping someone who was fighting for the Empress. His leg was wounded. It reminded me that killing goes against everything I've ever believed in."

"Then you'll never survive this world, Soren. Your captain kills."

"And I've begged him not to."

He frowns at me. "Your mother's compassion was never tempered with enough anger. You are evidence of the damage that was done because of it."

I swallow as he steps forward, his voice lowering.

"We need to balance mercy with anger. If anger serves greater mercy, use it, Soren. Nothing would be so merciful to all of Ipa as killing the Empress."

I lick my dry lips. He's not wrong...

"What happened on that enemy ship when Nkella killed everyone? I overheard someone talking about what almost happened—and what didn't happen."

My jaw clenches.

"Didn't that make you angry?"

I clear my throat and nod once. I almost forgot about thinking that some people do deserve to die. "There was so much blood."

"And Ipani who were stuck in those cages are now free."

"Yeah, that's true."

"So how could you not want to kill someone like the Empress? Someone who has babies in eternal torment as casualties of her wars."

I inhale sharply. I had forgotten about that. "I know."

"And don't you want to bring your mother back to life? She'll only keep coming after you."

"I know, I know. You're right. I just don't think I'm the one to do it. I *want* to kill her." My eyes well up again, and I fight back the tears. The rage is so overwhelming. I'm afraid I'll freeze. This is...so beyond my capabilities. I want her dead. I want my mother back. I want to bring back the dead, and I know the Empress needs to die in order for me to do it. "But what if I fail, Demitri?" My voice shakes as it gets louder. "What if I have the Sword in my hand and I freeze? And then you can't even kill her because you won't be able to take the Sword from me? We don't even know if I can give you the power over the Sword as you said. It's just a theory, right?" My voice is shaking, and I sit on the ground.

He lowers his voice to a whisper and places his hand on my shoulder. "As a Fate, you can take it without needing to make a sacrifice—I cannot. The rules of the card say a sacrifice must be made, and that sacrifice only pays for one use. But any Fate is immune to that rule. No one but you can use that Sword to kill the Empress.

"You told me once I can make the cards do whatever I want. What if I just tell it to give you the power to hold it without making a sacrifice?"

A surprised look flashes across his face, and a smirk dances on his lips. "You'd relinquish the power of the Ace of Swords over to me?" He shakes his head. "Either way, you still need to come into your power to do that. And—I thought about it. You're the one who needs to stab her with the Sword, not me."

"Why?"

"Because you need to take her place as the Fate of this world, even if you don't take the throne."

"You didn't tell me that before."

"I said one Fate needs to be here to keep the world from collapsing."

"Yes, but you didn't say I had to kill her in order for that to happen." I stand and dust myself off.

Demitri straightens his back. "Long ago, the Empress revealed to me that if one Fate dies, the Aō won't act quickly to find a new Fate—not if the potential Fate is here and inexperienced with her power. It'll be like you having an undeveloped ouma, unfit and without power. In order for you to become Empress, you must kill the current one. Then you can step down, and I will take over."

I squeeze my eyes shut. "And what if I fail?"

"My dear Soren, you won't fail. Not with me as your trainer."

I dry my eyes.

"Now, take a deep breath. And take a break. I'll see you here tomorrow morning before we disembark."

Before bed, I pull out the diary and flip to the next entry.

Dearest diary,

It has been an age since I last wrote. I was too afraid to reveal in these pages what I told Asteria. I fear that I am with child and Tetalla is the father. Words cannot express how afraid I am of my sister. She has become more obsessed with control over Ipa with each passing day. She was never so cruel in Greece, and I do not understand what has changed. I wish she could see the beauty of this world and of these people.

Love,

Adara

Pressing the journal against my chest, I think about how horrible it must have been for her to be in love with someone her sister was also after. The cards were never meant to be infused into the Aō. If only she knew what all of that would do down the line. I stick the journal under my pillow, knowing that the baby survives. I wouldn't be here if it didn't.

I dream of the enemy ship. I'm stuck inside a cage with the other unbound Ipani. This time, instead of the disgusting man who was there last time, it's Demitri looking through all the cages. He stops at me and shakes his head. "Pity," he says. "I had such high hopes for you."

Nangraku, the man with the snake tattoo, comes from behind him with a malicious grin. Then the one I was most dreading to see comes out from the other side—the man with beads in his sticky beard.

The other Ipani start screaming. There's something I'm forgetting.

My powers. I try to summon them, but at the moment, I forget what they even are. I have powers. I know I do.

Demitri's grin widens, and he starts to laugh. "What a useless Fate you are. Can't even remember your powers?"

I start panting hard. What were they? I need to get out of here. I need to release the other Ipani. I look down at my mark but gasp when I realize I no longer have one. Instead, my arms have stripes on them.

The Ipani are screaming even louder now, and some of them are banging on the cages. I squint to see what they're screaming at, but before I get a good look, blood is pouring over me. Nangraku blows up like a balloon, then Demitri.

I wake up out of breath. Lāri is sitting next to me rubbing my arm.

"Soren," she whispers. "You're dreaming."

Her short hair comes into focus. "I'm sorry."

"It's okay." She reaches beside her and brings up a canteen. "Do you want water?"

I take a sip and then gasp at the soft pinkish light coming in from the window. "I have to go."

"To your training?"

I jump out of bed and dress in double layers, wearing my green tunic, the shirt, and the coat Kenjō lent me. My knife is ready in case I need it—not that I've ever taken it off while on the ship.

I still don't trust Bronte and Demitri's crew.

Demitri is back inside the training room waiting for me. Doesn't he ever sleep in?

"Sorry I'm late," I pant.

Demitri stands straight with a smile on his face. "Please, no need to apologize. I thought we could speed things up today as we're disembarking in a few hours."

"How do you mean?" I walk over to where the target is.

"This time, I'll guide you through a memory."

"Oh. Okay."

"Close your eyes." He places his hands on my shoulders and squeezes. I take a deep breath and let it out slowly.

"Remember, whatever happens, aim your powers at the target. I want to see if you can do anything other than creating a web."

I don't respond. I can't imagine what else I can do...if there even is anything else.

"Imagine you're back in the enemy ship."

My eyelids flutter but I keep them closed. This is not something I want to relive.

"They've kidnapped you. Did they say what they wanted?"

"To hurt the captain."

"Ah. Most interesting. Take me through what happened."

I shift uncomfortably.

"Focus." He squeezes my right shoulder. "Find that anger. What happened when you were on the ship?"

"They took me down to where they were keeping the trafficked Ipani," I say. "They kept me down there for hours." My mark pulses and I am immersed inside my memory, just like a vision. I'm back at the gross, creaky brig with Ipani cages all around me. Their whimpers and cries make it all seem so real.

"Go on..." Demitri's voice sounds distant, but I can still hear him. I tell him what I see. Even though I know it isn't going to happen, and that Nkella is going to get here soon, I can't help but be afraid. The moment those footsteps start coming near the door, and the door creaks open, I hold my breath.

Seeing his disgusting face again makes me want to kill him myself. I felt fear upon seeing him in last night's dream, but now, rage courses through me, filling me with an intense urge to stab him with my knife.

A knife I realize I now have. I didn't before when this had happened.

Focus on my power.

The man with the beaded beard gets closer. I'm breathing hard. I don't hear Demitri anymore. "Demitri?"

I think I hear his distant voice, but I'm not sure about the sounds of the crying Ipani. I try opening my eyes, but for some reason now I can't.

I can't be trapped in a vision, can I?

Loud breathing and the sound of grunting make me look around only to realize it's coming from me. He grabs my neck and forces me up against the wall as he fiddles with his belt. I turn my neck. I remember what I did before—I punched him. But right now, I'm trying to focus on my power.

Blast this mother fucker.

He drops his pants, and I squeeze my eyes shut.

His hands slide over my mouth, and I start to jerk violently, but he grabs me harder.

"No." I pull away. "No. That's it. I'm done."

The man touches my shoulder, and I think he's making his way down my chest. I grab my knife and jab him hard. His eyes bulge, and he gapes at me. I feel the knife go through his guts, and he lets out a gasp as if the wind was taken out of him. I strike at him again and again, feeding my rage. I keep stabbing him. A croaked breath seeps out of his throat, and he lets me go.

The training room comes back into focus, and I'm out of breath. Then I scream.

Blood is pooling by my feet. I'm gripping tightly onto the black obsidian hilt of my dagger, but the blood drains from my face as I stare at the other end—it's buried deep inside a jugular. The body has multiple stab wounds, and I watch in horror as the man falls. "No..." I croak, falling over with him.

How? How did he get here?

"Help," I scream hoarsely. "Somebody help!"

A loud popping sound makes me jump, and I turn to look at Iéle while still holding pressure on his throat. Iéle leaves, and minutes later, Nkella barges through the training room door.

"Neyuro..." His face pales. "Is that Alec?"

26

TEARS STREAM DOWN MY FACE. "IT WAS AN ACCIDENT," I cry, disbelief in my voice.

Alec's eyes are wide open, and the sounds of eternal torment start to fill the training room.

"Alec?" I squeak. "No...please be alive. Please, please be alive." This can't be happening. How was he even here? Where was Demitri?

Nkella's face is awestruck as he approaches. "Soren... why?"

"I don't know," I stammer, my voice becoming high-pitched. "Please, tell me he's alive." Tears flow down my cheeks and land on Alec, my hands still holding the knife tight in his jugular, afraid that if I pull it out of him, more blood will spill.

Nkella shakes his head. "Koj. He is dead."

I let out an inaudible scream as I topple over his body. I killed an innocent person. "It was an accident," I croak. "I didn't know he—"

Nkella pulls my arm, lifting me up. "We have to go."

I gasp. "Are we leaving the ship now?"

"We still have a few hours. I will clean this up, daí? But you cannot be seen covered with blood. You killed the Swords Prefect."

I stare at him. His face is serious, but his tone is neutral. Realization paralyzes me. I killed the Swords Prefect. I killed Kenjō's fiancé.

290

The door creaks open. Demitri walks in, letting the door slam shut behind him. He stops, his mouth parting as he stares at Alec on the floor. He looks at Nkella, then at me. Nkella lets go of me and rushes at him, grabbing his throat, pushing him against the wall, and lifting him with impossible strength. His eyes flicker red, and Iéle advances on Demitri as well, drool dripping from her snarling teeth.

"Unhand me," Demitri croaks.

"You did this," Nkella growls.

"I wasn't even here."

"Daí? Why not?" he says, emphasizing the *"t"* in not. "You were training her. Why would you leave?"

I swallow and slowly walk up to them. "You left while I was lost in a vision, a terrible memory you led me to. What was Alec doing here?" I cry. "Where *were* you?"

Demitri croaks and slams his fist down on Nkella's arm. Nkella lowers him, but keeps him pinned to the wall.

Demitri coughs. "I left for only a minute. I was being called and did not want to disturb you. I'd hoped I'd see webbing on that target when I got back, not my friend, the Swords Prefect, dead on the floor."

Nkella lifts his chin. "Lies. You set us up. I should kill you for this."

Demitri rolls his eyes, his knuckles white from gripping Nkella's wrist. "I did not set you up. What good would that have done, when I need Soren for the Ace of Swords? She would never help me if I set you up, and I most certainly do not want Soren arrested. Now unhand me."

Nkella releases his stronghold, and Demitri rubs his neck, his eyes bulging.

"Shame. He was a good friend. Kenjō will be beside herself."

I bury my face in my hands and inch back, shaking my head. My hands still haven't stopped shaking. My whole body feels like it's vibrating. I refuse to look to my left. Nkella takes my arm again and wraps it over my shoulder, guiding me away.

"No one can know of this," Demitri says. "Not yet."

My breath hitches.

"Let's disembark first. Then—"

"How will we disembark from the ship without the Prefect?" Nkella demands.

"Last night, he made me second-in-command. We'll be safe with his Arcana guarding me, and us. But we can't let it get to the Empress. Not yet."

My eyes widen but I don't turn my head to look at him. The argument he and Alec were having resurfaces in my memory.

I cannot do it, Demitri. It would attract attention from the Tower if I make you second-in-command.

I glimpse Nkella's furrowed face. He's thinking something but stays quiet. Did Alec really make him second-in-command last night? After the argument they'd had when Alec told him he couldn't do it?

"As we're keeping this quiet—" Demitri starts.

"I will take care of it," Nkella says.

A red film spans across the room settling in the shape of a dome, and everything goes black and white. As long as no one walks inside the room and accidentally stumbles into Iéle's dome, we'll be invisible to anyone looking in. My eyes remain glued to Alec's body, but Nkella turns me around and walks me quickly back to our wing.

"Get cleaned up." He leaves me by my bed and turns around to leave.

"Where are you going?" I ask him. I don't want to be alone right now.

"To take care of it." He walks out, locking the door behind him.

For entirely too long, I stand still in the middle of the room, staring at the walls. I'm afraid to move for fear of leaving a trail of blood. This really happened.

I clutch my fist over my stomach and slowly walk to the washroom.

I turn on the pipe and let water fill the basin as I struggle to strip off my clothes. I stand in my bra and panties still staring at the blood smeared over my hands and fingernails. I have blood in my hair, and it's all over my black pants and Kenjō's tunic. Her fiancé's blood is on her clothes because I killed him.

I wish I could take it all back. Wish I could erase what happened. But one thing I've learned from the Past Fate is that she can't change the past—only retrieve objects.

I sit outside the basin waiting for it to fill. We don't usually fill the whole thing—to save water—but I'm doing it anyway.

The door creaks open. I'm still too shocked to move.

"Soren?" Nkella's voice comes through the door. When I don't respond, he slowly opens it.

Without saying another word, he walks inside the washroom and closes the door. Gently, He urges me inside the tub, and I let him, not caring about how I look right now or that I'm still in my bra and panties. He's not looking at me anyway. I sit inside the basin with the water up to my chest, and I hug my legs.

Nkella takes a sponge from the side and starts scrubbing my arms. I'm still shaking. Too freaked out to move.

He doesn't say anything the entire time; his features remain the same, fixed, neutral. He's probably the only person in the world who wouldn't judge me right now. A sob escapes me, and I look away.

"Neyuro, why do you cry? You did not know him, daî?"

"He was innocent," I whisper.

"As far as you know."

"Nkella, don't. He was Kenjō's fiancé."

"They were not aovate. She was pretending. Lying to herself."

"It doesn't matter. He didn't deserve for me to kill him like that."

He puts his hand down. "Tell me how it happened."

I take a deep breath and tell him how I met Demitri in the training room and what he was making me relive to ignite my power. I tell him how I thought I was stabbing the man he killed in my vision, and when I opened my eyes, I thought for a second that I had stabbed Demitri, but instead, I had killed Alec. Stabbed him repeatedly. My voice shakes and tears stream down my face again.

Nkella wraps his arms around me as I shake, his sleeves getting wet with the water. "I will take this burden from you, neyuro."

"What do you mean?"

"You did not kill anyone. You are not a killer."

I pull away and find his eyes. "But it's not true. You can't—"

"Sh. Koj. We have to be very careful now, daî? The Swords Prefect is missing, and no one can know he is dead." He sighs. "Unless Demitri tells the world Alec is dead and that you—or I—killed him."

My eyes bulge, but before I can say anything, he places a finger on my lips.

"Keep your voice down, daí?"

I nod.

"I killed him. Not you."

Tears sting my eyes. I have never felt more appreciation for Nkella before in my life.

"It was an accident," he says. "You are not a killer."

"It doesn't change anything. I still did it."

Nkella's eyes grow heavy as wrinkles crease his forehead. A strong wave of emotion pours in from him. He really wants to take the burden from me. He wants to erase what happened so that I don't have to endure the guilt. He wets the sponge and gently washes my back. "Neyuro..."

I turn my head.

"If you didn't need to come here"—he inhales—"would you have ever come back?"

After a few moments, I say, "Probably not."

He stays quiet the rest of the time he helps me wash away the blood.

My breathing is shallow the entire time I'm preparing to disembark. The look on Alec's face keeps flashing through my mind. Unexpected. Trust betrayed. He didn't have a guard following him around. Would they have been fast enough? It's not like any of them would have been able to read me—I wasn't even here. Physically I was here, but psychically I was somewhere else.

It isn't fair. He shouldn't have even been there.

It's all so surreal. Our room is still locked as Nkella goes to check on the clean-up; he recruited a few of our crew to help. He didn't want me to go anywhere near the training room. I know when he gets there and when the mess is cleaned up because Iéle pops in next to me, presumably sent by Nkella to check on me.

He told me to wait here, so I do. It's not like I want to be out there right now.

The door unlocks, and I sit back on the bed. Nkella walks in, followed by AJ, Kaehante, and Harold. Kaehante and AJ have blood on their hands, but Harold is squeaky clean and looks like he's seen a ghost. He walks right past me, not saying a word, and slams the washroom door behind him.

AJ slaps the sides of his pants as he stares at the washroom door and sighs. He shuts his eyes and turns back over to us. "Can somebody explain to me why in all the Aō's glory I had to get rid of the Swords Prefect's body!?" he whisper-shouts as he pants the last of the sentence.

Retching sounds come from the toilet.

"Be quiet, daí?" Nkella tells him, as he sits on the bed and pinches the bridge of his nose. I shudder. All of this is because of me.

Kae scratches his head and stares at AJ. They exchange a scorned glance and stare back at Nkella. "Captain? What did he do?"

Nkella sighs deeply. "Nothing Kaehante. He did nothing. I lost control. Again." He mutters. I gasp sharply. He's lying to the crew?

I know we don't have to say anything but, why can't we tell the crew? What would they do?

Nkella looks at me and gives me a warning stare. He doesn't want to incriminate them. Got it. But they just helped get rid of the body, so... Or is it because he doesn't want them to know what I did? That my powers are out of control, and I've become someone else they have to worry about.

Harold steps out of the washroom, wiping his face.

"Finally!" AJ runs past him and shuts the door. Kaehante grunts.

Harold glares at Nkella, who stares back but this time smiles at him.

"Maybe you should blow me a kiss too, daí?"

Harold scowls at him. "You are unbelievable." He starts to leave the room, but Nkella stops him.

"Where are you going?"

"To get some fresh air. Unless you want me to throw up again."

"Kh. Weak."

Harold gapes at him and walks straight up to Nkella. I gasp as Nkella's eyes burn with fire speckles. He tilts his chin up. "You do realize I have to go see Kenjō right now, right? She's going to be around me, and

I'm going to have to keep this horrible, horrible secret. Which by the way, I still don't know why!"

I hold my breath, trying not to cry.

"She will find out soon enough, but it cannot be from you."

Harold grunts and walks away.

"Harold—" Nkella calls after him.

"I know!" he shouts. "I'll keep my trap shut."

Nkella furrows his brows at the word trap, then sits back down on his bed. He looks over at me.

"You don't have to keep saying you did it," I whisper.

Kaehante flicks his gaze to mine, narrowing his eyes. Then he looks at Nkella. "What is this, daí? What is going on? Captain?"

Nkella sighs behind his teeth. "No more questions. This is for your own good."

I swallow.

Voices come from the common area, and the door opens. Lāri and Tessa come in carrying a few covered wooden bowls of food.

"Where did everybody go, mei?" Lāri asks, her eyes stopping at Kae's hand. She gasps. "Where is AJ?"

"In the washroom," I tell her.

Her eyes fall on me, then Kae, and finally Nkella. She sets the bowls down and crosses her arms. "What happened?"

"The Swords Prefect is dead," Kaehante mutters.

Tessa gasps. "Kae, what did you do?"

Brows rising, he points to Nkella. Tessa and Lāri exchange a glance but decide not to say anything else.

"We tell no one," Nkella repeats for the hundredth time. "Let Demitri handle the news of his disappearance or the Empress will be here to replace the Prefect."

"And we don't want that," Tessa agrees. "Right, then. May I ask what he did to deserve that? How he angered you?"

Nkella shakes his head and buries it into his hand.

"Don't tell me then," she says. "What a shame. He seemed like a good one." She drives her chair to her bed and starts gathering her belongings.

Lāri sits on her bed next to me. "Do you know what will happen when the Empress finds out another of her Prefects is dead?"

My breathing grows heavy.

"She will probably trap everyone in Piupeki and annihilate all Ipani."

"Why would she do that?" I breathe. "How would she know an Ipani did it?"

"She hates us all," Lāri said. "She will take it out on us, even if it isn't true. To teach a lesson as to why ouma is evil."

The blood drains from my face, and I stare at Lāri.

"She will not find out," Nkella says. "Not yet. And we will be gone before she does."

I slowly turn to look at him. I had just sentenced an entire island to death.

AJ steps out of the shower with a towel wrapped around his skinny waist. Kaehante who hasn't moved from his spot rushes into the washroom. AJ glances at Lāri and shakes his head, making his way to his chest to gather his clothes.

When everyone is ready to disembark, we head to the main deck to meet Bronte's crew and wait for the ship to make port. I can see the Arcana floating along the marina from here. The frigid cold wind smacks my face, and I have the biggest urge to go back inside our wing and bury myself inside the covers. I've lost all motivation for the day. The mountains' high peaks are vast and covered in snow. I stuff my hands into Kenjō's coat pockets to keep them warm, guilt filling my stomach to even be wearing it. But I don't have anything else to keep me warm.

People are laughing and chatting, going along their day, ignorant of the fact the Swords Prefect is dead.

Nkella walks behind me, I can feel his hard stare at the back of my head. Kaehante calls him over, and Nkella taps me on the arm, motioning for me to follow him. I start to, but my eyes find Kenjō sitting by the bow of the ship, staring out at the port. Harold isn't within my line of sight. He's probably staying away from her because he doesn't want to keep a secret he knows will kill her. I glance toward

Nkella who's distracted helping Kaehante bring down a barrel from the quarterdeck. I glance back at Kenjō.

I'm a horrible person.

I need to tell her. I take a step, but Demitri intercepts me.

"Leave her alone, Soren," he says.

"She has to know."

"And she will. Leave it to me."

"Is it true?" I ask Demitri. "Did I just sentence an entire island to death?"

"Who told you that?"

Shit. My crew isn't supposed to know. "It was... Nkella's worried that the Empress will take it out on the Ipani and use this as an example of what happens when people use ouma."

"Well then, we had better get you the Ace of Swords and have you trained up before the news leaks, shouldn't we?"

I gulp.

"Oh, and Soren?"

I blink at him.

"You did well during training."

"W-what?"

"The first kill is always the hardest. The next one you'll do with conviction, and the Empress will be easier. Harder to fight, but easier to get over."

"Y-you knew I would kill him." It wasn't even a question. A vulpine smirk slides on his face. "How?"

"Oh, Soren, I've seen that look on your face before. So frightened for your life, I knew if you were given the chance for a do-over, you'd save yourself without a second thought. And rightly so. Be proud of yourself. You're stronger for it now."

My mouth hangs open as he walks away.

Nkella finds me and heads over. "Stay with me, neyuro. Do not go far, daí?"

"Yeah, sorry."

I feel like the wind was just knocked out of me, but I don't tell Nkella anything—not yet. There's too much to think about right now. Demitri did this on purpose. He didn't want to get his hands dirty, so he used me instead. It had to be because of the argument they'd had; he wanted to be second-in-command, and Alec wouldn't have it, so Demitri needed him out of the way. *The first kill is always the hardest.* This was him training me and taking out two birds with one stone. That son of a bitch.

The ship pulls into port, and a row of Arcana soldiers with chrome masks and gold Swords emblems guards the entrance.

Nerves cause my stomach to tighten along with the loud metal clanking of the unloading rail being lowered onto the platform.

"We are almost out," Nkella mutters to us all. I crane my neck to see the rest of the crew. Harold has his back to the wall as he carries Quinn in her cage. He has a worried and serious look plastered on his face. His eyes meet mine, but my frown doesn't change. And neither does his. AJ has his arms wrapped tightly around Lāri, and Tessa is whispering something to Kaehante who's hovering next to her chair.

Demitri walks briskly toward the loading area. His eyes find mine, but I quickly avert my gaze.

I'm trying hard not to look at Kenjō, but a movement catches my eye. Her mother is talking to her about something, and Kenjō has a confused look on her face. She says something back, and her mom shakes her head. My heart stops.

Bronte wouldn't be telling her what happened now, would she? Not here. Not in front of everyone when we're just about to leave the ship.

That would be cruel.

But also, does Bronte know? Who has Demitri told? Surely, he'd confide in Bronte since she's the captain of this ship and Kenjō's mother.

Kenjō jumps from her seat and walks over to us. My heart starts to beat loudly in my ear, and my hands become clammy. She steps up to Harold. I hear her ask over the cold wind, "Have you seen Alec?"

I stare at Harold. Oh no.

Harold stammers and then shakes his head. He looks at me, his eyes wide. Then he shoots daggers at Nkella, who hasn't bothered to look behind him.

"He meant to be here by now," she says, "to ensure our safety."

My knees buckle, but I steel my spine and walk over to them. Nkella grabs my arm. I pull him toward me, and he follows, confusion coursing through the rikorō.

"Your mom," I clear my throat. "She doesn't know where Alec is?" I ask as we approach Kenjō, hoping to find out what her mom said or any clues as to what she knows.

"Koj," she says, "only that they are about to make an announcement. And that I should go downstairs for it, but she didn't press me."

Wow. Her mother is a grade A—

"If everyone can settle down," Demitri's voice booms from behind us, his voice somehow heightened, as if there were speakers around—but there aren't any. "There have been some...recent events."

Bronte comes dashing in and grabs Kenjō's arm, pulling her away from the wall. "I told you to go downstairs."

"Why?"

I close my eyes as I anticipate Demitri's announcement.

"Alec, the Swords Prefect...is standing down."

Kenjō's eyes light up in the shape of a cat. "What does that mean? Standing down?" She pulls away from the wall. "Alec is standing down as Prefect? Why?"

"In lieu of this," Demitri continues, "Bronte is the new Swords Prefect."

My jaw drops, and I turn around to stare at Demitri.

Bronte gives her daughter an apologetic look as everyone turns to her. Silence blooms among the pirates, an air of confusion blanketing the deck. AJ chews on his cheek, his eyes now glued to the floor. Lāri takes his hand.

"So, Demitri didn't want to be the Prefect?" I whisper to Nkella.

He tilts his head to me. "He cannot draw attention to himself, daí?"

I give him an understanding look and stare back at Demitri. He is now Bronte's second-in-command and has influence over all the Swords Arcana soldiers, creating his own army without having let the Empress know his whereabouts. And I helped him do it.

I never should have let him train me. I should have listened to Nkella.

Tessa whispers something to Kaehante, then she looks at us, getting closer. Her eyes fall to Kenjō who's being pulled away by her mom.

"So as long as the Empress thinks Alec is still alive, Bronte can do whatever she wants," AJ mutters under his breath.

"This is a take-over," Tessa says. "Convenient." She looks at Nkella.

He scoffs. "What are you implying, daí? You think I would want to give Demitri power?"

"I'm only stating the obvious."

"Kh." He breathes deeply, closing his eyes most likely to avoid showing their fiery glow to Tessa. This is the first time I've seen him give her attitude.

"He's an opportunist," AJ adds. "He saw an opening and went for it."

Tessa shrugs. "I suppose."

I chew my cheek. I hate lying to them.

Mūhī's voice booms overhead. "Listen up! Unloading goods should be simple. Everyone out."

Kaehante scratches his bald head. "Where are we going next, Captain?"

Nkella looks to me. "Away from Demitri. Then, we make use of daylight to head straight for the *Gambit*."

I swallow. I need to get to the Sword, but I haven't told him that yet. Demitri is never going to let us get away from him. "H-how far are we from the *Gambit*?" I ask.

"From here, it's a two-night journey if we leave now."

So we're two nights away from the Sword. That doesn't give us a lot of room to get far from Demitri. "What are you going to tell him? You know he wants to keep training me. And..."

"And what, neyuro?"

Tessa and Kae look at me expectantly.

I take a deep breath. "I am still planning to do what I said," I continued, not wanting to tell the crew about wanting to kill the Empress. "And for that, you know what I need."

"And why do you need Demitri for that?" he asks.

"You think I still want to train with him?" I snap.

Tessa furrows his brows. "Can't you train without him?"

I gape at her. "I—None of you know how to handle me if something goes wrong. He spent years—eons—with the Empress."

"He cannot be trusted." Nkella growls.

"I know." I huff. "But I don't think he's going to let us go—let *me* go that easily. He needs me so he can become Emperor, remember? How are we going to get away? Even if you use Iéle to hide us, he has oumala animals, and now an entire Arcana army at his command. We won't get far. We'll just end up causing a battle."

"She isn't wrong," Tessa agrees. Nkella scowls.

27

A CORMORANT FLIES SILENTLY OVERHEAD AS WE FOLLOW THE crew of pirates off the ship. I watch as it dips toward the icy water in search of fish, and disappears into the Aō with a low pop, almost like a thud. A shadow looms over the water's edge where the bird disappeared. My gaze cuts to the silent, chrome-masked Arcana soldier inspecting the waters for ouma. I hold my breath until it returns to the formation of Arcana soldiers watching us from just before the entrance to the village, probably satisfied that it was only a bird. What would it have done if it had thought it to be a spy?

The Arcana are split between those with Swords emblems—now Demitri's infiltrated soldiers—and those from the Tower. I don't know how they are communicating, but we are indeed not safe.

The marina is snowy and crowded with traders, fishermen, and pirates, but there aren't any ships being loaded. This is the only ship with anyone undocking as far as I can tell, despite the area being so busy, a testament to the island being held under siege.

Make it to the small village up ahead. This was the plan we'd briefly discussed. Get lost in the crowd. And try to lose Demitri and Bronte's crew. I peek over my shoulder to see if I can spot Demitri, but he's gotten lost in the crowd, most likely managing his plethora of ill-conceived cons to take full control of Piupeki...and Ipa. Nkella keeps a close eye, as he walks behind me. My fists clench the whole way, and I'm trying not to make eye contact with Kenjō.

Snow crunches under my feet as I step out onto the freezing early morning snow. The sea wind slams against us. We stay huddled together as we walk in the direction of the village center. A group of kids with soot all over their faces approaches us with sad and pleading eyes, and their hands cupped before them. Their little pointed ears have snow on the tips. My stomach wrenches as I watch them approach us, and I can feel Nkella's emotions start to stir. I can't imagine any warm foster homes for orphans in Ipa.

"We cannot help them all, daí, Captain?" Kaehante's voice cuts through the wind. I frown at him, but I can tell they're all wrestling with the inability to turn away from starving children. "We are a good target here," Kae continues. "We must keep going."

He's right. Knowing the type of crew we are—a crew that won't turn their backs on helping trafficked Ipani, he's right. Already, I can see Tessa and Lāri looking for coins, while members of Bronte's crew are literally kicking the children away. This is going to slow us down and get us caught. Nkella squares his jaw, and with regret in his eyes, he turns away from them, urging us to keep moving.

"We'll help them by finishing the Empress," AJ whispers loudly to us. My lips form a thin line as I look around me. This place is busy because it's riddled with starving families.

"I thought Piupeki wasn't under a full siege? Wasn't Alec allowing shipments?" I ask no one in particular.

Nkella shakes his head. "These are displaced children from families executed from using ouma." My breath catches in my throat. He urges me to keep walking. No wonder Alec told me he no longer agreed with the Empress's methods. He was hoping Bronte and Demitri's plans for a better future would work.

The Arcana soldiers fix their gazes on our group walking toward the village, slowly following us with their hollowed-out eyes. I shrink into my skin and keep my eyes trained on the village.

Someone grabs my shoulder. I spin around to face Demitri.

There goes our attempt at sneaking away.

Nkella grabs his wrist, his stare darkening at Demitri. A flicker of red ignites his irises as he growls out, "I do not care about the size of your army. Touch her one more time and your fate will be unsurvivable."

Arcana soldiers are surrounding us within seconds, their dark hollow gazes fixed on Nkella. The crew pulls out their pistols and points them at each of the soldiers.

Demitri's lips form a scowl as he takes his hand back. "So you did notice I now have an army. Would you like to test your threat, Captain Devil?" He stares at me. "Soren and I have a deal. Leave her with me, and you can move along if you don't want me around. But as it turns out, I know she's quite fond of you—your crew." He narrows his eyes and smirks at Nkella.

"Kh. I can murder you right now without lifting a finger. Keep talking." Nkella purrs with the promise of bloodshed in his voice. Dread claws at my stomach as I stare at the Arcana hovering around us, and my eyes stop at Demitri.

Demitri shifts his gaze from Nkella to me. "You still need me. Your little wolf can't get you through my soldiers, or the magic lock I have on your ship. And as I said, Soren and I have a deal." He looks down at my clothes. "Hide your sleeve inside your coat. And get yourself some new clothes before we head out."

I gape at my wrist and tuck the bloodstained fabric inside Kenjō's coat sleeve. I chance a look at Nkella whose features are pensive.

Demitri walks off smugly, knowing we aren't going anywhere without him now that we know he'll have guards outside the *Gambit*. We walk to the village, and I dig through my little pouch for the Piupeki gichang I had traded with the Hermit. The buildings are white plaster with straw roofs. The aroma of burning wood wafts through the air, hinting of cooked meat. We walk past a store that has different colored linens hanging from the outside, and Lāri points to a clothing shop.

AJ is bouncing on his feet, trying to keep warm. Nkella rummages through his coins and hands him a few to grab some coats.

I follow Lāri inside, grateful that Harold stayed back with Kenjō. I don't even care what the shirt or coat looks like, I just want to return Kenjō's coat.

Nkella stays at the door speaking to the rest of the crew; I can feel his eyes glued on me, but he leaves me alone with Lāri.

My stomach is still in knots; I wish I could tell Lāri what happened, what I did. So far, she probably thinks I'm acting weird because of Nkella. Lāri rummages through some coats and pulls out a tight, long-sleeved black coat with bone buckles. I nod, and take off Kenjō's coat, revealing the blood-stained shirt underneath. Lāri's eyes widen momentarily, and she shakes her head.

"You should not have to clean his mess, mei?"

She thinks the blood is because of something Nkella did. Avoiding eye contact, I take the coat from her to try it on. She can think whatever she wants for now.

Glad to take off the stench of blood, I quickly change into a new pair of brown pants inside a makeshift dressing room. Even though I can't smell anything in this cold, it's in my head, and that's enough for me to think I can smell it.

The coat is a snug fit, with wool lining the inside, and the collar covering my neck. At least, it doesn't have fur.

Staring at my reflection in the mirror, I button up the coat, and tidy back my messy hair. If I wasn't trying to hold it together, I might stop to appreciate how this new outfit makes my curves look. The tight brown leggings have fur on the inside, but grip my body in all the right places. I wipe my face, only irritating my red puffy cheeks more, and I gaze upon the bags under my eyes. I take a deep breath and give myself a fake smile.

Pulling aside the animal skin curtain, I find Lāri waiting for me right outside. Her eyes widen, and a grin spreads across her face. I scrunch my face at her.

"Soren, you look *simo*."

"Hmm?"

"Beautiful."

"Oh." My cheeks warm. "Thanks."

She grabs the clothes in my hand—I give her my pants and Kenjō's soiled tunic, but keep her coat.

"I will discard these for you." She turns to the merchant and hands him the gichang she was holding for me.

Outside, Harold is walking toward us with Kenjō, the chicken cage gripped firmly in his hands. My stomach clenches and I look away from her. Nkella's eyes soften when he sees me, and I go to him. I hold my breath, unsure what to do. I don't know how I'm going to keep this secret; I wish she'd just go away.

"Tell me more about how the snow is oumala," Harold says to Kenjō. "How do the trees thrive?"

"These trees only thrive in oumala snow. It is not like the other island, è?"

"Right. Should have guessed." He smiles at her, but sadness lingers in his eyes. He doesn't want to keep this secret from her either, and I know he's only trying to keep her distracted. He sets Quinn's cage down on the ground by Kaehante's feet.

"Have any of you seen Alec?" Kenjō asks us again. My lips part, Nkella stares at me, and I shake my head at Kenjō. She frowns.

Nkella looks at her. "You will make Soren the cure now, daí?"

Kenjō's eyes widen, and she smacks her face. "I am sorry! Yes, I need to get the ingredient, and then I will make it."

"How do you get it?"

"From Demitri. He did not want to tell me where it came from, so I cannot extract it myself."

Harold gapes at her. "You don't know whose ouma the cure comes from?" his voice rises. Quinn starts to cluck at the sound of his voice. "Why do you continue to trust that guy?"

She's about to retort when Nkella steps in front and leans into him. "It is the cure, daí? And Soren needs it. Argue about it later." His voice is low but direct. Harold purses his lips and shifts his gaze over to me.

I wince, bending my hands.

Kenjō stares at me, her forehead wrinkled. "You got new clothes."

"Oh yeah." I hand her coat back to her. "Thank you. I, uh—"

"I ruined your tunic, Kenjō." Nkella tells her, finishing my sentence. "When I was training Soren. I am sorry. Let me pay you for it."

"No, that is okay," she says. "It was an old tunic. I will go remind Demitri for the ingredient."

"You mean part of someone's soul," Harold mutters.

"Not someone," she snaps. "He says it does not come from an Ipani."

"Sure," Harold fake smiles.

"Wait," I step toward her. "Are you sure Demitri wasn't lying to you about where it came from?"

Harold cuts her off before she can respond. "Oh, you mean to make sure she behaves like a good little girl and does what he says? Because she doesn't want to kill people?"

I swallow a dry lump in my throat. Even though he wasn't shooting that comment at me, he might as well have.

"He did not lie, Harold," she argues. "I would have recognized the compound, è?"

Harold relaxes his shoulders. "Fine then, some poor oumala animal."

She grunts and starts walking back toward the Prefect's Tower where we left Demitri.

"So, do we follow her?" AJ asks, now wearing a thick brown coat that covers his neck.

"I'd rather we all wait here," Tessa chirps. "Keep Nkella and Demitri away from each other before an unwanted war happens."

That's a wise idea.

Laughter erupts from one of the wooden buildings. A few men walk out, dressed like they're about to go hiking in the snow.

"That is a rumor," one of them laughs. He wears a blue wool coat, a matching hat, and heavy boots. The other wears a similar outfit but in green.

"You will see when we get there. I saw it being dragged with my own eyes."

"È?" The other man chuckles, "And what did it look like?"

"Purple and blue hair. It was big but it was knocked out cold."

The man in blue shakes his head. "No one can take down a drakon, è? Someone was fooling you. In any case, my bets are on the āngaraeke."

My brows furrow as I turn to see the men walking past us, their conversation dying with the sounds of chatter coming from the Prefect's Tower. I squint at Nkella who looks like he heard the same thing. He pivots and catches up to those men.

The crew and I exchange a quick glance and follow him.

"Did I hear someone say they caught a drakon?" Nkella asks them.

The one man with the blue wool coat shakes his head and shoves his friend. "At least, that is the rumor going around. You know how the village likes to entertain, è?"

The other one rolls his eyes. "It is true. I saw it with my own eyes."

"I heard you say it had purple and blue hair. Anything else?"

The man furrows his brows. "What is it to you, è?" He turns to his friend, pointing at Nkella. "It is almost like he knows the drakon."

Nkella laughs a fake hearty laugh. "Koj, koj. My friend's daughter is sick, daí? She has never seen a drakon before and would like to know all the details."

The man's face drops at the sound of a child being sick. "Tell her it had big, crazy yellow eyes." He nods at us. "It was only for a second. The drakon opened its eyes, all droopy and drugged like this." He drops his head and sticks out his tongue. "I know it was drugged because it had a crazy smile, not like any drakon I have ever seen. They plan to make it fight against the āngaraeke. My bet is on the drakon," he chuckles. "If that creature is truly as crazy as it looks, it will murder anything."

"Nothing can beat a āngaraeke," his friend says.

"Where are these fights?" AJ asks with a tight smile. "We would love to attend."

"I would like to place my bets," Lāri agrees.

"Naó. It is at the fighting ring where all the fights are held."

Nkella looks at AJ, then back to the men. He tells them something in Ipani and waves them off. We wait until the men walk a bit further. Nkella turns to us. "It is out of the way of the *Gambit*."

"That sounded like Gari, though," I say.

"It could be any drakon."

"There are probably more drakons with blue and purple hair," Tessa adds.

"With crazy eyes?" I press. "The only other drakon I've seen had ferocious, serious eyes."

"Yeah," Harold holds the back of his head. "The one that guards the Temple is no joke. Gari seems a little..." He twirls his fingers to his temple indicating "crazy."

"We have to save him. I don't know how he ended up here, but it's gotta be him."

Nkella rubs his chin. "If he got away from the serpent, he could have washed up on shore somewhere, then gotten captured." Nkella lets out a sigh. "This is a detour, daí?" But he doesn't seem to be against the idea.

"So, we are doing this, mei?" Lāri perks up. "You know AJ and I are always up to take down oumala fighting rings."

"You know I am, too," Nkella says, "but we need Soren's cure."

"Kenjō's getting it now," Harold says. "I'm concerned about the mention of fighting āngaraekes. I would hate for it to be Alfred."

"It is unanimous then," Kae says from behind Tessa.

"How fast can Kenjō make a cure?" Nkella asks Harold. His concern for me brings a warmth to my center, despite Alec's face being fresh in my mind, and lingering in the forefront of my head. I no longer think Nkella only cares about me getting his sister back. No, I think he actually does care, or he'd be rushing to the *Gambit* without the cure, prioritizing this sister's return—and if the Death Card saved me, too, it would be a bonus. I smile at him. When he looks at me, he furrows his brows.

"Hn?"

"Nothing."

Harold scratches his head. "It's hard to say. I've never made it, and I refused to help Kenjō with anything involving rikorō, after learning what it does."

"That is admirable of you," Tessa tells him. Harold shrugs.

"Yes," Lāri agrees. "You are a good person, Harold."

"So is Kenjō," Harold says. "You don't know her like I do."

"I can tell she is," I tell him weakly. "You can't blame her for trusting her mom, and Demitri seems to be the only father figure in her life."

"I just don't understand how she can't see through him," he says.

"He's powerful in his own right," I tell him, "and he brings results. He's someone she can rely on. If she was raised with a dead parent, and one always at sea, then Demitri is all she's had, right?"

He nods. "When she found me here, she was living alone in the mountains, creating these potions by herself—hunting by herself."

"A girl from a small Piupeki village," Tessa adds. "It must have been lonely."

Footsteps crunch on the snow behind us, and I turn to find Kenjō running up, with a serious look on her face. "I have some bad news."

Demitri is just behind her. "We are going to have to extract ouma. Someone broke into my reserve and stole it."

"Kh. Convenient," Nkella says.

Demitri rolls his eyes. "Why would that be convenient? You think I wanted my stash stolen?"

"If you even had it to begin with."

"I need Soren cured just as much as you want her."

A surprised look crosses Nkella's face. AJ wipes his face to hide the smirk and walks away.

I choose to ignore the whole thing. "I can keep going," I say. When they stare at me, unsure, I tell them, "Really, I feel fine. We can keep going."

"We will need to go on foot. Even though I have my Arcana, the Empress's Arcana soldiers are still blocking the pathways. Arcana can go places, but they can't carry people. It is now forbidden."

"Her laws are becoming more strict," Tessa mutters. I'm sure it was to trap Demitri from teleporting via the soldiers.

Nkella cocks his head. "Where do you go to extract this ouma, daí?"

"And who are you extracting it from?" Harold adds.

Demitri grimaces. "That's top secret. But if you wait here, I will have a source bring me a vial, and then Kenjō can get to work before we leave."

"Is there a way I can grab it, using my power?" I ask.

Demitri shakes his head. "There are too many vials. You wouldn't know which one to grab."

I squint at him. It couldn't be that hard. "I could go into your memories and see which is the right one."

"I said no, Soren." He snaps at me. "Don't go prying into people's memories all the time. It's rude, you know."

My eyes blink rapidly. Not too long ago, he was encouraging me to practice my power. What's he hiding?

Nkella steps in front of Demitri, forcing him to take a step back. "And where would this source be coming from, daí? It wouldn't be in

Naó, where they are having āngaraeke and drakon fighting matches, would it?"

"So high and mighty coming from you" Demitri sneers. "What about your recent use of rikorō? Seems to me your priorities to save your crew outweighs your care for... well, anything else really."

Nkella lifts his chin. "At least, I do not tell lies. I am not a coward."

Kenjō gasps. "They are fighting āngaraekes?"

"You didn't know?" Harold asks her.

"Harold! Of course not!"

As Demitri adjusts his collar and steps away from Nkella, an Arcana soldier appears beside him. Now, I'm stepping in front of him and drawing out a memory as fast as I've ever done. If I weren't feeling like the scum of the earth, I'd be proud of myself.

A vision of Demitri sitting in the front row of the oumala animal rings, with people placing their bets all around him plays in the front of my mind. Someone sits next to him and hands him a vial.

I gasp. "Nkella's right," I say, out of breath. "It's at the fighting rings."

Kenjō shakes her head. "No. Tell me it isn't true."

"Soren's the Past Fate descendant, Kenjō. She's not lying," Harold tells her.

Kenjō's jaw drops, and she moves to stand next to Nkella, her eyes accusatory and fixed on Demitri. "This is why Alec was always curious about you spending so much time in Naó. This was your operation, è?" Her voice shakes.

"That's why I didn't tell you, Kenjō. Your heart gets in the way of results." Demitri responds. "If there is a way not to kill them while still extracting their ouma, I'm sure you can find it."

Kenjō gasps, her eyes full of tears.

"Kenjō," I reach for her. "You don't need to make me the cure. I have another way."

Kenjō stares at me, her mouth is slack-jawed, like she still can't believe it. We're both in shock for different reasons, but I feel for her.

"Seriously," I say to her. "It's fine."

"It is not fine," Nkella says, his eyes glued to Demitri. "You bring nothing but lies."

"Captain," Tessa warns. Arcana soldiers are closing in around us. "There's nothing we can do, and we're outnumbered."

"I'm with Tessa," I say. "He's not worth it." I've learned enough, and I have the diary. I can get the Sword to kill the Empress myself, and Iéle knows where the *Gambit* is.

Demitri glowers at me. I narrow my eyes. "We have a deal," he says.

I smirk. "Silly you for making deals with pirates."

Nkella glances at me from over his shoulder, and I don't miss the smirk on his face before he looks back to Demitri.

I cross my arms in front of me. "I'm not going anywhere with you."

Demitri narrows his eyes. "You still need me. I have the key to the *Gambit*. And you'll never make it through Swords alive without my protection. The Tower's psychic soldiers are stationed everywhere."

"Oh, we're resourceful," AJ says, leaning on Kaehante whose arm quickly morphs into shields from shoulder to fist.

Demitri steps back.

"Wait until Alec hears about this," Kenjō says.

Demitri's lips form into a smirk. "Why don't you go tell him? Let me know when you find him." He turns to the rest of us. "None of you are going anywhere. Soren and I had a deal. And I intend to make sure she keeps it. He snaps his fingers and we're surrounded by Arcana soldiers with chrome masks.

Harold pulls at Kenjō's arm, but her eyes are squinting at Demitri.

"Harold was right," Kenjō says. "You are a bad man."

"Oh, Kenjō," Demitri says. "That hurts my feelings. What would your mother say? She's been in on all my plans, you do know that."

Kenjō's face pales. "Alec will have you arrested."

"Kenjō," Harold whispers. "Stop..." He pulls at her, backing her away from the Arcana soldiers.

"È?"

The rest of the crew exchanges glances.

Demitri gives Harold a warning stare, then he passes the stare on to us. "When the Empress comes, you'll all end up in the Tower—not just me."

"And why would she come?" Kenjō challenges him.

Harold pulls her harder, and this time she stares at him. "We'll tell you later. Let's get out of here," he mouths to her.

"Tell me what? Just tell me now. Where is Alec?"

I swallow. "Kenjō..." My voice falters, and the chrome-masked Arcana closes in. Nkella steps away from Demitri to guard me from the Arcana soldier whose hollow eyes are fixed on me.

"Alec... " Harold starts.

"Alec is dead," Kaehante announces. "Sorry."

The blood drains from Kenjō's face, and I squeeze my eyes shut.

"No." She shakes her head. "That cannot be."

I open my eyes, tears welling in the corners as I stare at her shocked face. I can't hide this. I have to tell her.

"It's true, Kenjō..." Harold gently says. "I saw his body. I'm sorry I didn't tell you," His voice grows hoarse as he glances at Nkella. Kenjō follows his stare, her eyes growing wide in horror. I shake my head.

"No. It wasn't him," I say quickly. The crew stares at me. Nkella had told them all that he had been the one to kill Alec. This will come as a shock to the rest of them, but I can't have Kenjō hating Nkella for killing her fiancé. Besides, it would make things worse for us in Piupeki.

"Oh dear," Demitri says musingly, hiding his tone behind fabricated shock. I narrow my eyes at him. "We mustn't let this get out, though," he warns Kenjō.

"She should know," Nkella's voice darkens as he walks closer to Demitri, but loud enough for all of us to hear. "You had him killed, daí? To make Bronte Prefect, so you can get your army without the Empress suspecting anything."

My shoulders drop. He's not wrong. "I overheard the argument in your office. You asked him to make you second-in-command, and he said no. He stood in your way."

Kenjō gapes. "You...you killed my fiancé."

"Well, technically, Soren stabbed him," Demitri deadpans.

I forget to breathe. Kenjō's gaze finds mine, and I swallow. "I..." My voice is hoarse. "I'm so, so sorry, Kenjō..." I reach for her but she steps back, a yellow glow flashing in her eyes.

AJ and the others gasp.

"Kh." Nkella looks to her. "She had the knife, but it was he who made her do it."

"How?" Kenjō asks. "How could someone make you?"

"I didn't see him. I was trapped in a vision—"

"Brought on by Demitri," Nkella finishes. "She was not in control."

The crew talks around me, but it all becomes background noise as my vision focuses on Kenjō. Realization hits her face, but I'm not sure if she fully understands. She's clearly in shock. I get it. She might not ever forgive me, even though Nkella is right. But I should have had more control of my power. I shouldn't have let Demitri manipulate me like that.

"I'm so sorry, Kenjō," I croak.

Demitri snaps his fingers again, and the Arcana soldiers stop to stare at him. "Take Soren, kill the rest."

28

A SOLDIER GRABS ME FROM BEHIND, AND I SCREAM. ICE forms at my feet, not the muddy sludge that was there a minute ago. Full-blown ice. I slip, but the soldier keeps a hard grasp on my shoulders.

From the corner of my eye, Kenjō shifts into a giant cat, but I have no time to process it. She lunges for Demitri's throat, and he yells.

Nkella snaps his attention to me and raises an arm. A burst of wind slams the soldier back, but it takes me along with him, making me slip on the ice as I twist my arms away from his grasp. Nkella pulls me away from the soldier just as he lets out another giant gust of wind at the Arcana, sending them flying until they disappear in white smoke.

AJ and Kae are shooting at them from afar.

Demitri is screaming on the ground, and Kenjō has blood on her sharp teeth.

"Everyone, get back," Harold shouts as he throws something to the ground where Demitri is holding his bleeding neck. Blue smoke fizzles out. Screams come from the surrounding village. I had almost forgotten we weren't the only ones in the vicinity. Nkella stops to stare at Demitri among the smoke, hatred oozing out of his stare.

"Nkella, we have to go," Tessa tells him, aiming her chair cannon at the Arcana appearing behind him. Backing up, Nkella leaves him, and we start to run through the village. Chrome-masked soldiers gain on us, and I can hear Demitri throwing out commands.

We run through the village square, screaming for people to get out of our way. Kaehante takes down a gray animal skin awning from one of the shops with his head, as we jump through the muddy slush of the village.

People all around us run inside as the Arcana advance toward us. I run as fast as my feet can carry me toward Tessa, who's in the lead. She reverses in her wheelchair and fires her cannon a few times behind me. I don't see where Kenjō went, but as a cat, I'm sure she's far ahead of us.

Nkella stops and lets out another large gust of wind; this time it's so strong, it blows the roof off someone's building and crashes against two Arcana soldiers. From behind him, people are emerging, but instead of running away, they're advancing toward us. I gasp. Mūhī is there with other pirates I recognize from the ship. Nkella grabs my coat and urges me to keep running.

Mūhī forms his signature sandwhips from each arm, lengthening them toward us. I sprint faster, trying to keep track of the direction the crew is going. One of the sandwhips reaches over my head, and I scream. Nkella swings back, picks me up, and carries me out of Mūhī's reach. I cling to his back as he stomps hard on the ground, sprinting faster than before. I hold my breath as we reach the last building of the village center. An old lady sees us coming and runs back into her home. Nkella puts me down on thick snow, but we keep running, reaching the rest of the crew.

I arch my neck and glance back at Mūhī and his crew. The Arcana is spreading out to cover more ground.

We dodge into the trees. Tessa has lost speed due to the snow. Kaehante reaches his arm out, grabs one of her levers, and pulls. Gusts of black smoke pump out of her chair as it begins to hover on the snow as she did at the skull beach back at Wands.

A popping sound goes off in my ear, and we're covered in Iéle's gray dome.

"Keep heading to the trees," Nkella says. "They cannot see us, but they can still catch up."

"What took you so long, Iéle?" AJ says. He's out of breath. I slow my step as well, grabbing onto my chest.

Iéle growls but keeps urging us forward.

"She was far away," Nkella says, "but she is here now."

Looking behind us the rest of the way, we catch the Arcana coming out through the woods. "They'll never stop looking for us," I say.

Mūhī and a few of his crew start spreading out.

Searching for us.

Harold gasps for breath, setting the cage down by his feet. Quinn is clucking furiously, probably scared out of her wits. I can't blame her; she's just a chicken.

Iéle snaps her attention to Quinn and bites at the air. Quinn jumps, and with a loud popping sound, she disappears into the Aō. My eyes widen. Harold gapes at the empty cage.

"I thought you said she wasn't an oumala chicken," I say to him.

"They told me she wasn't!"

An Arcana soldier appears a foot from the front of the dome, his gaze snapping to where Quinn used ouma. I hold my breath. The soldier raises his hand, and ice immediately forms over us, revealing the invisible dome.

"Well, they lied to you," Tessa says, backing up.

Mūhī starts running toward us, forming sandwhips with his arms, calling for the others.

Nkella steps to the edge of the gray dome. He sends out a gust of wind toward the pirates. An Arcana soldier appears in front of them, blocking them from being blown away. The wind turns to snow and picks up speed, forming a snowy cyclone. Icy wind carrying hail gushes toward us. Nkella turns, telling us to run.

We duck and bolt to the side as the hail just about misses us, and the cyclone disperses in a random direction.

A growling bark makes me whip my face around to see three wolves appearing out of Iéle's dome. They charge after Mūhī and the rest, allowing us time to get away. I'm not normally happy to see wolves, but right now I'm glad Nkella has them.

I pick up my feet as high as I can as the snow becomes difficult to run through. Iéle still has her dome cast over us, and the ice is gone. We dodge toward a wooded area and keep running between the trees until we're far enough away to catch our breath.

"Hey, maybe don't arm the ice Arcana with wind?" AJ tells Nkella.

Nkella scowls at him.

Something jumps from the trees, and I gasp. Iéle growls, her eyes glowing red. What looks like a jaguar stares at us, and then shifts into Kenjō.

Harold takes her in his arms.

"Calm, Iéle," Nkella says.

"Kenjō," I whisper. "I—" I'm out of breath. I want to tell her how sorry I am, but the words can't come out. I've already told her I'm sorry, but nothing I can do can change what I did. It can't bring her fiancé back. Her face is pale as she looks at me, but she doesn't say anything.

"Later," Tessa tells us. "For now, we have to go."

My lip trembles, and I nod.

"What timing for your chicken to disappear, mei? Lāri stares at Harold.

"Don't blame Quinn." Harold scowls at Iéle. "This whole time she stayed in her cage—during a shipwreck, while running—and it took a wolf wanting to eat her."

Iéle's eyes glow red, and I shift my gaze to Nkella who is staring back in the direction we came from. A whistle carries in the wind.

"Time to go, daí?" Kaehante says as Nkella passes him a glance and nods.

"This way is good," Kenjō says. "It is rough and cold, but they may not come this way right away. With Demitri injured, it will buy us time, è?" She looks at Harold. "To wherever you need to go."

"I thought you were going to kill him," Harold says.

Kenjō scowls at him, then shifts back into a jaguar.

Harold shrugs. "Either she's warmer this way or she doesn't want to talk."

I don't blame her.

The wolf leads us through feet of snow up to my calves. Even though I'm fully dressed in my snow attire, I'm freezing to the point of shaking. Harold grumbles something about how he wished he still had his runic power. We're mostly quiet, not wanting to bring attention to ourselves. Every now and then, we hear Mūhī or another pirate's voice. So we keep trudging through the snow, following a wolf and a jaguar. In her cat form, Kenjō doesn't seem to feel threatened by Iéle. I can tell Iéle doesn't like it, but she knows not to attack Kenjō. I think she knows the difference between Ipani shifters and real animals, but Nkella said she doesn't like the smell.

Even though our telepathic connection is weakened, I still get currents of his energy from time to time, bringing in guilt and brooding emotions. Despite the quiet of the crew and the sound of our steps through the snow, I don't feel alone in my despair because of his energy coming out of him—toward me. Affection. Protection. Trust. That last part is something I've always refused myself. But I trust him now. More than ever.

"I think we finally lost them," Lāri says.

Kenjō shifts back to her human form. "I do not smell them from here. I think you are right."

"We need to make a plan, Captain," Kaehante says. "What is our heading?"

"We need food for supper," AJ says. He digs into his pack and takes out bread and fruit. "This is all I have, but the uncursed should eat. We'll want to hunt for more food before nightfall." He looks at me and Nkella, and then at Kenjō. "We can keep going. We don't really need to eat—well, except big boys like Kae whose hunger can endure a curse."

Kae grunts and smacks AJ in the back. "You think about food more than I do, daí?"

AJ chuckles and hands us the bread.

"Too bad about the chicken," Kae says. Harold rolls his eyes.

We stand around eating from AJ's pile. I nibble on a piece of bread, still unable to really stomach anything. My knees quiver from the cold.

"We have nothing to make camp with," Kenjō points out. "And we are on the opposite side of the yeti grotto, so we cannot go there."

"And any inn will have been told about us," Tessa adds.

"Great. Fugitives again." I mutter. Kenjō looks away from me. I know she's refusing to look at me.

"But the plan remains the same, mei?" Lāri asks, bending down to her knees. "We take down the oumala fighting ring?"

"We can't do that if we freeze to death." AJ rubs her shoulders.

Kenjō glances at Harold. "Make a fire, è?"

"Right," Harold says between bites of bread. "We'll make a fire at night and make camp. Does Iéle's invisible dome keep warm over a bonfire?"

Nkella nods. "We will not freeze. We will rest after we hunt and eat."

"Good plan," Kae agrees. "Get energy first, then we keep going."

"But for now, we'll keep going until before nightfall?" Tessa confirms.

Nkella unhooks his flask from his belt and takes a sip. "That is the best plan, or else, we risk them reaching the ring before we do. Demitri will know that is where we are headed first, and he will have Arcana waiting for us at the ship and at the Temple. We do not have time to waste, daí?"

We nod. Kae stuffs the bread into his mouth.

"If you are taking down the ring at Naó, I want to help," Kenjō says.

We walk for the next few hours, until the sun starts to dip on the horizon, bringing in a whole different kind of cold. I rub my gloves together, but my knees are quaking in this frigid snow. I don't know how Harold survived this island when he first came to Tarotland.

We finally stop to make camp—or what we'll call camp.

Nkella, Iéle, Kae, and Kenjō split up to hunt for food, while I stay back with Harold, AJ, Lāri, and Tessa. We clear an open area by the woods and find logs and branches to build a firepit. AJ and Harold get to work building the actual fire.

Kenjō and the other hunters return with fish and rabbits on poles. They skin the animals while AJ and Lāri prepare sticks for everyone. Tessa starts sharpening some branches with her knife. I haven't been hungry all day, and I'm glad for that. Otherwise, I'd be dying of hunger as the crew hunted and prepared the food.

I sit close to the fire next to Tessa, watching Nkella skin the fish. Normally, I'd find a way to pitch in, but right now, I don't want to move. And no one tries to get me to do anything. I think they understand I need some time to myself. If it wasn't for needing to stay warm, I would be sitting under a tree, alone in the woods.

Harold breaks the silence. "Look at the bright side." He takes a bite of his meat and chews. "At least now we don't have to walk through the Haunted Forest. Last time, we were avoiding being caught by the Prefect's Arcana, so we had no choice..." his voice tapers off. Kenjō turns away.

The fire dies down, and Harold moves to feed it. Kenjō snaps her attention to him. "Why don't you use your magic, è?"

"I don't have it," he retorts angrily, "remember?"

"Harold," Tessa asks, "are you alright?"

"Yeah, I think she's gone through a lot in one day, mate," AJ says to him.

Harold's shoulders droop, and he looks at Kenjō. "I'm sorry, I—" He sighs. "I'm just so far away from home, and I need to get back to Jötunheim. I've been cursed twice. And I don't know if I'll ever get back home."

Kenjō shakes her head. "You will," she says. "But you must use your magic, Harold. It is inside you, è?" He furrows his brows, and I do too.

She takes his hands and pulls him toward the woods. "Make them again. You can do it."

"It's not that simple," he says, allowing her to lead him into the woods.

After we eat, I lie back with the diary open.

Nkella is staring at the fire from across from me, his gaze intense and his features hardened. I wonder what he's thinking about after all this. The flames cause shadows to dance over his brutally handsome features, but he doesn't look up as others talk among themselves.

I don't feel like talking. I've been looking forward to some alone time, which is hardly possible when traveling with a crew, but they get it.

"Good thing your ouma is not to kill by looking at them, mei?" Lāri says to Nkella, but he doesn't respond. He doesn't flinch either. It's like he didn't even hear her. I glance her way. She shrugs and goes back to talking to AJ.

I take the diary out from under my shirt and stare at it.

Something wet runs down my nose, and I stifle a gasp as I touch it. Blood smears my fingers in the dark, but I quietly roll over so no one sees. There's no point in making anyone worry. I rub the blood away and wipe it on my pants; at least it isn't gushing out. Finding the Death Card is the only thing that'll save me now.

Kenjō's voice pulls me away. I shouldn't listen in, but I can't help wanting to know what she's thinking, what she's saying. I know she hates me. And I normally wouldn't care if some girl I met not too long ago hated me, but I did something so unspeakably horrible to her, she must be dreaming of tearing my throat open in my sleep. I'd be dreaming the same thing.

Nkella said Demitri manipulated me, that I had no control over it, that I didn't know what I was doing. I don't know what pains me more, that I killed someone innocent, taking someone away from someone else, or that I was able to be manipulated. I never trusted Demitri, and yet, I ended up trusting him. I wanted so badly to become powerful that I let him take me to a terrible memory so that I would be trapped in it, enough for him to somehow know how I would react. He even confirmed how predictable I was to him.

I hate him even more now.

I hate the Empress, and I hate Demitri.

Somehow, I can't affect people in my memories, I can only take objects. I'm not sure why that is.

"I think I always knew Demitri had ulterior motives," Kenjō admits to Harold, who is staring hard at a long branch in his hand. "I think I only wanted to believe he had the best intentions. But now I know it was stupid. Why would I think someone who was okay with killing Ipani for rikorō was a good person?"

"Don't be so hard on yourself," Harold tells her. "They taught you the ends justify the means. A lot of people get caught up on that, not just you."

"I don't know how to feel about my mother either." Her voice grows heavy, and I force myself back to the diary. I take one of the pages in my hand, but Kenjō's mention of her mom permeates my mind.

One thing that Demitri said to me still sticks. *The first kill is always the hardest.* I wanted him to be wrong. And in a way he is, Alec was innocent, and I'll regret it for the rest of my life. But the Empress killed my mother, and that is not something I can forgive...or forget. Now, even more than ever, pumped with adrenaline, anger, and hatred, I want her dead. Even though it was Demitri's manipulation over me—which I hate—it was still because of the Empress that all of this happened.

I'm still going to kill her.

Alec is dead because the Empress killed my mom. If she hadn't, I wouldn't have been training my power. Demitri would not have had a chance to get to me.

I flip to the last few pages of the diary. Maybe this will help keep my mind busy, if nothing else, it could have some useful information.

> *Dearest diary,*
> *Today Tetalla and I have decided to run away together. I will open a portal, and we will live somewhere in the past. I don't have the power to go to the present, but I can't wait to show him Greece.*
> *Love,*
> *Adara*

I flip to the next page.

> *Dear diary,*
> *It's hard to write this, and I'm afraid my tears are blurring my script as I do. Aletha did not take the news well, and it is so much worse than I could ever have imagined. His name means the bringer of death, as he is a warrior. And because of this, between Aletha's anger and the newfound power of our combined magic, he has become cursed as the incarnation of Death from our card game. Aletha always did love games, but she has taken this too far. He has vanished, and I can still hear his screams.*
> *Love,*
> *Adara*

She can still hear his screams? He just vanished? Confusion clouds me, as I flip to the next page.

> *Dearest diary,*
> *This might be the last I ever write you.*
> *I hear my sister calling my name, and I am only thankful Asteria took my baby and left. I don't know where she went, but as long as they're safe. My beautiful baby girl. Aletha has gone mad and is threatening to raise our little island high up off the ground. She has locked me in, afraid I'll escape and go find him. But I know not where he is, ever since she made him vanish. I feel it in my bones something isn't right with him. Why wouldn't he come, if he was here? I will never know.*
> *Farewell forever, my only friend.*
> *Adara*

I stare at the words I just read. My nose itches as tears threaten the rim of my eyes. The Empress told Adara she had made him vanish. I glance over at the crew. Tessa is lying on the floor next to Kaehante. AJ and Lāri are cuddled together. And Harold and Kenjō, surprisingly, are as well.

Nkella is still awake and staring at the flames with Iéle's head resting on his lap. I'm still not ready to talk, and I don't think he is either. He doesn't even look my way.

My eyes grow heavy, and I turn over with the diary in my arms, trying to make sense of what I just read. I recall the vision I had of her when she was scribbling in her diary and then threw it into the ocean. It makes sense now why she was in a hurry to get away, but...what became of Tetalla?

My mark starts to pulse, and suddenly I'm being pulled into a vision.

I'm standing on the beach outside the Tower, but we're high up in the sky. It's nighttime, and Tetalla is there. She caused the island to float high above so he would never reach it, but somehow, he found a way. His rage emanates from him, and I can feel it coursing through my bones as if he's directing it to me. It's worse than I've ever felt before. He's heartbroken.

He got word that the Empress killed his love, the mother of his child when she found out she had been disloyal to her. And he's furious. Fire sears out of him as he channels his ouma.

Within seconds, the Tower is caught ablaze, and in mere minutes, the entire building is burning. He keeps throwing fire over the flame like a child hitting a basketball against a wall, as his anger pours out of him.

She's dead.

The love of his life is dead.

And now he's going to kill the one who took her life.

The roof of one of the Towers crumbles to the ground. I watch as flames enter the building, consuming everything in its wake. An agonizing scream comes from Tetalla's mouth as he falls to his knees.

The memory takes me inside the Tower as it's burning. The Empress Aletha is in her nightgown, and she's sprinting down the hall calling for Asteria and Adara. She doesn't wear a mask. Her face is beautiful, flawless with porcelain skin.

She calls for Asteria but remembers Asteria has returned to their homeland. She isn't in the Tower. Why would she be calling for Adara? She's dead. She killed her. Maybe it was out of habit.

Except, then she opens a door and runs down the stairs. She slips and falls on the way down, blocking her fall with her hands. Why is she going downstairs, when she should have tried to leave the Tower? "Adara!" she screams. She screams and screams. She reaches a dungeon door and starts looking for something on the wall. Keys? Something crashes overhead; the ceiling half collapses around us. She finally gets the door open, and another part of the ceiling covered in flames collapses over Aletha. Her body catches on fire, and a spider half the size of her body falls over her, its web tightening around her like a cocoon, pulling her up. Her screams shake my bones, filling them with pain even though this is a vision, but what's worse is that she's still calling her sister's name.

The vision fast-forwards.

Aletha's face is burned to a crisp, as she digs through the rubble, sobbing loudly. With the help of the spiders, she uncovers wood, stone, and bramble. Finally, she uncovers a hand. And her crying intensifies.

Moving a heavy piece of wood, her sister's face emerges from the rubble. Cold, dead, burnt beyond recognition.

The blood drains from my face. The Empress was trying to save her sister from the fire. She hadn't killed her?

Smoke swirls around me as the vision takes me back to Tetalla. He's barefoot on the beach of Dempu Yuni, his clothes in rags and covered in soot. Demitri appears before him. Tetalla swings his sword from its sheath, but Demitri tells him something that makes him drop his weapon. Tetalla shakes his head and backs away. A Tower guard appears, holding a body beside Demitri. Tetalla drops down to the floor, as they uncover Adara's corpse. The screams that leave him make my blood run cold. He believed the Empress had killed her sister out of jealousy, but in his rash judgment, he had been the one to kill Adara. Black smoke starts to cover the scene, and I back away as Tetalla's eyes burn crimson, and black horns curve out of his head.

Images of fire to random buildings emerge as the scene fades away.

29

TETALLA KILLED INNOCENTS AFTER HE LEARNED THE TRUTH of what he had done. The Empress may not have physically killed her sister, but she still caused it to happen. Why couldn't she have just let Adara be happy? She lied to her—to them both—to get them to stop seeing each other, and in turn, she caused her sister's death...and has been alone ever since.

I lie awake, staring at the nautilus swirls of the bayoa twirling in the sky. My legs grow restless, and I decide to get up. I glance at the crew. It's still dark out, but the low flames dance over their bodies. Nkella has his hat over his face, and one arm over his head. Iéle lifts her head and stares at me.

"Sh," I whisper to her. "I'll be back."

She growls a little but lays her head back down.

As soon as I step out of the Aō dome, the crisp wind hits my face. It was really toasty in there; I even have sweat behind my neck. I grab a nearby branch lying on the ground and stick it up right where I stepped out. The dome hides them all so well, it's as if nothing is there at all.

I'll just walk along these woods for a little bit to take my mind off things. Arcana soldiers aren't going to be here; they won't have known to come this way. Stepping into the side of the leafless silver birches, I start walking away from the dome, my mind in a million places at once.

Alec. But I bury that down. I don't want to think about that right now.

My vision.

It's so sad. Tetalla didn't know she was locked away in the Tower.

The Empress lied to him. Or...someone did. Somehow, he thought the Empress had killed Adara. And in turn, he sought to set the Empress on fire. Considering how the Ace of Swords is the only thing that can harm her, it mustn't be easy to hurt a Fate, which means...he had some kind of special fire ouma that could.

I can't imagine a love as strong as theirs being forced apart. And then he went insane. He received the Devil curse, on top of him being Death, and he lost himself so fast. He must have been in so much pain.

"You should not be out here alone." Nkella speaks in a low, sleepy voice.

I gasp and spin around. "Sorry. I just needed to walk."

He walks up to me quietly. "Let's walk then."

"You don't have to—we can go back."

"Quiet, neyuro. Too loud, daî?" He half turns to me and winks.

A smile creeps onto my lips, and we walk in silence under the stars. Finally, I bring up the courage to ask him a question.

"Why did you ask me if I would have come back here if I didn't have to?"

He doesn't respond, and I think he either didn't hear the question or is ignoring it.

"I wanted to know," he says after a few beats.

"But why?" I stop at a tree, and he turns. I can see his frown through the starlight. He turns to face me completely and walks up. I steel my spine, letting him get close. A fiery spark lights up his eyes as they find my gaze through the dark.

"I told you when you got here," he says, his voice a decibel above a hoarse whisper. "I feared the Empress had taken the World Card to find you in your land..." He glances down at the snow between us. "You lived in my head for weeks."

"That doesn't answer my question," I whisper. He lifts his eyes to mine, but this time there's a different intensity about them. He gives me a long lingering look that makes my insides quake, and I'm yearning for him. A rush of emotions caves in, likely the last of the rikorō pouring out of him, only this time he's letting it.

His breathing is deep and hard. I can tell he wants to say something, but he's stopping himself. After a few beats, I gather my will and let out a long breath, forcing myself to pull away from the tree. There isn't any point in this. But he grabs my wrist and brings me back against the tree.

"I want you, Soren." My breath hitches. "But we cannot be together," he says with regret in his voice. "I will kill you." He takes my hand, eliciting goosebumps to ride up my arms. "I could never forgive myself. Please don't make me do it. I could not bear it if I lost you forever and it was my fault." His breath brushes against my skin as I glance up to meet his eyes.

I stare at the lines on his face, sincerity in them and in his voice. It takes everything in me not to reach his lips, to kiss him deeply. I give him a subtle nod and swallow. "Would you come to my land if you could?"

His lips part, and he moves in closer. Sparks skitter down my spine, my back presses up against the tree behind me, and I feel the stubble of his chin against my cheek. "To find you? I would never stop trying."

His eyes linger over my lips as his fingers caress my hand. Then he lifts it to his mouth, brushing his lips gently over my skin. His eyes close as he kisses the back of my hand, then lets me go. "We should go," he says.

"Yes."

It's early morning now, and Iéle's dome is still toasty. Nkella is about to start discussing the plan to save Gari, and I'm trying my hardest to listen. I want to save Gari. But it's nearly impossible to concentrate when I still have last night playing over in my mind.

"This is the plan," Nkella announces by the dying fire, and we all huddle to hear it. "Oumala shifters will infiltrate, daí?" He looks at Kenjō and Lāri.

AJ crosses his arms in a tight embrace around himself, his forehead crinkled. "I'm not worried about Lāri, because this is what we've always done. But Kenjō, are you okay doing this?"

"If it means undoing what Demitri has done, then yes," she says.

"But you're not trained," Harold presses.

"I will keep an eye on her," Lāri says, then turns to face Kenjō. "But if you are uncomfortable, stay with the crew in the audience. I can handle opening the cages on my own."

"Just tell me what to do and I'll do it. I like the idea of taking these fighting rings down," Kenjō says. "I need to do something active anyway to keep my mind off of..."

I lower my eyes to the hard-packed snow. Kenjō still avoids looking in my direction, but I'm just going to have to accept that she may never speak to me again. The faster I get that Sword and kill the Empress, the better. Then I can take the Death Card and bring my mom back, and never come back here again. Never face Kenjō again.

My eyes flutter to Nkella and the crew.

I can't let myself get caught up in them.

Home is where my crew is.

But it's also where Talia is.

"Iéle stays behind," Nkella says, "so we will be visible before approaching."

"We don't want Iéle getting caught and put it in the ring," Tessa adds.

Iéle huffs as if she can understand. She probably does.

"How far are we from the fighting ring?" Harold asks Kenjō.

"Half a day's walk. We should get there right before sundown if we leave now."

"And what time do the fights start?"

"Usually sundown," Lāri responds to Harold. "The trick will be to sneak into the back cages without getting caught. If they see we don't have an ouma dampener, they will give us one, and we won't be able to use ouma until we are in the ring. But it will be faster with the two of us to open all the cages and deactivate their dampeners.

"It's best if you go in first and start letting the animals loose as soon as you're left alone. The rest of us will be in the audience or on the perimeter for backup. If something goes wrong and you end up in the ring, we'll have to improvise."

"Let's hope nothing goes wrong," Tessa says.

We clean up any evidence of us being here after we eat. We spread out the firepit, but unfortunately with Iéle's dome containing the warmth from the fire, there is a large circle of melted snow. Harold and Kae kick mounds of snow to cover it up as best they can; this takes up a little of our time, even with the rest of us helping.

It's sunny today, too, which is great for hiking up this mountain as it's not as cold, but we could use a little snow to cover our tracks. It'll look weird to the psychic Arcana soldiers that randomly survey the area to see footsteps coming from a group of invisible people. They'll know we're traveling through an Aō dome.

My legs grow heavy with each step we climb. The crunching of our boots on the snow is rhythmic and no one is talking. Nkella and Iéle take the lead, creating the dome. Tessa goes from hovering over mounds of snow and rocky steepness to driving in the new heavy-terrain wheels the Hermit had given her, in order to not use up the potion that makes her chair hover. Kaehante is walking behind me—the strongest in the back I guess. Unfortunately, I have to stare at Kenjō most of the way, as she walks in front of me with Harold. They occasionally switch places with AJ and Lāri as they're walking kind of huddled.

My nose has already bled about three times since we've been hiking, and I've kept it quiet. It's happening more frequently now, and I'm not sure how long I have left. The Death Card will work. I have to believe it will, or all this is for nothing. I try to occupy my head with what I learned in my vision last night.

Whatever happened to Tetalla?

Where did he go after he lost himself? What did the Empress do with him?

We stop only once by a loud stream to rest, and then we keep going. We reach the Ancient Greek ruins of Naó just as the tip of the tallest mountain is starting to hide the sun behind us.

We stand on a hill full of pines, behind a few boulders. Large broken columns are scattered around the grounds. Foliage and trees break through them, evidence of something colossal having happened long ago. I'm told more of the building is hidden among the trees, farther up the mountain path. But from where we're standing, only scattered fragments of the ruins remain. The building is meant to be the Ancient Temple, where the Ace of Swords is kept.

People are entering a tall building up ahead. It is large and round and made from the same white plaster I saw in the village. My chest is starting to pound with anticipation. With all the current atrocities taking up residence in my head, the fact that we're going in to save Gari is only just hitting me.

I hope he's okay. And I hope it is him. Not that I don't want to save another drakon and other animals, but I've been worried sick over Gari. The fear of never seeing him again has been buried deep in the back of my mind.

"Right. Do we all know our positions?" Tessa asks, refilling small cannonballs in the back of her chair cannon. "Kaehante and I will be the back-up muscle, so we'll stay back here. Iéle will be with us, keeping us hidden."

"I'll be bringing in Kenjō and Lāri as new recruits," AJ announces, "and I'll weasel my way in to break the locks myself so you two can get out." AJ leans in and kisses Lāri on the lips. He looks at the rest of us and nods. "Once they're safely in cages"—he pauses and shakes his head at his own wording—"I'll head to the front to take on my 'annoying chap' persona and distract the guards in case you need a decoy."

Lāri stares at Kenjō. "Are you ready? Once AJ leaves, we wait until no guards are watching us, then we start unlocking the gates. We will leave the ones in the fighting ring for last. Any questions?"

Kenjō stretches her hands, bending one toward her. "What happens if no guards leave us alone?"

"Then you wait for my signal to attack at the same time. Some oumala animals will be ready to fight for freedom, but most likely they will have dampeners on them. You have to take those off as soon as you open the gates, mei? Which means you have to shift back to do it."

"How do we take the ouma dampeners off them?"

"Oh, right," AJ says. "I'll have to scope that potion out for you. The guards will have it on them."

Kenjō nods, uncertainty wrinkling her forehead.

"This sounds like a crap shoot," Harold says, and Kenjō furrows her brows.

"A what?"

"You're depending on guards not being around the animal cages for this to go smoothly? Why would they leave the cages alone?"

AJ leans to one side. "Because they won't be expecting anyone with the balls to take them on. We have done this many times before, and those guards are greedy but also lazy. Trust me. They take breaks to watch the show, especially knowing the animals are dampened and locked up."

Harold pinches the bridge of his nose. "I'll be in the audience with Nkella and Soren," he tells Kenjō.

The three of us make our way down together, while Lāri and Kenjō take another route to the back. They have oumala animals guarding the ring from inside the Aō, which is why Iéle couldn't take them hidden in her dome, but they'll be hidden from a distance. The idea that there are oumala animals protecting the fighting ring makes my stomach turn, especially knowing how much Iéle understands. I guess some animals only care about being fed, or whatever deals they've made with whoever they're bonded to.

"Let me do the talking to get us inside, daí?" Nkella looks at us both. I make the zipping mouth motion with my hand over my lips. He gives me a look from the corner of his eyes, and I know he's remembering my inability to keep quiet in Wands.

I won't make that mistake again.

"And pretend to like it," he adds. "Clap. Laugh. Cheer, daí?" He looks at us both. I grimace.

As we approach, smokiness hits my nostrils from a giant piece of meat cooking over a fire outside a round two-story building, its conical roof made of straw. A long line of people waiting to get food stands in front of the fire, and boisterous laughter and chatter come from all directions.

The fights have started, so we walk right up to the ticket collector. A few Ipani eye me and Harold. We look different from the rest of them— especially Harold with his blue eyes and blond hair. Red is still rare, but more common, maybe not as bright as mine, but still. I smile back, and they widen their eyes and look away. Nkella narrows his eyes in their direction, and a tiny smile threatens my lips.

Nkella pays our entrance fees, and we make it inside to look for seats. Wooden benches are displayed in rows all along the two-story building. In the center is a large circular cage that reaches from floor to ceiling.

Something crashes against the gate from the inside, and I jump into Harold. A pile of snow lands on the floor, and a full-sized gorilla stretches on its two legs and roars. Bolts of purple lightning spiral up the gorilla's arms and reach the top of the cage. Cheers erupt from the audience. My throat is still stuck in my throat as Harold pulls me away. I do a double-take as the pile of snow on the floor comes together like magnetic clay of sorts, morphing itself into what looks like a quadruped beast until it lengthens itself to become a polar bear.

My jaw drops. A bear that can turn itself into snow. Just when I thought I'd seen everything.

It backs up against the cage as the gorilla lets out a roar.

"Oy, move out of my view!" someone shouts behind me.

"Neyuro."

I dart my eyes over to where Nkella is standing next to three seats on the third row. He's next to the aisle for an easy exit. Harold and I hurry to take our seats. The foul smell of blood mixed with notes of alcohol and whatever animal they're cooking outside permeates the air.

Harold lets out a deep sigh as he looks at the exit. I know he's worried about Kenjō. I hope she and Lāri both made it in safely.

The gorilla approaches the polar bear, and the bear stretches his long claws, striking the gorilla across the face. The gorilla roars, blood shooting from its mouth. Then it turns and smacks the polar bear back. He raises his arm, sending a bolt of purple lightning down from the cage and into the bear. The bear staggers as he shifts into a pile of snow. That's a decent defense, but I imagine it could also be great camouflage to catch prey.

I'm at the edge of my seat in total horror and shock. "This isn't fair."

"The lightning gorilla comes from the jungles of Oleanu," Nkella mutters low enough for only us to hear. "He does not belong here."

I shake my head.

Harold leans in across from me. "This seems to have attracted a lot of attention, though. Why doesn't the Empress shut it down?"

"I actually don't think she minds them," I whisper, recalling the fighting ring in her Tower with both oumala animals and Ipani.

Nkella guffaws over the cheering. "This is legal, daî?"

"This is legal?" Harold almost shouts.

"Sh." Nkella retorts.

Makes me want to kill her even more.

Harold inches to the edge of his seat, his fist on the wooden bench.

AJ's laugh from the aisle row that leads to the door makes me do a double-take.

"Good. They are in cages," Nkella states in a low whisper. "That is step one."

"This should be quick then, right?" Harold asks.

"Sh." Nkella eyes him but then gives one nod. "Be ready."

The polar bear isn't moving, and the gorilla turns around, causing lightning to strike out of his arms again as the crowd roars. "It's almost as if he likes the attention."

"Oh, I think, he absolutely does," Harold whispers back, fake clapping.

The gorilla kicks at the snow pile, making the polar bear quickly shift back. He lets out a moan, and the gorilla picks him up over his head, turns around to face us, and begins to rip the bear apart.

I gasp, a squeak coming out my lips, as I shut my eyes and turn my head into Nkella's arm.

The crowd cheers, some scream.

"This is barbaric," Harold says.

Nkella wraps his arm around me and draws me in closer. His warm hickory scent sends me back to Wands for a moment. His hand reaches my face, gently shielding me from the view. I pull away, not wanting him to think I'm weak.

"There is no shame in hating this, neyuro," he tells me as if reading my mind.

The cheering dies down as the polar bear is taken away through a small cage opening at the bottom. The gorilla spots the opening and runs for it, but the cage is closed before he can get out. The gorilla grabs onto the cage and shakes it, letting out an angry yell.

"So, we're letting that thing out?" Harold whispers to Nkella who tilts his head, narrowing his eyes.

"Kaehante will put the dampener on that one. Enough time for everyone to get away."

"Why Kaehante?" I ask.

Nkella smirks. "Only a gorilla can understand gorilla."

I shake my head.

"And then what? Where do all the animals that don't belong go?" Harold asks.

I stare at him. "Valid."

"We don't have time to take them all home. I can send Iéle to find others who do this kind of job."

A speaker makes an announcement, and everyone quiets to hear.

"Have you had enough?" the speaker asks.

"Ko Ko Koj!" The audience booms.

"Then get ready, for next we have an even better match for Rod the Gorilla. An āngaraeke from your very own Piupeki. From āngaraeke grotto."

Harold grips the edge of the bench as they bring out what looks like a twelve-foot yeti. Harold's mouth drops and his eyes widen.

"Is that Alfred?" He stands up.

The yeti looks around and lets out a long moan, then his eyes stop on Harold, and he quiets. A few people look back at us.

"Harold." Nkella grunts, grabbing his arm and pulling him back down.

Harold stares at Nkella. "I'd recognize that stupid face anywhere. That's Alfred. We have to save him. What's taking the girls so long?"

Nkella eyes the door. Anticipation is starting to surge out of him in a wave, meaning he's not keeping his emotions in check right now. Something's on his mind. He's worried.

"Is this taking longer than usual?" I ask him.

The gorilla strikes down a bolt of lightning. The yeti—Alfred?—creates a shield, making the lightning ricochet off him and hit the gorilla instead. The crowd quiets as a few lightning flares strike the cage. Their champion gorilla flies against the cage, looking like a small dog in comparison to the yeti. He lands with a hard thud.

Rod picks himself up and uses his fists to walk around the yeti. Alfred stands there keeping his eyes on the gorilla. Rod motions to summon another lightning strike, but seems to think better of it and lowers his arm. He stands on both legs and starts pounding on his chest. Alfred stays put and lets out a loud, earth-quaking wail. Rod then runs at the yeti. Alfred knocks him out with one swing of his gigantic arm, sending Rod flying to the side of the cage. This time, when he lands, he doesn't get up.

My bottom lip shakes. I stare at Harold whose face has gone paler than usual. Nkella stands.

"Where are you going? Is it time?"

"Wait here."

"What! No way!"

"Something might be wrong. Be ready," he repeats again. I purse my lips as he leaves us.

"Who do you think they'll bring out next?" Harold asks.

I shake my head.

After they clear the gorilla from the cage, the speaker steps inside.

"Who will the yeti fight next? Will it be the drakon?"

My stomach sinks, and Harold and I exchange a scared look.

"Or will it be something new?"

I chew on my cheek, the anticipation killing me. Gari doesn't know Harold's friend, and he will defend himself against a yeti. I'm sure of it.

"Drakon! Drakon! Drakon!" the people cheer.

Nkella walks back to us quickly. "Change of plans." He takes a seat.

"What does that mean?"

Nkella leans toward Harold. "Get your smoke bomb ready, daí?"

Harold places his hand on his belt and nods.

"Kenjō was taken before AJ could break the lock on her cage. He secured Lāri, but someone showed up before he could go back for Kenjō."

I gasp. Harold's face reddens as he stares at Nkella.

"So what now?" I ask.

The little gate opens and they strike an electric rod behind a feline animal. I gasp as a jaguar walks into the fighting ring. Her prowl is low, as she stares at everyone in the front row. My heart nearly shoots out of my mouth. Harold stands and someone behind him shouts at him, but he ignores them.

Kenjō turns to the yeti, who let out a curious moan. Then Kenjō sits, and the yeti falls to his knees and scratches her head. Harold falls back on his seat letting out a nervous laugh.

"This works in our favor, daí?"

"È!" someone shouts. "They like each other?"

"Or they know each other!" someone else answers.

"I knew it was Alfred." Harold grins.

Someone approaches the cage holding a rod with a burning hot coal on its end and pokes it at Kenjō. She spins around and roars at him. The yeti roars, too, getting protective as he stands and grabs the rod through the cage. Suddenly, the light scones snuff out.

The audience starts to murmur, confused, asking what's going on. I turn to Nkella who nudges us.

"Do it now."

Harold throws one of his smoke screen bombs, and blue smoke fumes out, making people drop around us. I almost lose my footing as some of the smoke permeates around me. A wave of nausea forces me down, and I lean against the bench. I touch under my nose, and sure enough, there's blood. I wipe it away quickly, but a pain hits my temples, and I have to steady my breathing.

"Sorry," Harold says, keeping me upright. "Wait—are you okay?" His brows rise at the sight of blood on my hands.

Before he can say anything, I cut him off. "There's no time. I'll be fine."

He gives me an understanding nod.

People scream from the opposite sides of the building, but AJ appears on the other side and throws another bomb. He jumps over a guard and opens the gate of the fighting cage.

Kenjō jumps down, and Harold runs over to wave Alfred down.

On the left side of the building, people aren't affected by the potion. They're shouting and probably calling more guards. They scream as Alfred plants his feet flat on the ground and roars at them.

"Where's Gari?" I shout to Kenjō, ignoring the headache blooming at my temples. She shifts back to her Ipani form and ignores me as she runs to the back. We all follow her through a cold hall. Rooms are on either side with cages upon cages.

"Start opening them," AJ shouts. Nkella makes it into one room and I follow, opening the cages as soon as AJ hands me a pair of keys and a potion to drop on their dampeners. The dampeners look like the glowing bands that were placed on me and Nkella when we had our little goat heist. We hurry, letting out all kinds of animals from wolves, to bears, to otters. None of them hunt each other, as they're all trying to get away.

My heart is racing, worried that Gari either isn't here or that he's dead. Loud popping sounds come from all around us as oumala animals are released and pop back into the Aō.

Pounding comes from a door, and I stop. The pounding gets louder. Do I open it? What if it's a gorilla?

"Someone let me out of here," a gurgling voice comes through. I gasp and find the keys hanging from the side. I quickly unlock it and twist the knob.

Crazy yellow eyes stare at me from a dark room. Blue and purple hair poke out, and tears sting the corners of my eyes.

"Soren?" he says weakly. "Is that really you?"

"Gari!" I rush in and wrap my arms around him, ignoring the shouts and fights breaking outside.

"Quick, take this off me." He moves onto his back and shows me his hind leg.

I pour a few drops onto his dampener, and the gold twisted band releases him. I back away as he stretches and grows in size, his glow springing him back to life.

"I thought you died," I say.

"I thought I did too," he gurgles. "That serpent didn't like the way I tasted." He giggles. "I was washed away, and a kind family nurtured me back to health."

"They did?"

"Until the traffickers took me. I think they got paid for it. The family, I mean." He twists his body to lie on his back in the air, as he stretches himself out.

"Soren!" Lāri yells. "They're here." She reaches me and grabs my arm. Her eyes widen when she sees Gari.

"Who?"

"Demitri and his Arcana."

My eyes narrow into thin slits. I look back to Gari, and a menacing smile spreads on his wicked face.

30

BLASTS FROM ALL DIFFERENT TYPES OF OUMALA ANIMALS ARE coming from all directions. I duck as fire soars through my head from a pelican. Gari lengthens his body, shielding me and Lāri from getting scorched.

Popping sounds ring in my ears, as many of them flee the scene, while others stay to fight. Lāri and I run through the dark hall, a mess of melted sludge making me half slide and almost trip as I stop at another doorway, looking for the rest of the crew. AJ is in one of the rooms, still releasing animals. A strange four-legged animal with purple scales and a long nose jumps down from one of the cages on a shelf and waddles past me. Lāri enters and starts helping him.

"Where's Nkella?" I ask.

A blast comes from outside, and the three of us gape at each other.

"Is this the last room?" Harold barges in.

"There's one more down the hall," AJ tells him. "You and Kenjō take that one."

"We have to hurry. The Arcana just got here," Harold says as he runs toward the back.

AJ curses.

Another blast hits and I jump.

342

"Go, Soren," Lāri shouts at me. "We got this room. Go find our captain."

I take off running down the hall and through the main stadium. People have already left. I book it through the main door to find Kaehante outside with both arms covered in his armadillo ouma scales, and Tessa throwing blasts with her chair cannon. Flickering lights from torches illuminate the night around us. About a dozen Arcana soldiers are waiting for us outside. Three pirates are in hand-to-hand combat with Nkella.

He glimpses me. "Soren, run!"

A firebolt shoots past me and lands on the roof of the wooden building. My feet don't move fast enough to jump out of the way and a piece of the wooden roof falls beside me.

"Don't hit, Soren, you idiots!" At Demitri's voice, my gaze snaps to where he's standing. Two Arcana soldiers guard him on either side. "Kill the rest, bring Soren to the Prefect's Tower."

I back into the building. I have to get the crew out of here. Demitri shouts behind me as fire soars. An Arcana soldier grabs my shoulders and pulls me back. I fight him, "Let go of me, creep!" I will not let them take me from here. "AJ! Lāri!" I shout. "Get out!"

The soldier tightens his grip, but this time I take my knife from my sleeve and drive it into him. The Arcana soldier dematerializes in a gust of white smoke, giving me just enough time to escape out the door. I know he'll be back.

Fire blazes behind me. The Arcana have now taken out swords and started to fight Kaehante. Tessa keeps blasting them away, but it's only a matter of time before she runs out of cannonballs. I can't see Nkella. Fear strikes at every pore.

"Fine!" I shout. "I'll go with you. But let them go!"

The Arcana stop fighting and stare at me. Demitri hops down from a small hill, and his posse of pirates all smirk. Mūhī stands next to him, a stupid grin on his face.

"Get her," Demitri says to one of the pirates next to me. He has a smoky smell; he must be the one who burnt the building.

"Put out the fire first," I shout, as the fire roars behind me. My heart races in my chest. Nkella is about to run back in, but a soldier holds him back. The pirate grabs me, and I twist my arm to escape his grasp.

A blast of wind strikes him, blowing me back against the wall. Nkella's eyes are red, and the Arcana soldier has also been blasted back. Someone hooks my neck, and I yelp. I tug at his arm and kick back hard. He lets me go, and I stumble forward. The man's eyes are wide, his mouth agape with his tongue sticking out.

I back up as he grabs for his throat, his face is turning blue.

"What is this? What's happening?" Demitri asks. All around us, his pirates are also hitting the floor, their faces puffing up as air fills them. The only ones untouched are Demitri and, oddly enough, Mūhī, whose face is twisted in shock.

Nkella stares at Demitri, pointing at him with his sword. "Watch what happens when someone touches her."

Blood splatters all around us, as bodies explode from too much air. I shut my mouth tight and look away, as blood drenches the scene. My heart pants in my chest.

The Arcana soldiers take out their swords, and ice spreads over the ground, over the blood. They move in toward me and Nkella. Kaehante and Tessa back into each other.

"You might be able to kill Bronte's crew, but you can't kill the Arcana." Demitri's voice is steady, emotionless, despite him having witnessed men who had been on the ship with him explode. High on his hill, he's dry and untainted by blood.

Mūhī is shaking next to him, but Demitri ignores him.

A soldier grabs at me. Nkella spins and sends a blast of wind, knocking the soldier into the fire. The crew is still in the back of my mind. I hope they got out from the back door. I hope they're not trapped in there.

Ice blasts over Nkella as another soldier advances swinging a long sword. Tessa and Kaehante shoot at him, while Nkella turns to face Demitri head-on. He lifts his arm up in his direction, and I know what he's about to do.

"No!" I shout. Nkella stares at me and grimaces. "Don't," I tell him. A surge of anger mixed with restraint emanates from him, and I shake my head. Nkella's brows furrow, but he lowers his hand. He trusts me.

At the same time, I can feel the build-up of rage from the Devil inside radiating off him. His eyes glow, and he backs up, grabbing at his temple.

"Yes, don't," Demitri says. "Soren knows what she needs. Are you ready to come with me now?"

My sight zeros in on Demitri.

I steel my spine and walk through the carnage toward him.

He stares at me and smiles with a smug look on his face. As if he's already won.

My blood curdles.

He doesn't care about anyone but himself. I get wanting revenge, but he wants power.

He tried to kill my crew.

He's a trafficker.

He's used and manipulated me.

And he made me a murderer.

Nkella lets out a horrible wail, and I pause to look at him. He's hunched over, his eyes are ablaze, and his hat has fallen off his head to reveal his horns, which have grown a little bigger, twisted back. They're no longer stumps. His canines are tinted with blood as he stares at the Arcana, and rights himself. An Arcana grabs at him, and he punches the Arcana's chest with impossible strength, breaking through its robe. The sounds of breaking bones make me swallow a gasp. I blink, waiting for the soldier to dematerialize, but he doesn't. The soldier's body hunches over as he topples to the ground. Nkella lifts his arm and takes on the next one as the soldier lies motionless on the bloody ground. A memory of being on the *Gambit* when the Devil inside him took over flashes through my mind. He killed the Arcana soldier then too.

No one could understand how. And he didn't remember it.

Feral rage smolders in Nkella's gaze, as each soldier advances toward him. He's an unmovable, impenetrable force. Unstoppable. He takes each of them one by one.

Tessa and Kae handle a group on their own, and I fix my gaze back to Demitri, who's transfixed by Nkella's power over his soldiers. Mūhī backs into the woods. Good. Leave. As I approach Demitri, he cuts his gaze to me.

"Have you decided to come with me?" Demitri asks.

An eagle flies over my head and lands on the side of the hill. Gari follows in my peripherals, but that's background to me right now.

All I see is red. Fury courses through my bones, and my mark pulses. I aim my hand at him, and webbing shoots out from my fingertips, draping over Demitri. He shouts as he tries to move and lands on his knees. I keep forcing webbing out of me until his torso is tightly covered, but not his face.

I want to see his face.

"What are you doing?" he quakes. A wicked smile crosses my face as I pull out my knife.

Nkella falls to the ground in my peripherals. He grabs onto his head, and I know he's trying to regain control. His face snaps to me, and his glowing red eyes dim to black, and then he's back to normal as recognition hits his features. I give him a stare as he picks himself up, but then retrain my focus on Demitri.

Nkella runs to my side. "Soren..."

I stare at Demitri, and he starts to wriggle, noting that something in me has changed.

I'm ready to ignore Nkella's attempts to stop me, when instead, he walks behind Demitri and holds him in place for me. I stare into Nkella's eyes. He stares back at me with such intensity, amber notes flickering behind his irises when he's excited or when he's angry. But this time, it's excitement. The way he's looking at me, waiting for me to make my move.

"No. You don't want to do this, Soren. I'm not the one you want to kill." Demitri's voice shakes as he begs for his life. Something about that sends a thrill up my spine.

I take my dagger and plunge it into Demitri's chest, as I stare into his awestruck eyes. Blood gurgles from his throat as he tries to speak. I shove the knife in harder and twist. Blood runs out, and his gaze is glossy and wide. He stares at me, and I inch close to his face and whisper. "You were right. My second kill *is* with conviction." Then I pull the knife out and drop it.

Nkella lets Demitri's body fall to the floor. Something fierce flashes across his eyes and a swarm of emotion emanates from his pores. The way he looks at me is purely diabolical, something dark and animalistic glowing in the depths of his eyes. It's almost chilling, like he wants to devour me, right here, on top of all this carnage.

Then with all seriousness, he walks toward me with full force. He grabs the back of my head and our lips crash against each other, and I'm filled with primal, feral energy. He pulls away just a little to whisper against me, "No one will ever touch you again." His tone is breathless. And I catch his lips again. I don't even care that we're in the middle of a slaughter, and people are surrounding us. I don't care that we're both covered in blood. He pulls away to avoid my chest filling with air, but it's a struggle to pull away. I grab him, pulling him back to me, and we lock eyes. He flashes me a delicious grin that makes my stomach swim. It tells me he revels in this bloodshed. But it also tells me, he's allowing the Devil inside him to surface a little more.

Is it bad that I like it?

Stars dance inside my closed eyes as I lose myself in the feel of his lips against mine. If this is to be the last time we kiss, then I want to hold onto this feeling for as long as is humanly possible. Heat intensifies between us, and this time I know it's not because of the rikorō; it's only because of the rikorō that this is coming to light. His lips gently pull away, and I open my eyes. He stares at me with those intense, dark eyes, amber flickering beneath them. All his fury, his purpose, his passion. And I now know that I don't want to run from his darkness, I want to embrace it forever.

"Captain!" Kaehante's voice separates us. We stare at each other for a second, and an exasperated giggle escapes me as we stand over Demitri's corpse. His harrowing cries of entering the tortured dead surrounded us. It's the most carnage, most morbid, and yet most exhilarating experience of my life.

"Captain!" Kae calls again, and this time we turn to look at him.

Tessa reverses her chair and drives toward us, her wheels covered in blood and guts. "Something is happening with the Arcana."

"What's happening?" I rasp.

The two Arcana soldiers that had been attacking Tessa and Kae look as if they're stunned in place. Their heads are hanging low and their shoulders slumped as they float a foot off the ground. Their hollow eyes stare emotionless at the bloody snow. Kaehante shoves one with his sword; the soldier doesn't move.

"It's like they've been deactivated," Harold says, approaching, stepping over some of the carnage, but giving up on staying clean as he nears. Gari floats by and presses his face against one of the soldier's masks.

I smile. "I'm glad you all made it out of there," I tell them.

"Gari saved us," AJ says, stepping over the carnage. Lāri still hasn't shifted back—she probably doesn't want to step on all the guts on the ground. Kenjō is staring at Demitri's body. I move my gaze away from her. Something else she can hate me for. Despite seeing him for who he was, she was still close to him and probably didn't want him dead. It's okay. She can hate me. I've made my peace with it.

"What happened to the yeti?" I ask Harold.

"He shielded me and Kenjō the moment the fights started, but when Gari showed up to take us, we parted ways."

I nod.

Both the soldier's faces snap up to the sky, and I train my sight on them. They straighten their spines, and Gari backs away with his tail swimming through the air. Tessa loads a cannonball on her chair cannon, and everyone aims a weapon of some kind at them. But before we can attack, they take off in unison and fly toward the night sky.

Like clockwork, the sounds of airstrike sirens fall from the sky.

"Now we're fucked," Harold states.

Kenjō runs to us. "When Demitri died, his guise over the Swords Arcana shifted back to the Tower. They just reported everything!"

AJ gasps.

"The Empress is coming," Nkella says. "We have to go now."

A flicker of rage taps on my wrists at the sound of her coming. Part of me wants her to find me, but I need the Sword first.

I stare at Gari. "How many of us can you carry?"

"To where?"

"To the Ace of Swords," I say.

"Soren?" Harold steps toward me. "What are you planning?"

I ignore him.

Gari moves his head from side to side as he counts and measures us, expanding in length. "I'll have to come back for that one." He nods toward Tessa. "It isn't far."

Kaehante puts his hand on her shoulder. "I will wait with her."

Nkella walks to Demitri and starts looking through his clothes, then he pulls out a bronze key from his inside coat pocket. "The key for the *Gambit*." He tosses it to Kaehante who catches it in the air. "Keep it safe, daí? Go to the *Gambit* instead. We will meet you there."

Kae tucks the key inside his coat but shakes his head. "Koj. I am not leaving you to fight on your own."

Nkella hardens his jaw and places his hand on Kae's shoulder. "Then we go together, cousin."

"I can fly alongside Gari," Lāri says.

"In that case," Gari moves closer to us, his body lengthening. "Three of you hop on." Nkella hops on first, and I climb up behind him.

AJ holds onto me from behind, and Lāri shifts into her eagle form to fly inside Gari's Aō dome with us.

My arms are wrapped tightly around Nkella's torso; I take in the scent of his leather coat as the cold winds zip around us, and I rest my head on his back. Our surroundings are grayed out, except for a few lights coming from the night sky. Gari's dome works a bit differently from Iéle's, as the colors from the Aō come through.

Lāri glides close to us, her majestic wings outspread, and I focus on the beauty of her flying. Nausea overcomes me, but we're almost there. I'm almost there. I'll have the Death Card soon, and I'll be able to stop my own death and reverse it. And bring my mom back, and everyone the crew has lost.

AJ spits out my hair every few minutes, and I try to move it to my side. But we're not in the air for long.

The Temple comes into view, and Gari starts to steadily lower us.

"We've got company," he sings.

Glancing over the side of Nkella's arm, I spot Arcana soldiers guarding the area. Two people are standing on the Temple terrace. One of them is tall, with blonde hair and a reflective golden mask on her head. The Empress. The other one is shorter, but it's too dark to see his face.

My mouth dries. I wasn't sure how I'd react to seeing the Empress again, after knowing the truth about how my mom died. I clench my fists against Nkella's torso, and he grips it harder like he understands what I'm thinking.

A small smirk crosses my face. She thinks she beat us here and is trying to protect the Sword. I stifle a laugh. No, bitch. You're right where I want you. How nice of her to spare me the trip to the Tower.

A black and white drakon meets us head-on in the Aō dimension. I gasp, and Gari takes a dive. I grab onto Nkella as tight as I can, and he grabs my hand, making me feel secure. AJ squeezes his legs around me, and yelps.

The drakon chases us down.

"Hang on!" Gari gurgles as he makes a dive into the trees and zips through.

"Harold mentioned he had to fight a drakon to get to the Sword," AJ shouts. "I thought he said he killed it!"

"Only injured," I shout back.

"This one will tell the Empress we're here," Gari sings back as his body starts to do something weird underneath us.

"What's going on?" I bump closer to Nkella, and AJ squeezes me tighter from behind.

"Hold on tight!" he sings again. His body is getting smaller—uncomfortably small. I arch my neck and find the other drakon opening his large mouth, revealing pointy teeth. He snaps at us, and Gari makes a beeline to some rocks. I shut my eyes and press my face against Nkella's back.

"I'm leaving you here, and I will lead him away," Gari says.

"No way, you can't!" I yell at him. I can't let him get killed for real this time. One sea serpent fight was enough.

"Soren," Gari gurgles, "I can handle him. I'll be back with your crew."

I sigh deeply and nod my head against Nkella's back, my eyes still shut. AJ starts to scream, and Nkella curses. I open my eyes as we gain speed.

A startled scream escapes my mouth as we head straight toward a large crack between two boulders along the face of the mountain. I shut my eyes again and wince, bracing myself for impact, but Gari becomes skinnier as he goes straight through. We almost trip over each other and Gari's body for the way he slid inside the crack.

Gari makes a turn upward, leaving us on the ground inside the mountain, and flies over our heads right before the other drakon spots us. I stare at him in disbelief as the other drakon completely misses the fact that we're here. Instead, he's chasing Gari.

"Do you think he'll be alright?" I ask.

AJ wipes his face and slams his back against the wall of the crack. "He better be."

The silhouette of a large bird eclipses the moon as Lāri lands inside, shifting back into herself. She's out of breath and embraces AJ as her feet touch the ground.

Nkella takes out his flask and takes a long swing of it, then hands it to me. I refrain from chuckling as I take it from him. I think it'll help right now.

"What's the plan, Captain?" AJ asks.

Lāri stares at us through the darkness. "The Empress is there with a lot of Arcana. Should we wait? Or at least wait for the others so we have more firepower?"

Nkella looks at me, and my brows furrow.

"I don't want to wait," I say. "The Ace of Swords is right there, and the Empress is right where I want her."

31

"I THINK WE SHOULD WAIT FOR BACKUP," AJ SAYS.

I ball my fist. I want to get this over with.

"Even if you get there now, Soren, how will you get past the Empress? She's blocking the Ace of Swords Card. There are Arcana everywhere."

"But she could leave," I protest. "Once the Arcana search the perimeter and don't find us, she'll go back to the Tower."

"And then we'll ambush her with the *Gambit*. The ship isn't far from here," AJ argues.

Lāri takes a step toward me. "And what do you mean right where you want her?" she asks. "What are you planning?"

AJ's eyes widen as he gives Lāri a double-take, then looks back at me and Nkella. "You're not... Soren, what *did* you mean by that?"

My mouth forms a scowl. I stare back at Nkella who's been quiet and pensive against the wall. A small wave of emotion seeps out of him, and he stares back at me. I let out a cough and rub under my nose. There's a tiny bit of blood.

"I'm not doing well, guys," I say to them. "I've held on for a long time, but without a cure, I'm dying."

"Don't say that, Soren," Lāri whispers.

"I need the Death Card to bring my mom back, but also to cure myself. And it has to be now."

AJ nods.

"But there is more," Nkella tells them.

Lāri and AJ stare back at me expectantly.

I take a deep breath. "The Ace of Swords is the only thing that can kill her...so I intend on doing just that."

AJ's eyes widen. "Soren, are you sure?"

"As sure as death," I say. "She killed my mother."

"That sounds like revenge," Lāri says. "Mistakes happen in the midst of fury."

I lift my chin. "It's now or never. The sooner she dies, the sooner I can get the Death Card."

AJ runs his fingers through his hair. "I wasn't ready for this level of fight. I think we should wait for the rest of the crew."

I wince as something comes to mind.

"What is it?" AJ asks.

"I forgot something."

"Daí?"

I turn to Nkella. "I was going to use Demitri's memories to grab the Death Card. It's at the Tower."

Nkella's eyes widen.

"How do I get it now? The only reason I didn't use yours is because I didn't want to be tempted to take it before you all got cursed." AJ and Lāri exchange twisted glances. "Hear me out, as much as I might want to save you guys before it happened, it would have erased a lot from existence." I turn to Nkella. "As the Past Fate, I must never try to alter the past or it can change the future."

"That's how we know you are a good one," Lāri says.

I smile weakly at her.

"Yeah, we wouldn't want to change the past, Soren. It's okay, we get it," AJ says. "Our lives have changed with you in it—for the better."

I swallow a lump in my throat. Nkella comes close, and he gently touches my cheeks with both hands, pressing his head to my forehead.

"Use me," he says. "Take the Death Card after I am cursed. Do not hesitate."

353

"Are you sure?" I ask.

"I trust you," he breathes. My breath gets caught. Neither one of us trusts easily, and he's telling me he trusts me inside his head. I nod, squeezing my eyes to avoid tearing up. "Neyuro..." he whispers.

I open my eyes and stare into his dark eyes.

"Promise me something."

"What?"

"Do not lose yourself. Do not kill the Empress. Let me do it as I am already gone."

"No, you're not," I say heavily. "And I thought you liked me covered in blood?" I smirk.

"Kh. Not for vengeance, daí? Demitri had to be stopped. But you do not hate him the way you hate the one who killed your mother."

I reach for his hand. "You're wrong about being already gone, Nkella. You're not already gone."

"I am, Soren. I can feel the curse taking over. When I killed the Arcana...I was aware of it, and I remember doing it."

I shake my head. "It has to be me. Only a Fate can stop her with the Sword."

"Then let me make a promise to you." His voice darkens, and I blink at him, confusion swarming my emotions. "I vow to always protect you. And you shall let me."

"Why?" I ask. "Why are you saying this now?"

"Because I know the burdens that come after committing vengeful murder."

I screw up my face. I don't understand what he means by this, but we're wasting time. I take his arms and tug them down. "I can handle it."

"I promise anyway." He smirks.

"So, are we just going to walk up the steps and say, "Hey, Empress, how's the crown, eh?" AJ asks.

"You can't twist my arm to want to kill the Empress," Lāri adds. "But we need a plan, mei?"

"We sneak in from the side of the Temple," Nkella says. "Soren is right. If we go now while the drakon is distracted, we can catch the Empress by surprise."

AJ turns to look out of the cave. "What about the psychic Arcana? That's who she has right now, not the Swords Arcana."

"Leave them to me." Nkella grins.

I nod and look at each of them. "Okay, I'm ready."

We stealthily make our way through the trees and to the mountainside close to the Temple. It's a tall, cathedral-esque stone building, with only a few steps leading up to the entrance. Pines and silver birches outline the sides, which makes it a great place to take cover.

No signs of the drakon so far, which means Gari is still keeping him occupied. That's both good and bad. Bad because it could mean the crew is in danger. But if anything, Iéle will keep them hidden.

"What do you think she's waiting for?" AJ asks.

"If Demitri's Arcana reported things to her, she must know about Alec being killed," Lāri responds, "and about Demitri's plans for the Ace of Swords."

AJ gapes at her. "Do you think she's expecting Soren? His Arcana saw everything."

"It's entirely possible," I say.

We press against the Temple wall.

"I will distract them. You sneak inside," Nkella tells me.

I bite my lip. "Be careful."

A smirk slides on his face. "Neyuro, I am your fierce captain, daí?" He winks.

AJ shakes his head. "I'm right behind you, Fierce Captain."

I turn to Lāri. "You shouldn't come with me. When she sees me, and she will, she's likely to kill anyone near me."

"That's a good point, lover," AJ tells her.

Lāri nods. "I will cover you from here and wait for the others."

Nkella takes out his sword and raises a finger to his lips as he moves with his back pressed against the wall, toward the entrance of the Temple. The Arcana immediately snap their hollow eyes in his direction and start swarming him. AJ follows, shooting at them.

"Well, it's about time," I hear the Empress announce from around the corner.

Steeling my spine, I walk briskly against the stone wall and gaze upon the Empress and her new advisor. She walks down the steps looking so fluid and regal. Her black cloak is adorned with a silver web that shimmers in the starlight as it flows behind her. She turns slightly, allowing me to see her laurel tiara resting on her head, matching her gold mask.

I crouch low to the ground between a silver birch and the stone steps. Nkella walks in front of her, guiding her gaze to him and away from me. The Arcana lingers close by, but he walks with his sword switching positions from them to her. AJ holds his gun pointed at them.

"Capture them and take them to my Tower," she commands. "Leave the prince alive. I'll have to get more creative with the undead."

This is my chance. Swiftly, I crawl up the stone steps.

"Perhaps this time, I'll have each of their limbs separated from their bodies and spread out undersea."

Her new advisor backs into a corner. Not a very brave Hierophant, huh? This'll be easier than I thought. I back into the shadows along the wall, now inside the temple. Soft lights dance on the wall from scones lighting up the dark space. I take one glance at her new advisor, but he's still not paying attention, his eyes transfixed by the fight. He's huddled so tightly against the corner, I'd say he was scared. Not a very big guy either.

That one will get killed in no time.

The temple is tall, and the stonework spans three stories. Keeping a light foot, I stick to the shadows, ignoring the sounds of swords clashing behind me.

This might be the first time I'm thankful that the Empress is pompous enough to watch the bloodshed like it's a show—gives me time to move behind her.

Inside the second room, the stone walls act like a sound suppressor, and everything in here echoes while simultaneously making my ears pop. A few feet in front of me, a card floats over a gray stone podium. A wicked smirk crosses my lips. She won't know what's coming when I plunge this Sword into her chest.

Carved on the mantle below the floating card, Ancient Greek words are inscribed in the stone, and I watch eagerly as they transform into English before my eyes.

One worthy sacrifice to release the blade. Thence returned, unless by a Fate.

But I know it also means I don't need a sacrifice. A safeguard created by the two other Fate descendants as a way to save their world, in case one of them ever went rogue. I suppose they would have been making a sacrifice by killing their own blood. They just didn't expect it to reach so many generations of descendants.

A purple sheen slides over the face of the card where the Sword is. I pick it up, and its power tingles up my arm, making my mark pulse with recognition of its magic. The Sword comes to life in the card, as if I can reach in and pick it up, just like the Ace of Wands, and I do. At first, it's tiny between my fingers, but as I take a step back, the sword grows to a size of a longsword. The hilt is silver, and the inscription on the podium is also engraved on the Ipani steel blade. My reflection stares back at me in the steel, and I can almost hear the sounds of the Ipani who forged it —those with a special kind of ouma that makes steel come alive— judging sacrifices, choosing what is worthy, and commissioned by Tetalla himself before he lost the love of his life, and himself along with her. Before the Empress had all those steelworkers bound.

Feeling the weight of the sword in both hands and determination filling every pore of my body, I stride toward the woman who took my mother's life. I want her to look into the eyes of the daughter of the woman whose life she stole, the descendant of the sister whose life she ruined.

Walking slowly and lightly on the stone floor, I keep my eyes on the Hierophant, making sure he doesn't turn to spot me. He's busy cowering in the corner instead of helping the Empress fight. The Arcana are busy with their backs to me. Nkella is stalling, making the fight last to give me a chance to do what I need to do. He could take them all out in a matter of seconds. I glimpse the way he's fighting, deadly but beautiful.

I approach directly behind her, blocking out the fighting of my crew against the soldiers. Nkella glances at me, and I give him a little nod.

With a wicked grin, he blasts an Arcana holding AJ up with his ouma of wind. AJ drops to the ground but quickly gets to his feet. Nkella spins the wind under the Arcana, dragging the soldier to face the

Empress, to show her what he's about to do. With his other hand, he lets out a blast of wind to the other soldiers, and they all fly back. Lāri and AJ duck down to avoid being caught up in the crosswinds.

The Empress screams.

Nkella walks callously to the soldier and punches a fist through him. The sound of cracking bones echoes through the temple.

"How are you doing this?" The Empress gasps. Nkella turns to the other Arcana and begins to fill them all with air. The Empress starts to laugh.

I stay hidden behind her as she's distracted.

"I'm pleased to see that your curse is finally consuming you, turning you into the beast that you are," she says. But lies tinge her tongue. She's afraid of him. I know she is. The Devil curse has proven to be undeniably unstoppable. Strong. Powerful. If he is aware of killing the Arcana, something no one else can do, then the Devil inside him is taking over, and I don't think she'll be able to stop him.

With a wave of her hand, she makes another soldier appear. A soldier with a white mask from the Tower. "Let me see you do it to your sister, or I'll have her kill your crew like I had her kill your precious Queen of Wands."

Nkella fixes his gaze on his sister but doesn't let the soldiers down.

Now I press the tip of the blade against the back of her neck. "Let them go."

She freezes and then slowly turns around. Her green eyes glare back at me from behind her golden mask, her lacy spiderweb collar fans out around her neck, forming a tight bodice that forms into the cape around her long black dress. Her eyes grow soft behind her mask. I keep my hated stare pinned on her.

"I said let them go or I will kill you." I'm going to kill her anyway.

Arcana soldiers disappear from Nkella's side and re-emerge around me. A huge gust of wind flies them back as Nkella walks to my side. Behind him, AJ and Lāri are also coming into the Temple. Gari arrives in the back with the rest of the crew, and my smile widens.

The Empress's emotionless mask hides her lips—as well as any semblance of emotion, not that I'm looking for it.

"I was wondering when you would show up, Soren," the Empress says almost kindly. "I do not blame you for wanting me dead."

"Shut up," I spit, moving the Sword up to her chin. "I wanted you to see me kill you. You killed my mother."

"I did," she admits. "It was wrong of me."

My eyes flutter. She apologizes as if all she'd done was steal candy from a child.

"You have every right to be upset, my child. Know that I can leave, but I want to be here with you, I request for you to hear me."

"No," I say. She isn't going to make me feel sorry for her. Not now.

"Oh, but I think you'll want to listen." She motions to where her scared new advisor is hiding in the corner. "Come here, my child. It's okay."

A short, slender person comes out from the shadows, and my blood drains from my face.

"Hi, Soren," Talia says, holding one of her arms, her shoulders slumped.

"Stand up straight, my child, just as I showed you."

My mouth is gaping. No words can come out. No. No way. This can't be real. She... This is an illusion.

"Neyuro?" Nkella's voice comes from beside me, but I can't hear him now. "Who is this, daí?"

"Sh-she's..."

"Soren's sister," the Empress finishes for me.

My hands grow clammy and weak, and I almost drop the Sword, but I grip it hard.

"Soren, I can explain," Talia starts.

"Shush, child, that is all for now." I snap my attention to the Empress, a newfound hatred reaching my bones.

"Why?" I cry hoarsely, my voice and arms now shaking. "How?" She has the World Card, that's how. But...I look at Talia. "You were being adopted." I stare back at the Empress. "You kidnapped her!"

"On the contrary," a Tarot card materializes in her hand, and she shows me the face of the Magician. As she spins it in her hand, her form changes into that of the businesswoman I saw at the group home driving Talia away. "Did you find me too archaic to know how to impersonate someone from your modern world? I had time to learn and to pay someone handsomely to act as my suitor," she says coyly. "But it was all revealed to Talia, for I did not wish to lie to her. I told her this was all for you. She needs a family, Soren. I can provide her with everything she could ever want, and with you in our Tower, she will never want for anything. And you would never want to leave."

I gape at her, then look at Talia who's dressed in a black corset and form-fitting leggings. Decorative webbing lines the edges of her collar. My mouth snaps shut, and my eyes narrow.

"When I knew your mother, she was a threat to me," the Empress continues snapping my gaze back to her, "as I felt you were as well. But after you took away my power with the Ace of Wands, making me unable to unbind Ipani, I realized you are my sister's legacy. You are the Past Fate now who needs to sit in the Tower with me, to restore the balance." She's walking toward me now, and it catches me off guard, I take a step back. "Between you and me, we can bring peace to this world and finally have a balance. Asteria will see I've changed, and the three of us can be together."

"That's the wildest dream I've ever heard." I look to Talia. "I'm taking you home."

Talia shakes her head. "I don't want to go home, Soren. I love the Tower. There's magic here," she whispers loudly.

My heart thumps in my chest, and a swirl of emotions comes from beside me. I glance at Nkella, who's been standing there silently, his brows furrowed.

"Listen to your sister, Soren. She loves her room. She has oumala animals she can play with. And I'm training her to have the most powerful role in my Empire, apart from us. She's family. *Our family.*"

All this was one giant manipulation to corner me into relinquishing my power. She'll probably kill me and Talia if I put down the Sword and give in.

"My family is my crew," I point the Sword under her chin. "I'll never forgive you for what you did to my parents, for stealing my childhood, and for the horrible things you've done to all of Ipa."

"No!" Talia screams. "Soren, what are you doing? You're not a killer! Please don't! I like her!"

"You don't know what you're talking about, Talia."

From the corner of my eye, I see Lāri is slowly making her way to Talia, her arm reaching for her. Good. She can take Talia away from here. It'll be better if she doesn't see any more bloodshed. "This is no place for you, Talia. Go with Lāri now."

Talia shakes her head and moves away from Lāri. I train my stare back at the Empress.

Talia starts crying for me to stop, and my arm wavers.

"Are you certain you want your sister to watch you kill the person who saved her from a life in foster care?"

I swallow. The crew is standing at the foot of the Temple. Kenjō is in jaguar form, and I think she ran over here to give Gari more space to bring the rest of them. Kae and Tessa are armed and ready, and so is Harold. Nkella is close behind me, ready to protect me, ready to kill if he has to, but his words from earlier surface in my mind.

"Don't lose yourself, neyuro. Not for revenge."

I look to Talia, fear stricken in her features. Her eyes are wide, displaying terror plastered across her face. If she loves this sociopathic woman in front of me, she's being fooled, and that I know is a fact, but I also can't let her see me like this.

"That's right, put the Sword down, my child," the Empress says. "Hand it to me."

My eyes narrow, and I smirk. I still have one thing to do. "Never." With a blast from my fingertips, my webbing shoots out and pushes the Empress to the side of the Temple. She cries out, but the webbing wraps around her, tightening around her body. My smile widens as I walk over to her. I glance at Nkella who hides the shock in his face. Now's the time. "I need you," I mouth to him.

He strides over to me, and the manner in which he comes, as soon as I said I needed him sends every fiber of my body screaming with desire. I have to push down my impulses. There'll be time for that later.

"What are you doing?" the Empress demands.

I shoot more webbing, closing her in tightly. She tries to escape. To be honest, I wasn't sure she could be held by my webbing, since she has this same power herself. Can a spider hold another spider in place? Some of them are cannibalistic by nature. She's right where I want her.

I won't kill her, but I'll go back to my initial plan, and this time, I want to make her watch.

The Empress can't move, I have her tightly secured against the cold surface of the Temple. The Arcana start to move, and my crew fights behind them. Nkella glances at Ntaoru still suspended in the air, her hollow eyes staring at nothing in particular. Concern is swarming him, but I grab his hand.

"This is how we release her."

He stares deeply into me. "Do it, neyuro. I trust you."

The Empress's green eyes widen beneath her mask. I send more webbing to close in around her neck, leaving her able to breathe and see. I lift my chin and tell her, "I want you to see how powerful I am. I want you to watch as I undo the terrors you've done. I want you to watch as I bring my mother back to life."

"What—You can't."

"Oh, I think I can," I tell her. I turn to Nkella and hold his hands. Closing my eyes, I can feel my mark already pulsing and ready for me to enter his memories.

I'm in his memory. He stands before the Empress's bed. The Death Card is floating on her nightstand, and I wonder why she keeps it so close to her, separated from the rest of the deck. She opens her eyes. Her mask isn't on, the soft tissue, red and keloid, covers her once-beautiful face. The area around her eyes is engorged and red. A scream rips out from her throat, and she pushes him back out of her bedroom, but right before he steps foot outside of his memory, I turn and grab the Death Card.

I open my eyes and let go of Nkella with the Death Card in my hands. I stare at it, and a purple sheen illuminates a skeleton standing on a boat. Two curved horns are on his head, and he holds a sword and a shield in both hands. A smile creeps over my face.

"Neyuro, you did it."

I glance at him. "Thanks to you," I resist the urge to kiss him and stare back at the Empress, showing her the card. Her eyes become bloodshot.

"You mustn't."

"I absolutely must." I chuckle, my arms vibrating with power. I won. I got the Death Card. I could have done this sooner. They were right, chasing revenge only slowed me down.

"Stupid girl—"

A popping sound echoes in the temple, and I glance down at Philo who appeared on my hand, just like she had before I grabbed the Ace of Wands months ago. My little friend coming to— "Ow! She bit me." I gape at the spider, her mosaic glass pattern dancing shadows over my skin, and her large eyes glaring up at me. I swing my hand sharply. Philo falls to the floor.

"Listen to the spider, child. You know not what you're about to do."

"You turned her against me. What I'm about to do is bring my mother back to life." I'll check on Philo later. I'm sure she didn't mean to bite me—it was probably the Empress making her.

She struggles to shake her head. "You can't bring her back—" She chokes on the web, as I shoot more of it under her mask. Talia runs to me, but I ignore her. Soon, this will all be over, and I'll take my mom and Talia back home. "You don't understand!"

I'm already walking away from the Empress and Talia, Nkella by my side.

I stare at the card. How do I make this work?

"Soren, I'm sorry I didn't tell you," Talia says. "I wanted it to be a surprise because I thought you liked it here, and the Empress said we could be a family! And I'm okay, I really am. Now you don't have to work so hard and worry about adoption and renting an apartment. We can live in a castle! But Soren, listen to me. She says that card is bad. And it won't bring back your mom!" Talia cries.

"She's lying to you, Talia." I snap my gaze back to her. "All she does is manipulate. But don't worry, that'll all be over soon," I say under my breath.

I was able to reach in and take the Sword from its card, and with the Ace of Wands, I was able to do the same. But the rest of the cards are different. The Aō gives us a mark when we manifest attributions to the cards. But as a Fate, I can use any one of them, just like the Empress used the Magician Card to look like someone else and fool Talia.

The Empress yells at me, "Leave that card where it was, girl!"

"She is starting to free herself, neyuro. Hurry."

"The Arcana are coming closer," AJ warns.

A bomb explodes, but I recognize the sound as one of the cannonballs from Tessa's chair. They'll hold them off until I'm done. I look over what's on the card again.

The skeleton has devil horns on his head. He holds a shield and a sword, and there's black fire with purple tips all around. The Tower burns in the background. He stands on a boat. The symbolism for death and destruction.

But also new beginnings.

A small engraving in ancient Greek ripples in words on top of the night sky of the card. *Acceptance.*

My mark pulses. It's time. I hold the card up, and I squeeze my eyes shut.

"Bring back my mom," I command.

A voice whispers in my ear, and a warm breeze kisses my cheeks with the scents of sandalwood and tropical spices. *"Accept Me,"* it lulls.

Taking a deep breath, I whisper, "I accept."

The Empress roars, but Nkella holds her back.

The ground shakes beneath our feet, and everyone—including the Arcana—stop and look outside. In the distance, a bright purple light emanates from the sky. I run a full sprint outside the Temple for a closer look, my heart in my throat. Any minute now, the ground will release my mom. And it's working. Something is happening.

"You stupid girl." The Empress rushes past me, her eyes fixed on the sea.

What looks like a black cyclone mixed with cold and purple winds reaches from a cloud down to the sea.

"That is coming from Danū," Kaehante says.

Nkella approaches behind me.

My eyes are fixed on the cyclone. "It didn't work?"

The Empress turns to stare at me. "You released him," she accuses.

Nkella looks between us, confusion on his face.

The Empress stares at me, her large blue eyes widening with...fear. My blood grows cold. Her voice goes rigid, but there's an underlying tone of fear when she says, "The Death Card trades one life for the other, you stupid girl. You brought him back from the Deep. And now, with his army of dead, he will rain havoc onto this world until everyone is dead."

A shot of terror rips through my core. "No! That's not what I— It can't be—"

Whatever happened to Tetalla?

He was cursed. Cursed by the Empress to enact the Devil Card; he killed everyone, blinded by rage. And he lost himself instantly, sending himself down to the Deep.

"Who is back?" Nkella demands.

I turn to him. "T—" A surge of pain sears behind my eyes like shards of glass wanting to explode. The shards reach down to my throat, spreading to my lungs and heart. My mouth gapes open as I grab at my chest, stumbling back. My vision narrows, and then a dreadful cold washes over me.

A loud clatter hits the stone as my hand lets go of the Sword. Before I can process it, I'm falling. Nkella catches me as I drop to the floor. His beautiful, dark eyes search mine as he frantically calls my name, but his voice is merging with the background. I can't see the others, and my eyelids are so heavy I have to close them. My breathing slows to become one with the icy, slowing beats of my heart. Nkella's voice is a distant roar as he calls my name.

And then I take my final breath.

32

NKELLA

Koj.

My shoulders shake over her body. My insides quake. I see red. Darkness. Death.

Koj. Take control.

This is not right.

My breath shakes but then it turns into a furious hiss and my shoulders shake more.

I'm cradling Soren's body tightly in my arms. Her beautiful red curls fall over her fair skin. Exquisite in every way. The most striking girl who has ever crossed my path. My challenge. My perfect aovate. My bayoa.

I cannot bear the thought of living without her. That is why I swore to protect her.

My head is pounding with the torment of my curse. Loud. Quaking. Unstopping. She cannot be dead.

Her cries of eternal torment seep from her lips. Death has her. She goes with the suffering of the Deep.

The pounding grows harder. Rage fills me. My shoulders slump over her, and a violent cry I was not expecting tears from my throat.

She is gone.

My neyuro.

The land trembles around us.

"He has brought his undead army," the Empress says. "She should have listened to me. Stupid girl."

"Captain?" Kaehante grabs my shoulder. "We have to leave, Captain."

I shove him back violently. They will not take me from her. This is my fault. I allowed this to happen. I vowed to protect her, and I failed.

I failed. I always fail.

Soren's little sister runs to me. Her eyes are wet. Her tears run down her cheeks. She screams Soren's name. But I continue to hold her. I cannot let her go. Not yet.

The Empress reaches for Soren's sister. I take out my sword and point it at her. "Leave the girl." I hiss between my teeth.

The Empress cocks her head. "I am her new mother," she says. "With or without Soren, I intend to raise her."

Red fills my eyes. The Devil threatens to escape. I cannot let it. If I do, I risk killing everyone. My crew. The girl too.

Get back.

My breathing grows heavy.

"Talia," she tells the girl, "we're out of time. Soren released the worst Devil of all. He is Death and Destruction. We must go to the Tower at once and prepare our army to fight his undead."

She pulls on the girl's arm. I do not have the energy to fight her.

"Captain, there is a beast being unleashed in Danū," Kaehante warns me as if I do not know what is happening. My arms are shaking.

"The dead army is coming," he continues.

I look back to my neyuro. I brush her lips with the back of my fingers, and I lean down and kiss her soft lips. I ignore the tormented cries coming from her. This isn't fair. She needs to be alive.

"Danū won't be able to survive this," Tessa says.

You deserted our island. Your people are starving.

Ntaoru was meant to lead. Not me. I make things worse. I am

nothing without my crew. I vowed to protect them and my neyuro. But I have failed.

I'm a terrible prince.

And a worse captain.

"Captain?" AJ walks over, his voice low and shaking. The drakon floats beside him, his head bowed. I glance at AJ, and his sad eyes fall on Soren. Without AJ, would I have given her a chance when I thought she was an utwa?

Even then her spark had enthralled me. I had hoped she was not utwa.

AJ bends down next to Soren's sister. "We really do have to go. We can take Soren's body, and we can bury her somewhere we can visit."

The rage fills my body again. I shake my head. A tear falls from one eye and lands on Soren's face. I wipe it away. The sheen of her card glares at me from her pocket. My brow perks up.

"But we have to go now, okay?" AJ continues. "We need our captain to lead us now more than ever."

I nod at him. But they do not need me.

They need my sister.

They have always needed her. Danū has always needed her. Not me.

I glance behind me, pulling my gaze away from Soren for the first time. Ntaoru floats in the Arcana uniform of the Tower.

I stare at AJ, and then past him to the rest of my crew. I stare at Kaehante and Tessa. At Lāri. Even Harold. The Magician proved his loyalty to me. He is also my crew.

AJ's brows furrow. "Captain?"

I smile at them. "Take care of each other, daí? Make sure Soren doesn't do anything bancha."

His features twist, and I reach for the card.

AJ stands. "Woah! What are you doing?"

"No!" The Empress stammers. She grabs Talia and pulls her away from me.

My crew is now walking up to me, but I lay Soren down gently on the stone floor, and I hold the Ace of Swords in my hand. Harold runs at me, and I am prepared to fight him. I will not let anyone stop me.

"Wait!" he shouts, pushing AJ out of the way. The Empress acts like she is going to throw magic at me, but Harold turns and throws a smoke bomb at her instead. The Empress disappears in the blue smoke. The poor girl gets lost too. The rest of the crew is ready to hold her off for me. They can always be counted on. My crew.

"Don't do it yet," Harold shouts, the smoke is behind him, so now I can only see him.

I quirk a brow, but warn him with my stance.

His palms are facing me. "I know what you want to do," he says, "and I respect you for it, Captain." My face hardens.

"I am listening." The Magician rarely calls me Captain.

"Watch your wording. You can help all of us. Including your sister."

I nod to let him know I understand.

I square my jaw. I'm determined and ready. A glare reflects from the Sword in the card.

"Just reach in and pick it up," Harold says. "Then, say your wish."

I do it. The sword lengthens as I pull it out of the card.

With one deep breath, I say, "My life for my crew."

Then I slice my throat.

33

SOREN

My lungs threaten to burst open as I gasp in the frigid cold air.

"Soren?" Talia's voice jolts me up.

"What happened?" I groan.

The crew is standing around me. Tears are covering their faces, and Tessa is screaming.

The last thing I remember is holding the Death Card. Then, a cyclone came out from somewhere south of here, people were screaming, Nkella caught me, and I—

I gasp.

I think I died.

Talia wraps her arms around me, and I hold her arms.

"It didn't work," my voice shakes. "It didn't bring back my mom."

"Oh, Soren, I'm so glad you're okay." Talia cries. The Empress stands over her and bends to her shoulder. I wrap my arms more tightly around Talia, guarding her.

"Leave her alone," I tell the Empress.

370

"Dear, you will want her to come with me. Now that you've released hell on Fateland—"

I forgot Fateland is what she calls Ipa.

"—especially now that you don't have your captain to protect you," she finishes.

My brows furrow and I look out at the crew. They are huddled together, tears and horrible sounds coming from them. Harold and Kenjō are standing apart, staring at me.

"Where's Nkella?"

Harold shakes his head, and I climb to my feet, making my way to the crew. I push past them, and Kaehante is holding the captain in his arms. Blood covers Kae's hands, and I squint to see where it's coming from. I gasp and drop to my knees. Kaehante lets me in.

"No," my voice gurgles. "No no no no. Why? How could he?"

"He did it for you," Kaehante says.

"No," Harold says, walking close to us. "He did it for all of us." He points behind Kaehante, and we all turn.

Ntaoru is descending to the ground. Her feet hit the stone floor, and she stumbles a bit. Her mask falls off, and a beautiful girl, with long black hair and high cheekbones—unmistakably resembling Nkella— stands there, gaping.

I gasp.

"He used the Sword," Harold said.

"The Devil made his *Gambit* after all," the Empress says.

I take the Sword and swing it at the Empress, not caring about Talia seeing me kill her now. Not caring about anything. But the moment I strike her, she turns to smoke and takes Talia with her.

I drop the Sword and run back to Nkella, taking his head in my hands. Tears fall off my cheeks, as I press my hand onto his throat to stop the bleeding. His blood pools in my hand, the tormented sounds of his soul singing that awful cry of despair. I try to reach him with my mind, searching for those waves of emotion he'd leave me.

But there's nothing.

I can't feel him anymore...

"No. I need to bring him back." My shoulders shake violently as I let myself cry over his body. This isn't fair.

"My brother?" Ntaoru bends down next to me. "Is that Nkella?" she gasps, shaking her head. "Koj, what did he do?"

Harold bends down and places a hand on my shoulder. "Unfortunately, I don't think the same rules apply to a Fate. You can only carry the Sword and use it to kill. But the instructions don't say if whether you use it to make a wish."

I shake my head furiously, holding onto Nkella. "I don't know," I mouth.

Kenjō walks next to Harold and looks at me for the first time since she found out what I did to Alec. "He made a deal with the Deep, and it's going to collect. You can't undo a deal once it's made," she says.

I gape at them.

"Don't let his sacrifice be for nothing," Kenjō tells me.

I turn back to Nkella, tears running down my cheeks.

The land quakes hard, and we all fall to the side. I clutch Nkella's body.

"Tetalla's army?" Tessa shouts over the ground still ripping open.

A large tentacle comes out of the ground. Ice-cold water crashes in.

"It's the serpent!" Gari shouts in a gurgle. "We have to go now!"

I gasp, not wanting to let go of Nkella. The serpent's tail heads straight toward me, but I stand my ground, trying to back away, trying to carry Nkella's body away with me. Fast—so fast, it's almost impossible, the serpent's tail wraps around Nkella's body. I hold on tightly to him, but the serpent starts to tug, pulling me with him. The crew grabs onto me, pulling me back.

"You have to let go!" Harold says. "Don't let his death be in vain."

The serpent grasps tighter, pulling him hard, and ripping him away from me. I let out a shattering scream, which turns into wail as I watch it take Nkella down into the frigid cold waters, and into the Serpent's Deep.

THANK YOU

Thank you so much for reading *The Devil's Gambit!* I hope you enjoyed Soren's adventure into Tarotland as much as I loved writing it. Watch out for book three of *Chronicles of Tarotland*, coming out in 2024.

If you would like to receive updates on all my new releases, please join my mailing list at http://killian wolf.com/. You will also get access to my books at a discounted launch price when they first come out, along with an exclusive sneak peek or short story just for you.

Scan For Series

GET IN TOUCH!

Come say hi in my Facebook Reader group. In there, every day is Halloween!

facebook.com/groups/killianwolf

Please feel free to get in touch with me.

Website: http://killianwolf.com/

facebook.com/killianwolfauthor

x.com/killian_wolf22

instagram.com/killian_wolf_author

pinterest.com/killianwolf22

goodreads.com/killianwolf

amazon.com/Killian-Wolf/e/B07WHFB8FW

bookbub.com/authors/killian-wolf

tiktok.com/@killian_wolf_author

patreon.com/killianwolfauthor

FREE BOOK

Scan to get this free book and sign up for my mailing list.

"Don't kill" is a no-brainer. But what if it's for a good reason?

My name is Harold and my family is cursed. When my aunt made the tough call to pull my mother from life support, she enacted the curse of the Frost Giants, freezing herself from the inside.

To save her, all I had to do was step through the portal, but one wrong move sent me flying off to Tarotland, a place where the tarot cards have come to life. The good news is I still have my runes. The bad news? Magicians are illegal here. Not to mention, I haven't exactly come into my powers yet. . . and I can't get the portal to reopen.

My salvation is a breathtaking native. She makes me act like a Fool, but she also told me about a sword that cuts through any doorway. Power doesn't come without sacrifice, though. With a mysterious predator out for blood, and my name on every wanted poster, who knows if we'll make it before my aunt breathes her final breath?

ACKNOWLEDGMENTS

Writing this book was an emotional ride that kept pulling me away from my outline. Eventually, I decided to just go with it and see where it took me, and I'm glad I did. Having said that, it wouldn't be what it is without the help of some exceptional individuals.

A special thanks to Christian Thalman for continuing on working on this amazing language with me. I feel that the way the Ipani language has evolved had added a certain depth to the characters and their culture, making it so much more real.

To my critique partner Christina, you have been my rock from the beginning to the end of this book. Thank you for constantly sanity-checking me, and making sure I didn't stray too off course. Thank you for the impromptu brainstorming sessions over the phone and for helping me through plot issues. I always look forward to your hilarious and helpful comments, and cannot wait to work with you again on the next one—especially since I know you'll never forgive me for that ending if we don't. Seriously, thank you for believing in me and my books.

To Claerie, I know I've said this before, but I'll say it again: you're my sanity. Whenever I need to brainstorm or throw an entire idea out, you're there to talk me through the process, and it always works. Thank you.

To Alice, your belief in me and my books has become my light at the end of the tunnel. If I ever feel like my work sucks, I think of how much you enjoy it, and it gets me through my writing. You're awesome, and I can't wait to continue working together— and finish reading your series.

Mom, you continue to inspire me. Thank you for always believing in me and my books. If not for you, I probably wouldn't have discovered the possibility of sneaking off into other dimensions through books. And turning that power into writing.

To my husband, your patience and support mean more to me than you could ever know. I promise, one day this will all be worth it.

Lastly, a huge thanks to my readers, especially the ones making it all the way here. I hope you enjoyed reading these characters as much as I loved writing them, and don't worry, there's more to come.

ABOUT THE AUTHOR

 Killian Wolf is a Miami, Florida, native who enjoys pirates, rum, and skulls as much as she loves writing about dark magick and sorcerers. She holds a Bachelor of Arts degree in Cultural Anthropology and Sociology and a Master of Science in Environmental Archaeology and Palaeoeconomy.

Killian writes books about obtaining magickal powers and stepping into other dimensions. She lives in Florida with her husband, a tornado of a cat, and the most timid snake you'd ever meet. When she isn't writing, you might find her at an archaeological dig, rock climbing, or sipping on dark spiced rum while working on a painting.

GLOSSARY

IPANI VOCABULARY

á: Sound often used by natives of Sāgirang, used to represent a sound made in speech in a variety of situations, often used to ask for something to be repeated or explained or to elicit agreement.

Aō: [a.ˈo] world spirit

Āngaraeke: Yeti

Aovaṭe: (begisi aovaṭe) [be.ˈɰi.si a.o.ˈva.te] soulmate, destined partner (lit. betrothed by the hand of the world spirit)

Bancha: [ˈbaɲ.ca] empty, free of, lacking, fool, idiot, stupid

Bayoa: turning light in the sky, northern lights/Nautilus

Daí: Sound often used by natives of Danū, used to represent a sound made in speech in a variety of situations, often used to ask for something to be repeated or explained or to elicit agreement.

Drakon: Ancient Greek dragon with a serpentine body. Can both swim and fly, and pop in and out of the Aō dimension.

Engi: Thankful

Garisi: drinkable potion, as opposed to explosive potion

gembella: [gem.ˈbel.la] from gembe, prisoner, inmate

Gichang: currency, money

gichang rīrō: money from Danu, pressed ruby

gichachi: mark

guyuti: [gu.ˈju.ti] shrivel-ear, derogatory term used to describe a human

Hn: A sound made by an Ipani when thinking out loud.

Helāni: Descendants of the Ancient Greeks who crossed the portal with the Moera

hū raku (raku): [hu: ˈra.ku] poison gas: poisonous breath

iá: [i.ˈa] hailing; hello, ahoy, greetings

Iéle : [i.ˈe.le] moon

Imboe: [im.boe] Ancient Greek-Ipani creole spoken in Ipa.

Indakepoa: [ˌin.da.ke.ˈpoa] translation potion, liquorice

Ipani: [i.ˈpa.ni] of the World; the language of the World. Ipani (singular and plural)

Ipononchi: [i.po.ˈnoɲ.ci] cookie, pastry (lit.: little baked)

Kaehante: well prepared with a paddle (literal), or armed/prepared (figuratively).

Kenjō: [keɲ.ˈjo:] (Open Sky)

Ko: Negative, soft no

Koj: [koej] No, none, no! don't!

Mei: Sound often used by natives of Oleanu, used to represent a sound made in speech in a variety of situations, often used to ask for something to be repeated or explained or to elicit agreement.

Mikiroro: Black palm tree, the Danū crest

Moera: The Ancient Greek Fates

Mūhī: [ˌmuˈhiː] footprint [in the] sand

Muse: [ˈmu.se] spider

Nangraku: [naŋˈɾa.ku] poison tooth

Neyuro: [ne.yuro] brave

Nkella: [ŋˈkel̪.la] Hope, lifting, rising; first name of Captain Nkella Mkiroro

Ouma: [ˈow.ma] magic; magical

Oumala: [owˈma.la] mage, practitioner of magic, magic user

Rikorō: [ˈdik.oro] soul thief, plant

Rikwa: [ˈdik.wa] thief

Ruh: [ɾuo̥] wolf

saechi: peak berry, volcanic berry

solerie: [so.leˈɾie] soleri'g, solerigo (i) peppermint (lit.: ice-leaf), give you transparency, spectre, can be used for people and objects

Taevenye: [tae.ˌʋeˈɲe] cinnamon (lit.: cloud-wood), gives ability to fly, float, can be used in potions for people, and objects

Tetalla: [teˈtal.la]: habitual dead-maker

Utwa: [ˈu.twa] scout, spy

Places

Danū: "Six suns." Farthest Southeastern Island. Currently called Pentacles, Danū by the rebels.

Dempu Yuni: trading post island; Dempu: foot; (i) standing, located; (i) river mouth; Yuni: transparent, pure, clear

Ipa: [ˈee.pa] the global ocean, the World

Naó: Greek Temple

Oleanu: "Highwater" Island to the East. Currently called Wands, Oleanu by the rebels.

Piupeki: "Steelrock" Island farthest to the North. Currently called Swords, Piupeki by the rebels.

Ruta Helāni: Prefect's Tower

Rutavenye: "Cloudwall" The Floating island, location of The Tower

PHRASES

Ipani translations:

E hongu a songu: who waits, wilts.
Jovoe m'pate: Peace to you

CHARACTER ART

Captain Nkella and Soren

Milton Keynes UK
Ingram Content Group UK Ltd.
UKHW040134130324
439347UK00013B/167/J